J.W. McKenna

Delicious Daydreams

What the critics are saying...

ꟹ

PRIVATE DAYDREAMS

4 Hearts "PRIVATE DAYDREAMS is a recent release by J. W. McKenna and is good enough to have made this reviewer a fan! The pacing of the story is great, it has enough background to keep everything in perspective yet moves along fast enough to keep the reader enjoying every minute of guilty pleasure. [...] This is a good book to read and then share with your friends, who knows what you might learn about each other!"
~ *Love Romances and More Reviews*

"A steamy erotic tale of private longings and desires. Each fantasy may come with a price, though, and that's what lends a darker flair to the story. [...] J.W. McKenna not only focuses on the illicit and bawdy in PRIVATE DAYDREAMS, but also heeds the consequences for the girls' actions. This lends a more serious touch to an otherwise erotic tale that's also lightened up by a few needed humorous scenes as well."
~ *Romance Reviews Today Erotic*

An Ellora's Cave Romantica Publication

www.ellorascave.com

Delicious Daydreams

ISBN 9781419957819

Edited by Mary Moran.
Cover art by Syneca.

This book printed in the U.S.A. by Jasmine-Jade Enterprises, LLC.

Trade paperback Publication August 2008

DELICIOUS DAYDREAMS

PRIVATE DAYDREAMS

ꟸ

Trademarks Acknowledgement

ℬ

The author acknowledges the trademarked status and trademark owners of the following wordmarks mentioned in this work of fiction:

Bloomingdales: Federated Department Stores, Inc.

Cosmopolitan: Hearst Communications, Inc.

Donna Karan: Gabrielle Studio, Inc.

Google: Google Inc.

New York Times: The New York Times Company

PowerPoint: Microsoft Corporation

Realtor: National Association of Realtors

Sex and the City: Home Box Office, Inc.

Chapter One

The Leprechaun

ꟼ

The girls were having too much wine and too much fun. Yes, that's what they called themselves—"girls". Not women and certainly not ladies. They were four girls in the prime of their lives, real-life versions of *Sex and the City*, living and loving in Manhattan. Two were single, two were divorced, but all were veterans of failed relationships. They weren't afraid to speak their minds about men, relationships, bosses and life in general.

Now, after two bottles of wine, the women were zeroing in on their favorite topic—sex. It was Monday night, their regular time to get together and rehash the previous week. They were in Suzanne's living room instead of a restaurant so they felt free to let loose even more than usual.

"Six years!" Wendy Delano was complaining, her voice slurring a bit from the wine. She was the youngest member at twenty-nine and perhaps the most naïve. A petite woman with a short dark hairstyle, she had long given up on trying not to be "the perky one". "Six years we were married and Frank never once gave me the Big O! Was it me?"

It was a common complaint and the others commiserated with her.

"He obviously didn't do it right," said Carol Hopwell, an editor at a publishing firm who was still single at age thirty-three. She was an attractive brunette in a gangly sort of way.

"The mind has to be engaged as well as the body—maybe that was your problem," Suzanne Diggs noted, the unofficial "brain" of the quartet. She was a tall redhead who dressed impeccably thanks to her rich ex-husband's alimony payments and her regular job as a legal secretary. "You had issues with Frank and they extended into the bedroom."

"So you're saying sex is all in your mind?" Wendy asked.

"Well, sure," put in Diane Lesher, the oldest at thirty-five and the group's corporate-ladder-climbing career woman. She had beautiful ash blonde hair that framed a pretty face, but she claimed she never used her looks to get to the top. "We all have our fantasies. Maybe Frank just didn't measure up to yours."

They all hooted at the double entendre.

"Come on, Wen. Tell us your secret fantasy," Carol said.

"Uh-uh. You go first."

The other women laughed and called her chicken.

"No, it's all right if she's shy," Carol said. "Hey, I'm not shy. You should see some of the books that come my way every day. Whoo-ie! Did you know female erotica is the new 'chick lit'? Gives one a lot to think about. You want to know what turns me on?"

All eyes swiveled to hers. "Yes! Yes!" came the chorus.

Carol tipped her head. "It's not very politically correct."

"Ohhh now you have my full attention," cackled Diane. "Come on, girl, spill it."

"Okay. But remember, it's just a fantasy." She took a deep breath. "I have this fantasy—sometimes I even dream about it—of being dominated. Forced to submit. Maybe be spanked, you know, to soften me up? I'm not talkin' about rape. It's more about being under the control of a sensitive but demanding alpha male, you know?"

"Wow. I think I need to buy one of your publisher's new romance novels," Diane said, laughing.

"That's a very common fantasy actually," Suzanne said. "I read it in *Cosmo*. You're a closet submissive."

"Really? It seems to go against the grain of the modern feminist," Wendy said.

"It's our inner cavewoman," Diane said. "We can't escape it."

"Inner cavewoman? Is that real? Are we all just products of our ancient hormones?" Wendy marveled. "'Cause I like to think we've advanced a little bit since then."

"Come on," Carol said. "I told you my fantasy, now you all tell me yours."

"Oh gosh," Wendy demurred. "Please, someone else go before me."

"Okay," Suzanne said at once. "I'm game." She took a deep breath and gave her red hair a little shake. "I fantasize about having a one-night stand with a perfect stranger. Anonymous sex."

"Really? That sounds disappointing in a way," Diane said.

"Why?"

"Well, because if he's a lot of fun, you don't get to see him again!"

"I think that's just the point—it's something about the elusiveness of it. You know it won't last going in. You can be a completely different person just for the night and let your inhibitions fly to the wind. You see?"

"Ohh yeah, I can see that," Wendy said.

"Come on, Wen. It's your turn," Carol pressed.

Wendy looked around to see all eyes on her. "All right, all right. But you'll laugh."

"No, no! This is secret stuff. It goes no further than this room."

"Of course not," said Diane. "We're all friends here."

"Well..." Her face reddened. "I can't believe I'm telling you this..."

"Come on—you tell me yours and I'll tell you mine, okay?" Diane said. "Everyone else has already confessed."

"Okay—I fantasize about being a prostitute."

The other women's mouths opened in surprise then quickly closed so as not to hurt Wendy's feelings.

"Tell us more—I mean, you can't want to walk the streets in those ugly little outfits, can you?" Suzanne asked.

"You would think only of the outfits," Diane said.

"No, no. Not like that. I imagine myself being an exclusive call girl who caters only to rich businessmen and world leaders. But the sexy part comes when I must do whatever they want because they've paid me, see? I don't know—it makes me feel all dirty and naughty and sexy at the same time."

"I can actually see the turn on there," Suzanne said. "It's not all that dissimilar from mine, only in mine, the man doesn't pay me for the one-night stand. And I want him as much as he wants me."

"Or mine," Carol noted. "You have to do whatever the man said because he paid you, whereas I have to because he's so strong and virile and he just takes what he wants!"

They all had a laugh and poured more wine.

"Hey, now it's your turn," Wendy told Diane. "You promised."

"Yeah," the others put in.

"All right, all right. You'll probably think mine is the strangest of all."

"Ohhh now you have our full attention," Carol giggled.

"I fantasize that I'm on display somehow—you know, having sex in public. It could be a dark alley with a man taking me up against a wall, with the risk of people walking by, or it could be I'm making love in front of a class of first-year medical students while a doctor describes my performance. Just the idea that strangers might be watching us gives me a thrill." Diane took a deep breath. "There, now all our confessions are out there."

"That was a good one, Di. I've even lived that one!" Suzanne said.

"Which part?"

"The sex in the alleyway part. Except it wasn't an alleyway—it was a dark spot behind some bushes outside my college dorm room. My boyfriend just had to have me and I couldn't invite him up. So he fucked me up against the wall. It was kinda quick, if you know what I mean."

"Ohhh that's so sexy!" Diane said. "It should've happened to me!"

"I'm sure it sounds sexier than it was. But it certainly was naughty! My mother would've shit a brick if she'd ever found out!"

A moment of silence descended on the group as each thought about the others' fantasies.

"Well," Suzanne said. "Now that we've gotten sex out of the way…"

"Oh you think that's all we'll say about it tonight?" Diane said, and everyone had a good chuckle about it. Sex was always on their minds. And men.

"Ohhh yeah. I'm going to have to try Suzanne's trick one of these days," Diane promised. "All I need now is a boyfriend!"

The women nodded in commiseration and there was another odd silence. Almost as one, they all laughed at themselves and the spell was broken.

Diane took a deep breath. "For a complete change of subject, let me show you the new shoes I bought today," she said, and the others nodded, happy to put their strange little confessions behind them for now. She rose and fetched the bags she had stashed in the corner.

"Just a little 'retail therapy'," Diane said. "I'm still getting over Jimmy."

"That would've never worked. You can't get serious about a forty-eight-year-old man named Jimmy," Suzanne said.

"Yeah, that was funny. I tried to call him James or Jim, but he didn't like it. He was a Jimmy, like in Jimmy Carter."

Diane showed off her new black and white pumps with the two-inch heels and everyone said how pretty they were. She slipped one on and they admired her foot, turning it this way and that.

"Come on, what else did you buy?" Wendy said, eyeing the remaining packages.

"Well, if you insist." She laughed and dug out another box. "This is a silk blouse from Bloomingdale's. I just couldn't resist. And a Donna Karan skirt that matches."

She held up both so the women could see how they went together. The others made appreciative noises.

"How about this last box?" Wendy said, peering into the bag, not willing for the fun to be over.

"That…um, that's nothing. Just an eccentric ceramic. An impulse buy. I think I'll take it back tomorrow. It's kinda weird really."

"Let's see it," Carol said. "I love ceramics."

"Well, I don't know. You'll think I've lost my mind."

"No any more than the rest of us," Suzanne said, "especially after our confessions!" She hooted and the others joined in.

"All right." She pulled a small rectangular box from the bottom of a bag and held it up. "I was walking along 69th Street near the park and I saw this little antique shop. Sometimes you can find real bargains in places like that so I went in. There really wasn't much of interest, except for this strange piece of sculpture. It seemed to call to me somehow. So I bought it before I even thought about it. Now I'm having second thoughts."

"Enough stalling! Show us!"

"Okay." She opened the top and pulled out a small green leprechaun. He had his arms up as if gesturing and a big grin on his face as though he had a joke to share. It *was* a bit weird but it was also…strangely compelling. The three other women all stared at it for a minute before speaking.

"How old is it, do you know?"

"Where did it come from?"

"Can I hold it?"

"One at a time, girls, one at a time," Diane laughed. "Let's see. I don't know how old it is, but the shopkeeper—who by the way was *quite* handsome—said it was nineteenth century, which means—what?—1800s? Of course, he could've been lying. And he said it came from Ireland of course. I mean, look at it. He said he'd been meaning to have it appraised. It came in on consignment or something." She hefted it in her hands. "And yes, Carol, you can hold it."

She passed it over. Carol took it gently, as if it were a rare artifact, not a strange piece of ceramic. Then she jerked slightly, her eyes glazing over just for a second.

"Whoa! What was that?" joked Suzanne.

"Sorry, I just felt a sudden charge, like static electricity," Carol said. "It's nothing."

"Let me see it," Wendy said.

When she held it in her hands, she nodded to the others. "Yeah, I can feel it. It's like it's kind of alive or something."

"Oh come on," Suzanne said. "That's silly."

"Try it." Wendy passed it over.

Suzanne took it tentatively. "Wow. You're right. It seems hot or…maybe cool. I don't know."

"Really? It didn't do that in the store. I'm really not sure why I bought it." She took it from Suzanne and had a tiny spasm herself. "Jeez! You're right! It feels completely different now. I wonder why that is?"

"Maybe it's haunted with the ghost of its former owner," deadpanned Suzanne.

"Stop it! That's not funny. You'll make me nervous. I probably won't get any sleep tonight."

"So you'll take it back?" Carol said, looking wistfully at it. "Can I ask how much you paid for it?"

"I'm too embarrassed to say. It was too much, I can tell you that."

Diane put the object back in the box and packed up the rest of her purchases.

They moved on to other topics, talking over their hopes and fears and the dearth of good men. After another half-hour, Diane looked at her watch.

"Well, this has been a lot of fun," she said, rising and gathering up her bags, "but I have a big meeting in the morning and I'd better not show up looking haggard and hung over."

The gathering broke for the evening. The women collected their things and left as Suzanne stood at the door. "Bye, thanks for coming. We'll do this again soon."

She closed the door and leaned against it. She sighed, thinking how much she loved those friends. If her ex-husband had been a friend like that, they would never have gotten divorced.

She also wondered if she should go visit that little shop to see if they had any more strange items like Diane had found.

Chapter Two

Diane – Public sex

ꟹ

Diane woke the next morning stiff and out of sorts. She'd had many strange dreams of being naked in public, which she chalked up to her embarrassing "confession" the night before. What was she thinking, telling them that? She should've kept it to herself. Now her friends would probably think she's weird.

She shook off her lethargy and jumped into the shower. Later, as she was rushing out the door, her mind was preoccupied with the meeting she had scheduled at ten. It was an important presentation and the company CEO would be there. She mentally went over the points she wanted to make.

At the office, she grabbed a cup of coffee and reread her notes. There would be a PowerPoint presentation of course, but she wanted to keep the static graphics to a minimum and explain her report in words. Before she knew it, it was ten o'clock and time to gather.

Diane picked up her laptop and her sheaf of notes, heading for the conference room. She met Richard Duncan, her boss, in the hallway. He was an athletic man in his mid-forties and even though he was happily married, he enjoyed flirting with her a little. To Diane, it was innocent fun. She would never try to steal Richard away from his wife.

"Hey, beautiful," he said, keeping his voice low. "You're looking good."

"Well, hello yourself. Thanks."

"Listen, Paul's going to be a few minutes late, so do you mind if we start off with Kathy's report first?"

"Oh no, not at all," she said, pleased he wanted her to wait. Let Kathy be the warm-up act.

They filed in. Besides Diane, Richard and Kathy, there were four other junior staffers there, eager to soak up knowledge and observe the power plays that would be occurring. And Diane knew she was to be the star of the show.

As Kathy droned through her report, Diane went over her notes one last time. Her laptop had already been plugged into the A/V system so it was just a matter of waiting for Richard's boss.

The words on the page in front of her blurred and she found herself daydreaming. She imagined Richard's hand on her knee underneath the table. She wouldn't shake it off for fear it might cause a scene, but it was more than that—Diane found the idea arousing. Emboldened, he would move his hand up under her skirt. She had worn pantyhose that morning but wondered what it would be like if she had on stockings and a garter belt—and nothing else. Then her imaginary self could feel his hand on her naked thigh, close to the hot core of her.

"Are you all right?" Richard whispered from her right. She came out of her reverie with a start, feeling embarrassed. The daydream had seemed so real she dropped a hand to her thigh to make sure Richard's hand wasn't really there.

"Yes," she responded. "Just a twinge."

God, stop that! she told herself. She struggled to pay attention to Kathy. She was embarrassed to realize her fantasy had made her wet.

At that moment Paul Dartling walked in and apologized for being late. The CEO was a handsome, confident man with a barrel chest and a full head of gray hair. He was divorced and was rumored to have a girlfriend somewhere in the building, but no one could ever find out if it were true. If so, it would certainly be against company rules—ones he no doubt helped create.

Kathy quickly wrapped up and everyone settled in to see Diane's presentation. She stood and nervously brought up the first slide. She began to speak, finding her nerves calmed as she went through the facts, requesting backing for the new project.

Paul nodded several times during her talk, encouraging her. At one point, he asked a pointed question and she fielded it like a pro. He smiled and nodded his approval. When she finished, she sat down and Richard applauded, causing the junior members to join in.

"Thank you, that was very concise and to the point. I appreciate it," Paul said.

"Yes," Richard echoed. "Very effective presentation."

Diane smiled and nodded shyly. Suddenly another image thrust itself into her mind. She was lying on her back on the edge of the table, her legs spread, her pantyhose and panties gone. Paul was standing between them, his pants down around his knees, his fingers like talons on her hips as he pulled her to him. His hard cock speared her and it seemed so real she could almost feel him as he slid into her wetness. The others in the room were staring transfixed, but instead of being horrified, they were turned on by the scene. Kathy's hand was under her skirt and Richard was unbuttoning the blouse of a junior exec named Susie so he could grab her breasts.

The image was so sudden and so powerful, Diane gasped with the impact of it.

"Are you all right, Diane?" Paul asked.

"No, I mean, yes, I'm fine. I just…a cough got stuck in my throat."

He poured her a glass of water from the metal pitcher on the table. "Here. Wouldn't want to lose you now!" he joked, and everyone chuckled along with him.

She drank the water, grateful she could cover her gaffe. What was going on? Why would she think about that now?

She had never imagined herself as the boss's girlfriend before. Why now?

The meeting broke and they filed out. Paul pulled her aside. "Are you sure you're all right?" he asked, stepping close to her.

She knew he was flirting with her and she couldn't deny that she liked the attention, even if it was wrong. Her eyes dropped as she demurred and she could swear she saw his pants bulge with his erection. She had a sudden urge to touch it, right here in the hallway.

My god!

"Uh, yeah. I'm fine." It took all of her effort to raise her eyes to his face.

"Well," he said, trying to prolong the moment, "if you need anything, just let me know." With some effort he stepped back, but he made no attempt to disguise his hard-on. She glanced at it again and she knew he caught her doing so.

"Uh, yes, sure. Thanks, Mr. Dartling." She fled down the hall, shocked at what had just happened.

Richard caught her as she moved down the hall, her mind in turmoil, and asked to stop by for a debriefing.

"Diane, are you all right?" he asked when he had closed the door behind them.

Not you too! she thought. "Yes, sure. It was just a cough."

"Well, you looked pale and flustered there for a moment. I just wanted to make sure you aren't coming down with anything." He came over and touched her shoulder out of concern and Diane found the gesture pleasurable.

"No, really, I'm okay." Had she really made a scene in there in front of the CEO? She didn't understand what was going on in her mind.

She realized Richard was still holding her upper arm and she took a step back. This wasn't right. He was married! He was her boss! But another part of her said—*Yeah, do it! Right here in his office!*

He dropped his arm immediately when she resisted. She made an excuse and fled, heading immediately to the restroom near her office. Once inside, she was relieved to find it empty. She went to a stall and locked the door. Pulling her dress up, she looked down at herself. Her panties were soaked! She wiggled her pantyhose and panties down to her thighs and stared at the mess. God! This had never happened to her before! Diane grabbed several wads of tissue and began to sop up.

The touch of the tissue to her clit made her shake. She couldn't stand it anymore. Diane sat down suddenly on the toilet and pushed her pantyhose down past her knees, splaying them apart. Then she used her right hand to rub her clit. She was so turned on, she expected to explode at once but it was strangely unsatisfying. She didn't know why—all she wanted was a quick orgasm then she could get back to normal.

Almost by itself, her shaking left hand reached out and slid the deadbolt back, causing the door to come ajar. Even as her mind rebelled at the notion she was risking exposure, her mouth dropped open and she felt the rush of an approaching orgasm.

God!

Her left hand yanked the door open more until it banged against her knee and her right hand frigged her clit furiously until she came hard, her eyes rolling back in her head. She heard the bathroom door squeak open and she quickly slammed the stall door, throwing the bolt even as her other fingers were held tight to her sloppy clit, the waves of pleasure causing her to bite her lip to keep from crying out.

She stayed there for a minute and listened as the other woman entered a stall next to hers and peed noisily. Diane didn't dare move. She waited until the other woman left the stall and washed her hands. Finally she exited and Diane could breathe a sigh of relief.

What the hell had just happened to her? She had risked her very career here! Why had she opened the stall door? It didn't make sense.

She dried herself and adjusted her clothing. She came out and caught a glimpse of her reflection in the mirror—hair slightly disheveled, eyes wide, lipstick smeared. Diane quickly cleaned herself and left, her body shaking.

She stayed in her office the rest of the day, not even going out for lunch. She made excuses, telling people she had a lot of work to catch up on, and tried to concentrate on her next report.

At five, she got up and left with the streaming throng of employees, smiling and chatting as if nothing had happened but her mind was elsewhere. She went down the steps to the subway and stood on the crowded platform, waiting for her train. Diane purposely kept her mind blank, humming a tune and thinking of her friends. What would they say about her now?

When the train arrived, she pushed her way on with dozens of others. She caught a strap and stood there, swaying with the rocking motion of the train. She spotted a young man in a sport coat sitting near the window, reading a newspaper. He was an attractive man, she mused. Too bad he's married—she had spotted his gold ring right away.

Then another image forced its way into her brain—she was sitting on his lap, her legs on either side of him. He had his pants down and she had lost her underwear again. His erection rubbed against her clit and she reached down, pressing it hard against her.

"Fuck me, slut," he said, and she looked around to see the other passengers staring at her. A few even cheered her on. The sound electrified her and she rose up, feeling the head right at her entrance. She wasn't ready to end the show just yet, so she rubbed herself back and forth, exaggerating the motion of her hips as the crowd whistled and egged her on.

When she finally pressed down, forcing his engorged cock into her hot wetness, she had the most powerful orgasm she had ever experienced in her life.

Diane felt hands on her and she came to. Nearby riders looked at her with concern.

"Are you all right, ma'am?" a young woman asked her, gripping her elbow to keep her upright. "You seemed to have fainted."

She looked around horrified. Another rider held her shoulders from behind and she could feel herself leaning against his strong chest. She realized she had climaxed and passed out momentarily. She pulled herself upright on the strap and stammered, "Uh, yeah, thanks. I'm fine. I guess I just got a little hot in here."

The woman nodded but her eyes told Diane the truth—*I know what you just did.*

"I'm all right now really." She turned and nodded to the man behind her, who released her at once. "Thanks."

The rest of the ride was uneventful unless she counted her damp, hot pussy that throbbed like a drumbeat in her ears.

Chapter Three

Suzanne – Anonymous sex

Suzanne stood at the bar, sipping a martini and checking her watch. She was supposed to meet an old friend from work at seven, so why did she feel the urge to arrive at six-twenty? Did she want to get sloshed before she showed up?

She looked around, eyeing the man candy present. For some reason, they all seemed particularly attractive to her tonight. Especially the rugged-looking fellow with the fashionable three-day growth of beard and the shaggy brown head of hair. Was there some connection between the thickness of a man's hair and his penis size? she wondered. She laughed at herself. That would be a good question to pose to the girls.

The man caught her eye and Suzanne immediately flashed him a smile. *My but I'm being bold today,* she thought. He picked up his drink and came over at once.

"Hello," he said in a slightly foreign accent she couldn't quite place. Perhaps Greek? "You look lovely tonight."

"Well, thank you. You look pretty good yourself." Had she just said that? Her pussy seemed to be doing all the talking tonight. Men aren't the only ones who sometimes let their sex think for them!

"I don't think I've seen you in here before."

"No. My girlfriend and I heard about this place and thought we'd try it out."

He looked around. "Girlfriend?"

"She isn't here yet. In fact, she might've stood me up." That lie had come out of nowhere. It puzzled her. She squeezed her legs together as if to punish her talkative sex.

"Ohhh too bad. Well, I'd be happy to buy you a drink. My name is—"

She held up her hand. "No! No names. There will be no names tonight."

The grin started small and expanded until it filled his face. "What a wonderful idea!" he said.

They chatted over the next drink, which wasn't easy, for Suzanne didn't want to know what he did for a living or if he was married, engaged or dating someone regularly. She really had only one question. "Do you live alone?"

He did.

She checked her watch. It was ten to seven. Time to go or she'd have some explaining to do. She grabbed her purse. "Is it nearby?"

They left arm in arm. He hailed a cab and they got in. Once inside, he was all over her, his fingers caressing her breasts, her thighs, his lips planting hot kisses on her neck, cheeks and lips. She loved the way his soft beard rubbed her skin and the manly smell of him.

Suzanne was on fire herself. This was exactly what she needed, she thought. Since her divorce, she had lived like a monk, waiting for Mr. Right. Her mysterious Greek lover may not be Mr. Right but he certainly was Mr. Right Now.

The cab came to a stop and Suzanne pulled her clothes together, following the dark stranger out onto the curb. They were in a neighborhood of brownstones. She wasn't even sure where she was and she didn't care.

He led her inside and they went up two flights of stairs. Pausing outside a door, Suzanne could see 314 in gold numbers and immediately looked away, as if even that was too much personal information.

Once inside, he was on her and she was eager to comply. Her clothes were practically ripped from her body and she didn't care. When she was completely naked, he swept her up in his powerful arms and carried her to the bedroom. He threw her on the bed and undressed quickly. She watched, her legs slightly apart, as his clothes came off, exposing his well-developed chest. *Man candy,* she mused, her mouth coming open slightly when he slipped off his boxer shorts. His cock was just the right size and at full attention. Suzanne thought she could hear trumpets.

"Oh my," she whispered.

He crawled over her and began kissing her neck, upper chest and breasts. Suzanne swooned. God this man was making her hot!

They writhed together on the bed like desperate lovers. He bit her breasts and shoulders and she growled to encourage him. When his hand dropped down to her pussy, she knew she was well lubricated for him.

"My god, you are so wet," he commented.

"Just for you, baby, just for you."

He grabbed a condom from his nightstand as she spread herself open for him. She had never felt so alive, so responsive. When he was ready and the tip touched her, she could feel the orgasm building already. No other man had affected her this way, not even her ex. It surprised her.

"Yes, yes," she gasped, and he thrust into her in one stroke, as if he had to have her immediately—his overwhelming desire drove her to new heights. The lights seemed to explode in her head. She threw her head back, her mouth open in a comical "O", and felt the shockwaves of her climax wash through her.

"Oh god! Oh GOD! OH GOD!" Her hips thrust back at him as she felt his cock piston within her. He was just warming up. Sex had never felt so good. She had no time to think about it.

She came again and again, each one as powerful as the first. Her mind had come loose from her head and floated somewhere above her. She could look down and see her sweaty body clinging to this strong man, riding him for all she was worth.

When the stranger finally stiffened and erupted, Suzanne climaxed yet again, feeling each throb of his cock inside her. Then she passed into a blissful twilight.

When she awoke, it was morning. *Wow,* she thought, *I've never been knocked out like that before!* She lay in the damp sheets, her pussy delightfully sore. She heard the shower running. Her mystery lover was up already. A sudden urge overtook her. Without another thought, she grabbed her clothes and put them on. All except for her panties. Those she laid carefully on his pillow then tiptoed out of his apartment and into the new dawn.

Suzanne hailed a cab and went straight home. She knew she had to call her friend and make excuses as to why she hadn't shown. As the cab made its way uptown, Suzanne could feel her satisfied pussy practically purring.

Chapter Four
Wendy – Call girl

ꙮ

Wendy couldn't explain the twinges she felt. Ever since her confession to the others, her mind seemed to be preoccupied with sex! And not just any sex—the risky, prohibited sex she had fantasized about—being a whore. She imagined being handed a wad of cash by some mysterious man and ordered to fuck him or do things she had never done before. She chalked it up to their shared fantasies and wondered if the others were having similar thoughts.

Because Wendy was a "good girl", she didn't act on her fantasies. But at home Tuesday night, she did look online for *prostitution + New York City* and read several stories about arrests, convictions and the problem areas of town. That wasn't what she wanted, she decided. So she tried *call girls + New York City* and received several interesting hits. One in-depth story in the *Times* described the lifestyle and how "degrading" it was for the women involved. To Wendy, it sounded exotic and exciting for reasons she couldn't explain.

"Claire", the woman in the story—although that wasn't her real name—had agreed to talk to the reporter after her arrest, perhaps as some sort of warning to others. She had come to New York at age twenty to become an actress and, like many others, had taken a part-time job to make ends meet. But she had lost her job and no auditions had come through. She was too embarrassed to ask her family for help—her parents had told her when she left she was on a fool's errand and would soon come home, her tail between her legs.

In desperation, she had pleaded with the landlord to give her a break. His counter-proposal had startled her. If she would make love to him on six separate occasions, he would let her slide on one month's rent—twelve hundred dollars. Though at first shocked, it had seemed like a good deal to Claire—in a month, she could easily land another job, she reasoned.

The landlord wasn't an ogre either—he was a harmless little man in his late forties with a slight pot belly who had lost his wife to cancer three years before. Claire actually felt sorry for him. So she agreed. She made him wear a condom each time and didn't let him kiss her. Claire told herself she wasn't selling her body for money. This was a special arrangement, she told herself. A one-time deal.

However, the month passed and Claire still hadn't found work. Not only didn't she have the rent, she had no money for groceries or the utilities either. And she had to have a phone or how else would casting agents find her?

This time she approached the landlord with another proposal. She would "take care of him" as often as he wanted if he would cover those costs as well. The landlord agreed. In many ways it was like having a sugar daddy. The month went by quickly and Claire had somehow managed to compartmentalize her almost daily trysts with the landlord. He would come by, often at inconvenient times, and she would have to drop everything to satisfy him. Once he had followed her in after she had bought some groceries and fucked her over the arm of the couch, her pants yanked down and her groceries forgotten on the kitchen counter. A pint of ice cream had been ruined.

Still, Claire thought everything would be fine in the short term, just as soon as she found a job or secured a part. Another month went by. The landlord began to complain. Her expenses totaled eighteen hundred a month—even if he fucked her every day, which he didn't, he was still paying a lot to keep her. He began to put pressure on her to get a job or get new "clients". At first she hadn't understood, but she had quickly gotten it. It shocked her that she had in fact become a whore.

The landlord told Claire from now on, he would knock just one hundred dollars off her rent for every "session". If it didn't add up by the end of the month, too bad. It was up to her to bring in the extra money to cover her expenses.

As Wendy read this story, her hand was between her legs, pressing hard against her clit. Her clothes were in the way so she quickly stripped them off and sat naked in the chair in front of the computer, her hand rubbing herself. But it wasn't easy for her to come for some reason. She kept reading.

As the month wore on, the landlord visited Claire less and less. Perhaps he was growing tired of her. During the last ten days, she realized she had earned just nine hundred dollars in credit from him. Despite going on many auditions and sending out several applications, she hadn't been hired for any of the jobs.

Claire didn't know what else to do. How could she make up nearly one thousand dollars in ten days? So she had contacted a few escort agencies, just to test the waters. She found an ally in a service run by a woman—Sally—who was named in the story because she had recently been busted as well. She sent Claire to a hotel where she had met her first real john.

Wendy rubbed and rubbed herself as she read but couldn't climax. It was very frustrating. She finally abandoned the story, went to the bedroom and got out her trusty vibrator, which always worked. But she found that once she was away from the story about Claire, her ardor had cooled. Her clit felt oddly numb.

So she brought the vibrator out to the desk and sat there, reading the story as she held the vibrating tip against her. She succeeded in achieving a few little climaxes but the big one eluded her.

Claire had been very nervous. The man claimed to be a businessman from out of town but he could've been an undercover officer for all she knew. That would in fact occur later, but this time the man had been what he had claimed to be. He had paid her three hundred, which she had to split with Sally. After she accepted the money, he wanted to spank her. Spank her! Claire had been shocked but had gone along with it. After he reddened her ass, he put on a condom and plunged into her. He came within minutes and it was all over. All in all, she decided, it hadn't been too bad.

That was the beginning of her career as a whore. She went from a starving actress, not able to make her rent, to a wealthy independent call girl, earning eight to ten thousand dollars a month.

Wendy scanned the rest of the story and found it dealt with Claire's downfall—her arrest and realization of how low she had fallen. Therapy, recriminations...blah, blah, blah. She skipped it. To Wendy, the thrill was in her rise to the top of her profession.

The story made Wendy so hot she couldn't stand it. She wanted to be Claire and be forced to do things she didn't want to do, all because some man had paid her. It was the sanitized version of being a whore—no abusive pimps or dangerous johns. More like the *Pretty Woman* ideal, where every client was as handsome and polite as Richard Gere. The vibrator buzzed against her and she felt on the edge yet couldn't cross over.

She found herself dialing the number of her ex-husband Frank.

"Well, this is an unexpected surprise," he said. "What gives? Don't tell me you need money."

"No, Frank, that's not why I'm calling." She felt odd being on the phone with her ex totally naked. And especially since he had never given her the Big O she had needed. But she had no one else to turn to.

"I need, um, kind of a favor."

"But it doesn't involve money, does it?"

"No, not exactly."

"Whoa. What do you mean, 'not exactly'?"

"Oh Frank, don't embarrass me. I need… I haven't…" She couldn't say it.

"Wait a minute? Are you suggesting what I think you're suggesting?"

"Yeah, I am."

He cackled into the phone. "So you kinda miss me, huh?"

"Not all of you," she said, trying to flatter him but at the same time letting him know she didn't want to rekindle the relationship. "This is just a one-time deal, okay?"

"Sure, okay, sweetie. I guess I could help out my ex-wife in the sex department. Jeez, I figured you'd have two or three boyfriends by now."

"I'm not that kind…" her voice trailed off. "I mean, I haven't met anyone."

"Sure. I understand. So when do you want to do this?"

"Can you come over now?"

"Now? Wow, you must really be desperate! Well, sure, I'm not doing anything tonight. I guess I could."

Wendy suspected Frank hadn't had a date since their divorce, but she wouldn't say anything now. She needed him.

They hung up and Wendy dressed. It would be a bit too obvious to answer the door naked. She paced, waiting for him. She knew once he arrived she would have trouble climaxing if they simply had routine sex. But she suspected she might be able to reach her goal if she could convince him to pretend she was a call girl. Now how does an ex-wife broach that subject gently?

The doorbell rang and she ran to answer it, slowing to catch her breath just before she opened it. She didn't even use the peephole first.

Frank stood there, just as she had remembered him all those years they were married. It would be unfair to say they divorced because he couldn't give her regular orgasms but that certainly played into the mix.

"Hi, Frank."

"Well, hello, babe. Guess you just had to have me, huh?"

"Yeah. Uh, listen, I was wondering if you'd mind playing a little game with me." She was thinking fast, trying to come up with a plausible reason for her odd request.

"Yeah?"

"Well, the girls and I went out to a movie..."

"Yeah, what was it?"

"Uh, some art film. In French with subtitles." She almost smiled as she saw his eyes glaze over. "Anyway, there was a scene in it that was really hot. And I've been thinking about it."

"Yeah?" His interest perked. He probably imagined the film was X-rated.

"Yeah. The story was about a girl, I mean woman, who comes to, uh, Paris to find her fortune and falls on hard times..."

She went on to explain a lot of Claire's story using a French counterpart "Jacqueline". Frank seemed impressed, especially at how the landlord managed to get lots of sex from a hot young Frenchwoman. He seemed to gloss over the part about how expensive she was.

"So what is it you want to do?" he said when she finished.

"I want to pretend..."

"You mean..."

"Yeah. I want to be Jacqueline, just for tonight."

Frank gave her a big grin. "Well, okay." He took control. "Why don't you leave and this will be my hotel room, all right?"

"Yeah," she breathed, already feeling the sensations working through her. Her pussy began to grow wet just thinking of the scene about to unfold. "Yeah, and you act like the businessman from out of town."

He waved his hand. "Don't worry, I know what to do."

She left, standing out in the hall, trying to pretend she was in some fancy hotel. She knocked on the door. Frank opened it. "Well, hello there, little girl. Come on in."

His cheesy acting didn't help matters but Wendy went along with it. She came in. He tried to kiss her right away, even before he had the door closed. She held up a hand.

"Wait. We have to get the, uh, negotiations out of the way first."

He pulled back. "Huh?"

"You know. The money."

"Ohhh!" he said, understanding dawning on his face. "Sure." He pulled out his wallet and pretended to hand her some money. "Will that do?"

Wendy felt the sensations that had been building in her evaporate. "Uh, no, mister. You have to really pay me."

"Hey, I thought this wasn't going to be about money!" His face darkened. "Is this just some cheap scam to get extra cash out of me? 'Cause if it is, it ain't gonna work!"

"No! It's just that we have to make it real!"

"Yeah? And do I get my money back at the end?"

Wendy hadn't thought that through. "Uh, well, actually…" She was trying to figure out if she could pretend to really take it and give it back after she had climaxed, but her hesitation gave Frank the wrong idea.

"Forget it!" he bellowed. "You think I came all the way over here so I could be shaken down by my ex-wife? What kind of fool do you take me for?" He stormed out the door, slamming it behind him.

Wendy ran to her bedroom, threw herself on the bed and wept. What was wrong with her? Why was she doing this?

Chapter Five

Carol – Submission

ꟷ

For Carol it started with a dream. A dream unlike any she had ever had before. In it, she was in the company of a tall, good-looking man. She could tell from the way he carried himself that he was strong and very much in control. He wasn't cruel, in fact she found herself drawn to him. He made her wet.

He was fully dressed and she was in her nightgown. She felt embarrassed to be wearing such a scanty outfit and she tried to cover herself. He came forward, tsking.

"No," he told her. "Don't hide."

His hands roamed over her body and she shivered with desire. Everywhere his fingers touched grew hot. The nightgown was just in the way. It tore under his hands and she didn't care.

"You're beautiful," he whispered. "I can't wait to spank that soft, round ass."

"What?" She felt him pinch her nipple and it aroused her further. "God."

"You've been very bad. Here. Get over my knee."

She obeyed, unable to resist. Why was she doing this? The answer came immediately—because she needed it. Because she was naughty. The why didn't matter.

Her ass was up, waiting for his hand. Her pussy trembled.

Slap!

"Ohhh god." How could this be so good? Yes, it hurt at first but then faded into a fresh heat that made her push her bottom up to meet successive blows.

Slap! Slap!

"You need this. You've been disobedient."

"I have?"

"Call me 'Master'."

"Yes, Master," she found herself saying. Even the word thrilled her.

What had she done wrong? The questions evaporated with the next strikes, heating her and making her cry out. All she could think about was her reddening ass and his calloused hand. She would be good, she told herself. She would obey.

Slap! Carol thought she might climax right there. His hand began to stroke her, soothing her hot skin.

"There, there," he said. "That's enough. I like to see your little ass grow pink under my hand."

"Yes, sir, whatever you want."

"Here. Get up."

She rose and stood before him. He was still seated. He drew her to him until she was straddling his knees, her legs forced apart. His fingers brushed her wetness and she swooned.

"Oh god!" Her orgasm approached and she surrendered to it.

He pinched a nipple, bringing her back from the edge.

"Don't come until I tell you," he said. "You know the rules."

Rules? There were rules? It didn't matter. She would follow them. Anything to keep this overpowering feeling alive. She wasn't a career woman or a feminist at this moment—she was an obedient young woman, a purely sexual being, all in the thrall of this powerful man. It didn't seem wrong—in fact it felt exactly how it should be. He would protect her. All she had to do was obey him.

"Maybe I'll put in a ring here and here," he said, tugging at both her nipples gently.

Her knees nearly buckled. "Yes, Sir."

"And this will have to go," he said, tugging at the downy fleece between her legs.

"Really?" She looked down, proud of the hair that marked her as a woman.

"Yes. It's untidy. I prefer it bare."

She nodded, feeling the heat grow in her loins. "Whatever you say, Master." She shivered.

"See, that's the idea. Let go. Submit to me. I promise to take good care of you."

"Ohhh." She closed her eyes. Where had this man been all her life? She could see the other men she had dated. They were nice guys—polite, respectful. All very modern. But no one had swept her off her feet. Could it be they were all too nice? Dare she say wimpy? Had the women's movement ruined men? Where were all the big strong men today? The kind of man who would grab her and crush her against his chest. Or be so turned on by her that he couldn't stand it. A man to take her breath away. A man who was strong but not cruel, who was masculine and yet sensitive.

Did such men even exist anymore?

Her dream lover pulled her to him and kissed her breast. Carol wanted him. She could almost feel his hard cock entering her. She looked down and saw the bulge in his pants and smiled to herself, knowing that her nakedness caused it. She was desirable. She was needed.

She understood now how they fit together. She needed his strength and he needed her submission. It wasn't wrong. Instead it was beautiful. The yin and yang of the sexes. Rather than fight for power and position and try to beat men at their own game, she would find true happiness by letting go. She would get what she wanted by giving him what he wanted.

"Yes," she whispered. "I'm yours."

He eased her back and stood. Bending down, he picked her up as if she weighed nothing. She felt safe in his arms. He carried her into the bedroom and lay her down gently on the bed. In an instant his clothes were gone and she saw his naked body for the first time. His chiseled chest tapered down to narrow hips. Dark hair couldn't hide his hard cock that thrust out toward her. She reached out to stroke it.

He playfully slapped her hand. "No, you wait."

She nodded. Where had this man been all her life?

He climbed over her and brought his mouth down to hers. She lost herself in his kisses. She could feel his hard cock brush against her leg and she wanted him inside her. But that wasn't up to her. She must be patient, let him control the pace of their lovemaking. It was somehow freeing, allowing him to take over. She trusted him, that was the key, she realized.

He pulled her hands up over her head and suddenly her hands were tied to the frame of the bed. "Ohhh," she said. "You naughty man." Now she was helpless, unable to stop him from doing anything he wanted to her.

He brought his kisses down to her neck, causing her to shiver. Her breasts were next and her mouth came open with the sensation of his soft lips on her nipples. Her pussy quivered in anticipation.

Just fuck me! she wanted to shout.

But the man was deliciously deliberate. His kisses trailed down her stomach and Carol spread her legs for him, grateful they weren't tied as well. When his tongue touched her clit, she climaxed and saw spots in front of her eyes. She wanted to take a minute to recover, but her mystery man wouldn't have any of that. His tongue was insistent and she came again.

"Oh god," she murmured.

Finally, he climbed up over her and she felt his hard cock touch her hot core. She knew she would come again and didn't know if her body could take it.

His cock slid in effortlessly, the shaft teasing her clit. When he bottomed out, she climaxed for the third or fourth time—she had lost count. He began to move and Carol became lost in the sensations. Orgasms crashed in on her, rocking her body and short-circuiting her brain.

No one had ever affected her like this before.

"I want you to be my submissive," he whispered in her ear.

She nodded. *Of course, sir.*

Carol woke in a sweat, immediately disappointed. It had all been a dream! She looked down at her naked body and found the shreds of her nightgown all around her on the bed. Her pussy and nipples were sore. She realized she had torn her own nightgown from her body and had been rubbing herself in her sleep. Her pussy was weeping and Carol knew she had come more than once. There was an odd taste on her tongue—it took a minute to realize she had been sucking her own fingers after they had plunged into her grasping hole.

"Oh god, that was incredible," she whispered, wondering why she had dreamed with such intensity.

She got up and showered. The morning routine couldn't erase the images in her mind. Why couldn't she find a man like that in real life? Was her dream trying to tell her something?

Later at work, she sat in her office trying to proofread a novel onscreen and found her mind wandering. She clicked over to the Internet and brought up Google. With shaking fingers, she typed in *submissives* and hit enter.

The number of responses startled her. She found a definition and brought it up—

In human sexual behavior, a submissive is one who enjoys having any of a variety of BDSM practices performed upon them by a "Dominant"; or one who holds a submissive position within a relationship based upon dominance and submission – Ds or D/s. This enjoyment can spring from a simple desire for submission or an enjoyment of the interplay of wills involved in such a scenario.

Carol felt a rush of emotions and pressed her legs together until the feelings passed. She clicked off quickly and looked around, afraid she might be caught. There was no one else around of course. She was being silly.

Is that what I am? she wondered. There was no denying the thrill it gave her. *When did I become a submissive?*

Chapter Six

Comparing notes

ཨ

Monday night. Another meeting of the girls, this time at Carol's place. She still felt deeply aroused by her dreams. They had come every night, sometimes featuring the same man, sometimes with others. In her last dream, there had been three men and they all had spanked her, made love to her. She could do nothing but obey. In each case she woke panting and horny, her breasts and clit rubbed red.

She didn't think she should tell the others about her disturbing dreams. Perhaps it would be better to find a competent psychiatrist and get it all worked out. The girls might think she'd flipped out.

The doorbell rang and she answered it, trying to act normally. Wendy and Diane came in, handing her two bottles of wine they had purchased.

"Hi, it's good to see you," Carol said, a little breathlessly.

They exchanged hugs and Carol asked about Suzanne.

"I dunno," Diane said. "She said she would be here. But I haven't seen her all week so I don't know what she's up to."

"Really? I haven't either," Wendy said, and then asked Carol, "Did she call you?"

"Uh, no. I guess she's just been busy. I'm sure she'll show."

They went into the kitchen where Carol had prepared canapés. They opened both bottles of wine, grabbed glasses and plates and returned to the living room. They sat on the couch and gossiped about their lives. As the wine flowed, the women all felt more relaxed, yet no one volunteered to discuss their strange behaviors. They all believed they were alone in their dreams and waking fantasies. It would be too embarrassing to just come right out and say it. Each thought the others would think they were nuts.

The doorbell rang and they all exclaimed, "There's Suzanne!" Carol ran to the door. Suzanne entered, carrying another bottle of wine. She had a big smile on her face that somehow seemed out of place.

"Hello, hello!" They air-kissed and sat down.

"It's about time," Wendy said.

"Boy, Suzanne, you look distracted," Diane remarked. "What have you been up to?"

"Oh nothing," she said without conviction. Her smile widened into plastic territory.

"Come on, spill it!"

"Nothing happened!" She tried not to sound testy.

"Sounds like man trouble," Diane said. "So you might as well tell us who he is."

Suzanne looked away, tears forming at the edges of her eyes.

"Come on, this is us here, girl. You can trust us," Carol said, pouring her a glass of wine.

Suzanne took a healthy sip and said, "I'm not sure you would approve."

"Why wouldn't we? I'm just jealous, that's all," Diane said.

Wendy had a sudden urge to confess her own little secret just to make Suzanne feel better. "Hey, whatever happened to you can't be any worse than what happened to me. I got so horny, I called my ex-husband!"

The girls laughed and teased her, breaking the spell. More wine was poured. Suzanne finally relaxed a little.

"It's okay, you don't have to tell us if it's really bothering you that much," Wendy said, putting a hand on her forearm.

"No, I probably should. Because I don't quite understand it myself."

They waited. No one wanted to try to force information out of her. They knew she would tell them when she was ready.

"Okay, here it is. I slept with a man Tuesday night."

"That's it? B.F.D.," Carol said. She was thinking about her own dreams of being "forced" to submit and felt a little shiver of desire run through her.

"Well, that's not it. I slept with another man Thursday night."

"A different man?" Wendy asked.

"Yes." She took a deep breath and had another slug of wine. "And Saturday night I slept with another man."

"Three different men in a week!? Wooo-hooo!" Diane said, fist pumping the air. "Who says women can't be equal to men!"

"Yeah, but men are considered worldly when they sleep around, women are called sluts," Suzanne pointed out.

"So who are these guys? You think you'll date them again? And by that I mean, not all at once," Carol said, trying to make a joke. But Suzanne wasn't laughing.

"The reason I'm late tonight is because I stopped off and met another man at a bar earlier." Suddenly she burst into tears.

The other girls sat, shocked. They had never seen Suzanne behave this way before.

"What's going on?" Diane asked. "What's gotten into you all of a sudden? This isn't like you."

"I know!" She grabbed a tissue out of her purse and dabbed her eyes then blew her nose. In a quiet voice, she said, "And that's not the worst of it."

The other women looked at each other. What could be worse than sleeping with four men in less than a week?

"I don't know any of their names..." she said, her voice trailing off to a whisper.

The girls sat shocked. How could that be? Wendy finally vocalized what they were thinking. "You didn't get any of their names? How did that happen?"

"No. I...I didn't want to know."

"Oh my god," Diane said. She put a hand to her forehead. "Oh my god."

"Don't make me feel worse than I already do!" Suzanne said, and cried anew.

"No, I'm sorry. I wasn't thinking of you. I was thinking about something that happened to me." She told them about the visions that had come to her during her meeting last week and how in the days since she couldn't stop thinking about having sex in front of others. "And let me tell you, these aren't run-of-the-mill daydreams. I was rocked by them."

"Oh shit," Carol said. "I've had strange dreams too." She told them about the dream where the handsome man and others had dominated her in such a wonderful and loving way.

All eyes swiveled to Wendy. "How about you?" Suzanne asked, still blotting her wet eyes.

"Uh. Well. Yeah. I've had, uh, urges too."

"Let me guess," Diane said. "You got turned on when you thought about being a prostitute."

Wendy nodded wordlessly.

"That's why you called your husband," Carol said quietly.

"Yeah," Wendy responded, her voice low. "Except he wouldn't play along."

For several seconds, the four women sat and stared at each other, each lost in her own thoughts. Finally Suzanne broke the tension.

"This is just like our fantasies. I mean, they're coming true."

"Come on," Carol said, desperate to come up with another explanation. "I mean, why now? We've all had these fantasies for years, right? Why all of a sudden would they manifest themselves?"

As one, all eyes slid over to Diane.

"The little leprechaun," Suzanne said.

"No way! That old thing? That's ridiculous."

"Do you still have it?" Wendy asked, holding her breath.

"No, like I said, I returned it the next day. It really wasn't me."

Suzanne and Carol jumped up. "We've got to get that back!"

"I can't believe it! You guys are going off the deep end," Diane said, shocked.

"Then please explain to me how else this could be happening," Carol said. "Everything we said during our little confessional last week has come true. I am having very powerful dreams about being, well, a submissive. Wendy is having call-girl dreams. Suzanne is having a series of one-night stands and can't seem to stop. And you, you are imagining fucking your boss in the conference room in front of everyone, just like in your fantasy!"

Diane had no response. It sounded crazy. Could it be true?

"Remember the little electric shocks we got?" Wendy said.

"Yeah, like static electricity," Suzanne added.

"My god. What if we can't find it?" Carol said. But inside a voice said, *Would it be so bad?*

"I'll be known as the biggest slut in New York City," wailed Suzanne.

"At least you won't get arrested," Wendy put in. "Or get beaten up by a pimp."

"Yeah. I wonder how my boss would react if I were caught fucking some guy in front of everyone? I think my career would take a nosedive. I wonder what time that little shop closes?" Diane asked, checking her watch. It was almost eight. "It could still be open."

"Let's go. Maybe we can get there in time." Suzanne grabbed her purse and led the group out into the hallway.

"What are we supposed to tell him? And what are we supposed to do once we get it back?" Diane asked.

"I don't know. But maybe we can reverse it somehow. The key is, we have to have that fucking leprechaun."

The girls hailed a cab and Diane gave him the address. They arrived at eight-thirty only to find the store closed.

"Shit! It says it closes at seven-thirty, Monday through Friday." Diane squinted at the placard in the window.

"What about tomorrow?"

"Ten a.m."

"All right, there's nothing to be done. We'll just have to meet here at ten tomorrow."

"But what about…you know."

"Nothing's going to happen," Suzanne said. "Just lock yourselves in your apartments and take sleeping pills."

"Easy for you to say," Wendy pointed out. "You've already gotten your stranger out of the way tonight."

Suzanne glared at her. "Hey, do you think I like it? I can't help it if my secret fantasy is legal. It still makes me a slut."

Wendy hung her head. "I know. I'm sorry. That crack was unnecessary."

"It's all right, we're all on edge," Carol said.

"Okay," said Suzanne, taking charge. "Let's all call in sick, at least for the morning. We'll meet here at ten and hopefully, we'll be back to normal by noon."

They agreed it was really the only solution.

Chapter Seven

The shopkeeper

ꕤ

Promptly at ten, the four women met on the corner near the store. It was still not open so they stood and compared notes. Suzanne had slept pretty well but the others all had increasingly erotic dreams about their chosen fantasies and appeared haggard, worried.

Diane had arrived wearing a skirt with no panties, just a garter belt and stockings. She hadn't been able to stop herself. She rationalized it by telling herself no one would know, but why then did she have the urge to let her skirt fly up in the morning wind, showing her bare pussy to the strangers walking by? Just the thought of that made her so wet she could barely stand it.

Wendy had actually called an escort service that morning and inquired about jobs there. This came after she awoke in a sweat, her mind filled with images of strange men in anonymous hotel rooms. Fortunately, the service suspected trouble and hung up on her.

Carol awoke with her trusty dildo in her hand, thrusting it deep into her wet pussy, moaning with desire as she dreamt her mystery man was forcing her to entertain him and two friends.

They were all nervous as cats as they waited. Little was said for they could tell at a glance each woman was on edge.

Finally, the door was unlocked and they all hurried in. The proprietor was a tall, handsome man in his early fifties with a full head of black hair speckled with gray. He seemed surprised to find four good-looking women in his store first thing.

"Well, what can I do for you lovely ladies," he said, returning to his post behind the glass counter.

"That leprechaun sculpture I bought and returned. Do you still have it?" Diane said in a rush. She stood close so she could press her clit right up against the low counter. She hoped her friends wouldn't notice.

"Whoa. Wait a minute. What sculpture?"

"The green one. It looked like he was laughing? It was kinda weird-looking?"

"Oh yes, I remember that one! I was disappointed to see you bring it back. I really thought you liked it."

"Yeah, yeah—do you still have it?"

"Uh, no, I'm sorry. That particular piece was on consignment. When you returned it, I let the owner know. He came in the next day and picked it up. He seemed rather put out."

An anguished cry went up from the women. The storekeeper was taken aback. "Well, if you felt that strongly about it, why did you return it?"

"It was a mistake," Diane said. "My friends, uh, convinced me it was right for me." She had a sudden desire to flip up her skirt and press her bare mound against the edge, watching the eyes of the proprietor as she did. She bit her lip.

"Well, I'm sorry, but we have many fine pieces—"

"NO!" the entire group said at once.

"Can you tell me who owns it? We'd be willing to buy it back." Diane pushed up on her toes, increasing the pressure to her sex.

"Oh I'm sorry, my consignment customers are confidential. You wouldn't want someone rummaging around in your private business, would you?"

"Yes, but we're willing to give the owner more money for it," Suzanne put in. "Can you at least call him and let him know? Maybe he'll talk to us."

"Normally, I might, considering just how desperate you ladies seem to be. But this client said it was no longer for sale."

A collective groan went up from the group.

"But I'm the original buyer!" Diane pleaded. "And I want it back!"

"That is unusual. But he was quite insistent."

Diane stepped back with great reluctance and dug into her purse. She handed him her business card. "Listen, this is urgent. I can't express just how important this is. Please tell the owner to call me at this number anytime." She wrote her home number on the back. "We just want to talk."

As she handed him the card, she felt a surge of emotions when their fingers touched and glanced into his eyes. He smiled.

"Well, I don't know… I'll have to think about it." His words held weight and she felt drawn to him. Diane was suddenly hot. She stepped back and followed the women outside.

"Now what?" Wendy asked.

"I don't know," Suzanne said. "Can you girls hold out okay?"

"God, I don't know," Carol said, a sentiment echoed by Diane.

"Well, you can always do what your urge tells you to do in a controlled environment, can't you? Like Wendy tried to do with her husband."

Wendy blushed. "That didn't exactly work out like I had planned." She explained how Frank had gotten angry when she wanted him to pay for the right to have sex with her.

The women nodded—they completely understood. They knew how powerful their urges had become.

"I probably could've given it back afterward," she said.

"I doubt it," Carol put in.

"Well, it's worth a thought," Suzanne said. "Let's get together tonight and see what we can come up with. Can we meet at my house? Say seven?"

They agreed and split up, the worry beginning to line their faces. Two of the women were going uptown, one downtown. They offered to share cabs but Diane said she had some errands to run before she went back to work. All three women eyed her carefully.

"Don't get into any trouble," Suzanne warned.

Diane felt as if her friend somehow knew she was naked underneath her skirt. "I'll be okay," she quickly assured her.

When the women left, Diane waited a bit then returned to the shop. The shopkeeper smiled when he saw her again, as if he had expected her.

"You're back."

"What's your name?" she asked.

"Uh, Ray. Why do you—"

Without another word, she flipped up her skirt, exposing her wet pussy to him. His mouth came open and then closed suddenly. Diane found herself moving toward him, almost as if she were in a dream. "I really need to talk to the owner," she cooed, her pussy on fire.

He recovered quickly. A smile came to his eyes. "I don't know," he said coyly.

"Would you like to touch it?"

He nodded and stepped from behind the counter.

Diane came close and reached down for his hand. She brought it to her hot core and breathed out when he touched her as if a great weight had been lifted from her shoulders.

"You're all wet," he whispered.

"Yes. And I'll let you rub it until I come if you'll give me his phone number." It was all a game—they both knew she would let him do it anyway for nothing. He could see the lust in her eyes.

Still, he played out their little charade. "He'll be mad. He might not bring me anything else to sell."

"Trust me, he's waiting for my phone call, I can assure you."

His fingers began moving in small circles around her clit. Diane nearly came right then. With effort, she stilled his hand. "The name and phone number," she insisted.

The man grinned and made her heart melt. "I'd like to do more."

She glanced down and saw the bulge in his pants. Diane almost whimpered with desire. "Okay, but I control how it's done, all right?"

He nodded.

The man went back behind the counter and found a tin index card box. He rummaged through it until he came up with a card. "Peter O'Grady." He rattled off the phone number. Diane wrote it down on one of her business cards.

"Okay. Your turn."

"Come here, sit down on this chair." She pointed to a folding chair sitting next to the display case. She turned it so the back was to the front door, not fifteen feet away.

He looked puzzled. "But what if someone comes in?"

Diane shivered with delight. "Yes, that would be horrible, wouldn't it? Come. Sit. Do you have a condom?"

He shook his head.

"Wait. I think I do." She rummaged through her purse and found one, lost among the debris on the bottom.

"Come." He sat and she reached down to unbuckle his pants. His cock was invitingly hard. She unwrapped the condom and slipped it over his erection, her hands shaking. Spreading her legs, she straddled him and pulled her skirt out of the way. He stared at her damp, hot pussy. She used her fingers to spread herself open for him, giving him a good show, then eased herself down on his cock. Her wet pussy made the passage easy. When she was fully seated, she could look outside through the glass door and see people walking by. Her fingers went to her blouse and unbuttoned it, exposing her bra. If they only knew just inside the door, a semi-naked woman was riding a man's cock. She rocked up and down, rubbing his shaft hard against her clit.

"Oh god!" she cried. The sensation was wild! She'd never felt this good before. Diane increased her speed and felt the man responding beneath her.

Suddenly through the door, she watched as an older woman in a wide-brimmed hat turned out of the sidewalk traffic and entered the shop. The bell above the door jingled.

The man gasped when he heard it and tried to rise. Diane gripped the back of the chair, holding him in place. She never stopped moving up and down on his shaft. At first the woman didn't see them then her eyes focused on the bawdy scene in front of her and she cried out in surprise.

"We'll be with you in a moment," Diane gasped and came in a rush, made all the more powerful because a stranger was watching her.

The woman turned and fled.

The shopkeeper with his back to the stranger was still able to maintain his erection and he came a few seconds later. Diane could feel his cock throb, triggering another orgasm. She suddenly felt quite satiated. She stood and felt his cock plop free.

"Thank you so much," she breathed. "For the number."

"Uh, you're welcome." The man stood, stripped off the damp condom, pulled his pants into position and looked nervously around the shop. "Who was that?"

"Some woman. She didn't see your face."

"Yeah, but I own this place. It's not like she wouldn't recognize me!" He shook his head slowly. "You're crazy." The way he said it sounded more like a compliment.

"Yes, I suppose I am." Diane winked at him, shook her skirt back into place. On the way out the door, the man called to her. She turned.

"Come back anytime," he said.

She nodded and flashed him a big smile. As she stepped outside, carrying the number tightly in one hand, she realized her pussy felt satiated for the first time in days.

Chapter Eight

The noose tightens

ജ

When the girls gathered that evening at Suzanne's, they were met with a big surprise. Well, it was a surprise to everyone except Diane. The three of them had arrived in two taxis, one right after the other. They met on the sidewalk and exchanged meaningful looks. No words were exchanged. Carol rang upstairs to be buzzed in. At first nothing happened. Frowning at the others, she tried again. Suzanne's breathless voice came through the tinny speaker.

"Oh is that you, guys?"

"Yes," they all shouted.

"Okay, give me a sec then I'll buzz you in."

They stood on the stoop and waited.

"You don't suppose…" Wendy said.

"Nah, she wouldn't do that, would she? I mean, she knew we were coming at seven," Carol responded.

Only Diane kept her mouth shut.

The door buzzed and they marched through. They took the elevator up to five and as they were coming out, they spotted a man, still tucking in his shirt, his pants unbuttoned, being pushed out the door of Suzanne's apartment. He smiled weakly at the girls and caught the elevator.

Suzanne stuck her head and a bare shoulder out the door. "One second!" She disappeared inside.

"Oh this is getting bad," Wendy said.

"How about you?" Carol asked. "How are you holding up?"

"Just okay. I've called six escort services. No one will talk to me much on the phone so it seems to work out as a good delaying tactic. But I'm going to have to start visiting places soon, I can tell. How about you?"

"I must be putting out pheromones or something. I swear I'm being ogled by every alpha male in the city! It scares me and makes me horny at the same time."

Carol and Wendy turned to Diane. "And you?" Wendy asked.

"I'm, uh, okay." She flashed a thin smile.

Suzanne came back to the door, wearing a loose dress she clearly just threw on. "Come in, come in! Sorry about that."

"Your urges get the better of you?"

"I don't know what gets into me! I knew you guys were coming, but I just had to make a quick stop at the local bar and find a guy. I'm horrible!"

"Don't say that. We're all struggling with it," Carol said. "Well, except for Diane here. She looks like the cat that swallowed the canary."

Suzanne, now that she was satiated herself, could see that same look in Diane's eyes. "Well, well, what did you do today?"

"Oh nothing much." She smiled.

"Come on, we're all in the same boat here," Wendy said. "I've been telling you all about my whorish urges. Don't hold out on us."

Diane reached into her purse and pulled out the paper. "I got the ceramic guy's name and phone number."

For a moment no one spoke then they all jumped in at once.

"How did you do that?"

"Don't tell me you fucked that shopkeeper!"

"Not in public, I hope!"

Diane gave them a brief rundown of her adventure, including being interrupted by the woman in the wide-brimmed hat. "You should've seen the expression on her face!"

They laughed then caught themselves.

"You should be careful!" Carol said. "You could've been arrested."

"Or beaten up!" put in Wendy.

"No, he was very nice." She felt a tiny shiver run through her as she remembered the feeling, riding his cock as that woman came in. "But it *was* risky nevertheless. So let's call this O'Grady guy and ask him how to break the spell that thing has on us."

With shaking fingers, Diane dialed the number and listened. "One ring. Two. Three— Oh hello? Is this Peter O'Grady? Oh is he there?"

Suzanne mimed that she should put it on speaker. Diane nodded and pressed the button then replaced the receiver.

After a few seconds a gruff voice with a distinct Irish accent barked, "Aye, this is O'Grady. Who is this?"

"I'm Diane Lesher and I bought that cute little leprechaun ceramic you had at the antique shop on 69th Street?"

"Oh you're the one. Ray said you changed your mind and demanded your money back."

"Yes, well, I was hasty. I want to buy it back."

"Oh really? And why would that be now?"

Diane didn't know if she should explain its seeming powers or if O'Grady already knew about them.

"Uh, well, I just decided I really liked it after all. But the shopkeeper said you came and retrieved it."

"Yes, I did. I'm not going to have me country's work insulted."

"So it did come from Ireland?"

"Aye. It's very special."

"Well, yes, I've become quite, uh, fond of it. Would you be willing to sell it back to me?"

"Maybe. Why don't you come by and we'll talk about it?" His voice sounded like a leer.

"All right. But I want to bring some friends with me."

"Oh? In case I try some funny business?"

"No, no, they're just some girlfriends for moral support."

"Girlfriends, hmm? Okay. Why don't you come by tomorrow morning, say eleven o'clock?" He gave the address.

"Wait! Can't we come by tonight?" Carol jumped in.

"Who was that?"

"Oh that was just one of my friends. She, uh, really liked the piece too and thought I was crazy to return it."

"Yeah, well, it's too late tonight. Tomorrow, eleven a.m." He hung up.

Diane closed the phone. "Another night of dreams," she said.

"God, can we survive it?" Wendy asked.

"We'll have to."

* * * * *

Only Diane and Suzanne slept well that night. They both had dreams as before, but because they had satisfied the leprechaun's alleged curse, they weren't as intense as they might've been. In her dream, Diane was fucking Paul Dartling at a basketball game, not caring that people around them were jeering. At one point, they were displayed on the giant scoreboard screen and the audience cheered. Even the game came to a halt as the players watched them. She had an orgasm in her sleep that was so strong it woke her.

Suzanne dreamed of another bar, another stranger. She would make love to him then return to the bar to select a new man. Her body didn't seem sore—in fact, she had one delicious orgasm after another.

Carol, both attracted and repelled by the inherent dangers of her fantasy, didn't go out for fear she'd succumb to her carnal desires and wind up under the control of a dominant man. She wasn't sure how she was supposed to have her fantasy and yet control the risk. She tried to masturbate, thinking of strong, hard men, but her orgasm wouldn't come. When she did finally drift off into a restless sleep, she dreamt of the same strong man who both thrilled and scared her. She'd wake, feeling restless and horny, and the process would start all over again.

Over at Wendy's house, it was a different story. The young woman couldn't sleep at all—the itch was too strong. She went into her bathroom to splash cold water on her face and found herself toying with the razor there. Before she knew it, she was in the shower, shaving her legs, underarms and finally all the hair on her buzzing pussy. She bent down to make sure she removed every stray strand as far back as she could reach.

After she dried, she strode naked to her closet and picked out the tightest, shortest skirt she had—a black miniskirt she hadn't worn in years. Frank had bought it for her on a lark and she had worn it just one time for him outside their home. It had been scandalous. Wendy had no idea why she had kept it.

It was a little tight—she had to wiggle her hips to get it on. Of course, she didn't bother with underwear or stockings. Once it was on, she turned this way and that, looking at herself. The hem came down to just below the globes of her ass and it excited her to think about men trying to get a peek underneath. He bare breasts were still firm and perky at her age and she cupped them in her hands, pointing them at the mirror like twin six guns. Her fingers pinched her nipples, causing her to squeal in delight. She squeezed them again and watched as they stood erect.

Wendy found a purple tank top and slipped it on. It too was tight. But it sure made her breasts stand out! Her nipples threatened to poke someone in the eye. She walked around the apartment pretending she was a streetwalker. She wondered why she was doing this—hadn't she wanted to be an expensive call girl? No respectable hotel would allow her across the lobby in his outfit!

Not that she had any intention of leaving her apartment! No, this was just for dress-up, to ease the itch in her pussy that made her wiggle her ass and pinch her nipples. She tried to convince herself she was just about to take off the slutty clothes and go to bed! But the urge wouldn't let her. Wendy checked her watch—nearly one. Dammit! She was supposed to be at work at eight-thirty. Now how was she going to get up and look alert if this itch kept up all night!

Deep down, she knew what she had to do if she wanted to sleep. That damn leprechaun wanted his pound of flesh. Diane and Suzanne had succumbed to its power—only she and Carol had managed to hold out. But both of their fantasies were so dangerous! How could she ever have thought sex with strangers for money was a good fantasy to have? Not that she had any real control over it!

Even as she thought it, her pussy contracted. It seemed like a very good idea right now. Wendy walked around the small apartment again, like a caged animal. She stopped to look at herself in every mirror, seeing a slut on parade, just begging for it.

"Come, sailor, I fuck you long time," she said in a singsong Thai whore accent. She reached underneath her short skirt—which was embarrassingly easy considering how short it was—and rubbed her hot pussy. It felt numb somehow, like before. She knew she would not be allowed to bring herself off so easily.

She paced again. Suddenly she snapped her fingers. Mr. Townbridge! The older man lived alone three doors down from her. Every time he passed her in the hall, he smiled at her and often told her how pretty she looked. She knew he was interested in her. He seemed like such a nice gentleman. Of course he was a little too old for her, probably close to fifty! But maybe…

She shook her head. What was she thinking? *Good god, woman. You would ruin your reputation pulling a stunt like that. Sure, he probably would jump at the chance to fuck you like a common street whore, but you could never face him again! Especially once this damn curse was lifted. No, forget it.*

Wendy went into the bedroom and lay down. She tried to sleep but her thoughts were too jumbled. She got up again and resumed pacing. Her urge drove her actions. She went to the nightstand and pulled open the drawer, rummaging around until her fingers found what she was looking for—a condom. She held up the small square package, pleased with herself.

Now you can be a whore and not risk anything, her mind told her, as if it made perfect sense. She already knew Mr. Townbridge was harmless. Wendy found her black shoes with the stiletto heels and strapped them on. She stood, admiring herself in the mirror.

She grabbed her key and tucked it into the tiny pocket in the front of her miniskirt then left before she really thought about what she was doing. She strode down to Mr. Townbridge's apartment and knocked. Wendy stood there a long time knocking before a sleepy voice said, "What? Is the building on fire?"

"Mr. Townbridge? It's Wendy, from down the hall. Can I talk to you for a minute?" She heard the locks disengage and the door cracked open. His sleepy face peered out, his brown hair tousled. His eyes widened when he saw her outfit.

"Wen-Wendy? Is that really you?" The door came open wider and he looked up and down the hallway, as if he were afraid someone might see her. "Come in. Come in! Why are you dressed like this?" He was wearing pajamas and had a rash of stubble.

"It's kind of an initiation. I'm trying to join this select club and I'm supposed to pretend I'm a streetwalker," she lied glibly.

"Really? Which club?"

"Oh I can't say. But what I have to do is get at least one customer so to speak."

"One…customer?" One eyebrow threatened to take off.

"Yes. It would be dangerous for me to go out dressed like this. So I thought of you. I know you kinda like me."

"Well, sure, I like you. But…but…"

"Oh it's just for tonight! After this, we can both pretend it never happened, okay?"

"What never happened?"

She held up the condom. "This."

Now both eyebrows shot up. "You mean…"

"Well, only if you pay me for it."

"Pay you?" His eyes narrowed and for a minute Wendy thought he might react like Frank did.

"Yes. What do you think this is worth?" she said quickly, lifting up the edge of her dress to show her cleanly shaven pussy. His mouth dropped open.

"Uh, uh, uh…"

"I think fifty bucks would be a real bargain, don't you, Mr. Townbridge?"

"Please, call me Bob. You want me to pay you fifty bucks…and then you'll let me…?"

"Fuck me? Well, yes, that's what hookers do, don't they?" She smiled sweetly at him.

"And this club wants you to do this as part of an initiation?"

"Yes. Something like that."

He seemed suspicious, as if this were far too good to be true. "I've never heard of a club like this before."

"Does it really matter, Bob? I've seen you look at me when we pass in the hall. This may be your only chance to make love to me. Do you want to pass it up?"

"Nooo," he breathed. "Let me get my wallet."

He counted out fifty dollars, two twenties and a ten, then led her into the bedroom. Wendy realized she hadn't brought a purse and the tiny pocket on the front of her skirt was too small. *Something to remember for next time,* she told herself. For now, she placed the money on the floor next to his bed and stripped off her skirt and top. She left her shoes on.

She jumped onto the bed and watched while Bob yanked off his pajamas and crawled in next to her. They kissed and hugged for a minute then Wendy pushed him back impatiently. "Come on, let's get to it."

He crawled over her, his cock a hard spear. "Tut, tut," she said, holding up the condom.

Bob looked at it then at her lovely, firm young body laid out beneath him. "I'll give you another fifty if you let me do it bare."

She smiled and tossed the packet across the bed. "Deal."

He entered her in one smooth thrust and her breath was nearly knocked from her body. She realized that was the leprechaun's treat for her. Now that she finally did what he demanded, he was providing her reward. *I'm being paid one hundred dollars to fuck this man,* she thought and her pussy contracted, sending new waves of pleasure throughout her body. She came once then again in quick succession before she felt Bob's cock erupt inside her. Wendy grabbed him and hung on, feeling another powerful shockwave rock her.

And then it was over. He rolled off her and seemed ready to fall asleep. She got up and dressed quickly. She poked him and held up the money.

"Get another fifty out of my wallet on your way out," he said. "Oh and thanks so very much, my dear. You made my year." He drifted off to sleep, a slight smile on his lips.

Wendy found his pants and fished out his wallet. There was close to two hundred in there, she noticed. If she were a crooked whore, she could take it all. But she felt satiated for the first time in days and didn't want to punish her first paying customer. She took another fifty and tossed the wallet back on top of his pants.

She felt his seed seeping out of her and she reached down, scooped up some on her fingers and tasted it. Wendy experienced a pang of disappointment that she didn't get to suck him off and the thought startled her.

I'm sorry because I didn't get to blow him too…?

She shook her head to get rid of that stray thought. No more! But she had to admit, it had been so easy! She had worried over nothing! She let herself out and returned to her apartment. In minutes, she was sleeping dreamlessly.

Chapter Nine
Peter O'Grady

ℌ

At eleven the next morning, the women exited a cab in front of the address Peter had given them. Of the four, only Carol appeared haggard and weary. The other three were almost cheerful. *Just give the little man what he wanted,* Wendy thought. *Or was that what* we *wanted*? She shook her head—it was so confusing.

The address turned out to be an expensive, newly remodeled townhouse in an upscale neighborhood. Diane rang the bell and they waited nervously. A formal, white-haired man dressed in a black suit answered the door.

"Yes?"

"Um, we're here to see Mr. O'Grady?"

"Your name?"

"Oh I'm Diane Lesher..."

"One moment please." The door shut in their faces.

"Well, he's not very nice," Suzanne harrumphed.

"Peter must really like his privacy," Diane suggested.

The door opened and the butler stepped aside. "Please come in. Mr. O'Grady is expecting you in the library."

They followed him through an ornate foyer into a small room filled with floor-to-ceiling bookshelves. Behind a desk in the corner sat a small man dressed in an expensive gray suit, his tie knotted tightly at his throat. He appeared to be somewhere between sixty and seventy years old, although it was hard to tell. His gray hair was still thick and neatly combed over his head. He had a snifter of brandy before him.

But what really caught the women's attention was the little green ceramic leprechaun that seemed to laugh and dance on the desk in front of him.

"There it is!" Diane exclaimed at once. "How much do you want for it?"

The man ignored her and waved the butler away. The door closed softly behind him. "Wow, four of you," he said. "I'm impressed. I daresay that's a first." His Irish accent was strong. He stood and came around. The women could see he was only about five-six in height. "I'm Peter O'Grady, at your service."

"Yes, it's very nice to meet you, now about the statue..." Diane started in.

Peter held up his hand. "Not yet. First we talk." He gestured to the couch and two wingback chairs around a coffee table. Reluctantly, the women sat, three on the couch and Suzanne on one of the chairs. Peter took the other. They introduced themselves and he nodded in turn.

"Now tell me why you want this little statue so badly," he said then sat back and waited.

The women looked at each other. Finally Diane said, "You must know about the, uh..." She didn't want to say it.

"What? You mean the power to make your dreams come true?" O'Grady flashed a smile.

"Well, we were thinking it was more of a curse," offered Suzanne. "But yes."

"So tell me, did all of you ladies experience this, uh, curse?" He looked around and saw them all reluctantly nod. "Excellent. Really. I have never seen this before."

"Please, you've got to remove it!" begged Carol, twisting her hands in her lap.

"First, tell me what you wished for."

"We didn't wish for anything!" Diane said. "We were just talking and we passed it around..."

"Don't waste my time. You don't have any to waste." His eyes bore into Diane's. "Let's start with you. What happened? What were you talking about?"

"Oh god, do I have to? It's embarrassing."

"Yes, you have to. Or you can all get up and walk out right now."

Diane and Suzanne eyed the statue, both thinking the same thing. *I'll bet we could grab it and be out of here before that little man could catch us.*

"Tut," Peter said, catching their expressions. "The statue won't do you any good without the secret incantation to remove the, uh, power. Do you want to remain as you are…forever?"

"No!" Diane took a deep breath. "We were talking about our…secret fantasies," she said, her face coloring. "You know. Girl talk. Innocent fun. Then afterward, just by coincidence, we all passed that strange little ceramic around…"

"And what was your secret fantasy?"

"You little pervert," Suzanne put in.

"Fine. Go. And good luck to ya."

"No!" Diane said. She turned to Suzanne. "Don't." Her friend reluctantly nodded.

Diane faced the Irishman. "Mine was, uh, that I have…sex in public."

"And what have you done about that in the last week?"

She stared at him for a long few seconds but he remained firm. The others knew their turn was soon to come. "I've had visions, dreams about…having sex with my bosses, uh, in front of others. And two days ago, when I went to the shop to get your number, the shopkeeper was reluctant to give it. He said you valued your privacy. So I, uh…" She looked over at the other women, embarrassed to relive it in front of this nasty little man.

"Go on."

She sighed. "I made love to him in his store in exchange for your number. And while we were doing it, a woman walked in. It was…strangely satisfying." She hid her head in shame.

Peter smiled. "Sex in public. That's a good one." He turned to Suzanne in direct challenge. "How about you, Suzanne?"

She held her head up high. "I mentioned right before I handled the damn thing that I had a fantasy about having an anonymous one-night stand. Since then I've had several different lovers—and I never wanted to know any of their names."

"And you can't stop yourself, can you?"

She shook her head silently.

"Amazing." He turned to Wendy. "And you, my dear?"

"Oh god, I'm so embarrassed!" She put her head into her hands.

"Nonsense, Wendy. The others have talked about theirs, now it's time to hear yours."

She looked at the floor as she said in a monotone, "Uh, my fantasy was to become a call girl, a whore. Being paid by men and forced to do things I wouldn't normally do."

"And what have you done about it?"

"Nothing really," she lied. "I mean, I called some escort services but I haven't gotten around to actually going there."

The room fell silent. Peter studied her carefully. Then he stood abruptly and plucked the small ceramic figure from the desk. "What do you think, leprechaun? Do you think she's telling the truth?"

He put the statue back. "He says you're not telling us everything. So I guess you don't mind staying the way you are…"

"*No!* I mean, how would you know what I did or didn't do?"

"I can tell. For one, you're calmer than she is." He pointed to Carol. "If you hadn't done anything, you'd be just as nervous right now."

Wendy put her head in her hands. "Oh please, don't make me tell!"

The other women perked up—clearly Wendy had been holding out on them!

"Come on, Wen," Diane said. "I told you about my encounter with the shopkeeper!"

"All right. But it isn't me, you understand."

"This isn't any of us," Suzanne pointed out. She turned to Peter, "Although I'm not sure why you insist we tell you the lurid details."

"Consider it part of the reclaiming process. I have to understand what happened in order to help you." He paused. "Because right now I'm a little surprised at the intensity of your experiences." He looked pointedly at Wendy.

"All right!" She took a deep breath. "Last night, I was so antsy, I went down the hall and played being a hooker for one of my neighbors."

Carol gasped in surprise. "You did?"

Wendy nodded. "Yeah. Mr. Townbridge. I made him pay me fifty bucks." She decided not to share the last bit of information.

Peter nodded. "And did you feel relief afterward?"

"Oh yes. I slept very soundly after I came home."

"Good. Right. Now, Carol, it's your turn. I can see you've been resisting your fantasy."

"Yes. Because mine is too dangerous. I don't know what I was thinking having a fantasy like that! I…I imagine I'm being forced to, er, submit. Like being under the control of a strong man. An 'alpha male' type."

"Ah," O'Grady said. "A dominate/submissive scenario. Part of a BDSM fantasy."

"It's a common fantasy," Suzanne assured her. "I'm sure many women share it."

"Yeah, but what if I became attracted to the wrong man? In my fantasy, it's like they are more in control or experienced, you understand? In real life, I could be murdered! Or held as some kind of sex slave!"

Suzanne and the others nodded sympathetically. Then they all turned to the Irishman.

"Okay, you've had your jollies," Diane said. "Now can you remove the curse?"

"Like I said, I needed to understand what was happening in order to help you. It's not supposed to work like that."

The women appeared puzzled and frankly worried.

"You see, this ceramic has a long and ancient history. It's much older than nineteenth century actually. It, um, encourages the owner to achieve their innermost desires. Say for example, Diane, if you had a secret desire to visit Paris in the springtime. That idea would stay with you. Over time, you'd find a way to make it happen. You would fulfill your dream."

"But it's much more powerful than a mere suggestion," Diane said. "It's making us crazy."

"Yes, that's the part that puzzles me. But I assume it's because you spoke your innermost thoughts out loud before you touched it. Normally, it's much more subtle."

"There's nothing subtle about this," Suzanne said. "Now how can you stop it?"

"Wait a minute, Suz," Diane put in. Something was bothering her. She pointed at O'Grady. "If it's so valuable, why did you put it up for sale at that shop?"

He smiled. "I do that from time to time. The sculpture always comes back to me. It amuses me to know that somewhere out there, a man or woman is achieving their secret desire."

"That's despicable!" Wendy said.

"It's supposed to be a good thing," he said, shrugging.

"What gives you the right to play with people like that?" Diane asked.

"Because I'm the last of the leprechauns," he said, eyes twinkling. "It's what we do."

"Bah," Diane said dismissively. "There's no such thing!"

"Who do you take us for, fools?" Suzanne snapped.

"Then how do you explain what's happened to you?"

They had no good answer for that.

"If you're really a leprechaun, why aren't you back in Ireland then, sitting on a pot of gold or something?" Wendy asked.

"I travel around," he said simply.

"All right, putting aside who or what you are, can you help us? I mean you've got to do something. You've just about ruined us!" Suzanne said.

"Yes, you have to remove it," Carol said. "I'm desperate here."

"Yes, well, that could be a bit of a problem."

He had the women's full attention now.

"Because the statue is only supposed to suggest action, I'm not sure how to undo what's been done."

"What about the secret incantation?" Suzanne asked.

"Well, I might've fibbed about that. I didn't want you to try to grab it and run out of here. That would only make your desires intensify. Trust me, the last thing you want to do is to hang on to that ceramic."

Any thoughts the women had of stealing the ugly little statue evaporated.

"You have to do something," Carol begged. "Please."

"I could try to modify it..."

"Yes!" they all said at once.

"I'm not sure it would work..."

"Anything's better than this!" Wendy said.

"Very well. Unfortunately, I can't do anything yet." He faced Carol. "You have not yet fulfilled your fantasy as the others have. You'll have to do that first. You're all linked now, you see. You started this journey together, you have to walk it together."

"Oh god!" Carol wailed. "I could be killed!"

"No you won't," Suzanne said. "We'll simply do it in a controlled environment."

"Yeah, we can hire some guys to play like dominants," Wendy said.

"You think that would work?" Suzanne asked O'Grady.

"It might. As long as it satisfies her itch. She'll know. But you have to take that step before I can attempt to modify its power. If I can at all."

"Don't say that! Of course you can!" Diane said, casting a wary eye at Carol.

"Okay," Suzanne said, standing up. "We'll run out and get Carol taken care of then we'll come back here a little later, all right?"

"Yes, that would be fine. Say five o'clock?" O'Grady stood. All of the women were taller with the exception of petite Wendy.

"We'll be back," Suzanne warned. "Don't try to pull a fast one on us."

"I feel a certain responsibility here. I'm not an evil man."

"Yeah, whatever," Diane said. She still didn't believe in such fairy tales.

They left, gathering on the sidewalk outside to map their strategy.

"God, I was supposed to go back to work," Carol cried. "Now I have to go be someone's sex slave!" She shivered, but it wasn't from fear—it was desire.

"Oh stop. We'll control everything. You'll be fine." Suzanne was always the rational one.

"Where are we supposed to find some Dom who won't go too far?" Diane asked.

"Give me a minute to think."

*****

Inside the town home, Peter sat back in his chair and laughed out loud. His voice echoed across the walls and down the hall. The butler heard him and shook his head. He was well aware of his master's mischievous ways.

Chapter Ten

Carol takes the stage

ࢻ

It was all set. While Wendy took Carol home to watch over and protect her, Diane and Suzanne went down to the theater district. It took a bit of doing, but they found a tall, handsome actor in his mid-thirties waiting tables at an off-Broadway café who agreed to listen to their request that he "dominate" their friend.

"Come on," the man said. He had introduced himself as Dirk—a stage name if there ever was one. "This is a gag, isn't it?" He looked around as if trying to spot a hidden camera.

"No, this is legit," Suzanne said. "It's, uh, part of her secret fantasy."

"Yeah," Diane put in. "It's coming up on her birthday and we thought that would be the best gift."

He eyed them. "I don't know…"

"Hey, if you don't want to, I'm sure I can find some other out-of-work actor who could use a hundred dollars…" Suzanne said, gathering up her purse.

"No! Wait! A hundred dollars? For how long?"

"An hour to an hour and a half. But you'd have to be convincing. You'd have to act the part of a Dominant, you understand?"

"How far would you want me to go?"

Suzanne looked at Diane. Her friend nodded.

"Sex might come into it," she admitted. "But you'd have to wear a condom!"

Dirk raised an eyebrow. "Sure. But this sounds like a setup."

"In what way? We're offering you the opportunity to make love to a beautiful woman," snapped Suzanne.

"It just sounds too good to be true. In order to protect myself, I'd feel more comfortable bringing along a friend." He jerked his thumb at another waiter, a shorter but solidly built man talking to a nearby customer. "That way she can't cry rape halfway through."

Diane and Suzanne huddled privately to discuss this wrinkle. They didn't like it but they could understand Dirk's reluctance.

"What do you think?" Diane asked.

Suzanne looked over her shoulder at the two men. "I don't know. She did say she had dreams about more than one man. It might be all right."

Diane nodded and shrugged.

"All right," Suzanne told Dirk. "But no real rough stuff."

Dirk agreed. He introduced them to his friend Sam, who stood about five-nine but had a thick chest and arms that could only come from continuous weight training. He listened to the proposal with a startled expression and said, "Hell yes!" when they were done. He high-fived his friend Dirk.

They all took a taxi to Carol's apartment where they huddled outside with Diane while Suzanne went in to explain the rules to Carol. Wendy just sat in the corner, her eyes wide, listening in.

"You think this will work?" Carol asked.

"Of course it will. This will be your fantasy, just as you want it. These men really won't hurt you—they'll behave just like the men in your dreams," Suzanne assured her. She found two condoms in the nightstand and placed them on top.

"There's two men?"

"Yes, he insisted that he bring his friend. Is that all right?"

Carol nodded, thinking about being under the control of two dominants. A frisson of desire ran through her body. "Okay. What do I do?"

"In a few minutes, you're going to leave and go down to the store and buy a newspaper or something. When you return, the play will begin. All right?"

She nodded again. "And they won't really hurt me?"

"Of course not! You think we'd allow that? We'll be right outside anyway, just in case."

"Outside the apartment or outside the bedroom?"

"Which would you like?"

"I'd prefer that at least one of you was in the apartment—just stay out of sight unless I need you."

Suzanne nodded. "All right. But don't worry. Now wait here for a few minutes before you leave. Give me your spare key. Wendy, you come with me."

The women left and met the group in the hall. "Okay, we're all set. Let's go upstairs until she leaves then you two go in and pretend to be someone she knows—her dominant lovers. You understand?"

The two men nodded. They all trooped upstairs and listened in the stairwell. They heard Carol leave and lock the door, her footsteps echoing down the hall. When she had gone downstairs, the group returned to the apartment and Suzanne unlocked the door.

"Okay, you guys hide and 'surprise' her. Just remember, don't hurt her! I'll be hiding in the spare room so don't go in there."

"We've got it," Dirk said. He and Sam went in. Suzanne turned to Diane and Wendy. "I guess you guys should hide somewhere. Or maybe go get a cup of coffee."

"We'll get coffee," Diane said. "We'll come back in about a half hour."

"You sure we should?" asked Wendy.

"Yeah, she'll be fine. We have to give them a little time. I don't want to stand around in the hall while they're playing their games."

The women left. Suzanne went in and nodded at the two men then disappeared into the spare room.

Carol came home ten minutes later. The two men heard the key in the lock. She came in with a small sack and pretended not to be nervous but her heart was pounding.

Dirk was standing in her kitchen, a cruel smile on his lips. Carol sucked in her breath, suddenly afraid.

"Hello, my little slave."

Sam stepped forward out of the shadows, took the sack from her and placed it on the counter. Dirk grabbed her upper body and snarled, "You've been very bad! You need to be punished!"

Despite her friends' assurance, Carol felt almost out of control with fear. "No!"

"Grab her feet!" he ordered Sam.

"Wait!" He ran to the bag and looked in.

"What are you doing?"

He pulled out a quart of milk. "Don't want this to spoil." He put it in the refrigerator.

He returned and picked up her feet as she struggled. They carried her into the bedroom and threw her on the bed.

"You're ours now, slave," Dirk said in his tough-guy demeanor. "You need to learn the rules."

"Yeah, babe," Sam put in. Dirk gave him a funny look.

They jumped on both sides of her and Dirk began unbuttoning her blouse, careful not to rip it while at the same time trying to appear menacing. For Carol, the experience had an otherworldly impact on her. Her fears began to evaporate. These men were clearly acting—not at all like the men in her dreams. Those men were deadly serious. These men were…clowns.

Stop, she thought. *Give it a chance.*

They managed to get her blouse off and began working on her skirt. Sam had some trouble with the zipper and finally had to ask Carol to get it started for him. She then lay back and tried to rekindle the feeling of helplessness she needed for her fantasy to be fulfilled.

The men got her stockings off—no snags or rips!—and Sam carefully folded each one, placing them on the nightstand. Soon they had her naked on the bed. She just lay there limply.

"Aren't you supposed to fight or something?"

"Yeah," Sam said.

"Oh sorry." She tried to sit up and Dirk pushed her back down. That sent a little shiver of fear through her. It was strangely delightful. He turned her over, exposing her ass.

He slapped her cute round ass and she jerked. Her mouth came open. *Yes,* she thought. *Oh god, yes.*

Dirk spanked her again. The blows weren't hard and she wanted—no, needed—them to be. She wanted to be really punished. For what, she didn't know. It was difficult to get into her role—these men were about as far from the men in her dreams as one could get.

Dirk stopped after a few swats. He climbed up over her and unbuckled his pants. She saw his cock spring out and gave a little scream but not out of fear—he was rushing things. He slapped her face as if he were patting her with powder, using just the tips of his fingers. It wasn't Dom-like at all.

"Shut up, slut!" It sounded as if he were reading from a bad script.

He steered his hard cock toward her and she screamed, "Condoms!"

"Oh sorry," he said, and grabbed one off the nightstand.

As he was trying to fit the condom over his erect cock, Carol couldn't help herself. She began to laugh and rolled to her side, covering her face with her hands.

"Hey!" Sam said. "That's not nice!"

"I'm sorry! I'm sorry!" She rolled back. "Okay, where were we?"

Dirk's cock deflated and he tried to coax it back upright with his fingers to no avail. He snapped off the condom and turned to Sam. "Help me out here, wouldja?"

Sam leaned over and began sucking on Dirk's limp cock. Carol scooted up against the headboard and grabbed the sheet to cover her. "You guys are *gay*?"

Dirk looked up, surprised and a little hurt. "Does it really matter?"

Sam pulled away. "You don't have some sort of prejudice here, do you?"

"No, no! It's just that…" She began to laugh again.

"Hey, now you're hurting my feelings," Dirk said.

"I'm sorry! But I just never expected Suzanne would hire *gay* dominants for me!" Her laughter burst out.

"For the record, I'm bisexual. Sam is gay."

She turned to Sam. "And were you going to have sex with me too?"

"Well, I figured Dirk would handle that," Sam said. "I saw myself in more of a supporting role."

"Suzanne!" she bellowed, her sides hurting from the hilarity of the situation.

Suzanne burst into the room. "What? What's wrong?"

She saw Carol, naked and giggling, holding the sheet up to cover her body. The two men squatted next to her on the bed with perplexed expressions on their faces. Dirk had tucked his cock back into his pants.

"What the hell is going on here?"

"You hired *gay* dominants," she cackled.

"Oh god," Suzanne said.

"They were so polite! He put away the *milk*! I thought they'd iron my clothes as they removed them."

"I'm *bisexual*," Dirk repeated. "I can play this part."

"No, no. You're a fine actor," Carol said. "But it's just not *right*, you understand? It's all too fake."

The men climbed off the bed and faced Suzanne. "What now? Do we get our money or not?"

"Clearly this isn't working out. Let's say fifty bucks apiece for your trouble."

"Yeah, we're going to *go in another direction*," cracked Carol, still holding herself. "We're looking for sort of a Brad Pitt meets Christopher Walken." She buried her face in the pillow. Suzanne could see her sides moving with mirth.

The men accepted their pay and left. Diane and Wendy came by a few minutes later and rang the buzzer. Suzanne let them in while Carol dressed, still chuckling and shaking her head.

"Gay dominants?" Wendy said incredulously when Suzanne explained what had happened.

"What were we thinking?" Diane said. "I never thought to ask them."

"Well, duh. I hear there are a few gays in the theater," Wendy said, starting to laugh.

"Hey, this isn't funny!" Suzanne snapped. "We still have Carol's problem to figure out or none of us will be getting rid of this curse."

That put a damper on Wendy's giggles. She sobered and realized how much trouble they were really in. During their coffee, Diane had confessed that the urge to have sex in public was growing again. Wendy had nodded in understanding—her need to find another trick was building within her as well.

"You mean we have to do this all over again—this time with straight actors?" Diane asked.

"I don't know. I guess we do—we don't really have a choice, do we?" Suzanne began, but was interrupted by Carol's appearance. She was fully dressed now.

"What don't we have a choice about?" she asked.

"About how to get your fantasy fulfilled without any risk," Diane said.

"Yeah, well, about that. I realized something when I was in there. It won't work."

"What? Of course it will, if we hire the right guys—"

"No, you don't understand. The feeling wasn't there." She turned to Wendy. "Remember how you told us you felt numb when you tried to, uh, masturbate your itch away? And, you, Diane, couldn't really climax until that woman saw you with the shopkeeper? Well, that's how I felt. I knew deep down that it was all an act. So the leprechaun wasn't satisfied."

"Shit," Diane said.

"But it's too dangerous..." Suzanne began.

"I know! But it can't be helped. It has to be real."

"No way," Diane said. "We're not going to risk you."

"What choice do we have? You heard O'Grady. We have to go back as a unit, all having satisfied our fantasies at least once. You all have done it, only I remain. And I have to do it soon."

"All right, give me a minute to figure something out," Suzanne said.

"No," Carol told her. "You three go back to work. I'll take care of this."

"How?"

"Leave that to me."

"No way! You could get hurt!"

"It's a risk I'll have to take. Besides, look at the risks you're all taking! Wendy went to a neighbor's for sex, Diane fucked a man in a public shop and Suzanne, you've had countless one-night stands. It's all risky behavior."

"What will you do?" Suzanne pressed.

"I have a plan. You'll have to trust me."

"Is it a safe plan?" Suzanne asked.

"I think so, yes."

"But you won't tell us about it?"

"No. I really feel I have to handle this on my own, just as you did."

A silence fell as all four women were momentarily lost in thought.

"When would you be, uh, done?" Diane asked.

"I don't know. It could be as late as tomorrow morning sometime."

"Oh no, another night?" wailed Wendy. She began thinking about Bob again.

"Yeah, I may have to flash someone," Diane added, trying to make a joke out of it, although she wasn't joking.

"Stop it! There's nothing to be done about it," Suzanne snapped. But already she felt the urge growing. She knew by late afternoon the desire to pick up a stranger would be overpowering.

"Easy for you to say," Wendy muttered.

"Come on, let's not fight among ourselves," Carol said. "We're all in this together."

"All right. I'll call O'Grady and set up something for tomorrow morning," Diane said.

They hugged and the three other women left. When Carol was alone, she immediately called work and told them she wouldn't be returning. Then she headed for her computer.

Chapter Eleven

Diane thwarted

ꟷ

Diane returned to work and tried to concentrate on her reports. The fact she wasn't wearing panties again made her mind wander. Her pussy was wet and needy, framed by her garter belt and stockings. Just a public quickie would satisfy her, she knew, but how to do it? She wondered if she could find someone to sneak out with for a few minutes. Just up against the wall of an alley—one, two, three and she would be fine. But who could she ask in the office? The gossip would ruin her, not to mention she'd suddenly have a moony-eyed boyfriend she didn't need.

She realized that last part wasn't really true. She wouldn't mind having a boyfriend who loved risky sex, but she didn't want to start picking up random guys for it. *Leave that to Suzanne,* she thought. *Dammit, I picked a fine time to be between boyfriends!*

She gritted her teeth and tried to concentrate. She was startled when her intercom buzzed.

"Yes?"

"Diane? This is Paul Dartling. Have I caught you at a bad time?"

Her hand immediately went underneath her skirt and pressed against her damp clit. "Uh, no, not at all."

"I, uh, was wondering if we could discuss the presentation you gave the other day. I have some follow-up ideas I'd like to run by you."

The CEO wanted her input? For a moment she forgot about her need. "Oh sure, Mr. Dartling! When would you like to do this?"

"Well, how about right now?"

Diane checked her watch. It was one-thirty. Her next meeting wasn't until three. "Sure, I'll, uh, be right up."

She stopped at the restroom and dried herself as best she could. She didn't want to come into his office smelling like a woman in heat! Then she washed her hands, fixed her makeup and took the elevator upstairs.

Dartling's secretary greeted her and sent her right in. She smoothed her skirt and put on a happy face then opened the door and walked in. The CEO's office was immense with large picture windows covering two walls that looked out over the city. He was seated behind his massive desk but he came right around to greet her, shaking her hand warmly and putting his other hand on top of it. It all seemed so innocent until she happened to glance down and see the bulge growing in his pants.

Oh so it's like that, huh? She wondered if she dared to have sex with the CEO. Almost immediately, she realized that wouldn't be enough. Did she dare to have sex with the CEO *in public*?

"Please sit down." He gestured to the couch.

She sat. He sat in a chair opposite, adjusting his pants as he did. "Can I get you anything?"

"No, I'm fine." She could hardly keep her eyes away from his cock. She glanced up at the huge windows and pictured herself naked, spread-eagle, against it while he fucked her from behind. The office workers across the street would have a magnificent view.

"…all right?"

"Huh?" She shook herself. "I'm sorry?"

"You seem distracted. Are you all right?"

"Oh yes, sure. I'm fine." She could feel the blush spreading up from her chest to her face. Her pussy wept with need.

"Let me get you a sip of brandy. You really don't look well." He stood and she could tell his erection had grown. It threatened to burst out of his pants. She stood and went to him, unable to control herself.

He paused, not sure what she wanted. She didn't know how to take the next step either. They stared at each other for a long moment, lust evident in their eyes, then she reached out and touched the outline of his cock in his pants.

He grabbed her and crushed her in his arms. She swooned, knowing this was wrong but not caring. His lips found hers and she returned his kisses. She felt his hand on her breasts and ached for him to expose her.

He began fumbling with the buttons. "I've wanted you for a long time," he gasped.

The heat she felt began to ebb and she knew what she needed. "Please," she whispered, "let's get closer to the window."

"What?" He pulled back and looked at her face.

Her blouse was half-opened. She thrust her chin at the windows. "It's always been my secret fantasy to make love in a high-rise building near the windows," she said. It was mostly true. But she didn't want to be near the window, she wanted to be up against it, naked and on display.

He smiled and nodded. "Okay, but we have to be discreet."

Nooo! she thought, but said nothing. They moved near the window but not close enough for her. He unbuttoned the last buttons and murmured, "This is against all company rules, you understand. We can't tell anyone."

He kissed the top of her breasts and Diane felt the heat rise in her. Encouraged, he slipped her blouse from her shoulders and continued kissing her shoulder, neck and the upper curve of her breasts. She reached back and unsnapped her bra, shrugging it off.

"Come, let's go back to the couch," he said, trying to move her.

"No!" She realized how that must sound. "I mean I like it here by the window. Don't you ever have a fantasy about having sex…when someone is watching?"

His gaze told her he didn't. Sex to him was a private affair, especially when it involves coworkers, she realized. She felt this opportunity was slipping through her fingers.

She stepped back and walked around him toward the large window facing the office building across the street. She unzipped her skirt as she went and allowed it to puddle down as she stepped out of it. Behind her, she could hear Paul gasp when he saw she was naked except for garter belt and stockings. She walked right up to the window, giving the workers across the street a good show then turned to face the CEO.

"If you want me, you're going to have to fuck me right here," she said. "From behind while I face the other building."

He seemed torn. His erection was massive but his conscience clearly bothered him. "What…what's up with you, anyway? Are you some kind of exhibitionist?"

"Yes, that's exactly what I am." She could feel the power of the leprechaun coursing through her and knew being on display like this was pleasing the little statue—but it wasn't enough. He wanted her to have sex as well.

She leaned back against the window and spread her legs. Reaching down, she began to rub her clit in circular motions and crooked the finger of her other hand. "If you want me, come and get me."

He came toward her and she thought she had him. She could almost hear the leprechaun laugh. On the way, he stooped down to pick up her bra, blouse and then skirt. He handed them to her and said, "Get dressed and get out. I'm not going to lose my job over a cheap tart like you. I really thought you had more class."

A wave of disappointment rocked her. "No!" she gasped.

"Get out or I'll have a security guard escort you out," he said, moving toward his desk.

Defeated, she put on her clothes and headed toward the door.

"Oh and Ms. Lesher?"

She turned, her body shaking with shame and disappointment.

"If I were you, I'd start looking for another job."

Her mouth dropped open. "You can't fire me!"

"I'm not firing you. But from now on, your opportunities are limited in my company. I won't have blatant exhibitionists working here, trying to ruin our reputation."

"You were willing to have sex with me in private but not in public, is that it?"

"I was willing to have sex with you before I realized what a nutjob you were," he said. "And if you are thinking about filing some sort of sexual harassment claim, I wouldn't. You won't be believed. Now get out."

She was in tears as she fled the office.

Chapter Twelve

Wendy feeds the beast

ꟸ

Wendy knew the urge would build in her all day and night until she couldn't stand it. To head off the inevitable, she decided to follow through with her plan to visit escort services. She called in sick the rest of the day then went to her closet. She found a longer miniskirt this time—no point in making it too obvious—and a blouse that was a bit tight. Underneath she wore her best lacy underwear.

She took a cab down to the area just south of Times Square where many of the services were based. The first three places rejected her outright, saying they didn't need anyone. Wendy suspected they thought she might be an undercover cop. But on the fourth stop, she got lucky. A Vietnamese woman who was shorter than Wendy ran the place. They met in her cramped office. She looked at Wendy a long time before she responded to her inquiry.

"You want chob?" Under her dark hair, tied up in a bun, her eyes were steel, giving her a menacing appearance.

"Yes. I want to be an escort."

"You been escort before?"

"Um, not professionally. But as an amateur."

"You know what escort does?"

"Well, they go out with people who can't find a date and, um, other things as necessary."

"You a cop?"

"A cop? No, of course not."

"We have cop in here alla time, trying to bust us. We run clean operation."

"I'm not a cop."

"How I know? Cop lie."

"If you run a clean operation, why would it matter if a cop comes by?"

She scowled. "Before I hire you, you have to prove you not cop."

"I'm not sure how to do that."

"Take off clothes."

The request startled her but under the circumstances, it didn't seem outrageous. She stood and unbuttoned the tight blouse, laying it on the desk. The skirt soon followed. The woman came forward and examined her underwear carefully, running her fingers along the edges. Wendy shivered.

"You wear wire?"

"No, I'm not."

Seemingly satisfied, she returned to her desk. "As escort, how much service you willing to provide?"

Wendy sat down, feeling exposed. "I don't know. I've never done this before, I mean, not like this."

"You like to fuck men?"

Wendy colored. "Yes."

"Women?"

"I've never done that. I don't think I'd be interested."

The woman nodded. "You clean?"

"Clean? Oh you mean…"

"Yes. All whores tested, every month. Wear condoms alla time."

"That's, uh, fine with me." Actually it was a relief.

"One final part of chob application," the woman said, moving things around on her desk to clear an area.

"What's that?"

"You fuck my man here. We see if you really whore."

Wendy wanted to protest but she felt the urge take over her emotions. "Yes, okay."

"Take off underwear."

Wendy slipped off her bra and panties and piled them on her other clothes.

"Now lean over desk. Ass up."

Oh it's like that, she thought, and did as she was told.

"Spread leg." Wendy moved her legs apart and knew the older woman could see how wet she was.

"You must make man happy. You unnerstand?"

"Yes, I understand."

"Not about you. You don't come, too bad."

"I understand." She had no problem coming.

The woman went to the door. "Roger!" she shouted.

Wendy couldn't see but she felt very aroused by how she was being treated—like meat, like a whore. She shivered in delight.

She heard a man's voice but didn't turn her head to see who it was. "Yeah? Oh! Hey!"

"New girl. You fuck. Here condom. Make sure she not cop or faker."

"Sure, Mrs. Tueh, sure."

Now she turned to see a powerfully built man with an undersized black T-shirt stretched over his chest standing close behind her. He was probably the bouncer, she thought. *I'm about to be fucked by a stranger!*

She turned away and laid her face sideways on the desk. She heard him unzip his pants and prepared herself for his cock. Wendy felt his big hands on her small ass and wondered how well endowed he was. She jumped when the tip of his cock spread her wet labia. She sighed and tried to settle down.

But something was wrong! The itch wasn't being scratched! She tried to get up. The man held her down.

"What wrong?" The woman's sharp voice pierced her thoughts.

"He has to pay me! It doesn't matter how much. Just something! Otherwise, it's no good."

There followed a shocked silence. Then Mrs. Tueh barked, "Give her dollar."

The man fumbled for his wallet and Wendy felt a dollar bill being thrust into her hand. The relief was palpable.

"Good," she sighed. "Good."

He entered her smoothly and Wendy was transported to a high she'd never experienced before. Her mouth dropped open and she sucked in a breath. "Oh god, that's good," she moaned. She climaxed almost at once. Nothing in her life had prepared her for the intensity of this moment. It was as if she could feel every vein on his cock.

"Oh yes, fuck me, fuck me," she panted. "Put it in deep. Fuck me, baby."

She was out of her mind and she didn't care. She just wanted to stay in the moment for as long as she could. The bouncer pumped into her and she had two more orgasms before she felt his cock twitch deep within her. She wished he wasn't wearing a condom—she had a sudden urge to feel his hot sperm splash into her warm and welcoming cunt like it had with Bob. They stayed together for a long moment, Wendy trying hard to cling to the sensation. She was a slut, a whore, a cheap tart.

He pulled out and Wendy immediately felt let down. She wanted another cock, another payment. She lay there unmoving as Roger buckled up and left.

"You hire. You start tonight. You name Brandy. We call, you go to man's place. You charge one-fifty for blowjob, two-fifty for fuck. We get sixty percent, you forty. They want any funny stuff, charge more. You stop by here to give money every night. No try to cheat!"

"I won't," she said. With some effort she pulled herself up and began to dress. Now that she had been a whore, did she really need to show up for work tonight? After all, tomorrow the mysterious O'Grady would remove their spells, wouldn't he? She decided to worry about that later. For now, she finally felt the relief she had urgently sought.

For most of the rest of the afternoon, Wendy felt good, great even. She shopped, went to the library for some new books and enjoyed playing hooky from work.

By late afternoon however, Wendy felt those old urges returning. She knew if she didn't go meet a man, she would be pacing around all night, unable to sleep. For a short time, she entertained the notion of visiting Mr. Townbridge again but the idea paled next to what she might experience at the hands of Mrs. Tueh's customers. The leprechaun was pushing her.

The first phone call came at six-thirty. It was Mrs. Tueh. "You go to Hotel Diablo. Room 356. Meet man. He want you one hour. Regular fuck. Get two-fifty first."

Wendy dressed in a new miniskirt she had purchased just that day and wore a scoop-necked pullover over it. She had on a bra but didn't bother with panties. She slipped some condoms into her small purse and left, catching a taxi to the hotel.

Once there, she felt a pang of nervousness as she walked across the lobby. Not because she was going to whore herself out but because she might be stopped by the desk clerk. He ignored her. She rode the elevator up to the third floor.

She knocked on room 356 and it was opened at once by a fat man wearing a large, unbuttoned white dress shirt. His slacks were tight over his ample belly.

"Come in! You must be Brandy!"

"Yes." She felt the power of the leprechaun within her and it eased her fear.

The fat man tried to kiss her and Wendy turned her head. "Let's take care of business first, okay?"

"Oh sure." He reached into his pants pocket and pulled out a wallet. "Let's see, it was two hundred, right?"

"No," she said at once. "Two-fifty an hour. How many hours you want?"

"Just one." He slipped her the bills. She counted them carefully and put them in her purse.

"Okay." She smiled. "How do you want it?"

"First get me hard then we'll go from there."

She unbuckled his pants and eased down his voluminous boxer shorts. His cock was tiny amid all the flab. *God, is this what whores do?* she wondered. *Fuck ugly fat men?* She realized, yes, this is exactly what they do. It gave her a little thrill.

She began to suck on his small cock, which barely budged. At least he didn't smell too bad, she thought.

"Wait," he said. "It'll be better if you get naked."

Of course! She's not being a very experienced whore! Wendy quickly stripped off her clothes and bent down to try again. His cock stirred and she encouraged it, like a starving woman trying to start a fire in a rainstorm. She kissed and sucked and teased him until his cock speared out at her.

"You want to fuck now?"

"Not yet. I want to spank you."

Spank? Was that a special service? Wendy didn't know. She decided not to push it. "Okay."

He sat on the bed and she lay over his lap, careful not to hurt his cock. She could feel it next to her hip. He began to spank her, the sound loud in the room. It hurt! She wiggled her ass, trying to avoid the blows, but his meaty hand was all over her. As much as it hurt however, her inner leprechaun was delighted.

At last he finished and picked her up, tossing her on the bed. She rolled over onto her back, spreading her legs, even as she winced from the pain in her ass. "Come, big guy," she said. "Fuck me."

He loomed over her. She realized almost too late that he would crush her. "Wait! Go easy!" His mass enveloped her and she couldn't breathe. She hit him with her fists, trying to suck in some air. His cock stabbed at her and she shouted, "Condom! You have to wear a condom!"

The fat man cursed and rolled off her. He grabbed the condom and slipped it on. Wendy felt better but a part of her was disappointed, remembering how good it had been with Mr. Townbridge. Then her thoughts were blotted out when his bulk returned, nearly crushing her. She felt his cock at her slit. He pressed it in.

The man was quick once he was inside her. He pumped a few times and Wendy felt his cock twitch as he emptied himself. Despite the impossible circumstances, she had a powerful orgasm and briefly saw spots before her eyes. The fat man finally rolled off her and she gasped for air.

The room was silent for a time.

"Well, I'd better go." She started to rise.

He grabbed her. "Oh no, we've got a half-hour left. Come, sit on me."

In the back of her mind, she could hear the leprechaun laugh.

* * * * *

Wendy dragged herself back home at one-thirty in the morning. She was exhausted and sore. She had fucked four men during her inaugural stint as a call girl and it didn't have nearly the glamour she had fantasized about. After the fat man, there had been the Arab businessman who paid her to dance naked for him for a half-hour before he fucked her. He had paid her five hundred dollars for about ninety minutes work. Then there was the bachelor who was getting married in a week. Why he needed to fuck a whore, she didn't understand. That was the best gig of the evening, for he paid her full price for regular sex, no funny stuff.

The last call had been the toughest one. She had gone to another hotel room where she was supposed to meet a businessman from Toronto. Instead, she found herself in a room with two very large black men. She had no prejudices about blacks but she did object to being lied to. When she tried to leave, they easily overpowered her. They made her suck them off and ejaculated on her face and breasts. Then they spanked her with their massive hands on her already sore bottom. Finally, they fucked her, their huge cocks spreading her tender pussy to the breaking point. Wendy had the presence of mind to convince them to use condoms by shouting, "Remember what happened to Magic Johnson!"

After two hours they let her go and handed her a fistful of money to keep quiet about it. She counted out six hundred dollars. All in all, she had made sixteen hundred dollars total, of which she got to keep more than six hundred. As she turned over the wads of cash to Mrs. Tueh, the Vietnamese woman smiled broadly at her and said, "You good whore. You make lotta money."

Wendy didn't have the heart to tell her she was quitting after tomorrow.

Chapter Thirteen

Carol submits

Carol sat at her computer, her fingers hovering above the keyboard as if it were a hot iron. She rubbed them against her palms and started again. It hadn't been hard to figure out what she must do. She knew what sites to look for. She had even visited a few out of curiosity, just to give herself a little thrill.

This time however, it would be different.

She called up a popular BDSM website and began to scroll through it. In just a few minutes, she had identified a Dom who regularly responded to people's questions. He called himself "Master K". Steeling herself, she emailed him a quick note, asking for his help in finding a trustworthy Dom in the New York City area. She briefly outlined her desire to "explore" this lifestyle. It felt odd for she was of two minds about it. She imagined that's just how the others felt before they gave in to their secret desires.

Within an hour he had responded. He wanted to know more. What was she into? Spankings? Bondage? Nipple play? Piercings? Water sports?

Carol wasn't even sure what some of those meant. She wrote back, saying she was just curious and wanted to go slow. She would work out those issues with the Dom, providing he was gentle and understanding. *Dammit,* she was thinking, *just give me a name and stop asking questions!*

He responded almost immediately this time. *Try Blue Dom – he's in NYC. He has links to this site.*

Carol looked up Blue Dom's email and wrote to him, asking for some information. She hoped he would be understanding.

Apparently Master K had alerted him for Blue Dom responded quickly. He gave her his Instant Message address and she contacted him right away.

Yes, I believe I can help you. I frequently work with "newbies", he wrote. *I would only go as far as you needed until you learned what gave you the most pleasure. However my services are not free.* He outlined a fee arrangement.

Carol felt vaguely insulted, although his fee was remarkably reasonable. It galled her she'd have to pay to get the leprechaun off her back. She wrote back and agreed. She felt as if she were moving too fast, yet she knew the other women were relying on her. In fact, she was moving too slow, she realized.

Blue Dom told her he could meet her that weekend—three days away.

No! She wrote back at once. *Can't it be today?*

Blue Dom: You are in a hurry. Is this part of some sting operation?

Carol: No, of course not.

Blue Dom: Then what's the rush?

How could she tell him? It could ruin everything. He might object when he realized this would be a one-time event. She planned to be cured by tomorrow.

My husband's out of town, she lied. *And my son's staying with grandparents. I'm alone now but by Friday, both will be back. I've been thinking about this for a long time and if I'm going to try it, it would have to be today.*

She smiled at her quick thinking. This would explain both her rush and the need for it to be a one-time deal.

Blue Dom: Very well. Meet me in two hours.

He gave an address on the Lower West side. She knew the neighborhood. It was a decent area, full of working-class people. It cheered her a little knowing he didn't live in Harlem. Idly, she wondered if he was black or white or something else.

Then again, did it matter?

Carol knew her friends would want her to call them so one or more could accompany her and make sure she was safe. But she didn't. She wasn't sure why. Perhaps each had to experience their inner desire alone. Suzanne didn't ask for anyone to come to the bars with her when she picked up men. And Diane had fucked that shopkeeper by herself. No, she would have to straighten her spine and do it, despite her fears.

But she couldn't deny the secret thrill it gave her.

She took a taxi to the address and found it to be a brownstone in a recently revitalized area. She was early so she waited in a coffee shop across the street, her eyes on the door. No one entered or left during the half-hour she sat and sipped her hot drink.

Steeling herself, she walked across the street, raised the heavy knocker on the door. It opened almost at once, as if he had been watching her approach. Carol stepped back, ready to run. The man who appeared in the doorway was just an inch or two taller than she was, probably five-ten. But he was solidly built with a thick chest and powerful arms that filled the sleeves of the dress shirt he wore. She guessed him to be about thirty-five, close to her age.

"Carol?" He had a slight accent, possibly European.

"Y-yes." She wondered if it had been wise to give him her real name.

"I'm Barry. Known as the Blue Dom online. Please come in."

He seemed surprisingly calm and, well, nice, she noted. He didn't act like a Dom. She stepped through the portal and watched as he closed the door behind them. Was she trapped now? She struggled to make small talk to calm her nerves. She looked around. They were in the living room.

"You have a nice place."

"Thank you. I inherited it from my parents. Come, I'll show you around." They went from room to room downstairs and Barry acted the perfect host. When he showed her his office, Carol suddenly realized how he had come up with that odd screen name. A large painting adorned one wall—a reproduction of one of Picasso's paintings during his famous "blue period". She smiled, visualizing him sitting there, his eyes on that painting. She felt a little more at ease.

They moved on, passing through the clean, well-appointed kitchen and dining room. Carol noted however, that he didn't show her the upstairs.

They returned to the living room and he asked her to sit. "Coffee?"

"Uh, no, no thanks. I had some a little while ago."

"You came early." It was a statement, not a question.

"Y-yes. How could you tell?"

"Well, someone who contacts me and wants immediate action would probably show up early to check out the place, correct?"

"Uh, yes."

"So tell me, Carol. What is the rush? Why act now?"

"Uh, well, like I said, I've had these feelings for a long time and my husband doesn't—"

"Please don't lie to me. You aren't married."

Her mouth gaped open. How did he know?

"You're not wearing any rings on your left hand."

"I-I could've removed them," she pointed out.

Barry shook his head. "You have no tan line on your finger, which tells me you don't normally wear rings there. Now why don't you tell me what's really going on?"

"I-I can't. You wouldn't believe me."

"Then I suggest you find another Dom. I'd prefer not to get involved in something I don't understand."

"No!" The idea she'd have to start over frightened her. She liked this man, even trusted him a bit, if that was possible in her situation.

"All right," she said. "But you're not going to believe me and you'll probably think I'm crazy."

"Give me the benefit of the doubt," he said.

Carol took a deep breath and began telling him the strange story of the leprechaun sculpture and its effect on her and her friends, watching his face for signs of derision. To his credit, he listened with rapt attention, eyes registering understanding and a certain amount of disbelief at the same time.

"That's your story?" he said when she was finished.

"Yes. It's the truth. I told you, you wouldn't believe me."

"Strangely enough, I want to believe you, although it's an impossible story."

"I know. It's impossible for me to believe too. For all of us."

"Give me the phone number of this Suzanne you mentioned."

That startled her but she gave it to him. Barry rose and went into his office. She could hear the murmur of his voice. He returned in a few minutes and sat down across from her, nodding his head. "She backs you up. Hard to imagine…"

"I wish it weren't so. I'd give anything to go back to the way we all were."

"She also said I'd better take good care of you or I'll have the wrath of your three friends down on me." He smiled.

She laughed. "Yeah, that's them. They're very protective of me."

"And this O'Grady character, he says you have to act out your fantasy in order to have this curse lifted?"

"Yes."

"So this is a one-time deal then, right?"

She lowered her eyes. "I hope so." Would he refuse to help her?

"Very well. I appreciate your honesty. I assume you brought your checkbook?"

Carol looked up, eyes alight. "Yes! Oh thank you!"

He held up a hand. "Don't thank me yet. I believe if this is going to work, you'll probably need the full-on treatment, albeit abbreviated."

"Yes, that would be good," she said, her stomach fluttering in anticipation. She wrote him a check on the spot, her hand shaking. He took it from her and pocketed it.

"Stand up."

She did, her nervousness almost causing her to faint.

"Relax." He stepped close. "You're perfectly safe. You know that, don't you?"

"Y-yes, I think so."

"Good. Remove your clothes."

She gaped at him. "Just like that?"

"Just like that."

Her fingers fumbled with her buttons. His eyes never left her—he seemed to be enjoying her discomfort.

"Come on, I don't have all day." He reached out and casually slapped her hip.

Carol jumped and began to peel off her clothes more quickly. Her body tingled all over. He stepped back and watched as they came off. It felt strange, being under his control. Intellectually she rebelled but emotionally this was just what she needed.

She paused when she was down to her bra and panties, but when Barry signaled her, she stripped them off as well. She stood there covering herself, embarrassed.

"Come, come, my little submissive, don't be shy."

Her hands came away and she felt her skin heat under his gaze. "God," she breathed. "This is so unlike me."

"That may be true, but it's what you need. I can tell."

She nodded. Was that really what she needed for herself or just to satisfy the leprechaun? Then again, it really didn't matter. She needed to stop thinking, she told herself.

Barry walked around her, taking in her beauty. Carol watched him, wishing she could cover herself. She felt like a gangly kid, unworthy of his attention.

"Do you understand the nature of the dominant/submissive roles?"

"Yes, sir." The formal address just came naturally to her.

"And do you see yourself as a submissive?"

"No," she said at once. Then—"Well, today I do."

"Ahh, you see, that's your problem. I believe you've always been a submissive—otherwise that would not have been your secret fantasy. But you've repressed it to the point that you deny it, even as you stand here naked."

She could only nod.

"You have to give yourself permission to let go." He reached out and took her hand. "I realize this is sudden but you set the timetable. Normally we would go slower. Come, I will help you."

He led her to the stairs. Carol looked up warily, afraid. What lay in store for her up there? A dungeon? Or would he simply take her to his bed and rape her? She tried to resist and he caught her forearm.

"Trust. It's a difficult concept in this situation, I know. But think of it this way—you paid for the service. What kind of businessman would I be if I harmed my customers?"

She smiled. "Okay. I'm just afraid."

"Don't be. I plan on asking you to give a recommendation on my website." He slipped her a sly grin.

She laughed and allowed him to guide her up the stairs. Her fears abated. He opened a door at the top of the stairs and eased her through it. Carol stopped and stared.

"Oh my god, it *is* a dungeon!" The room contained whips, chains, restraints and other strange devices that seemed medieval to her. She started to back out.

"Whoa. Relax. You are the most nervous sub I've encountered." He waved his hand at the room. "About ninety percent of this stuff you can ignore. It's not for you."

For some reason, Carol felt a frisson of disappointment. Very strange.

"Here," he said. "Let's put these on you." He held padded leather cuffs and began fastening them to her wrists.

Another wave of pleasure and fear ran through her. But she stood still while he buckled them in place then bent to put similar cuffs on her ankles.

"What are you going to do?"

"I'm going to free your inner sub." He led her to a thick wooden post in the middle of the room. There were rings hanging from the sides, near the top and bottom. He pressed her up against the smooth wood and clicked her cuffs to the rings above her head. He bent down and used short lengths of chain to fasten her ankles to the post. She could move her feet about six inches, no more.

"What are you going to do?" she asked again.

He moved out of her vision and she could hear something being taken down from the wall. *Oh god,* she thought, *he's going to whip me!*

"No! You can't!"

He came close and showed her what he held in his hand. "Relax, my little sub. This is a suede cat o'nine tails, my softest whip." He rubbed it against her shoulder. It *was* soft, but she shivered regardless.

"You can't," she whispered.

"Of course I can. Consider it part of your training."

He stepped back and she heard the whisk of the whip in the air then it struck her. She jumped, although she could tell he hadn't put much force into it.

"See? It's merely for focusing the mind." He struck her again, harder.

The whip warmed her skin and made beads of perspiration appear. She shook her body and the rings rattled. Carol was trapped, helpless.

Slash! The whip cut across her rump. It stung and then made her hot. Her clit swelled and she could smell her own arousal. How could this be?

"Oh god," she whimpered. She couldn't describe her emotions. They swirled and churned within her. But for some reason, she felt a sense of trust with Barry. He certainly seemed to know what he was doing. Her fears were pushed back and she decided to let go a little and see where this took her.

He began to strike her again and again—not too hard, but hard enough to sting her flesh and raise her temperature. She trembled. Hot tears ran down her cheeks. Her whole body felt as if it were on fire.

She found herself moving out of her body. She was looking down, seeing this shapely woman being whipped, her skin red and pink. Barry looked so masculine and in control, standing behind her with the whip. Carol watched as the woman began to thrust her ass back to meet the blows. Then she was tipping her hips, trying to expose more of her pussy to him. *Fuck her,* she told him. *She wants it.*

Barry stopped suddenly and dropped the whip. She came rushing back into her body, feeling the desire overwhelm her. He grasped her shoulders with both hands. "Tell me," he gasped. "Tell me what you want."

"Fuck me," she gasped through her clenched teeth. "Fuck me."

"Now you're beginning to understand why women enjoy being the sub," he said. She heard him behind her, unzipping his pants. She couldn't wait and pushed her hips out to make it easier for him. He took a few extra seconds to put on a condom and Carol was impatient.

"Just do it!"

He slapped her rump. "You don't give the orders, remember?"

"Oh god, please." She waited until he was ready. The tip of his cock touched her wetness and slid inside. An instant tremor rocked her, a mini-orgasm. Carol hung by the cuffs, wishing she were free so she could bend over more and spread her legs in order to feel the full effects of his hard cock.

"Please," she said.

He slapped her ass again and she shut up, letting him have his way. She wasn't sure she could come this way, not as if she wanted to. Carol realized this was for his pleasure, not hers. Was that the sub's duty? Not to be pleasured, only to please?

She had much to learn.

He sped up and she whimpered. His body pressed her against the wood, her breasts and clit felt ignored. She wanted to be pinched and slapped and rubbed until she came—it wouldn't take much.

Suddenly she felt his cock erupt within her and she cried out in frustration. Another mini-orgasm shuddered through her and she found herself begging.

"Touch my clit! Please touch my clit!"

"No." He held her close. "You're not ready."

He pulled out and she could feel her wetness leak out. Barry pulled off his condom and tossed it in a nearby trash can.

"Please," she said again.

He came close. "Subs have to learn. Orgasms have to be earned."

"Oh god."

He freed her and she was so weak she could barely stand. Her body felt lightweight and sweaty. He wrapped an arm around her and helped her to a bench.

"Rest here for a minute. Then we'll start again."

"Oh my god." All she could think about was an orgasm. Suddenly, she realized, the leprechaun was gone. For the first time in days, her mind was clear.

Chapter Fourteen

Another visit with Peter O'Grady

ꟹ

Carol tried to walk normally as she met Wendy, Suzanne and Diane outside O'Grady's townhouse at ten o'clock the next morning. After her amazing experience, she still felt aroused, several hours later. Her back and ass still felt warm from the whip and her clit was teased by her underwear, reminding her of her extraordinary experience. There was a red scrape on her cheek from the post that she couldn't quite cover with makeup.

But she had never felt more alive in her life.

"My god," said Suzanne. "Look at you! I was so worried—I'm glad you had him call me last night."

"Who called? What happened?" Wendy butted in.

Suzanne turned to her. "Carol met with a BDSM guy last night."

"Oh my god!" She put her hand over her mouth. Her eyes gave away her curiosity. "Um, how was it?"

Carol gave her a sly smile. "Pretty good. He was the real thing, that's for sure," Carol said, gingerly touching her cheekbone.

"Wow. Did he hurt you?" said Wendy.

"No, I would have to say he didn't," she responded, her body still tingling.

"How did you find him?" she asked.

"Online of course. You know, there's quite a society of Doms and subs in New York."

"Did he…?" Diane trailed off. Her expression told Carol she thought her question indelicate.

Carol decided to let her off the hook. "Fuck me? Oh yeah," she said.

"Was it horrible?" Suzanne asked. She knew it was a stupid question as soon as the words left her lips. But Carol's answer surprised her.

"Actually, it was just what the doctor ordered." She didn't want to tell them how she had begged Barry for it and how she wanted more. It wouldn't sound right to her modern, feminist friends.

"Well, at least you're all right," Diane said.

"Yes, and the leprechaun was satisfied. I feel almost normal today. How about the rest of you?"

The others averted her looks. "Uh-oh. That can only mean one thing."

"Yeah," admitted Wendy. "But it doesn't mean we're still not in sync. I mean, we've all succumbed to the wishes of the leprechaun's curse. So we're even, right?"

"I hope so," Carol said. "I'm not sure I want to do this again." That was a lie. She knew she could see Barry again and give her body completely to him. It thrilled her to think of what demands he might require for her orgasms.

"Well, come on, let's get rid of this curse," Suzanne said, and knocked on the door. The same butler opened the door. "Ah, ladies. Mr. O'Grady is expecting you."

They came in, hope in their hearts, and were led to the library. Peter, as before, waited for them behind his desk.

"Ladies!" he said cheerfully. "Top o' the morning to ya."

"Knock it off, O'Grady," Suzanne said. "We've come to get rid of the curse."

"Please sit down. Tell me what's happened since yesterday. Especially you, my dear girl," he said to Carol.

"Oh no, not again," Diane said. "Can't we just get on with it? You said we all had to have experienced some of what the leprechaun demanded. Well, we have. So if you don't mind, we'd like to cut to the chase."

"That's not the way it works," he said evenly, cutting off argument. "Carol, let's start with you. Do you believe you fulfilled your secret fantasy?"

"Oh yes," she said. Carol briefly outlined her visit to Barry's dungeon.

"Hmm. All right. Diane, you seem reluctant to talk. What's happened since your last visit?"

"Dammit. I don't like this True Confessions crap."

"Come on, Diane, let's just get this over with," urged Suzanne. "I know O'Grady is getting his rocks off listening to it, but if that's the price we have to pay to get rid of this curse, so be it."

"Easy for you to say. All you did was pick up another anonymous fuck. I lost my job yesterday."

There came a chorus of sympathetic voices. Diane explained as quickly as she could the disaster that occurred when her CEO made advances toward her.

"But you didn't actually lose your job," pointed out Wendy.

"No, but the clock is ticking," she said. "I destroyed my career. Or should I say, that *thing* destroyed it." She pointed with a shaking finger to the ugly little statue on Peter's desk.

"Wendy, your turn."

"Oh god. I gave in. I went to an escort service and they sent me on four tricks last night."

She endured another round of shocked responses, followed by much sympathy. She just nodded and folded her arms over her chest. O'Grady, the bastard, made her describe her encounters. She tried to be brief as possible.

"Now you've heard our sad stories. Can you fix it before we all die?" Diane demanded.

"I will do my best," he promised. "I called back to the home country and talked to some of my relatives. They too were surprised by the little guy's power. They chalked it up to an unusual confluence of events." He began ticking them off on his fingers. "One, it was a full moon that night, two, you all confessed your deepest, darkest secrets out loud to each other and three, you're all clearly very close friends. So you all got a double or triple dose of your wishes."

"Fine, so stop it. Please," Suzanne said.

"Very well. They told me what I need to do. It's a little unusual, I admit. But my relatives swear it's the only way."

They waited, eyes wary.

"Are you willing to do exactly what I say?"

Four women nodded.

"First, you must all remove every stitch of clothing and put them in a three-foot circle here on the rug."

"What!? No way!"

"I'm not doing that!"

Peter simply waited them out. "You're wasting time."

The friends realized they had little choice, even if the idea seemed crazy. Slowly they began peeling off their clothes, making a crude circle. Bras, blouses, skirts and panties soon littered the floor. They bent over and adjusted the clothes into the desired shape as directed by Peter.

"Good," he said at last. "Now, get into the circle and face inward, putting your arms around each other. Yes, do it tightly like that." He was rewarded with a view of four delicious asses, pointing in all directions. He moved around the circle, helping them to adjust arms and feet, making sure they were all even.

"Now let me get my book of incantations." He went to the shelf and pulled down an old dusty volume. He found the page he needed and approached the women.

"Now close your eyes," he said, and he began to read in Gaelic.

Tha mi fo ch˜ram a dhiu ro eileadh
Tha mi fo ch˜ram's fo mhoran tursa.
'S mo cheist air c˜irteir a' bhrollaich ghlË-ghil.
Tha mi fo ch˜ram a dhiu ro eileadh.
Tha mi fo ghruaimean
'S gur fhad o'n uair sin
Mo ghaol a' bhuachaill
'S cha chual e fhËin e.

When he was finished, he was silent for two long minutes. The women stayed huddled in their nakedness, eyes closed, waiting for their ordeal to end.

"Very well. The curse is almost lifted."

"Almost?!" exclaimed Suzanne. "What now?"

"No, I'm sorry, I misspoke. Please, you may all get dressed now. I'll explain more fully in a minute."

They all scrambled into their clothes. When they were seated on the couch and chair again, their eyes burned holes into Peter as they waited.

"Please," he said, holding up a hand. "Relax. The power of the 'curse', as you call it, has been greatly diminished. Now it's back to where it's supposed to be, just a mere suggestion. Like something you'd all like to do one day."

"I think we've done quite enough, thank you," Carol said.

"Yeah, I never want to have any more fantasies about being a call girl," noted Wendy.

"Or an exhibitionist."

"Or a slut." They all laughed nervously at Suzanne's crude description of her escapades.

"So then we won't have these strong desires anymore? You promise?" Carol wanted to be sure.

"Not according to my clan, who are experts in this. They say such a thing should have never happened. It has never happened before."

"Yeah, we should sue," said Diane. "I'm going to be losing my job over this."

"Maybe not. You could go back to your boss and explain that you were hypnotized or something."

"Well, I'm just glad it's over," Wendy said. "Now I want to go back to my regular life."

"What will you do when your escort service calls?" Diane asked.

"I'll tell them I retired. Effective immediately."

"At least you made six hundred bucks," Carol said wryly. "I had to pay the man to whip me."

"I lost my dignity," Diane said. "I'll trade you."

Suzanne stood. "Well, if that's it then we'll be going." She turned to the Irishman. "But if anything else happens, can you fix it?"

"I can redo the incantation again if necessary. But I doubt it will be. Consider yourself cured."

The women nodded and left, much relieved. Outside, they stood on the sidewalk and chatted for a few minutes.

"That little scene in there was weird," Diane said. "I mean I'm the exhibitionist so I kinda liked it, but it was weird, wasn't it?"

"Yeah, it almost seemed like some practical joke or something. I mean if it wasn't so serious," added Wendy.

"But how do you feel? Do you feel different?" Carol looked around anxiously.

"Yes, I do actually," Suzanne said. "I don't feel like picking up any more men, that's for sure. Maybe I'll become a hermit."

"And I'm glad I have my clothes on," Diane added.

"Good. Then I can sleep easy tonight," Carol said, trying to hide her disappointment in not needing Barry's services any longer. "Thank god."

"Don't you feel better too?"

"I guess. But I think it's so fresh in my mind. I mean it was a powerful experience."

"Of course," Suzanne said, patting her arm. "Just give it time."

"Well, I'd better get back to work. Anyone going uptown?" Wendy flagged down a cab.

"I will," Carol said, and they jumped in it together.

"You going downtown? I can get us a cab," Diane said.

"Yeah." But Suzanne stood there, looking pensive.

"What's wrong?"

She shook her head. "I don't know. Nothing. It's just this whole thing has me rattled."

"That's the understatement of the year. Come on, I'd better get back to work while I still have a job."

* * * * *

The butler returned to the library and approached Peter's desk. He picked up the dusty volume and read the cover. "Gaelic poetry, sir?"

"Were you listening?"

"To some of it. I used to know that poem in English. It goes something like—

I will climb no more

To the wilds of the moorlands;

I will climb no more.
I received a letter from Edinburgh
Saying I must not go to the moorland…

"I can't remember the rest."

"That's very good, Emmon. You have an excellent memory."

"What about the ladies?"

Peter laughed. "You know, I've never gotten four at once like that. That's as rare as a four-leaf clover, don't you think?"

"Yes, sir. But you really think it was wise, leading them on like that?"

He shrugged. "Probably not. But it was fun, getting them starkers and all. That little bit of nonsense should keep them for a while. The power of suggestion, you see."

"And then what, sir?"

Peter looked around his favorite room. "I think we might've worn out our welcome here in New York. What do you say we pack up and try France for a while? I'd love to snare a lovely young Frenchwoman. I hear they're very passionate."

Emmon smiled. "Very good, sir. I'll make the arrangements."

Chapter Fifteen

Tendrils

ℰ

For the women, the week crept by in blessed peace, disturbed only by occasional dreams that served to remind them of their individual fantasies. They chalked it up to the "suggestion" left by the curse and moved on to repair the damage in their lives.

Diane reached out to Dartling by sending him a note to tell him she had been hypnotized at a party recently and was made to think she was an exhibitionist. *I fear in my nervousness in meeting with you in your office, I may have regressed into my hypnotized state and acted inappropriately*, she wrote.

He called her back up to his office the next day.

When she was in his presence again, Diane tried to pretend that she had little memory of their previous encounter. Dartling remained skeptical.

"This story sounds farfetched," he told her. "I saw you with my own two eyes. You wanted to stand naked in front of that window and have sex!" He pointed with emphasis at the large window facing across the street.

Diane followed his finger and found a sudden pang of desire. It shocked her. She covered it well. "Oh my god!" She hid her face in her hands. "I am so sorry! I don't remember everything that day. I can't believe I did that!"

"What do you remember?"

"Well, I remember you were very nice to me. We were talking and you asked if I needed a brandy. And I remember touching your, uh…" She trailed off. Her boss looked away, embarrassed. "Then…my memory is hazy after that."

He softened, but only a little. "This sounds like 'damage control'. I never knew hypnosis could make one do something they wouldn't normally do in real life."

She looked up. "Sir, I think I know where this came from." She didn't have to act during this part—she could feel the blush rise in her face. Taking a deep breath, she described her "secret fantasy", just as she had done for her friends earlier. He looked shocked.

"That's something I never told anyone before because it's so embarrassing. But I believe this explains why I was able to be hypnotized in that way."

"That's…that's incredible. So at this party, did the hypnotist make you, uh, do things like that?"

"Yes, although I don't remember. He told me he made me cluck like a chicken and other routine things, but I suspected that more took place. The others at the party seemed quite amused by me. It was only after I confided in a friend who was also at the party that she mentioned that the hypnotist made me flash the crowd. It was nothing more than unbuttoning my blouse, she told me. It was actually quite innocent, but I think it caused something to be tripped in my mind. That was why I was so strange that day."

She saw his surprised expression and quickly added, "I'm not really crazy. I feel I was pushed into it. But I'm better now."

He nodded. "Very well. I'll give you the benefit of the doubt—but only because Richard spoke up in your defense. You may return to your office. You've given me a lot to think about."

She stood and thanked him for his time. She noticed with some secret pleasure that his cock had again grown hard in his pants.

* * * * *

When Wendy's service called that night, she told Mrs. Tueh she was quitting.

"What? You just start! You make good money!"

"I know, but it's just not me. I thought it was," she said. "Turns out I'm not a whore after all."

And that was it. She was furious and cursed her out in Vietnamese and Wendy simply hung up on her. In an exaggerated motion, she dusted off her hands and tried to put the ugly incident behind her.

It wasn't easy. She met Bob in the hallway often and always turned bright red when she remembered how she had fucked him. And that was the proper word—not "make love" or "have sex". She had fucked him like a hooker.

"Hi there, Wendy," he would say, giving her a nod or a wink, and she'd blush and turn away.

One evening, not long after the incantation, Bob stopped her in the hall and asked her if she had been accepted into that club.

"What club?" she asked foolishly before she realized what he meant. "Oh that club! I, uh, decided not to join after all."

"Really? You seemed willing to do anything to get in before. I was hoping your initiation might be repeated." He tipped his head knowingly.

"No! I mean, no, I don't think so. It was kind of an aberration. Please, can't we just forget about it?"

He nodded sadly. "Ah well. I suppose it was too good to be true. But I want you to know that you made my night—hell, my year—and if you ever change your mind, I'll be around."

She thanked him and scooted away. Surprisingly, she felt guilty. He could've become a very good customer, she thought. A little pang of desire thrummed in her.

* * * * *

Suzanne stayed away from bars—and men—for several days. She went to work, came home and went out only for groceries. She didn't even contact her best friends, nor did they contact her. It was as if they all wanted to forget everything and just looking at each other would remind them. She hoped their friendship wasn't ruined forever.

Friday afternoon, a coworker invited her to join a small group for drinks at the bar down the street. She almost said no then decided it was silly for her to continue to deny herself fun. "Sure," she said. "Just for a little while."

She met two other women in her department in the lobby downstairs and they headed off to the bar to complain about their bosses and discuss projects. It was an enjoyable evening. Suzanne even caught sight of a man she'd like to meet but resisted the urge.

One of the other women—Alice—caught her roving eye and told her she should go for it. "Come on," she urged. "Pam and I will be fine. He's a hunk and he only has eyes for you."

"No, I don't think so," she said, turning her back to the man. "I'm not in a place to meet guys right now."

"Oh really? When does that ever happen for women?" She meant it playfully but it struck a nerve.

"What? You think I'm just out to pick up men all the time?" She regretted her words instantly and apologized. "I'm just a little on edge. I broke up with a guy recently..." She waved off any further details.

Even as she spoke, she felt that familiar heat in her loins and realized she missed having a man around. When the stranger sent over a round of drinks to the table, she turned with the others to raise their glasses in thanks and she saw the other women were right—he only had eyes for her.

He came over. Pam and Alice nearly squealed with excitement. Suzanne steeled herself.

"Hi," he said, smiling with even white teeth. He was ruggedly handsome and dressed in an expensive suit. He would look at home chopping wood at a mountain cabin or in a boardroom. "My name is..."

Suzanne found herself gripping the edge of the table so hard her fingers turned white.

"Ben. Ben Samuelson."

She smiled. The world didn't end because he told her his name. The curse must really be gone, she decided.

"Hi," she said. "I'm Suzanne. This is Pam and Alice."

* * * * *

Carol wrestled with her conscience over the next few days. She knew she was cured yet she wanted to see Barry again. The idea of submitting to the strong, handsome man sent shivers down her spine. Why was that? Perhaps it wasn't the leprechaun but her own needs coming to the surface.

She almost called him a couple of times but stopped each time. She also didn't like the idea of having to pay him. That wasn't right. If she was going to find someone with whom she could explore this D/s relationship, she damn sure wasn't going to pay for it! She had more pride than that!

But it was right, the way it had gone. By paying, she had become the customer. It was a business arrangement. She smiled to herself as she rode the subway home and caught the eye of the man across the seat. He smiled back, thinking she was flirting with him. Carol averted her eyes.

At home, she allowed her curiosity to get the better of her and sat down at the computer. She called up various bondage and D/s websites. She looked at pictures and read some stories. They excited her and she removed her skirt and pantyhose. Her hand was busy between her legs. Carol brought herself to three orgasms before she finally tore herself away and went to bed.

Lying there, she could recall the home page of one of the sites, a personal favorite. There to the left had been a list of links she had tried hard to ignore. But now, in her mind's eye, she could see the link to *BDSM Chat* and wondered if she would have the nerve—or the need—to explore this lifestyle further.

Chapter Sixteen

Realization

ꟸ

Monday night, the weekly bull session of the girls almost didn't happen. But Suzanne called and insisted they come to her house to talk over everything. She had her doubts about what had happened at O'Grady's townhouse and wanted to hear what the others thought.

They trooped in at seven, looking tired and anxious. Looking at them, it would be hard to imagine the cheerful, funny, bitchy women who had filed in to Suzanne's just two weeks ago.

"Anyone want a drink?"

There came a chorus of affirmatives. Suzanne poured everyone wine. For several minutes they sat and drank without speaking a word. Then Suzanne broke the ice.

"I know no one really wants to be here. Trust me, I felt the same. Not that I don't love you girls to death, but I just wanted to be alone with my own thoughts and see if this curse was truly lifted. Since we're all in this together, I wanted to discuss it with you."

The other three nodded. This was like a trip to the dentist—painful but necessary.

Suzanne went on to describe how much better she felt and how she hadn't had the urge to pick up men…except for that odd little incident when she met the man on Friday and had to grab the table in panic when he told her his name.

"I just thought that was strange for a woman who's 'cured'. Did anyone have any similar experiences?"

Diane described her attempts to make amends with her boss. "It seemed to go pretty well but I'm not sure he's convinced."

"Yes, but did you feel any urges? You know…" Suzanne pressed.

"Well, there was a twinge I felt when I saw his big picture window again. But I chalked that up to the fact the leprechaun still is 'suggesting' things to us. It seems controllable…"

"Wendy? How about you?"

"I quit the escort service of course. The only thing now is I'm embarrassed to see Mr. Townbridge in the hall."

"Well, that's good news," Suzanne said. "That's really good news."

"Yeah, except that…"

The others leaned forward, their faces tense.

"Well, he was really nice to me. Mr. Townbridge. He was what I would've called a 'good customer'. I still have that feeling about him."

"Oh shit," Carol said.

"Did you feel something too?"

"Yeah. I mean mostly I felt this, uh, curiosity. But I haven't acted on it…yet."

"Yet?" Diane asked.

"It's hard to explain. Barry—the Dom I visited that one time—was really nice. So I've been doing a little research into the subject. And I have been having some dreams again."

"Shit," Suzanne said. "We've got to call O'Grady. We might have to have another incantation." She got up and went to the phone. Standing there, she could see the worry on her friends' faces and hoped another session would do the trick. The phone rang and rang.

"Dammit! There's no answer. And no answering machine."

"Well, he's probably out, doing whatever it is leprechauns do," Wendy said. "Try again later."

The four women tried to talk about other things—work, relationships, mothers—but soon the conversation trailed off. Suzanne tried to call O'Grady again and got nowhere.

"Tell you what," she said. "I'll stop by there tomorrow and talk to him or his weird butler and let you guys know what's up."

They all agreed. Looking at each other, they realized they had nothing more to say. They made their goodbyes and left. Suzanne looked at her watch—seven-forty-five. Normally, the girls would've stayed until nine-thirty or ten.

The next day, Suzanne took a taxi to O'Grady's during her lunch hour and stepped out, determined to get to the bottom of all this. She froze immediately. There in front of the building was a Realtor's sign.

"Oh no," she whispered, and ran up the steps. She pounded on the door. There was no answer. "Oh no," she said again, and hurried to a window. Peering inside, using her hand as a shield, she could see only an empty room.

"Oh shit, oh shit, oh shit!"

Grabbing her cell phone, she dialed the Realtor's number.

"Hello? Yes, I'm inquiring about the property on Lancaster? The townhouse?"

"Oh yes, isn't it lovely?" the smooth voice of the Realtor said. "Just came on the market first of this week. I'm sure it's going to go fast. Would you like to see it?"

"I'm really more interested in the former tenant. A Peter O'Grady. He left rather suddenly and I need to get in touch with him."

"Oh I'm sorry. He said he was going back to Europe and that he'd be contacting me later, after the house has sold. He left me the name of his attorney in Dublin, if that would help."

"Oh yes!" She wrote it down, thanked him and hung up.

She checked her watch. Let's see, they were about five hours ahead so she might just catch him in his office. Suzanne dialed the international number.

"Hello? Mr. Patrick O'Malley?"

"Yes, this is he," came the melodious Irish voice.

"Thank god! I'm calling from America—New York City. I'm Suzanne Diggs. It's imperative that I get in touch with Peter O'Grady…"

"Peter O'Grady, you say?"

"Yes! It's very important!"

"Well, he has no set address yet. He'll be callin' me when he's settled in, wherever that it."

"You don't know where he is?"

"No, Peter roams around. He's a regular gadfly, he is."

"Please, can you get a message to him as soon as he checks in? It's urgent."

Suzanne gave him her name and number, and O'Malley promised he'd get it to Peter as soon as he called in. She hung up, feeling the terrible weight of dread pressing on her.

* * * * *

The women met again Tuesday night in Suzanne's apartment. She told them about O'Grady's sudden move and that all she could do was leave a message with his lawyer.

"Oh no," Carol said. "Why would he suddenly leave?"

"I don't know. But it seems very odd," Diane said. "But let's not panic now. We all feel better, right?"

One look around the room and that hopeful notion was quickly put to rest. All four seemed drawn with worry.

"We had the incantation, we'll be fine!" Wendy said with false cheeriness.

"Yeah, about that," Suzanne said. "I've been thinking about it."

"Yeah?" Diane frowned.

"Something O'Grady said bothered me. I didn't think it through at the time but now, in light of the fact that he left so suddenly, it came back to me."

"What? What?"

"He was talking about calling his relatives, who he said gave him the incantation. Then he said, 'They say such a thing should have never happened. It has never happened before.' My question is, if it has never happened before, how did they know what incantation would work?"

A terrible silence filled the room.

"You don't think..." Diane began.

"I'm not sure," Suzanne responded. "We do feel better, right? I'm just wondering...did he make all that up? Was the incantation a hoax?"

"It did seem very strange to have us all get naked like that," Carol said.

"Yeah, if I hadn't been so anxious for it to work, I would've thought he was getting his jollies or something," Wendy put in.

Everyone nodded.

"Shit. Does that mean...?"

"What? That the curse isn't lifted? No, that's nonsense," Suzanne quickly said. "It just seems strange, that's all."

There was really nothing more to be said. Each realized she would have to face her demons on her own. After some dispirited goodbyes, they left, each deep in their own thoughts.

Epilogue

Six months later

ꟹ

Suzanne spotted the man across the room and did her best to ignore him. She felt that familiar thrum in her loins as she stood at the bar, ordering a glass of wine.

As she turned away and raised the glass to her lips, she caught sight of him staring at her with unabashed lust and she had to look away for fear she'd climax right on the spot. There was something about him. He was a handsome man, over six feet tall with dark shaggy hair and piercing brown eyes. She knew if he approached her, she would be helpless to stop herself. Already her pussy began to lubricate in anticipation.

Stop it! she told herself. *I can't go on doing this!*

She turned away, fighting her emotions. She scanned the other side of the room, looking for a friend or coworker to distract herself from the man's eyes.

"Can I buy you a drink?"

She turned, startled to see him standing at her elbow, and knew she was lost in that moment. Up close he was even more handsome, if that was possible, and she could see the muscles pressing against his shirt. And he smelled wonderful! A scent of aftershave mixed with a musky, manly odor, as if he had worked outdoors all day and had jumped into the shower just before coming to the bar.

She had to get this man into a bed.

"Sure," she said, trying to keep her voice cool, although she felt anything but that.

He ordered her another glass then turned back to face her. "I should introduce myself. I'm—"

She held up a hand. "No names."

He looked puzzled. "No names?"

"No. Humor me, okay?"

He gave a half nod. "All right, Miss X. We'll play it your way."

"Good. You'll find it's better that way."

"Am I to assume that you don't want to know anything about me? Where I work or what my dreams are?"

She thought about that and gave him a smile. "Work, okay—but be generic." Suzanne was curious about what he did that kept him in such good shape.

"I'm a steelworker."

Suzanne had a sudden image of him pounding rivets, sweat pouring off his dirt-stained body and had to grip the bar for support.

"Are you all right?"

"No. I mean, yes, I'm fine. Just a little dizzy there for a second."

"Well, okay then. Can I ask what you do—generically of course."

"Legal secretary."

He grinned. "So we have Beauty and the Beast, brains and the brawn."

"Something like that."

"Looks like we've just about run out of conversation though. That is, unless you want to know more about me."

Yeah, like what do you look like with your clothes off? "You're right. We do seem to be at an impasse."

"Well, this goes against everything I've been taught about women—you know, about taking it slow and getting to know each other. But if we can't talk, we might as well go to my place and fuck."

Another wave of pleasure coursed through her. She put her half-empty glass on the bar. "I thought you'd never ask."

She took his arm and they caught a cab outside. They rode the eight blocks in silence. Suzanne never let go of his arm, feeling the bicep press against her breast. Her pussy was wet with her need.

They got out and her mystery man paid the driver. She looked up at the apartment building and nodded. It was typical of what a construction worker could afford—not too fancy but certainly safe and clean. They rode up in the elevator, the silence stretching out between them.

Once he unlocked the door, Suzanne felt the dam burst within her. She didn't protest when he turned and grabbed her, kicking the door shut with his foot and pressing her up against the wall. He kissed her and she kissed him back hard. She loved the feel of his arms around her, crushing her to his powerful chest. He made her feel small and weak and helpless.

They kissed again and again. They were animals, unable to control themselves. She felt his hand on her breast and wanted those damn clothes out of the way. She needed to feel his fingers on her flesh.

Her fingers went to her blouse and unbuttoned it as quickly as she could. He helped her and soon her blouse was open and his hand went into the cups of her bra. Her skin felt hot.

She didn't stop him as he yanked her blouse from her shoulders then unhooked her bra. Her breasts spilled free and he immediately took a nipple into his mouth. Suzanne's mouth came open and her knees grew weak. Only the wall was holding her up. The wall and the man's powerful arms.

As he alternated between her nipples, his fingers dropped to her skirt and he found the catch, releasing it. The garment puddled around her feet. Suzanne cursed her pantyhose for there was no sexy way to get them off. Her pussy cried out for release.

"Wait, wait," she said, pushing him away. "Let me get these off."

He stepped back and she peeled her pantyhose down off her legs and threw them across the room. She reached for her lace panties but the man caught her arm.

"No, leave them for now. They look sexy on you."

Whatever you say, mister. Her pussy grew even hotter.

He bent down and picked her up easily, as if she weighed hardly anything. Suzanne, who was the tallest of her three friends, loved the sensation that she was petite compared to him.

He carried her to his bedroom. For the first time, she got a look at his apartment and found it clean and neat. Could this man be any more perfect? His bedroom was also organized, the bed made. He laid her down on the covers. She tried to act demure, fighting the urge to spread her legs wide and crook a finger at him.

She watched as he stripped, like seeing the wrapping being pulled off a long-desired present. As his shirt came open, she marveled at his physique. Well-defined chest and six-pack abs made her swoon. Her legs came apart on their own accord.

He pulled off his pants and she smiled when she saw the penguins on his boxer shorts. He looked down at himself and smiled back. "A gift from an old girlfriend," he said.

"I like them." *What idiot let you go?*

But she liked the bulge underneath more. God, he was well hung! His cock made a tent of the material. He had to pull the waistband out wide to ease it over his turgid member. Suzanne's mouth came open when she saw it—she couldn't help herself.

She got to all fours and crawled to the edge of the bed. Grabbing his hips, she pulled him close and took his cock into her mouth.

"Oh god," he moaned.

She had learned how to please a man well over the years—her ex-husband had been a particular fan—and her recent experience with strangers only improved her technique. She sucked and licked and played with his balls until she could tell he was about to come. Then she pulled away and shook her head at his dismayed expression.

"Uh-huh. Don't want to waste it."

"Hell no." He pushed her back and crawled over her. Thankfully he didn't thrust into her right away, although Suzanne was in no position to delay. He bent down and sucked on her nipples and she threw her head back, marveling at this wonderful man. He seemed to know just what to do.

He kissed her again and again until Suzanne's mouth ached. Their hands clutched at each other. She opened her legs for him and reached down to feel his tumescence. She didn't think she could stand to be without it another minute.

"Please," she begged.

"Well, if you insist," he said, and pressed the tip to her hot wetness.

"Oh god," she whispered. "Oh god."

Though his cock was large, it slid in smoothly. It was as if she had been made for him. Sparks went off in her head and she clung to him as he pressed it all the way in. The heat, the size, the power, of it made her not want to let him go.

But when he began to thrust within her, Suzanne thought she could very well die right there and be perfectly happy. All the other men in her life—including sadly her ex—seemed inadequate in comparison. His cock touched all the right spots. And he knew how to use it.

They rode together and she had one climax on top of another. He was indefatigable! Her pussy was the center of her universe and the rest of her body seemed to be sucked into it, like an exploding star.

After her fifth or six climax, when she thought she couldn't stand it anymore, she felt him stiffen and erupt within her, triggering her last orgasm. She cried out and her mind short-circuited for several seconds as the pleasure washed through her.

Suzanne was barely aware when he pulled out. Just a sensation of sadness, mixed with her exhaustion. She felt him pulling the covers down from underneath her and she could barely help him move—her body felt light yet she couldn't seem to find the controls. He crawled in next to her and pulled up the covers. She snuggled up against him. Her last conscious thought was how great he smelled.

She woke the next morning and looked over at the man. He slept easily. She admired him for several minutes until he stirred and opened one eye.

She put a hand on his cheek. "Thanks, Ben. That was wonderful."

"Oh you're back to normal now?"

"Yes. At least until next time."

"I still don't quite understand it all, Suz. But I have to admit, the game's a lot of fun."

She smiled. She could never expect Ben to really believe she'd been cursed. He was too down-to-earth.

"Yes, it is fun, isn't it?" She pulled back the covers, suddenly ravenous. "Come on, I'll fix you breakfast."

* * * * *

Carol knelt on the rug, naked, her knees apart, her head down, hands at her sides. She could hear the whisper of Barry's clothes as he approached her.

"How is my pet today?"

"Good, Master."

"Tell me about your day."

"I got home from work an hour ago. I cleaned the kitchen as you asked, and I answered some of your emails."

"Any prospects?"

"Yes, sir. A couple in Albany want you to train the wife. I called them and got them both on the phone. She's been hiding her submissive desires for years and now that it's out in the open, her husband is curious to explore them."

"Very good. Did they express curiosity about you?"

"Oh yes. The wife asked me many questions."

"Were you honest with them?"

"Yes, Master," she blushed, remembering how intimate the questions had become once they realized she had been ordered to answer all their questions honestly.

"Tell me some of their questions."

Carol knew that was coming and she felt the blush spread from her neck to her face. It pleased him to embarrass her by making her describe intimate details.

"Um, she asked if you whipped me regularly, and I told her yes, you did. She asked if that hurt and I said it did, but then the sex afterward was so good you forgot about the pain. That seemed to really excite both of them."

"How could you tell?"

"She kinda gasped and her husband chuckled."

"What else?"

"Well, she asked if I was marked and I told her I was."

"Be specific."

"Sorry, sir. I told her I had a ring in my clit hood that bounces against my clit all day long, keeping me aroused. Oh—I told her I'm not allowed to wear panties too. And I told her about the tattoo on my ass that looks like a swirling design but that it has your initials inside."

"Good. What else did she want to know?"

"She wanted to know if you ever made me fuck other men."

"And?"

"I told her that was an individual choice. You prefer to keep me to yourself but that they might decide otherwise."

"Anything else?"

"Well, he asked if you, uh, showed me off and I told him you did and how embarrassed I got."

"But you know you love it."

"Yes, sir."

He came close and put his fingers under her chin to lift her eyes to his. "I'm very pleased with you. You've become a great help to me."

"Thank you, sir."

"I shall reward you. Come."

Carol rose at once, her body on fire, and followed him upstairs. He took her to her favorite machine, the Sybian, a saddle-like device with many amazing attachments. This was their newest model with an extended front. He let her pick out the dildo she preferred, the six-inch model with the ribbed edges. Already she found herself becoming wet and her fingers fumbled to attach the dildo. Once in place, she climbed on, centered herself over the rubber cock and eased down. It filled her nicely, not too big and not too small.

He tapped her rump and she raised herself up, placing her hands well forward. This caused her clit to be pressed harder against the rise of the saddle and brought her ass into target range. Her hands rested on wooden dowels that stuck out from the sides. Barry tied them in place with rawhide laces—not too tight, but tight enough so she couldn't release her grip. She waited while Barry buckled the straps around her thighs and ankles, trapping her. She looked as if she were riding a horse, bent forward, striving for the finish line.

He picked up the remote. He would be in charge of her pleasure—and pain. She watched as he went to the wall and breathed a sigh of relief when he took down the suede cat o'nine tails, her favorite.

He caught her expression and smiled. "See how wonderful life can be when you please me?"

She nodded, impatient for him to begin. He thumbed a switch on the remote. Carol felt the cock inside her come alive, a low vibration sending waves of pleasure through her.

He reared back and slashed the suede whip against her ass. She rocked forward, her pleasure evaporating as the pain crashed through her. The straps allowed her some movement but only forward, to press her clit harder against the leather and to expose more of her ass to the whip. While she was in that position, he struck her again, lower this time.

Carol soon found her rhythm, rocking forward and back, getting a sharp jolt, followed by a wave of pleasure. He upped the vibrations and she soon found herself saying, "Oh god, oh god, oh god," like a mantra. The cock seemed alive in her, sending out waves of pleasure that at first alternated with the pain then began to counteract it.

She knew this was the beginning of a massive orgasm. It built upon itself, each time rising higher until she found she needed the whip to prolong it. She was riding now, her body coated with sweat, her mouth open, hair hanging in her eyes.

Everything was concentrated on her pussy and ass. *Whack!* Ohhhh! *Whack!* Ohhhh! Each time she climbed higher.

Her vocalizations rose with her emotions and her words ran together. "Ohmygod ohmygod ohmygod OHMYGOD OHMYGOD OHMYGOD!"

She screamed aloud and pressed her clit hard against the saddle as the orgasm rocked her. It was like being in the middle of an avalanche. She was swept away and she collapsed down on the Sybian.

Barry stopped it at once and left her there a few minutes to calm down. He rubbed her back and told her how much he loved her.

"Oh my god, that was incredible," Carol said when she finally came to her senses.

"Maybe we'll show that to our new customers when they come down for training," he said.

She groaned, knowing how that would embarrass her, yet she knew deep down it was what she needed. She couldn't deny her desires and Barry knew just how to play her.

* * * * *

Diane kept her eyes on a handsome older man at the front of the stage, ignoring the rest of the droolers and the drunks as she gyrated to the loud music. Tom was fifteen years older than she was, but he was the nicest of the men who came to watch her perform.

The club was packed tonight and she spotted Morty, the manager, standing by the bar, smiling at her. They both knew many in the crowd had come to see her. They loved to watch her strip and she could only imagine that it was because she enjoyed it so.

She unclasped her brassiere among the hoots of the crowd and tossed it to the stage, exposing her breasts, covered now only with pasties, complete with tiny tassels. She shook her torso, rotating the tassels in opposite directions.

Tom Stedman seemed pleased. He was fifty with thick dark hair speckled with gray. He wore wireless glasses and had an open, friendly face. As usual, he was impeccably dressed in a designer suit.

Diane had met him shortly after she had come to work at Club Femme, not long after she had been fired from her job. When the urges had returned, she was caught having sex with Richard in his office. He was demoted but she was canned.

Dancing at the club satisfied part of her needs but not all of them. She needed the looks of the men as she stripped, their eyes helped feed the leprechaun. As she danced, Diane wished she could pick a man out of the crowd, bring him up on stage and fuck his brains out. Preferably Tom. Now *that* would be public sex! Not that Tom would go for it.

She turned and wiggled her ass at the crowd, enjoying the hoots. Her fingers slipped into her short-shorts and she teased them for a little while before she eased them down, exposing her thong. Too bad she was required by law to keep it on, she mused. The thought of dancing completely naked made her wet with desire.

Fortunately, Johnny Law didn't seem to mind if she flashed the crowd a little. It also might explain why the audience had grown in the two months she'd been a featured dancer.

She had met Tom a month ago and they had chatted several times during her breaks. She had found him to be charming, generous and sexy, despite their age difference. And he seemed completely smitten by her.

Of course he wanted to "take her away from all this", not knowing that she needed it. She doubted he would be able to handle her libido now that it had been ramped up by that damned leprechaun. All she wanted was a safe way to satisfy her urges. Dancing semi-nude at a club brought her almost all the way there.

She turned back to the group of cheering men and yanked one of her pasties loose. It always stung but she covered it well with an open smile and a broad wink. The crowd went nuts when they saw her exposed nipple. Diane danced for a few more minutes, hearing in the music the approach of the end of her set and removed the other pasty. Now her breasts were free and she shook them at the crowd. Men flashed dollar bills at her and she allowed them to thrust them into the top of her thong. Whenever she spotted someone with a ten or a twenty, she would pull aside her thong for a quick glimpse of her shaved pussy. It was dangerous but the law hadn't busted her yet.

The music ended and she turned at once and left the stage. It was always best to leave them begging for more. She came back out for a brief bow and collected more money.

"Isn't she great?" boomed the manager who doubled as the emcee. He stepped out on stage, signaling Diane it was time to leave. She nodded at him and he flashed her a big smile. She turned and winked at Tom as she exited, stage right.

Backstage, she slipped on her silk robe, collapsed into her chair in front of the mirror and began repairing her makeup. Dancing always took its toll on her. At thirty-five, she was a good ten to fifteen years older than the other girls. She didn't know how much longer she could keep it up.

She hoped someone like Tom might steal her away as long as he understood her needs and how to satisfy them. The jury was still out on that however. Fact was, she hadn't yet told him of her secret. She meant to but the opportunity just hadn't come up. She knew it would have to be soon or else she'd have to find another sugar daddy, one with looser morals. Problem was, she *liked* Tom.

The music started for the next dancer and Diane smiled to herself, knowing that would be Brenda, who was just twenty-one and terrified to be showing her body. But the money was so good, it paid her way through college so she did it anyway then came backstage crying almost every night. Diane just wanted to slap her. *Get a job at a pizza parlor if you feel that way about it!*

Ruby, the fifty-something stage mistress with the big wig of platinum blonde hair, came back to hand Diane a single red rose. She winked at her, for they both knew the rose had come from Tom. He'd been giving her one every time he came to see her dance.

"You gonna marry that man?" Ruby teased.

"Ah, he'd never have me. I'm just a stripper," she said, self-deprecatingly.

"Hah! That's what Anna Nicole Smith said and look at what she accomplished!" she cackled, and left to round up the next act.

Diane looked at her watch. Ten-forty. She had one more set to do that night before she could go home and masturbate, and think about all the men who had seen her naked. She would have to pretend her dildo was one of them.

She tied the robe tight around her and went out to have a quick drink with Tom as was their ritual. She spotted him at his regular booth, near the back. It was one of the few places in the joint where one could actually hear conversation over the music.

She slid in next to him and pursed her lips for a kiss. He was a good kisser and it gave her a thrill. Diane had an image of them standing and kissing, his hard cock thrusting into her, and pushed it out of her mind.

"Hi, Tom."

"Diane, you look lovely as always."

"Oh you're so kind."

"When are you going to give up this life? It's not really you, is it?"

"We've talked about this before. I need the money." *And I need the exposure,* she thought.

"I'm sure a smart woman like you could find another job in marketing. I mean that was your career, wasn't it?"

Diane had danced around the topic so to speak for many weeks. She decided to let him in on her little secret. If it scared him off, so be it. She was tired of living a lie.

"Tom, about that. I didn't tell you why I changed careers so suddenly. I know you've been curious."

He leaned forward, all ears.

"Well, I've been repressing a secret desire, you see." She wasn't sure how to go about explaining it without sounding crazy. But she had started so she plunged ahead. "Every since I was a teenager, I've had this strange need to, well, expose myself. Isn't that weird?"

"No, no," he said at once, as if that were the most normal thing in the world. "Actually, it's kind of exciting."

"Yeah, well, I ignored it for years. But after I lost my job due to downsizing," she wasn't going to confess why she'd been fired, "it just seemed a natural way to kill two birds with one stone."

"I'm surprised, if you felt that way, why you didn't get into this line of work when you were in your twenties."

Diane sensed Tom was thinking she was too old for this and he was right.

"I was too focused on my career then," she said. "But it was only much later that I became disillusioned with the field."

"Hmm. So how is it? Do you get what you wanted out of it?"

She paused, not sure how to continue. "Well, yes and no." She reached out and put her hands over his. "I'm kinda, um, oversexed, I guess."

Tom picked up on it right away. "So what you're saying is the dancing isn't enough for you. You'd like to do more."

"Uh, yeah. But I don't want to get arrested!"

"No, of course not." He smiled and it grew bigger and bigger on his face. "I think we can work something out."

"Really? You aren't shocked?"

"No. Not in the least. I find it very exciting. But just how far do you want to take it?"

"I'm basically a one-man woman, you see, so if you're thinking that I'd like to pull a train or something, forget it. I just get a thrill out of sex in semi-public places, that's all." She added quickly, "Safe, semi-public places."

"That's quite a fetish," he said. "Where do you suppose that came from?"

"I don't know," she lied. Trying to explain the leprechaun story would label her a loon. She leaned forward. "So you don't think I'm crazy?"

"No, I think you're a dream come true." He looked at his watch. "What time is your next set?"

"Uh, eleven-forty. I should be all done by twelve-thirty."

He nodded. "Okay. Loosen your robe."

"What?" That familiar thrill ran through her.

"You heard me. Loosen your robe."

Diane's fingers fumbled to obey. Her pussy felt hot and her nipples tingled.

"Now scoot over here close to me."

She did, keeping the edges of her robe tight in front of her.

"No, no, you've got it all wrong," he said, pulling the edges apart. Diane gasped when a breast popped into view.

"Tom! What are you doing?" But it was the pre-leprechaun Diane talking just then. An automatic response to the shock of being exposed so suddenly. She pulled the robe together, covering herself, and felt a pang of disappointment.

"No, leave it loose. Just a little bit, okay?" The robe came open again, exposing the soft valley between her breasts all the way down to her hot wet thong.

"I—I could get arrested." Diane swooned with desire. Her legs came apart a little more.

"I'll protect you." She felt better hearing that.

Diane looked around. So far no one seemed to have noticed her.

"Now slip off your thong and put it on the table."

"What?"

"Come on, this is what you want and you know it. So get busy."

She raised her ass up off the cushion and eased her thong off and down her legs. She canted to one side to free it from her feet and handed it to Tom.

"No, on the table."

Diane dropped it and stared at it as if it were a snake. Deep down, she thought she could hear the leprechaun laugh.

She startled when she felt Tom's hand on her thigh.

"Relax," he said. "Just watch the dancer."

She raised her eyes to see Brenda, that shy, cute little college student, gyrating like a pro to the hoots of the men along the stage. Diane's mouth came open and her eyes glazed as she watched. She felt Tom's fingers move to her hot core and she allowed her legs to come apart to encourage him.

The robe came open a bit more, exposing part of one nipple. Diane kept her eyes on the stage, pretending she was up there, dancing, even as she felt his middle finger slide down her very wet pussy. She took in a breath and let it out slowly. She made no move to stop him.

His finger slipped up and down and Diane was lost to the sensations spreading through her. She didn't notice when Tom used his free hand to pull the robe apart, exposing both breasts.

Now some of the men began to notice the little show and they gathered quickly, forming a semicircle around the booth. One reached in for her breasts, but Tom barked, "No touching! Just watch or go away."

They nodded in unison and left her alone. Diane's legs were well apart now, exposing Tom's hand busy between them, rubbing, rubbing, rubbing.

"Oh god," she breathed, and the men smiled at her, knowing she was close.

The orgasm crashed over her suddenly and she cried out, falling backward against the padded back of the booth. Her legs came together, trapping Tom's hand. She rolled to the side, pulling the robe over her as she was rocked by the waves of pleasure. The men cheered. Diane couldn't move. She sat limply on the seat.

The show was over now and the men began to drift away. The manager came by, a frown on his face. "What's all this now?"

Diane managed to sit up. "Uh, nothing, Morty," she said. "I was just doing a table dance for Tom here."

Morty eyed him, knowing he was a good customer but not believing for a minute her story. "Well, don't shout out so. This place is probably crawling with undercover officers just dying to bust us." He left.

Diane took a deep breath. Tom took her hands into his. "Diane, this could be the start of a beautiful friendship."

* * * * *

Wendy knocked on Bob Townbridge's door, wearing her little black dress and high-heeled strappy shoes. And nothing else. "Hi, Bob," she said when she saw his smiling face. "You got something for me?"

"Yes, yes, I do, Wendy. Come in."

She entered and spotted another man inside. He was about Bob's age, late forties, and seemed nice enough. He was dressed in a white shirt, blue tie and dark slacks. He wore wire-rimmed glasses. He smiled nervously at her.

"I'd like you to meet my friend Steve," Bob said. "Steve, this is Wendy."

"Uh, hi." He thrust out a hand.

Wendy came over to him, took his outstretched hand and placed it on her hip. "Hi, Steve. Nice to meet you."

"Uh, yeah, me too."

"Oh you're not nervous because of me, I hope," she said coyly.

"Well, I've never done anything like this before."

"I can tell. But don't let that worry you. You'll know what to do when the time comes."

He smiled and nodded. Wendy half turned toward Bob. "Now did Bob explain the rules?"

Steve nodded. "Oh yes. One hundred dollars for forty minutes and I have to wear a condom. Right?"

"Right. And we pay up front."

She stepped back as he fumbled for his wallet, counting out five twenties. He placed them in her hand. The touch of the money nearly gave her an orgasm on the spot.

She turned and handed the money to Bob. "Now Bob here is going to keep this for me. He's going to watch some TV and leave us alone, okay? He's only here to protect me—not that I need any protection from a nice guy like you! We can go back into the bedroom and have some fun."

Wendy led the nervous man down the hallway while Bob sat on the couch and turned on the television.

Once inside the bedroom, she checked the clock. Eight-ten. Good. She reached down and pulled her loose dress up over her head in one smooth motion.

Steve gasped and his mouth came open. "You're...beautiful."

"Thank you." She came to him and felt his hard cock. "You're pretty beautiful yourself, big guy."

He blushed and she began unbuttoning his shirt. He let her, running his free hands over her breasts. Her hands went to his belt buckle.

"Ohhh that feels good," she cooed, quickly getting him out of his clothes. When he was down to his boxer shorts, she eased down and played with it through the material.

"What do we have here?"

She pulled the waistband down, making sure not to scrape it against his turgid cock. Wendy leaned in and kissed it as she allowed his shorts to slip down his legs. She felt in complete control and she loved it. She may be a whore, but she was good at her job. She took more of his cock into her mouth. Thankfully he bathed regularly.

"Ohhh," Steve said. "Careful!"

Ahh, she thought, a preemie. *I'll have to make sure he doesn't lose it before we get to the main event.*

"What do you like, Steve? Do you like sucking or fucking?"

"Well, uh, both. But you have me so turned on, we'd better get to it or else..."

"Sure." She rose and led him to the bed. Wendy found a condom in the drawer and opened it. "Allow me." She knelt down and slipped it over his cock. "How's that?"

"G-good. Real good."

"Now don't be afraid. Wendy's going to take good care of you."

He nodded as she pulled him onto her and lay on the bed. She spread her legs. "I'm so hot right now. I can't stand it."

He grinned and reached down to steer his cock toward her wetness. The leprechaun helped her get wet so she wasn't faking it. She felt the tip touch her and she shivered with delight. "Oh that feels good," she whispered. "You have such a nice cock."

Steve pressed it in and she settled, letting him take the lead now. He pumped vigorously a few times and stiffened, shooting his load. Wendy could feel his cock pulsating within her. She hugged him tightly. As she did, she glanced at the clock. Eight-twenty-one. Ha!

They hugged for several minutes until Steve calmed down from his release. Then she kissed him and told him what a great lover he was and how she hoped she could see him again. By the time she had him dressed and out the door, less than a half-hour had passed.

She sat on the couch next to Bob and collected sixty dollars from him. Forty was his for bringing her the client.

"That was quick," he commented.

"Yep. I'm good, didn't you know that?"

"Oh yeah. I remember."

"We got anyone else tonight?"

"No, that was it. Sorry."

"It's okay. I'm glad you're being careful. I don't want to risk any more than I have to." *Just enough to satisfy the leprechaun*, she mused.

"Good, because I'm not the most effective pimp. If I had my way, I'd keep you all to myself."

"Yeah, well, you can't afford me."

"Got that right. But I do like the benefits."

She turned to him. "Yeah? Why? You feeling a bit frisky?"

"I could go for a quickie."

"Come on," she said, rolling her eyes as if in exasperation, though they both knew she was kidding. "If I have to, I have to." She took his hand and tugged him to his feet.

"Hey, it's all part of doing business." As per their agreement, he handed her a dollar before they went into the bedroom. Wendy felt the little thrill she always got when a man paid her for sex.

She paused and took his face in both hands. "You know I really appreciate what you're doing for me, right?"

"Of course. I know that leprechaun can be a real bastard sometimes."

She nodded and pulled her dress off over her head. "I'm all yours. You've earned it."

* * * * *

Halfway around the world, in a small antique shop in the Paris suburb of Saint Denis, a small ceramic sculpture attracted the attention of Bridget D'Arbo, an attractive blonde in her late twenties. It was an odd little thing, she thought, but it had a certain charm. She picked it up and noticed how the little leprechaun appeared to be laughing at her, as if he had some kind of joke to share. She felt drawn to it.

"How much for this?" the Frenchwoman asked the shopkeeper.

"Oh that's very rare. Nineteenth century, I've been told." He quoted a price that seemed quite reasonable to her.

"I'll take it," she said impulsively. "I'm not sure if it will fit into my décor but I feel it belongs somehow."

"I'm sure you'll know just what to do with it," the shopkeeper said. "I'm told it will bring luck to whoever owns it."

"Really? That's funny. I'm sure my roommate will be pleased to hear that, she could use a little luck—with men, that is!" She laughed. "In fact, we both could." She handed over her credit card.

She watched as the shopkeeper wrapped the ceramic in paper and put it into her bag. For some reason, it gave her a little thrill, like a jolt of static electricity.

DELICIOUS BLACKMAIL

ഗ

Trademarks Acknowledgement

ꕤ

The author acknowledges the trademarked status and trademark owners of the following wordmarks mentioned in this work of fiction:

BMW: Bayerische Motoren Werke Aktiengesellschaft

Boy Scouts: Boy Scouts of America Corporation

Gone With the Wind: Turner Entertainment Co.

Greenpeace: Stichting Greenpeace Council

Ryder Cup: The Professional Golfers' Association of America

Velcro: Velcro Industries B.V. Limited Liability Company

Vera Wang: VWK Licensing LLC

Victoria's Secret: V Secret Catalogue, Inc.

Chapter One

ຣ

The doorbell rang just as Janet Mann was finishing her workout in front of the TV. She was sweaty and tired but pleased with herself. As she approached her thirty-seventh birthday, it was becoming harder to stay in shape. The doorbell bothered her because she knew at this time of day—close to eleven in the morning—it would probably either be a salesman or a religious fanatic. For a moment she debated just pretending no one was home.

She rose and grabbed the towel from the arm of the couch. Flicking off the TV, she moved toward the front door, flicking her blonde hair back and wiping away the sweat from her neck and face. She peeked through the peephole and was shocked to see Frank Ramon, the CEO of Springfield Mills, her husband's employer.

She opened door at once, panic rising in her voice. "What? Has something happened to Bill?"

Frank, a tall, handsome man in his early forties, put up a placating palm. "No, no! Nothing like that! Your husband's just fine." He was dressed casually in tan pants and a blue polo shirt with the company's logo on it.

Relief washed through her. "Well then, what brings you out here? I mean, Bill is still at work—isn't he?"

"Yes, of course. I need to talk to you about something." He stood there expectantly and it took Janet a moment to realize he wanted to come in before he would discuss it.

"Oh! Please come in." She stepped aside and he entered, giving her a short nod. "Can I get you some coffee?"

"That would be wonderful, thank you." He followed her to the kitchen. There was enough left for a cupful so she poured it for him and placed it in front of one of the stools that lined the counter. She stood on the other side waiting. He got the message and sat down, keeping the counter between them.

"Aren't you having any?"

"No. I've already had two cups. That's enough for me today." She waited.

"I'm sure you're wondering why I came out."

"Yes."

He sighed. "Well, no doubt you're aware of the difficulties our company has been facing."

Oh no, she thought. *Is Bill going to get laid off?* She steeled herself for the news.

"If it weren't for the damn Japanese dumping steel on the market, we'd be fine. I'm sure Bill has outlined the problem for you."

"Yes, he said they are trying to control the market, run Springfield and other American mills out of business so they could grab market share. But you've been petitioning Congress to do something, haven't you?"

"Yes. We hope they will impose tariffs that will level the playing field. I mean, we're all for competition—we can handle that. We just can't handle unfair trade practices."

Janet nodded, wondering where this conversation was going. Why would Frank come to her with all this?

"As you know, we've had to lay off about eighteen percent of our workers in the last two years just to stay afloat. The board is up in arms, the stockholders are angry with us and I'm just hoping we can hang on until we goad Congress into action."

Janet couldn't stand it any longer. "Please! Are you trying to tell me Bill is losing his job?"

He looked at her for a long moment then said, "I'm not sure yet."

Her mouth came open in surprise and she could feel the blood pound in her body. *What will we do?* She didn't work and their savings might carry them for a few months. After that…

He went on. "You see, the workers have taken the brunt of the cutbacks. Administration has remained intact. But the board is under pressure to reduce headquarters staff as well. You know, share the pain."

"Oh no…" she said softly. Bill was a project manager, one of about fifteen working out of headquarters.

"Yeah. I've been resisting the board on this. I've been keeping it under wraps while I tried to get them to back off. Well, last week I got the edict—I have to lay off three people or else I'll lose my position. And the new CEO they hire will come in and do it anyway."

"But not Bill! He's been there longer than you!"

"I know! It's a very tough choice. There's no 'fat' to cut. Every person contributes to the success of Springfield. I'm not really sure how we're going to manage once the cuts have been made."

Janet was still confused. "But why tell me? Why not talk to Bill about this?"

"That wouldn't do any good. I mean, if he's the one I have to lay off, it won't help to warn him. I came to you because I wanted to see if you could come up with a reason to keep him on."

Her brow furrowed. "Me?" She launched into her support of Bill. "Well, for one, he's a long-time loyal employee. I mean, he practically runs that place! He's been there for fifteen years. He expects to retire there…" She couldn't understand why he would ask her. Surely he must know all this!

Then she caught his expression. It was a frank appraisal of her. She knew she looked good, even if she was hot and sweaty at the moment. Frank wasn't the only one who gave her the eye or joked about how she kept herself in shape. But the circumstances seemed so inappropriate here she was taken aback. She stared at Frank, her brain not comprehending.

"I really don't understand all this."

"There are fourteen people at headquarters including myself. There's also an IT guy Howard Baines, whom I absolutely cannot lay off since he keeps the computers up and running. I don't know if you're aware, but it's very hard to keep a good IT man around."

Janet just stared at him.

"Since I'm not going to lay off myself, that leaves twelve people. Nine men, three women. I have to lay off three of them. Who should it be? That's what I wrestle with every day."

"And you come to me, why? Because you think I can help you decide? It's easy. Don't pick Bill. He will keep your company running, making sure your projects get done on time. Without him, you'll start missing deadlines."

"I wish it were that easy. I have others who could step in and fill Bill's job if it came to that. The problem is Bill is one of the older workers. He's, what, almost fifty now?"

She colored slightly. "No, Bill is only forty-seven. You know that."

"Statistics show that older workers cost companies more money. Not only in salary but also in healthcare costs. The board would probably be pleased if I chose Bill."

Janet felt a flush creep up from her chest into her neck. It was clear to her now what he was getting at and yet he wouldn't come right out and say it. It was so aggravating! Janet was tired of playing this stupid game. She made one more effort to get him to speak up. "So why don't you lay your cards on the table? What is it you want from me?"

He allowed his glance to drop to her breasts before returning to her face. "I want you to give me a reason not to put Bill on the list."

"Dammit! Just say it!"

"No. You have to say it."

She sighed, exasperated. "If I agree to fuck you, you'll allow Bill to keep his job. Is that it?"

"Wow, that's an interesting suggestion. I wouldn't have thought of that myself," he said. "But you do add another element to my decision-making process, that's for sure. I'll have to think about it."

"And what's to keep me from telling Bill about your little unauthorized visit here today? Not to mention your coy suggestion."

"I'm sure you could gauge his reaction. He'd probably march down to the office and punch me out. Or maybe even shoot me." He gave her a thin smile. "Because I have to make this decision tomorrow, I've arranged to have two security guards in place. If an employee made a scene, it would make my job of deciding whom to lay off that much easier." He paused. "Of course if he didn't know about it, things would go much more smoothly…"

"And what if the board were to hear about this? You're talking about blackmail, sexual harassment. I doubt you'd have your job for long."

"Well, it really was your suggestion, wasn't it? But you could be right. That is, if they believed you. It might seem to be the anger of the wife of a disgruntled employee talking."

"He's not a disgruntled employee!"

"He would be if he's laid off."

There it was, naked blackmail, in all its ugliness. If she told Bill or the board, he would be fired and Frank would take his chances with the fallout. The irony was, Janet had always liked Frank. She had found him to be funny, caring and easy to get along with. Not like some bosses. She had considered Bill lucky to have Frank as a CEO and had told him so more than once.

"How could you? We've had you and your wife over to dinner! We even went sailing together a few times!"

"Yes, my wife. I'm sure you heard about our divorce. Very sad. She got the house and the kids, and I got an apartment near the mill."

"Well, don't take your anger out on us! We don't deserve this!"

He sighed. "I don't like following these orders. I fought the board tooth and nail to prevent it. I gave them all the arguments you just gave me. But in the end, they say the perception is just as important as the cost savings. Workers have been cut back nearly twenty percent, administration has to take its cuts too."

She stood fully erect, her eyes flashing. "You're a monster. A despicable monster!" She grabbed his coffee cup and poured the contents into the sink. "Get out of my house!"

"Very well." He stood. "I'm sure Bill can find another job, although probably not with another steel firm—those jobs are hard to come by now. And you're still young. You could probably go back to work. What were you before you married Bill anyway?"

Janet could feel the blood rush to her face. She had been a cocktail waitress when she had met Bill ten years ago and she was sure Frank knew it. "Fuck you, Frank. Get out of my house."

He nodded and headed for the door. "Please give me a call before ten a.m. tomorrow and let me know of your final decision. After that, I'll be busy calling the three employees in to give them the bad news."

"Wait!" A sudden thought burst in her brain. "Are you approaching all the wives like this? You know, to fuck you or see their husbands fired?"

He didn't speak, he just stood by the door, leveling his gaze at her.

She pressed him. "Are you going to try and get Brenda and Susan and Dorothy and the others to agree to this madness?"

Again, he just stared at her. She began to think about it. She had seen them all at the last company picnic. Brenda was a dull, plain woman and Susan was fifty pounds overweight. Dorothy seemed a bit of a lush—she had gotten a little tipsy and her husband had had to take her home early. Janet couldn't pick out too many beauties from the wives of the headquarter staff. In fact, she could remember many of the husbands coming over to flirt with her. Had she really been the prettiest woman there?

Reality began to dawn on her.

"This is just about me, isn't it? You're not approaching anyone else. You don't want them. In fact," she continued, "you wouldn't dare go to anyone else. Word would get out… We would all march on the board and get you fired. If we all told the same story, they'd probably believe us. So this is just about me."

Frank just stared at her, same as he did before. Finally he spoke. "You have the power to control your future. Only you."

He gave her a quick smile then left. Janet stood in the living room and stared for a long time at the closed door.

Janet debated for hours whether to tell Bill. She knew he would be furious. At one point during that bleak afternoon, she went to the bedroom and opened the drawer to Bill's nightstand. Nestled there was his pistol, an ugly .38 that he kept "for burglars". Since Bill's son Andy was grown and living on his own in another state, Bill didn't have to worry about keeping it locked away.

She picked it up and felt its weight. She didn't know much about guns but she knew it was fully loaded—she could see the noses of the bullets in the chambers. Janet wondered if Bill would be so angry as to take the gun down to the factory and shoot Frank. If he did, then she'd lose her husband for sure. She quickly unloaded the gun and hid the bullets in her underwear drawer.

Could she really consider what Frank was demanding? Janet had actually been attracted to him, as hard as it was for her to believe now. He exhibited a quiet strength, which she had always found sexy. She remembered one incident while sailing in Frank's boat. Mary, Frank's wife at the time, had been on deck with Bill while she and Frank had gone below to fix lunch. Bill was enjoying being in control of the sleek craft and Mary had been helping him with the rigging.

In the tight quarters of the galley, a sudden shift in wind caused the boat to tip. She had bumped chest first into Frank. She was immediately embarrassed and apologetic, but she couldn't deny the heat she had felt from the encounter with his broad chest. It resonated in her loins, which had shocked her. She had always been a faithful wife, but in that moment, she felt a visceral attraction to him. She couldn't help but make a mental comparison between that fit, robust man and her thin husband with his little pot belly. Frank had placed his hands on her upper arms to steady her and she remembered he had left them there a couple of seconds too long. And she hadn't protested.

It was innocent flirting really. But it had given Janet a thrill. Her lovemaking that night with Bill had been especially satisfying. She had quite forgotten about it until now.

Clearly Frank had developed some strong feelings for her too. Did that contribute to his divorce? Had he been carrying a torch for her all these years? Her mind drifted to Bill. They were both on their second marriages. They had met twelve years ago. After dating two years, she had agreed to marry him. Bill had been a comfortable choice and she hadn't any other prospects at the time.

Sure, she supposed she loved him, but the passion had waned over the years. She couldn't remember the last time they had made love. At least two months ago. They had fallen into a rut it seemed. He would come home, give her a peck on the cheek, grab a beer and sit in front of the TV. She'd call him for dinner and they'd talk a little about their days as they ate.

Lately, he'd been complaining quite a bit about the cutbacks at work. Afterward, he'd return to the TV and she'd putter about until bed.

Not very passionate. But very safe. Wasn't it? She wondered how their lives might change if Bill lost his job. It would be hard for him to find another one at his age. Frank had been right—Bill probably could never find work in the dying U.S. steel industry, which would mean a middle-age career change. What would he do? Who would hire him? They had maybe three months of savings. She would have to go back to work, a prospect she did not relish. Recalling those days of serving drinks to grab-ass businessmen in a smoke-filled bar sent a shiver up her spine.

Bill, who was already a subdued man, would probably become more despondent and morose as the months went by with no job prospects. Their predictable marriage might easily crumble under the strain.

Her mind drifted back to Frank. He was a rich, powerful CEO of a major company. Even if he were fired over this episode of sexual blackmail, he could probably land on his feet somewhere else. His skills as an executive manager would be in demand.

She wondered what he might be like in bed…

She caught herself and shook her head. How could she even think about such a thing! What was wrong with her! Bill was a loyal husband and she should be ashamed of herself!

"It's blackmail!" she said aloud. "He's an asshole."

Ah, but it just wasn't that easy, was it? Frank stirred something in her, something long repressed and forbidden.

Don't go there, she warned herself.

She went back and forth over the next few hours. Tell Bill, don't tell Bill. Agree to Frank's terms, don't agree. Keep his "suggestion" to herself, alert the police and file a sexual harassment charge. Each time she veered from option to option, she found it really wasn't so much a matter of right and wrong—in that case, the decision would be easy. No, it came down to a battle between her ego and her libido.

The ego wanted to fight Frank, challenge him, get him fired, make him suffer for even suggesting such a horrible thing. But her libido found the whole idea stimulating. Certainly naughty. And not the least bit boring. That was it, wasn't it? She was attracted to the cad. Why? Maybe it was because he was risking his career for her. Her! He believed she would not report him because deep down he sensed she desired him too.

What other man in her life had gone out on a limb for her like this? Certainly not her first husband David, who had seemed so nice at first but, after they were married, had turned out to be an indecisive man who left all of life's difficult decisions up to her. It became so aggravating she'd had to get out. She had wanted a "real man" but settled on Bill. He was another safe choice who didn't cause any sparks to fly. At least not lately.

Frank, despicable as he might be, made her feel desirable. Like a throwback to another era when a man rode into town, swept up the woman he wanted, threw her over his saddle and rode out again. Her life had been filled with safe, boring men and suddenly along came a rogue, a cad, a bounder—but one who excited her like no one else.

By three o'clock, she couldn't stand it anymore. She went to her bedroom and fished her vibrator out of her nightstand—Bill didn't even know she had one!—and brought herself to a quick and satisfying climax. As her toy buzzed against her, nosing into her wet opening, she imagined it was Frank's hard cock teasing, probing, and she came again.

Chapter Two

ꝏ

Janet did not tell Bill. Not that night and not by the next morning when he headed off to work, distracted as usual. Not because she had already decided but because she knew it would set their lives on a course she could no longer control. She wished she could confide in him. That they could sit down and have a conversation about it, discussing the pros and cons without anger.

"How was your day, dear?" he would say.

"Well, I had the strangest proposal today, hon. Your boss dropped by. He wants to fuck me. And if I agree, he won't have you fired."

"Really? You don't say. Why would he have me fired?"

"Seems the board is pressuring him to lay off at least three of the headquarters' staff to match the layoffs the workers have had to endure."

"Wow. I'd heard rumors about that but I didn't think they were true. So what do you think we should do?"

"The way I see it, we have three choices. I can refuse and take our chances that you won't be among those laid off. He might be bluffing, you know. Or we can go to the board and the police and try to have Frank fired. Or…" She trailed off.

"Yes," Bill might say, "you can fuck him and guarantee that I'll keep my job. Hard choices. What would you like to do, dear?"

"Well, I've always been attracted to Frank. I mean, he is a good-looking, wealthy man. And secretly, you know, I'm kinda flattered. I mean, I'm the only wife he's approached."

"You know I'm behind you no matter what you want to do, sweetheart. If you really wouldn't mind sleeping with Frank, it would make our lives a lot easier. I really just have one question—is this a one-shot deal or an ongoing thing?"

Janet sat up straight on the couch suddenly, her fantasy talk with her husband shattered. She pulled the edges of her robe tighter. The morning coffee churned in her stomach. *My god—we didn't discuss that!* Frank had been so obscure that she hadn't thought it through. At the time, she supposed it would be a one-time occurrence but now she wasn't so sure.

She checked her watch. Nine-forty. She had to call within the next twenty minutes or Frank would assume she rejected his offer. But this seemed like a pretty big complication. Why hadn't she thought of it?

There was really nothing to do but call him and ask. She forced herself up from the couch and dialed the office number, her fingers shaking. She sat on a kitchen chair and tried to compose herself. Disguising her voice in case Jenny, the receptionist, recognized her, Janet got her to put her through by pretending to be Frank's insurance agent.

"Yes?" Frank's voice came on the line, startling her and sending little shivers down her spine.

"It's me, Frank."

His voice instantly relaxed. "Ahh, Janet. So nice to hear from you. To what do I owe this pleasure?"

"I've been thinking about your offer."

"My offer? I think you are mistaken. It was your suggestion."

Janet realized Frank feared the conversation was being recorded.

"Relax, Frank. I'm not taping this."

"Of course not. Now how can I help you?"

"Your, uh, 'the suggestion'. I was thinking you were referring to a one-time deal. Is that what you meant?"

"No," he said simply, sending another wave of chills down her spine. What wasn't clear was whether they were chills of danger or anticipation. She looked down and found she was squeezing her thighs together. She forced herself to unclench.

"If you make your decision today and Bill's name isn't on the list, then once would be enough it would seem to me. You lose your leverage."

"No. There's been a slight change over here. After much last-minute lobbying, the board has agreed to let me lay off just two positions for now, but wants me to closely monitor the situation. If our productivity doesn't meet certain targets, I'll be forced to lay off one more in the future."

Dammit!

Good!

The two conflicting emotions rocked her. What was happening to her? Why did it seem so thrilling to be forced to give in to this horrible man?

Because it's exciting. It's naughty. And he desires you… And you desire what he offers…

Boring old Bill would never think to treat her this way. As if he couldn't wait to have her. That he would risk his career to have her. It made her feel in a way she hadn't felt in…well, forever.

"Well?"

She took a deep breath. "Okay," she found herself saying. Part of her was shocked and part thrilled. "But this can't get out of hand."

"Of course not. Meet me at the Hotel Rincana on Route 9 at noon tomorrow. Ask for Mr. Ayers."

"But! But that's Saturday! What will I tell Bill?"

"I'm sure you'll think of some excuse." He hung up.

Janet sat there, holding the phone, wondering what she was getting herself into. The bigger question was, was she doing this to save Bill or to save herself? As she stood, she realized she desperately needed the relief her vibrator could provide.

* * * * *

Janet pulled up in front of the old hotel and sat in her car for ten minutes before she moved. It was not quite noon—in her worry not to make Frank think she was standing him up, she had arrived early. Or had she hurried due to the anticipation? She had to admit, her pussy had been throbbing all morning long and her nipples seemed tender. Bill had easily accepted her explanation that she would be out shopping with friends and merely waved to her from his spot in front of the TV, tuned into a sports pregame show. She supposed he actually looked forward to spending the day without her around to nag him for watching mindless television.

She checked her watch. Five 'til. Taking a deep breath, she got out and walked inside. Her legs felt stiff and she imagined everyone would be staring at her, secretly knowing she was some sort of slut here for a tryst.

But the only person in the ornate but aging lobby was the bored desk clerk.

"Yes, can I help you?" He was elderly, probably in his seventies, almost completely bald.

"Y-Yes," she managed. "I'm, uh, supposed to meet a Mr. Ayers."

"Ahh," he said, giving her a smug little smile as if he knew why she was here. "Yes, Mr. Ayers has already arrived. Room 212. Up the stairs and to the left."

She followed his directions, certain he was staring at her back. And why not? She *was* a slut and a whore. Cheating on one's husband was just that, even if she tried to tell herself that blackmail forced her hand. Yet somehow this felt less as if she were being forced to and more as if she wanted to.

She climbed the stairs, holding on to the old walnut railing so she wouldn't fall. Her legs were weak. But her pussy was alive with anticipation.

Dammit, she told herself. *Stop looking forward to this!*

Reaching Room 212, she knocked. It opened almost at once and Frank's smiling face appeared. He was dressed in jeans and a white golf shirt with thin blue stripes. He stepped aside and gestured for her to enter.

"Janet! What a pleasant surprise!"

"Knock it off, Frank—you forced me to come."

He did something unexpected that startled her and made her lower her guard. He reached up with his right hand and cupped her cheek. The gesture was so gentle and tender she found herself pressing into his palm. She had to catch herself and remember why she was there.

"Please. Don't be nice."

"Why not?"

"Because I'm here to save my husband's job. That's it. So let's get it over with."

"Oh come on. You know it's more than that. You've known ever since that day you bumped into me on the boat."

She looked up, startled to see how beautiful his gray-green eyes were. "You, you remembered that?"

"How could I ever forget?"

"So this…all this stems from that one day?"

"That and other times I saw you. I've desired you for years, Janet."

"Is that what broke up your marriage?" She hated to ask but she had to. Was she a homewrecker as well as a tramp?

"Of course not. That marriage was coming apart for years. You had nothing to do with it."

Janet breathed a sigh of relief. "Good."

"No, this is about you, Janet, and what you need. And what I need from you."

He stepped close and she could feel his strength rippling through her. It made her hot and weak. He put his arms around her and she didn't protest. His hands felt good on her back. He dropped them to her waist and she rested her head against his shoulder. Her breasts pressed against him, not unlike that time on the boat. Only this time it seemed to last forever. For a moment Janet allowed herself to believe this wasn't wrong. She had been living a lie for years, bound by her loyalty. Now she felt emotions that had long been denied her.

My god, is this how it's supposed to feel?

She put a hand on his broad chest and with some effort pushed him back. "What do you mean, what *I* need? This is all about you. You're the blackmailer."

"Technically, yes. But it's really about seeing a beautiful, sexy, hungry woman going to waste. I had to do something to save you from that dull existence."

Before she could protest, he brought his lips down and kissed her. She surprised herself by responding hungrily, as if he knew how lonely she had been in her marriage. He kissed as a man should kiss—forceful but gentle at the same time. Her body tingled. They kissed, locked in their embrace, for several minutes. Finally he pulled away.

"See, it's not so bad being blackmailed."

She caught her breath. "Y-You're being very kind, I must admit. I was afraid coming here."

"Afraid of what? Me?"

Janet waved her hand over the room. "This. You. The whole thing. I've never been unfaithful to my husband before."

"Janet, I've known Bill for years and I have to say, I just don't see the two of you together. Forgive me for saying that."

"What do you mean exactly?" She knew, but she wanted to hear him say it.

"He's an introvert, a drone. Yes, he's competent at his job, but he seems to go through life in a daze. Whereas you, my lady, you are a breath of fresh air. A real live wire who yearns for something more."

"Well, thank you, I guess. I'm not sure how you could tell that from the few times we all were together."

"Oh trust me, I could see it. I saw a wonderful, exciting woman being held back out of loyalty to a dull husband."

"He's not so dull," she said, coming to his defense even as she agreed with Frank.

"Hey, this is me you're talking to. You can speak your mind here."

"He's a good man," she said lamely, realizing it was a backhanded compliment.

"He doesn't deserve you."

"Oh? And you do?"

He kissed her again. "Yes, I do." Bending down, he swept her up into his arms. She felt like a teenager again and giggled. He eased her down on the queen-sized bed.

"Is it safe to assume you're on the Pill or will you be insisting that I wear a condom?"

His concern made her smile. She nodded. "I'm safe." Then she added, "You are a despicable man, Frank Ramon."

He tipped his head. "Yes, I know. At your service." He unbuttoned her blouse and she watched him, feeling the heat rising from her loins to her chest. God this man turned her on!

I am a horrible wife!

The good girl in her made one final effort. "I shouldn't be doing this, you know. This will lead to nothing but trouble." Even as she said it, she smiled, for that was the same thing her mother had told her more than once many years ago.

"'Nothing but trouble'—that's me all right." He flipped open the sides of her blouse, exposing her lacy bra. "Ohhh nice. Did you wear that just for me?"

"This old thing?" She smiled again. Of course she had worn it for him. She was such a slut.

"Can't wait to see if the panties match."

"Maybe you'll have to force me." The words just came out. She meant it as a joke, but at the same time, she realized she enjoyed being the helpless maiden about to be ravished by the handsome cad. That's what she realized about her situation. She had been forced. It was out of her hands. So why did it feel so good?

Frank pulled her into a sitting position and yanked off her blouse. She gasped with the suddenness of his actions. He owned her and he wasn't going to stop. God! Her pussy contracted and grew wetter. He was a stark contrast to Bill, who made love gently—and often too quickly. His lovemaking lacked power and drama. She was getting that in spades today.

He reached around her and unsnapped her bra, roughly pulled it from her shoulders. Her breasts fell free and she hunched her shoulders instinctively to cover her nudity.

Frank wouldn't have any of it. He gripped her shoulders and growled, "Don't be shy. You know you need it like this. You want to show off for me."

Her mouth dropped open. God he was pushing her buttons! He eased her back down on the bed and unfastened her skirt. He slid it off her then it was his turn to gasp in surprise. She was wearing a garter belt and stockings above her matching panties—not pantyhose.

"Ohhh baby," he breathed. "You really know how to turn me on."

"I don't like pantyhose," she said as if that were the only reason she had worn such a sexy outfit.

"You're wet," he said, and she tried to close her legs, suddenly overcome with embarrassment.

He slapped the inside of her left leg, causing her to suck in a quick breath. "Don't be shy. Remember?"

"Yes, sir," she said in mock terror. But she *was* a little afraid. Frank seemed to be Bill's opposite—rough and hard and decisive. He was impossible not to obey. Janet opened her legs again.

"Yes, you definitely are wet. Is that for me?" he teased her.

She closed her eyes, too embarrassed to answer.

Frank was unfastening her garter snaps. He rolled down the left stocking smoothly, touching her leg all over as he went. She shivered. There was no doubt in her mind that her wetness was growing. He tossed the stocking to the floor and moved to the other leg. In seconds she was bare, her garter belt hanging loose above her lacy panties.

"Let's get this off," he said, pulling her upright again. He fumbled for the catch and pulled it free. Now she was dressed only in her panties.

"What about you?"

"Don't worry about me. I like to see you naked while I'm dressed. Maybe I'll keep you this way."

It sent chills through her, even if she didn't quite understand him. Would she be naked, eating dinner while he sat across the table fully dressed? Or might he insist she be naked in the living room while they ate popcorn and watched a movie?

His hand touched the hot core of her and she jumped. She could smell the scent of her own arousal and chided herself. *God! It shouldn't be this easy to blackmail me.*

Then another part of her responded, *Oh come on! You're only fooling yourself. You know you want this.*

Frank moved up and kissed her, holding her body tightly in his arms.

"This is so wrong, you know," she whispered.

"I know. But I hated to see a woman living a life of quiet desperation."

"So you blackmailed me."

"I just pushed you in the right direction."

"And now you have me. What are you going to do with me?"

He kissed her gently but she could feel his strength just under the surface. "Everything."

Chapter Three

ࢱ

Janet never experienced the intensity of lovemaking she felt with Frank that afternoon. Both David and Bill were pleasant, competent lovers, like a cup of coffee on a cool spring morning or a ride on a tire swing. But Frank was a shot of one-hundred-year-old brandy, a rocket to the moon. He didn't pleasure her body as much as he owned it. His lips and hands were everywhere, setting her skin on fire and making her cry out with desire. And his cock! It was an extension of his personality—forceful, demanding, a little bit cruel and very, very kind.

She felt turned inside out. Her orgasms didn't come so much as crash upon her—her mind screamed, her body ached, her toes curled. He did things to her she had only imagined could be done to a woman.

He made her turn her mouth into a sexual orifice. Sure, she had had oral sex several times in her life but never in the way Frank demanded. He was both gentle and forceful. He taught her how to love his cock. Her pussy spasmed with need, her breasts ached for his touch. When he was done and her mouth yearned to taste his sperm, he pulled back, leaving her hungry for more.

Then he turned his attention to her body, her pleasure. Tit for tat. He kissed her until she thought her body might melt. His lips were both soft and hard and he made her head swim. He made love to her breasts with his tongue, his hands, until she could feel her pussy leaking all over the bed, begging for his cock.

And when his mouth dipped down to her hot core, she gasped and came for the first time as soon as his tongue touched her sensitive clit. Then again. Each one causing her to cry out and beg for mercy. And more. He knew how to pleasure a woman. She couldn't imagine how any woman could let this man go. He was an animal in bed.

When he finally loomed over her, his hard cock a spear pointed at her sex, Janet thought she couldn't possible stand any more. Her body tingled, her breath came in shallow gasps. All doubts about what she was doing had vanished. He was all man and all sex.

Then he entered her and she cried out as another orgasm shook her. Just like that! The mere presence of his cock in her grasping cunt made her shudder with desire. And that's how she thought of it—a cunt. Not a vagina or a pussy or any of those polite words, no, he was fucking her cunt like a beast. When he began to move inside her, she held on for dear life. His cock felt huge inside her, like an obscene presence with just one purpose—to make her lose her mind. She came again. And then again.

He sped up and Janet thought she might die from fucking. How many women can say that? She became aware of her own voice rising in cadence but making no sense. It was, "Uh, uh, uh, oh! Oh! Oh! OH! GOD! GOD! GODDAMN SON OF A BITCH!" Another orgasm took off the top of her head and her brains seemed to scatter out all over the pillow.

When he finally climaxed, it was as if she could feel each individual sperm cell shoot into her. *Wow! Bang! Crash!* She came for the last time and completely passed out.

When she became aware of her body again, Frank was still over her, his cock still inside her. Thankfully he had stopped moving. She had survived riding The Beast.

"Goddamn son of a bitch," she breathed.

"That's right. You are one sexy bitch," he said, smiling.

"Really?" She wondered if she had kept up with him. At times, it hadn't felt like it.

"No, really. That was wild. You are a very hot woman."

She smiled. "So does Bill get to keep his job?"

"Yeah. For now. But I'm not giving you up so don't get any ideas."

"Well, I am a married woman. I'm not sure I can do this regularly. I mean, for one thing, I'll die." She laughed. Could she survive a steady diet of Frank Ramon? And how had he gotten like this?

"To tell you the truth, I'm not like this with anyone else." He seemed to realize how that must've sounded since he hurried on. "I mean, in my life before this."

"I can't believe that."

"It's true. There's just something about you. You bring out the beast in me."

She felt inordinately flattered. "Aw, I bet you say that to all your girlfriends."

"You think I have a lot of girlfriends?"

"A lover like you? If word got out, they'd be camped on your doorstep."

He had the decency to blush. "Ahh, come on."

"No, seriously. If I were Mary and married to you, I would have never let you go."

"Well, Mary was…more reserved in bed. If I had tried to make love to her like I did to you, well, she probably would've called the cops. Or her priest."

Janet laughed at the image. "Her priest?"

"Yeah, she was quite religious. I'm more of a hopeless pagan."

"How did the two of you get together?"

"Oh I don't know. When I was younger, I thought she was the safe, proper choice. My, uh, appetites didn't develop overnight."

"Where *did* you learn to make love like that? God, I thought I was going to die."

"Like I said. You bring it out in me."

"I'm flattered. But now I must go. Bill is probably wondering where I am."

He rolled off the bed and sat on the edge. Janet got up and walked bow-leggedly to the bathroom. She sat on the toilet and wiped the copious fluids from her reddened pussy. But it wasn't complaining—the damn thing almost purred. She washed then came out and began getting dressed.

"This isn't over, you know." He lounged on the bed, still naked.

She felt a thrum of something she couldn't quite define. A belonging, as if she had somehow become his. It made her breath quicken. "So you've said."

"I'm going to make love to you again. You know it and I know it."

She stopped, her bra half on. *No!* her mind said. *Shut up,* her id responded. "It could get complicated."

"I don't care. I've been waiting for you all my life."

"That's just your dick talking."

He laughed. "Doesn't matter. In this, my dick and my brain are one." He tapped his limp cock then the side of his head and gave her a coy grin.

Janet chuckled and resumed dressing. "You talk like you own me."

"I do."

It was a flat statement yet she knew it to be true. She was married to Bill, but after that amazing lovemaking session, she would have to have more. Her pussy clenched and she could feel more of his sperm oozing from her. It certainly belonged to him now. *Where your pussy goes, the mind must surely follow.*

"I don't know," she said, trying to convince herself.

"This started with blackmail, I know. That was just an excuse to break through your barriers. But it's become something else now. I can tell you with some certainty that the next time I show up for you, you'll welcome me into your arms. And your pussy."

"Hush. You don't know that." Satiated as she was, she believed she could resist him. Give her a few days to think about it however, and all bets were off. She had started making love when she was seventeen. That's twenty years of men. Some were competent, some were clumsy, some—like David and Bill—were comfortable and maybe a bit boring. But no one was dangerous like Frank. Doesn't a woman need a little danger now and then?

He grabbed her arm and drew her to him. She felt his nakedness against her hot skin. "I'm not ready to let you go yet."

She stopped, her panties in her hands. "You can't be serious." She looked meaningfully at his limp cock.

"There are other ways to make love."

"Oh no, my pussy's too sore. You ruined me, I think."

He stood and took her into his arms. She felt small and helpless and it seemed just right. She enjoyed it and it scared her a little. Janet knew she could lose herself in this man. She tried to push him away. It was like pushing a wall.

"You shouldn't go home without a shower. Come." He plucked her panties from her hands and tossed them on the bed. His hands found the catch of her bra and it joined them. She was naked again. Naked and in the arms of a dangerous lover.

"I really should be going," she said quietly.

"I'm going to soap you and wash you all over."

Her eyes closed and she could *feel* his soapy hands on her, the water pouring over her. She gave a little shiver and melted into his arms.

"But Bill..." she said, her voice tiny now.

"Fuck Bill."

They spent a long time in the small stall washing and stroking and touching each other. Her body felt abused and alive at the same time. Janet was torn between her need for him and her conscience, which demanded she go home immediately. But his hands on her body pushed those thoughts away.

They dried off with thick hotel towels and she returned to the bed to pick up her underwear. Frank grabbed her and held her close, telling her she couldn't go yet.

"I insist," she said, her voice sounding hollow. "We just showered. I'm all clean."

"Then I'm going to dirty you all over again."

God! This man! He was incorrigible. "Frank, really..." she said then his lips were on hers and he pulled her tight to him, the shaft of his suddenly hard cock rubbing against her sex. Her body swooned, her pussy gushed.

What a slut! she told herself.

She didn't stop him as he eased her down onto the bed and kissed her bruised lips. His hands plucked at her tender breasts. His cock knocked at her wet entrance and she spread her legs for him.

I'm such a bad wife, she thought.

Their lovemaking was slower this time, more languorous, for which she was grateful. They'd had the main course, this was dessert. Still, she managed to climax once before she felt him stiffen. This time his cock throbbed but his sperm supply was greatly depleted. Not that it mattered. Feeling his organ inside her spasming made her come again. She held him close.

Finally they separated. "Now I'm all messy again," she teased.

"I like you messy. I want to keep you messy. I want to mark you."

That startled her and gave her another shiver. "Mark me?"

"Yeah. Maybe just a spanking at first so I can see the imprint of my hand on your ass. Later a nice tattoo or some small gold rings."

"Oh pshaw," she said, trying to cover the heat she felt. "That's ridiculous."

"Oh it will happen. Trust me."

"Yeah, like I could explain that to Bill."

"Doesn't matter. Bill doesn't matter. Only you and I matter."

"That's your lust talking."

"True. But it's talking the same language as your lust."

"Look, don't get any ideas. I'm married."

"Yes, you are. For now."

She rose, feeling disconcerted. "I have to go."

"Of course. I'll let you. But one day, I won't."

Janet felt as if she couldn't breathe for a moment. She didn't dare think about having a man like Frank in her life full-time. God, she would die! Or their sex would pale and become ordinary. The intensity couldn't be maintained. This was pure lust, that was all.

She got up and began to dress, feeling her wetness mixed with his seed. She looked down at herself and was not surprised to see red marks where he had clutched her breasts, arms and thighs. Was that a hickey on her breast? They had all better fade quickly or how would she explain them to Bill? She laughed to herself—as if he would notice her.

Frank watched her dress, a certain sadness in his eyes. As though he couldn't bear to see her body hidden. Her skin felt hot. She could imagine herself kept by him like a rare pet. She would wait for him to make love to her, naked and anxious.

She gave her head a little shake. *Stop that!*

"Thanks," she said when she was fully dressed. "I had… It was, uh, nice." God, that sounded so lame! It embarrassed her.

He just watched her, bemused. He looked like a lion in repose, his soft chest hair glinting in the light. Her gaze dropped to his cock one last time. She had to force her eyes away. Dammit! What was happening to her!

"Bye," she said, and almost ran for the door.

"Janet," he called when she had her hand on the knob. "I'll be in touch."

She could only nod and then she was gone.

* * * * *

"Hi, hon, how was shopping?" Bill was in front of the TV as usual watching baseball.

"Fine."

"What did you buy?"

Your fucking job back. "Nothing. Just window shopped."

He craned his head around at her. "You were gone four hours and you only window shopped?" His voice was incredulous.

"Yeah. Couldn't find anything I liked." Boy, what a big fat lie *that* was! What was she supposed to say? *Oh I found the perfect item – it's long and fat and it makes me come a dozen times!*

He returned to his game, merely shaking his head as if to say, *Women!*

So much for the suspicious husband. She had half a mind to strip off her clothes and show him her reddened skin, her well-fucked pussy. *He's ruined me for you,* she wanted to shout. It was sad but true. She knew, sure as she stood there, that she and Frank would be making love again soon.

Chapter Four

ꟗ

The days passed by and there was no word from Frank. Had it merely been a one-time fling for him? Slam, bam, goodbye, ma'am. What was worse was how she felt. As if she needed him, yet he was forbidden—she was married! It was a bad combination and preyed on her insecurities. Had he lied to her when he said he owned her? Or was that just talk, something to say to an employee's wife to make her stick around for seconds? And why was she even considering seconds? What was wrong with her?

She had just decided she hated him and would spit in his eye if she ever saw him again when the doorbell rang one afternoon about one-fifteen. Could it be? No, of course not. She ran to the door and stopped just before opening it to compose herself. She peeked through the peephole—Frank!

Her plan to spit in his eye and throw him out vanished. She threw open the door. "Well, it's about fucking time," she said.

"You got that right." He grinned and came into her arms. They kissed like long-lost lovers and Janet's anger melted away. God, his lips made her so hot!

"Wait," she said, quickly closing the door behind him, an awkward feat with his body in the way. "What if the neighbors see?"

"I don't care. Let them see. One day, I'll parade you naked down Main Street, telling everyone this is my girl."

Janet swooned. She felt owned again, just as she needed to be. "Where the hell were you?"

"Oh more boardroom drama. I've been busy putting out fires."

"Don't tell me they want to lay off more people."

"No, thank god. It's still too early for that. But now that we've reduced HQ staff, we're having trouble processing everything. I told 'em."

Janet nodded but she didn't want to hear about work. She wanted to hear about them. And yet she couldn't shake the scolding voice of her conscience. She allowed it to speak for her.

"Frank…"

"Yes?" His lips kissed her neck.

She fought to maintain control. "Dammit, Frank, we need to talk."

He pulled away with effort and looked at her, his head tilted sideways. "No we don't." He held up a hand before she could speak. "Oh I know what you're going to say. That this is wrong, that you're married, etcetera, etcetera."

"Well, yeah…"

"I don't care. I've wanted you for years and now I have you. I'm not about to let you go."

"But we can't just ignore Bill! If he found out, there would be trouble."

"Yes, I imagine there would be. But in the end, you would be mine."

Janet shivered with the thought. The idea that Frank would own her body and soul was almost too much to bear. Bill was comfortable, like an old pair of slippers. But Frank! Well, Frank was sex personified. To use the same analogy, Frank was a pair of red stiletto pumps that made a woman walk like a hooker, hips swaying. Frank was dangerous.

She tried again. "But really, Frank! I don't want to hurt Bill."

"I think it's quite the contrary. You sacrificed yourself for him. He still has his job. Think of how hurt he would've been if you'd told me 'no'."

"That's not nice! You make me sound like a whore."

"No. I don't think of you that way. I think of you as an incredibly sexy woman who was going to waste being married to that drone. I'm sorry, but that's how I see it."

"I married that drone. I love him."

"You mean, you loved him. He can't possibly excite you now."

"Women aren't like that. We just don't leave someone because the thrill fades. Why, if what you say is true and we wound up together, who's to say the same wouldn't happen to us?"

"It won't. Trust me on that."

"Easy to say now. I can remember when Bill…" She paused. She couldn't remember when Bill had as much passion as Frank.

"What? When Bill made you feel like you did with me last time?" He barked out a laugh. "Ha! I doubt that."

She colored. "Well, maybe not, but he did please me…uh…" It sounded so lame, even to her.

Frank laughed again. "I'll show you pleasure." He bent down and picked her up in his arms.

"Frank!" she protested, but her stomach was doing flip-flops. This is what she had expected when she was a young girl, imagining her married life. Some man would love her so much he couldn't stand not to touch her, to take her. "But, Frank…" she added weakly, glancing out the windows. She imagined the neighbors were all on their porches, tsking and shaking their heads.

He ignored her protests and carried her into her bedroom. "No!" she said when she saw her marital bed. "Not here!"

"Yes, here." He tossed her down. She tried to get up but he was on her, kissing her face, her neck, the soft hollows of her collarbone. Janet melted.

"Oh please…"

His fingers deftly unbuttoned her blouse. She let him. There was nothing she could do, she told herself. He was stronger, more insistent. His unrelenting desire for her body made her wet with desire.

God, I'm horrible!

For several minutes no words were spoken. Only the rustle of clothing as Janet allowed herself to be stripped. When she was naked, her body felt hot and she gazed at him while he quickly shucked off his own clothes. His body was magnificent. Not like Bill, who had let himself go with middle age.

Then Frank was on her and she hugged him close, smelling the manly scent of him, an odor quite different from Bill's. She was a slut, a whore, a very bad wife. And she didn't care, not right now. Recriminations would come later. For now, her body cried out for the release only Frank could give her.

When his hard cock touched her wetness, she gasped. But he didn't press it in. Instead he teased her, rubbing it up against her until she couldn't stand it anymore. "You bastard," she finally gasped, and he laughed.

"Tell me you're mine."

"No," she said, her teeth gritted.

Again that sweet cock, rubbing, rubbing, rubbing. "Tell me you want me."

"Nooo." It was becoming harder to concentrate. She didn't even know why she was being stubborn. Here she was naked on her own bed with another man and she was playing hard to get?

"Tell me you'll do whatever I want with you."

Rubbing, rubbing. The tip of his hard cock was slippery with her juices. Her vagina seemed to suck at it.

"God, Frank."

"Tell me."

"Okay! I'm yours! I'll do what you want. Just fuck me, dammit!"

He plunged into her, causing spots to explode in front of her eyes. Her head tilted back and the orgasm hit her body all at once, from her groin to the tip of her head. She made incoherent noises and her mind went to other places, as if it were on a giant rubber band, stretching away from her. Then she came back to her body, to that delicious pumping and knew she was going to climax again. Frank was grasping her shoulders, thrusting hard into her. Her legs were around his thighs, pulling him into her with each stroke, her eyes half open, her mind blasted with neurons all firing at once.

"God, god, god," she muttered, not even aware she was speaking. "Oh god, god, god…"

The second orgasm hit her and she went off again, lost in a twilight world of sensations and pleasures. Even now, in the depths of her thrill, she knew she would do anything for this man if he would fuck her like this regularly.

Frank sped up and Janet knew he was close. She hung on, feeling the heat in her loins, the hard shaft rubbing against her clit, the oncoming train of another climax and when he thrust deep into her and she felt his seed spill, she shuddered with the power of another orgasm, her body shaking, tears flowing from her eyes.

For a long time, they clung to each other. Finally he sank down and rolled to the side.

"God…damn." His voice was hoarse.

"Yeah." She had no words to describe what he did to her. Why was it so good? She had no answer. It just was. Frank had ruined her and it had all started with blackmail. Delicious blackmail.

"You really are a cad, you know," she said, gently running her fingers along his cheek.

"Yeah, I know." He turned and kissed them.

"You fucked me in our marital bed. That's just not right."

"No, it's not. Tell Bill that I apologize."

She laughed at the incongruity of his statement. "Like he'd even notice."

"See? That's what I'm talking about. You're wasted on him."

"You think? You think I'm just too sexy for Bill?" She was fishing for a compliment but she couldn't help herself.

"Oh yeah." He propped himself up on one elbow and leaned in to kiss her. "And you know it too."

"But what are we going to do? I can't sneak around like this forever."

"I can't tell you what to do in this case. I can in other areas but not this."

"Are you saying you don't want me to leave Bill?"

"I'm saying I can't make that decision for you. And I won't pressure you. I mean, other than coming over to fuck you regularly. If you want to go on the way we're going, that's fine with me. I can live with it."

"Really? You don't want me all to yourself?" She was disappointed.

"Of course I do. But I'm not going to tell you to divorce him. That's a big step. You have to think about it for a while."

Janet nodded. "Yes. I will. Bill's a good man..." She always found herself describing him as if he were a scoutmaster not a husband. "I just don't know how much longer you and I can go on like this. I think even Bill might start to get suspicious."

"Yeah. Well, you can always tell him you saved his job."

"Oh stop. He wouldn't like that at all. He might very well punch you in the nose."

"Yeah, I know." He stood and began putting on his clothes. She sat up and watched him.

"Just like that, you're leaving? Slam, bam, thank you, ma'am?"

"Yep. It has to be this way for now. I have to get back to work. But someday..." He let the promise hang.

"Someday you'll make an honest woman out of me?"

He smiled. "Someday, I'll own you completely."

The way he put it made her body tremble. As if she were his property. She wasn't sure how she felt about that. Part of her objected—but another part swooned. What kind of modern woman was she anyway?

"And if you 'owned' me, as you say, what would that mean?"

He stopped, his belt undone, his shirt untucked. "It means, my good woman, that you'll give yourself to me without question. I will own that pretty body of yours. I will do with it what I want, when I want to."

His words made her wet again, yet she still wasn't sure. "I'm not sure I want to be owned. I'm a modern woman."

He crawled up on the bed and kissed her, taking her breath away with the forcefulness of it. "I think you'll learn to love it," he said after he pulled away. "I'll be your caveman."

He got up again and finished dressing. She was still naked.

"Wait," she said as he was about to leave. He turned. "What about what you said the first time? That you'd like to mark my body—you were kidding, weren't you?"

"No. We could start with a small gold ring here and there. Or maybe a tattoo. I want to own you and that would be the proof." He grinned at her and left before she could respond.

She lay there, her body slowly cooling, and thought about how it would be to be possessed by Frank. Would it be too much? Would he scare her with his intensity? Right now, she didn't worry. He was a rich dessert in a land of bland dinners. Wouldn't do to have too much of him.

Chapter Five

ℵ

"Bill, do you still love me?" Janet was sitting on the couch next to her husband, who was watching Thursday night football. Janet always hated the fall for it meant Bill could watch football, baseball, golf and hockey. More reasons to ignore her. And when she would protest, he'd look at her incredulously and say, "But it's the *playoffs*!" or "But it's the *Ryder Cup*!" as if that explained everything.

He turned three-quarters toward her, keeping one eye on the game. "Of course I do, honey." He puckered his lips for a kiss.

Janet sighed. "You pay more attention to that TV than you do me."

A commercial came on. He muted the set and turned fully toward her. "What's wrong, hon? You seem out of sorts."

"I'm bored with all this. You go to work all day and you come home and watch TV. I feel ignored."

"I'm sorry." He put his arms around her. For a moment it felt good and Janet thought maybe they could rekindle their romance. He kissed her on the cheek. Instead of feeling warmer toward Bill, it only reminded her of Frank.

Then the commercials ended and Bill let her go, turning his gaze to the set. Janet grew angry.

"Bill! I swear, if you don't stop ignoring me, I'm going to go out and fuck someone else!"

The words just slipped out before she even had a chance to think. She was suddenly embarrassed and afraid she might give herself away.

Bill stared at her as if she had grown another head. "You really mean that?" In his eyes, she could see his confusion. "What brought all this on?"

She was on dangerous ground now and realized she had better tread lightly. "Oh nothing. It's just that we've gotten into a rut. You don't pay attention to me like you used to. And I try to keep myself in shape and everything! I should just start eating and get fat!"

"Oh no, honey! Don't feel that way!" He did something that pleased her—he shut off the TV. He turned to her and took both of her hands in his. "I know I've been distracted lately. What with all the crap going on at work—I really thought I was going to lose my job!"

Janet blinked back tears, thinking how close he had come.

"And so when I come home, I just want to relax and zone out. I'm sorry. I didn't mean to ignore you like this. You're the best thing that ever happened to me."

Oh god, she thought. *I'm a horrible wife.*

"That's nice to hear," she said, tears beginning to leak from her eyes now. "You don't know how lonely I get around here all day."

"Maybe you need a hobby. Or a job..."

The words stung her. "A job?"

"Well, I just mean..."

"You want me to go back to work in some bar? So we can earn a few extra bucks?"

"No! Not that! Make it a hobby then! I was just thinking you could volunteer or something. Do something that would keep you busy so you don't feel so alone all the time."

"I feel alone because my husband ignores me!" She felt her anger growing even as she knew she was being irrational. She couldn't help it.

"Janet, calm down! I'm just offering some suggestions. I can't be here all the time and when I come home, I'm exhausted and need some down time. Surely you can understand that."

And I need a man who will fuck my brains out, Janet thought. She reined in her anger. "Yes, I understand. We seem to be at cross purposes."

"Yes. But I admit I could be paying more attention to you. I apologize for that. I've been worried about work so much… I was thinking, if I lost my job, what would we do? Where would I find a new one? It could mean we'd have to sell the house and move. I've just had a lot on my mind."

Janet wanted to tell Bill that his job was safe, he shouldn't worry. But that would never do. He'd start asking questions. He would be devastated to find out she'd been fucking Frank to keep his job. Of course, that's how it all started. Janet knew deep down she could tell Frank she was done and she doubted he would retaliate by firing Bill. It had started as blackmail but it had evolved into something else. Now she needed what he gave her, even as it scared her.

"But didn't they lay off some people recently? Doesn't that take the heat off you?"

"Yes, for the short term. But with the steel industry the way it is, I think it's only a matter of time before we all lose our jobs."

"Then what would you do? Have you thought about it?"

"I think I've been trying to avoid it. That's why I've been zoned out in front of the tube. I can let my mind think about something else for a change."

"Oh Bill…" She drew him to her and hugged him. He hugged her back and she felt his shoulders shake. He was crying!

"I'm sorry," he said into her shoulder. "I've just been so worried!"

"It's going to be okay. We'll figure out something, no matter what happens."

Janet believed at that moment that if she told him she was fucking his boss in order to save his job, he might actually be grateful instead of devastated. But she wasn't about to do that.

She realized just how much Bill needed her. How could she hurt him?

He pulled away and wiped his eyes. "Sorry. I'm not supposed to be the weak one."

"Oh? And I am?"

"You know what I mean. I'm supposed to go to work every day, earn a living, be the man of the house."

"That's rather old-fashioned, don't you think?"

"Yeah, but I was never happier than the day you quit your job at that horrible bar. I felt great knowing I made enough money for both of us."

She paused, now embarrassed that she had gotten her back up about finding another job. "You know, Bill, maybe you're right. Maybe I should get another job. Just to bring in some extra money so we'd have a cushion…you know."

He nodded. "It might be a good idea. Just for the short term, until I know what's going on at work." His eyes were wet and he looked like a puppy dog. "But I don't want you to go back to any bar."

"Where could I go? I'm not exactly trained in anything." She hadn't gone to college and it had always embarrassed her.

"Don't rush into anything. Just look around, see what's out there. I'm sure I'll be okay for a few months. It's just if they come around for another round of cuts…" He couldn't go on.

Janet checked her watch. It was barely nine. "Come," she said. "Let's go to bed early. I think you could use a back rub."

His eyes lit up. She felt so sorry for him. Carrying all that weight of the world on his shoulders—no wonder he clammed up and watched TV when he came home! Janet felt like a real heel at the moment and she was determined to make it up to him. But could she give up Frank?

For a moment she felt like Scarlett O'Hara. *I'll think about it tomorrow.*

They went to bed and Bill stripped down and lay on the sheets. Janet couldn't help but mentally compare her husband to Frank. Where Frank was hard and fit and powerful, Bill was soft and white and weak. But she had married him, for good or bad. She took off her clothes, leaving her bra and panties on, and climbed up on his back. She found the oil in the nightstand and squirted a little into her palm. As she worked it into his back, she could hear him softly groan.

Using her hands gave her mind time to wander about what a mess she'd made of things. It wasn't her fault and yet it was. She could've said no and damn the consequences. She could've been loyal. Now she was embroiled in an affair—one she didn't think she could give up.

Damn it, Frank! How am I supposed to go on? I can't leave poor Bill and I can't imagine how dull my life would be without you.

She kneaded Bill's back, working down to his legs. He moaned with pleasure, telling her how good it felt. When she asked him to turn over, his cock was semihard. Janet couldn't help but compare it to Frank's and found it wanting. Nevertheless, she leaned down and took it into her mouth. It stiffened and she smiled to herself. She pumped him until she could tell he was about to come and didn't want to waste it. Quickly stripping off her panties, she mounted him and eased herself down over his shaft.

"Oh Jan. That's so good," he moaned.

"Yes," she said, feeling a little let down at how…well, *average* it seemed inside her. When she had nothing else to compare it to, Bill was a more than adequate lover. But now… Well, that's a different story.

She moved up over him, encouraging him as he began to thrust from underneath. It didn't take long. Within seconds, he erupted into her and sank back into the sheets. Janet pretended to climax as well, even though she hadn't come close.

Frank had ruined her.

Chapter Six

ꝏ

Friday, they met at the same hotel as before. This time they arrived at the same time and came in together. Janet hadn't wanted to but Frank dismissed her concerns. It was as if he were exerting his control over her and she was helpless to resist.

She had made up her mind to talk about this affair and what it was doing to her and her marriage. When she left the house, she had been determined to put a stop to it. Now in his powerful presence, she found she was beginning to waver.

Frank paid the elderly desk clerk and received a key. Janet thought the old man had winked at her just before he turned away to his newspaper, as if he knew she was a cheater. They went up to Room 224, down the hall from the site of their first tryst, and he unlocked the door. Janet braced herself for "the talk".

"Frank," she said, turning to face him as soon as she was through the door. "We need to talk."

"We will," he said. "But first, I have to see you." He began unbuttoning her blouse.

"No, Frank, wait!"

"I promise you, we'll talk. I know you have some things on your mind. So we'll talk. But I simply must see your beautiful body first."

How could she resist that? So she allowed him to strip her. She had not worn stockings today so her clothes came off quickly. He pulled the covers off the bed and eased her down.

"Really, Frank. I'm distressed here."

"Okay." He lay down next to her and began running his fingers over her body. "Talk."

God, he was making this difficult! He was still fully dressed and she felt naked and vulnerable. Yet she knew if she insisted he remove his clothes as well, they would be making love within seconds, all thought of talking lost.

"Frank, I had a talk with my husband..."

His fingers stroked the side of her neck, moving down to her breast then circled the nipples.

"Stop that! I'm trying to say something here."

"Okay." His hand moved away but only to her arm where it rested like an inviting presence, just waiting for the chance to pleasure her again. She took a deep breath and tried to concentrate. Why did he have to be so sexy all the time?

"He's very worried about his job. He thinks he dodged a bullet during the layoffs and that he might be next."

"Did you tell him his job is secure thanks to you?"

"Of course not! And don't joke about that!"

"Sorry." She could tell he didn't mean it.

"Anyway, we began talking about our financial situation. And it makes sense if I got a job."

"A job? Like as a cocktail waitress?"

"No. Not that. I mean something else. Something I could do during the day while Bill is at work."

"And what about us?"

"There is no us, not really! This is just blackmail, remember?"

"You don't really believe that, do you?"

His hand had returned, stroking her breast, her side, moving down to her hip. She squirmed away but he reached over to her other hip and pulled her close again.

"I don't know what to believe! I'm a married woman, dammit!"

She didn't feel much like a married woman lying there naked, her pussy announcing her availability by lubricating her warm passage. *If he touches my clit, I'm lost,* she thought.

"So let me get this straight. Bill is worried about money. So instead of telling him that his job is secure because you're making love to me, you're going to go out and get a job you don't need?"

"You really think I'd tell him I'm fucking you? You can't be that crazy."

"No, but he's going to find out eventually. When you become mine."

"I'm not yours! I may never be yours!"

His hand was roaming again, making gooseflesh appear where his fingers touched, causing her to squirm. She could smell the odor of her arousal and felt like a terrible person.

His hand moved down and forced her legs apart.

"Wait," she protested weakly, "we're not done talking yet."

"Talk. I'm just checking something out." His fingers found the loose flap of skin of her labia and he pinched it.

"What? What are you doing?"

"I think a small gold ring would look great right about here, don't you?"

Janet was completely flustered. "What? No way!"

"I could have it inscribed. Something like *Mine*. Simple and straightforward."

"Stop that! What I'm trying to tell you is that I'm going to be working. We won't be able to do this anymore."

His fingers pinched the other side and she gasped. "Or maybe a matched set. What do you think?"

Janet sat up and closed her legs. "I don't think you're taking me seriously, Frank."

He reached up and pinched her left nipple, just enough to make her gasp. "Eventually, I'd like to see some small gold hoops here too."

Janet became exasperated. "Oh? And where would the tattoo that says 'Frank's Slut' go?"

He half turned her and lightly slapped her rump. "How about right here?"

"Stop it, Frank, just stop it!" She sat all the way up and leaned against the headboard, breathing hard. But it wasn't fear that caused it—it was lust and she knew it. Furthermore, Frank knew it too.

He sat up and Janet could see the enormous bulge in his pants. She had to turn away, but in her mind, she saw Bill's smaller penis from the other night. She knew unless she regained control over her emotions, she would soon be on the receiving end of Frank's large cock.

"I'm just telling you that I have to end this. I can't go on."

"Why not? Because of your loyalty to a dead marriage?"

"It's not dead! Part of what caused it was Bill's worry over his job. You should've seen him the other night. He practically cried."

"So what kind of a job do you think you'll get?"

"I don't know. Something in retail maybe. I'm not going to waitress again, not even in a nice family place." She shuddered from the memory of aching legs, bad tippers and lecherous bosses.

"How much do store clerks get?"

"I don't know. Probably minimum wage, I guess. Maybe more."

"And you'd work about how many hours a week, do you think?"

Janet shook her head. "I haven't thought it through. I'd guess twenty hours or so."

"Okay. Let's do the math. Minimum wage is about six-fifty an hour. Times twenty hours, that's one-thirty. Minus taxes, you're looking at about one hundred a week or four hundred a month."

It didn't sound like very much the way Frank put it. Nevertheless, Janet tried to sound defiant. "Yeah, about that. So we could save some money in the event Bill loses his job."

"Well, I know exactly how much Bill is getting paid. It's a little under four thousand a month take-home. So you'd have to work about ten months to add one month of Bill's salary to your savings. Of course, you'd have to subtract the cost of working, including car or bus transportation, clothes and other expenses. Make it a year for each month of what Bill earns."

Tears came to Janet's eyes. "What else can I do? I don't have any skills."

"Yes you do. Your skill is here with me. You are the best lover, the most exciting woman I've ever had."

"Yeah, fat lot of good that does me." Then an inkling of what he was getting at flowered in her mind. "Hey…you're not saying what I think you're saying…"

"Sure. I'll pay you to fuck me. Two hundred a week, twice what you could make at any menial job."

"That's obscene!" She jumped up and began to dress. Frank made no move to stop her.

"You think I'm some kind of whore? Here to fuck you whenever you crook your finger? You bastard! And I thought you were a nice man!"

"I am a nice man. I'm offering to help you out. In exchange, I get what I want. To me, it's a win-win."

"I'm not a prostitute," she spat, yanking her clothes on, her face hot with anger. "Just because you forced me into this doesn't mean I have to put up with your insults!"

"I'm not insulting you. I'm telling you that you are the most amazing woman I've ever known and best lover I've ever had. If you have to get a job to help out Bill, I'd rather hire you myself. I'd prefer to make love to you for free. But I certainly don't want you getting some crappy job and not having any more time for me."

Janet was too mad to listen to his logic. She tucked in her blouse and headed for the door. Frank got up and grabbed her arm before she could open it. "Please, just look at it from my viewpoint, all right? I'm not hiring you as my prostitute. I'm simply offering you a way to explain how you're getting your money to Bill. You could tell him you got a job at a dress shop and turn over the money to him every week. It's up to you. The alternative to me is that I lose you. And I don't want to lose you."

It did make some sense, but Janet was in no mood to think of it in any other way. He offered to pay her for sex. Pay her! Damn him! She shook off his arm and left, slamming the door behind him.

She fumed all the way home. Inside, she yanked off her clothes and put on her exercise outfit. Putting in a tape of the most energetic workout, Janet stood in front of the TV doing kicks, bends and stretches until she was exhausted and sweaty.

Then she took a long shower, washing away the sweat and Frank's fingerprints. They seemed to burn where he had touched her. *That bastard! How could I have ever thought he was a nice man?*

When Bill came home, she had prepared his favorite dinner—meatloaf and mashed potatoes with string beans on the side. A bland dinner, she reflected, but that's all right. Bill may not be flashy and slick but he's solid and dependable.

"How was your day, dear?" he asked.

She froze for a second then hurried to cover up her gaffe. "Oh it was fine. I went around looking for job openings."

"Really? Did you find anything promising?"

"Not yet, but I'm thinking I could probably find something in retail. You know, at some upscale woman's clothing store or something."

"That sounds good. But just make sure it's something you enjoy doing."

Janet closed her eyes, thinking about Frank above her, thrusting into her, making her weak with passion. She shook herself. "Yes, that's what I was thinking too. I know I don't want to go back to waitressing."

"No, I agree." They sat and ate silently for a while.

Bill spoke up. "Have you thought about how much you might earn? We'd want to make sure it's worth it."

"Um, not really." She didn't want to use Frank's numbers, the bastard.

"'Cause if it's just minimum wage, it might be better if you just stayed home."

"Why do you say that?"

"Because it'd hardly be worth the effort to get there. And you'd come home all tired and cranky like me and then there'd be two of us bitching about our jobs!" He tried to make a joke of it but she knew it was true.

"I'm not sure what I can get. I probably can't earn more than, uh, one hundred dollars a week after taxes. I mean, unless I worked full-time."

"No! I don't want you to do that. Part-time is fine."

There came another silence as they ate. Janet finished and cleared the dishes. They went into the living room but Bill didn't turn on the TV.

"One hundred a week?" he finally said. "That's not much."

"You don't think so?"

"I just don't know if it'd be worth it."

"Well, I'll certainly try to find something that pays better."

"If you can't, just forget the whole thing. We'll make do. I should probably start dusting off my resume and sending it around though."

Janet sat up, alarmed. "Why? Have you heard something?" Did Frank get mad and retaliate already? She couldn't believe he'd do that.

"No, no. Nothing new. Just the same old rumors. But we're not stupid. We can all see the handwriting on the wall. When you've got the Japanese selling steel for less than it costs us to make it, well, we know we're in trouble."

"I thought Congress would do something."

"They can't really. It's a global economy. If they impose tariffs, the Japanese or the Chinese might retaliate and impose tariffs on goods they sell here. And our trade deficit is huge with those guys. No, we're kinda stuck. I think we're all going to have to accept lower wages or we're going to go out of business."

The news was crushing to Janet. "So you might lose your job anyway?"

"Yeah, eventually. So I'd better jump before I'm pushed."

"How long do you think you've got?"

"I don't know. It could be a few years, it could be a few months. It just depends on when the company decides to pull the plug. Already we're hearing rumors that scouts for Springfield are checking out land along the Mexican border. They can get labor there for one-fourth the cost here."

"So I'd better find a job that pays pretty good so we can boost our savings."

"Well, I don't want to worry you. It's just that in light of our conversation the other day, I want to make sure I'm not just keeping all this stuff to myself. I feel much better when we can discuss it."

She nodded, distracted. *My god,* she was thinking. *It's worse than I thought. And maybe Frank has been doing more for Bill than even I realized.*

* * * * *

Janet called Frank the next day shortly after Bill left. "Hi," she said when he came on the line. "It's me."

"I was wondering if I'd ever hear from you again."

"I think I might owe you an apology. Bill told me about the situation with the company, that it's worse than he let on. Is it true that you're looking for land along the Mexican border?"

"He told you about that?" His voice was sharp.

"He said it was only a rumor."

"Ah, well. You can't stop rumors."

"But is it true? Are you thinking of moving some operations to Mexico where the labor is cheaper?"

"Janet, I can't talk about that. The board would have my head. Not to mention the S.E.C."

That was all she needed to know.

"Okay, that's fine. I don't want you to lose your job. But this tells me we have a limited window here, doesn't it?"

"I can't talk about the internal operations of Springfield Steel other than to say I've done what I can to save jobs."

"I know. And I want you to know that I appreciate it." She took a deep breath. "And if the offer is still open, I'm in. But for two-fifty a week."

"Really?"

"Yes. I'll have to come up with some excuse about how I'm getting the money. I'll look around for a nice dress shop and say I'm working there."

"You understand under this new situation, I'm going to demand more."

Her breath caught in her throat. "What? What do you mean?"

"I want to own you."

"You can't! I'm married!"

"We can work things out. I don't want to jeopardize your marriage. Not right now anyway."

"I don't know what you could 'work out'. I'm not getting a tattoo!"

"No. Not yet. But we can do other things. Fun things. Things that will make you melt with pleasure."

"I don't want to melt," she said, but it was a lie. His words struck a chord in her. She realized she was heading down a dangerous path.

"It means you'll have to be available to me whenever I want you."

"Not when Bill's around!"

"Sometimes even then. You'll have to come up with excuses. Tell him you're working."

"You're going to get me into trouble. If I lose my marriage…" She didn't know how to finish that statement.

"Don't worry. I'll be discreet. But I'm looking forward to having you at my beck and call."

"Didn't you have me that way already?"

"Yes, but not like it will be. I'll call you Monday morning." He hung up.

Janet replaced the phone and sat very still on the couch. Her pussy tingled but her stomach roiled uneasily. *I'm going to get in so much trouble*, she thought.

Chapter Seven

ꕥ

Frank called at nine-thirty Monday and told Janet to meet him at his apartment in a half-hour. He gave her directions and said, "Now here's what I want you to wear..."

Janet was taken aback. "You're telling me what to wear?"

"Yes. Consider it an order from your new boss."

That familiar little tingle went through her. She licked her lips and breathed a little heavier into the phone.

"Put on some slippers or sandals and that satin robe you had on the boat the last time, the blue one?"

"Yes," she responded, curious now. "What else?"

"Nothing else."

"What? You want me to drive across town naked?"

"You won't be naked. You'll have a robe on."

"But what if I'm stopped?"

"If I were you, I'd obey all traffic laws." He hung up.

Janet paced the floor, worried about what she was getting into. At the same time, her body betrayed her. This was the most exciting, stimulating, terrifying thing she had ever done in her life. She felt alive and close to the edge. Frank was pushing her already and she wasn't sure how she felt about it.

In the end, she cheated. She slipped on a strapless sports bra and a pair of shorts underneath her robe before leaving the house. She drove across town very carefully. When she arrived at Frank's apartment complex, she parked near his unit and looked around to make sure she was alone. Then she slipped off her robe, discarded her bra and shorts, leaving both on the floor of the car. Quickly, she put her robe back on, feeling a shiver of fear and arousal run through her.

Janet got out and pulled the sash tighter before locking the car. The keys went into her side pocket. She hurried up the steps to his door and knocked. She wondered how he was going to be able to get away for these little trysts on a regular basis. He's supposedly tied up trying to save his company, how can he fit her in? Would he really pay her for a full week's "work" if he only saw her a couple of times? Or would he demand she come over at night too?

The door opened and Frank smiled at her. "Hi, come on in."

She scooted past, hugging the robe tight to her. "I'm so embarrassed—" she began, but Frank cut her off.

"You aren't making a good start at earning your money," he said, shaking a finger at her in mock anger.

"Wh-What do you mean?" She unfastened the robe and flashed him. "See? I'm naked underneath."

"Come here." He led her to a spare bedroom he had turned into an office. Janet was confused. Frank picked up a video camera from the desk. "Through that window you can see the parking lot." He rewound the tape and ran it. It showed Janet, sitting in the car, clearly removing garments. The camera zoomed in on her naked breasts and she flushed.

"Well, yes! I couldn't drive across town like that! I might be arrested!"

"Yes, but if the owner of a dress shop asked you to do a task and you refused, wouldn't they fire you—or at least dock your pay?"

She put a hand on her hip. "What are you going to do, fire me?"

"No, but I will punish you."

"What?" This didn't sound fun anymore. She started to leave.

He put a hand out to stop her. "Don't worry. I'm talking about a little spanking. I think you'll actually enjoy it."

"A spanking? That's a little, uh, kinky, isn't it?" For some reason, Janet felt her loins twitch and her ass became more sensitized in anticipation. Was she looking forward to this? What the hell was wrong with her!

"Sure, it's a sexual fetish, you might say. All part of the job duties here."

"You make it sound so ordinary. Do this or what? You'll fire me? Or am I simply an employee who could be easily replaced?"

"Oh no, you're one in a million."

"Yeah? How so?"

"You're a natural submissive, waiting to be set free."

"A…a…what?" Is that what she was? It didn't seem right and yet it made her wetter.

"Submissive. I've known it since that day on the boat. And the sad thing is, you're married to a man who doesn't recognize it."

Janet realized her mouth had come open. She gathered her thoughts. "And you do?"

"Of course."

Was that what was wrong with her marriage? Did she really want a man to "own" her, to be strong and masculine? Bill wasn't any of those things. He was simply comfortable. Okay, a little boring too.

"So if I take this 'job', part of my duties will be to be your little sex slave?"

"You put it so well!"

She shook her head. "This sounds too kinky."

"How about this. Give me a week. If at the end, if you're not enjoying yourself, you're free to go. You can go get your dress shop job and we'll part friends."

"And what about my husband? Will he still have a job if I go?"

He tipped his head. "Your husband will have to take his chances with the rest of us."

"But if I stay, you'll do everything you can to protect his job?"

He gave a little nod of his head. "Of course. That was the original deal."

"All right." She shrugged off her robe, kicked off her sandals and stood defiantly nude. "Where do you want me?"

She was determined not to enjoy this. She would put up with his little fetishes for a short time then call it a day and go home to her husband. This could easily get out of hand!

Frank led her to the living room where he had her place herself over his knee. She felt faintly ridiculous yet it did cause that familiar tingle in her pussy. Was she really a submissive? Was that why Frank turned her on so?

The first slap was laughably soft on her firm pale cheek. She wiggled her ass at him as if to say *Is that all you've got?* The next blow was harder and she settled down.

Whack!

"Ow!"

Whack! Whack!

"That hurts!"

"It's supposed to."

"How many are you going to do?"

"As many as I feel like doing."

Whack! Whack! Whack!

Her ass began to turn red. She could feel the heat. Now she was wiggling in earnest, trying to cool off the sting. *Whack!*

"Please!"

Whack! Whack!

"Please what?"

"Please stop!"

"Call me 'Sir' or 'Master'."

"What!?"

Whack! Whack! Whack!

"Okay! Okay! Sir!" God! It was almost surreal.

He kept spanking her with his open palm. Her loins boiled with lust and she knew she was dripping wet now. Surely he could he see that. What would he think of her?

When he finally stopped, Janet's eyes were blurred by tears. "Ow, ow, ow! You hurt me!"

"No I didn't." His hand returned to stroke her hot bottom. She sucked in her breath. Her feelings were all jumbled. Then his fingers went down between her legs. She tried to close them and he slapped her ass again, sharply. Her legs came open immediately, giving him access to her most private spot.

"Ohhh you're so wet."

Janet flushed with embarrassment. She didn't know why—he had seen her naked before. He had touched her there many times, even fucked her. But somehow it was different now. There had been a power shift—and it made her extremely wet.

His finger was quickly coated with her juices and she ached to have him touch her clit. One touch and she would climax. "Please," she said.

"Please what?"

"Please touch me there. You know."

Another slap pushed her pleasure away. "Ow! What did you do that for?"

"You didn't say 'Sir', and you asked for something submissives are only supposed to wait for."

"Well, I didn't know!"

Slap!

"Sir!"

He stroked her bottom, soothing her.

"This is getting out of hand…" she started.

"Shhhh." He stroked her. His fingers returned to her slit. She opened her legs more for him, trying to encourage him to let her climax. "That's a good girl. Open yourself for me. That's what I like."

Janet began to bite her lip, trying to keep from begging Frank to touch her in that one special spot. She rotated her hips up to bring her clit in contact with his fingers but he pulled away each time.

"Oh god."

"That's right. I own this body. I can do what I want to it. If I want to prolong your pleasure, I will do that. If I want to spank it or mark it, I will do that."

She found herself nodding. Anything to be allowed to reach her release.

"Here, sit up on my knee." He made her rise and face him. She straddled one knee and sat down, rubbing her wet slit against his pants. She thought she might be able to bring herself off that way.

He brought his sopping wet fingers to her lips and told her to open them. She tasted herself and found it sweet. Meanwhile, she continued to rock back and forth against his leg.

"Shhh, stay still," he said, holding her in position. She pouted, the frustration evident on her face. She liked it better when he simply fucked her hard and fast.

It was difficult being made to wait. She realized he was teaching her to be submissive. Or was he simply allowing her natural submissiveness to flower?

He touched her breasts. She offered them to him. Her nipples were fully erect and eager. Was that a product of the spanking or from his simple touch? She tilted her head back and reveled in the sensations. As jobs go, this wasn't too bad, she decided. It certainly beat some boring old retail job, waiting on demanding customers.

Although, come to think on it, Frank was being quite demanding.

Suddenly he pinched her nipple.

"Ow!" She shrunk back.

"Sorry. Just seeing how sensitive you are."

"Well, I'm pretty damned sensitive!"

"Uh-oh."

"What?"

"You didn't say 'Sir'."

Janet eyed him for a long moment. "So that's how it's going to be, huh?"

"Yes. I want you to experience your submissive side. Trust me, you're going to enjoy it as much as I do."

"I don't know. It seems, well, unusual." She paused. "Sir."

He smiled. "Good girl."

"I think you're getting off cheap. Sir."

"Really?"

"Yeah. Two-fifty a week? I should charge five hundred a day!"

"No. You're not a whore. You're my secret lover. We're both getting a good deal. We're both getting what we want."

Janet had to admit that was true. At least the sex part was true for her. She wasn't so sure about whether or not she was submissive. He had told her she was and that he could tell. And it did stir strong emotions in her to give in to him. He was so powerful and Bill was so, well, ordinary, the contrast was startling.

She began to rub against his leg again, feeling the friction there. She decided to play along a little. What could it hurt? "Please, Sir, may I come?"

Frank nodded. "That's better, my little slut. Ask for permission. I'll let you come. In just a minute." He pulled her to him and she frowned, her pussy still unsatisfied.

"You're still dressed."

"Yes. I like to see you naked while I'm dressed. Maybe I'll take you out sometime like this."

She recoiled. "No! I'd be arrested! And Bill would surely find out. That would ruin your little party. Sir."

"I want you to do something for me," he said, kissing her on the cheek, making her melt into his arms. She waited. "I want you to go into the bathroom and fetch me my razor, shaving cream and a wet towel."

She sat up. "What?"

"I'm going to shave you here," he said, grabbing a handful of the soft tawny hair between her legs. "Oh you'd better bring some scissors as well. You'll find them in the medicine cabinet."

"I can't do that! What would Bill say?"

"Just tell him you decided to shave to be more sexy for him. Might improve the marital relations."

"You're…you're going to get me into trouble." Yet her body thrilled with the idea of Frank shaving her pussy. It was such a statement of ownership. But what about Bill?

"You're asking for more punishments. I'm being lenient this first day. But I won't tolerate disobedience."

She rose, her body trembling, and went into the bathroom. She had never felt so aroused! Not since, well, since that first day with Frank in the hotel room. Once out of sight, she debated bringing herself to a quick climax but believed Frank would somehow know. She found the items and wet a towel then returned to the living room. He was sitting on the couch waiting, a bemused smile on his face.

He had her lie down on the couch, her legs in his lap. He forced one to the floor, the other up over the cushions, exposing her pussy to him. It buzzed with anticipation.

"Don't cut me."

"I won't. Shhhh."

He began by snipping the hairs with the small scissors, carefully catching the loose strands and putting them on the coffee table in a neat pile. She watched fascinated as he trimmed her most private spot. How would she explain to Bill that after ten years of marriage she suddenly decided to shave it? Her heart beat loudly.

Frank was finished trimming, leaving mere stubble on her mound. He dampened the area with the wet towel and squirted a little shaving cream into his palm. She gasped when he began spreading it onto her skin. It wasn't that cold but it represented a transfer of power that took her breath away. She was a helpless little girl being "forced" to give in to the big bad man. Janet licked her lips.

Frank took the razor and began to shave her carefully. He made her move her legs wider until she was showing him everything. Her stomach did flip-flops and she held her breath to keep still.

Little by little her naked skin emerged. He moved down between her legs, getting every hair along the wet folds of her pussy. She thought she might be able to come just from that. Her mouth came open and she felt dizzy. Her labia slipped out of his grasp and he pulled away immediately so as to not cut her.

"I need some help here," he told her. "Grab this and pull it aside for me."

She was made to facilitate her denuding. It was embarrassing and very, very sexy. Janet held the skin away from the razor as he slipped it down along her slit. First one side then the other. When he was done, he wiped the area clean. She stared at herself. She looked like a little girl again. Was that what Frank liked? Little girls?

She brought her gaze up to his and they just eyed each other silently.

Frank seemed to read her thoughts. "No, I'm not trying to turn you into a little girl. I like to make you do things for me that signify ownership. Besides," he said, gently pinching her naked labia, "it will make it so much easier to put in a small ring here."

She gasped and pulled back. "No." But her body was on fire. She wondered what it would be like now to fuck him. Would she be able to tell the difference, now that her hair was gone?

He gave her a little slap on the outside of her leg. She jumped.

"No, what?"

"No, Sir."

"I want you to keep it like this for me, okay?"

She nodded, afraid to disobey him.

"Now," Frank continued. "About your punishments."

"What? You spanked me already."

"Yes, but you've been challenging me at every turn. Another punishment is in order."

"I haven't been—" She realized she was challenging him again so she closed her mouth. Janet had trouble letting go of herself as Frank wanted. She was a modern woman and yet he was pushing her buttons. Right now she would agree to just about anything if he would fuck her. She could see the bulge in his pants and wanted to free his beautiful cock. She forced herself to wait. Let Frank control the pace.

"I'm glad you're bare here. It's the perfect place for your punishment."

"What!?" Janet tried to close her legs but Frank was still in between them.

"Relax. Just a few slaps with my bare hand. But it will help focus your mind."

A few slaps? There? Janet was confused. Her mind said one thing, her pussy said quite another. It weeped, it tingled, it cried for release.

But wait, her mind said, *this isn't right.*

Shut up—you're not the one he's going to slap! Was that her pussy talking?

The mind shut down. Janet lay back and watched, her body alive with sensations. His hand went up, her eyes followed it. Down it came.

Slap!

It didn't hurt so much as startle her. And there was something else. Her pussy, which had been quietly waiting its turn, suddenly came alive. *Wow!*

Maybe it was kinky but it sure felt good. Well, good and bad. Naughty. Depraved.

Hit me again!

Slap! Harder this time. Her pussy wept with the pleasure and pain. Janet knew her juices were flowing freely now. The bare skin made a lot of difference, she noted.

Slap!

He held up his hand and she could see her wetness on his fingers. "Oh god," she breathed. "Oh my god." She looked down and could see the faint pink outline of those same fingers across her mound. Her clit looked like a wet marble, trying to free itself from its fleshy prison.

Slap! Slap!

Janet thought she might actually die from being kept on the edge of release. Was that possible? Would police find her body later with a big smile on her face, her pussy sloppy wet and still twitching?

Slap!

"Oh please, Sir," the word just came out automatically. He was a "Sir" now. He held her pleasure in his hands, even his fingers.

"Are you beginning to understand now what I want from you?"

"Yes, Sir."

Slap!

"And what is it? I want to hear you say it."

Slap!

Her body was shaking. "Uh, obedience? And nudity?"

He laughed. "Yes. Both. And more."

"But, Sir, I'm still married…"

Slap! Slap!

"Of course you are. You have to trust me. Can you learn to trust me?"

"Yes, Sir."

"Good." He moved back, leaving her there, spread wide, her pussy burning with need. She wanted him to slap her again. Or rub her clit. She wanted to cover herself. She wanted him to fuck her. Janet took a breath and let it out, trying to control her emotions. It was up to him. And that, she realized, was what her life would become if she stayed in this crazy "job" he offered. He would make her his. He would own her, just as he said.

Could she? Dare she?

It was about trust. She wanted to trust him yet she wasn't his. She belonged to Bill. It would ruin Bill if he found out. The issue rattled about in her brain like a steel marble in a coffee can.

"Sir?"

"Yes, my pet?"

"I want to trust you, let go, as you say, but I still have a big issue with Bill. You understand, don't you?"

"Of course I do. And you should learn to let me take care of that issue for you as well. All you have to do is what I say. Don't worry about anything else."

"Okay," she said, but she didn't feel it as completely as she wanted to.

"Now would you like to come?"

"Oh yes, Sir! Please!"

"All right. Wait here." He got up and left her. She stared after him, confused. He returned a minute later with a video camera in one hand.

"Oh no!" She sat up and covered herself with her hands.

"Do you trust me?"

"I want to but you're putting me in a very uncomfortable position."

"Don't worry. This won't end up on the Internet, if that's what worries you. If you don't trust me, you should get up now and leave. We'll call the whole thing off."

Janet thought about that. She knew she should get up and go before things went too far. That's what she had told him when this started. *"We can't let this get out of hand."* And here she was, about to be filmed having sex with a man who wasn't her husband.

"I can't do it," she said. "I can't let you film us having sex."

"Who said anything about me?" He sat at the other end of the couch and pointed the camera at her. "I want you to masturbate for me. I want you to come very noisily."

Janet knew she could come easily but was disappointed he wasn't offering to slip his hard, wonderful cock into her. Not that she wanted to fuck him on camera. God, it was so confusing.

"You want to film me…doing that? Why?"

"Because it pleases me. And I can watch it anytime."

"You promise not to show it to anyone?"

"No, I can't promise that. I might want to share it sometime. You'll have to trust me not to embarrass you with it. That's all. Now please begin." The little red light came on in front of the camera. Janet was still sitting there, hunched over.

"I'm not sure about this, uh, Sir," she said. "I'm very shy."

"Nonsense. You're all worked up. You can't wait to climax. I can see it in your eyes, your body posture. Please. Do it for me."

"I can't believe this is my 'job'," she said, leaning back and letting her hands drop, exposing herself for the camera.

He waved his hand at her and she let the fingers of her right hand drift to her wet slit. She could hear the sounds it made as her middle finger moved up and back. A shudder went through her. Somehow the combination of the spanking, the slapping and the camera made her incredibly horny. It surprised her that she enjoyed performing for him. It was so unlike her. Wasn't it? Her finger stroked her sensitive clit and she forgot about the camera, about Frank. She closed her eyes. Her breaths became shallow. Her fingers moved faster, her mouth came open. It didn't take long. The orgasm came on her suddenly, catching her by surprise. Janet shook and she clamped her fingers hard against herself.

"Ohhhh, ohhhh," she cried. It was nice, but it wasn't the big release she needed.

"Again," he coached. "Do it again."

She did and it took longer this time. Her fingers moved, making those squishy sounds. This time she kept her eyes open, watching Frank watch her, recording her. It made her climb that stairway again. Her fingers became a blur.

"Oh god!" She threw her head back. "Oh my god!" The orgasm roared through her and she felt slutty, naughty—and very, very satisfied.

"That was better. I liked that one."

She hardly heard him, lost as she was in her own world. When she came back to her senses, Frank was still there with the camera, filming. He stood and moved around the coffee table, putting the camera down carefully and aiming it at her from the side, using the display screen to center her tightly in the frame. She didn't move. Even her legs were still splayed open.

He stepped back, letting the camera run, and unbuckled his pants. Janet watched him hungrily. He stripped off his clothes and came around to crawl between her legs. She opened her arms to welcome him, her eyes on his hard cock. She no longer cared about the camera, only his cock.

"Oh yes," she breathed. "Oh my yes."

Frank centered himself and entered her suddenly with one thrust. She gasped and fell back against the cushion. "Yes, baby, yes!" she cried out. He thrust hard into her again and again, driving her up against the arm of the couch. Janet hung on to his arms and rode with him. She could hear the noises of their congress, the slap of flesh, the wet sounds of her pussy, the vocalized gasps of pleasure.

He bellowed suddenly and shot his seed into her. She climaxed again and fell back against the cushion, exhausted. They rested for a few minutes then he pulled away. He came around and shut off the camera.

"So ends your first day on the job," he said with a twinkle in his voice.

It took her a moment to find her own voice. "My god, I'm not going to survive this!"

Frank began to get dressed. "I'm sorry but I do have to get back to work. You go on home and wait for my call. It might be a couple of days."

"Sure," she said, staggering to her feet. She found her robe and put it on along with her sandals. Her fingers closed about her keys in the side pocket.

"What time is it?"

"Eleven-thirty."

That whole wild escapade had taken just ninety minutes. It had seemed much longer.

He stopped her by the door and gave her a long, lingering kiss. "You were wonderful today," he said.

"Thank you, Sir. You weren't so bad yourself."

From the office, he watched her scurry back to her car and get in. She didn't try to put on her underclothes this time, he was happy to see. She started the car right up and drove away.

Frank smiled to himself and closed the door.

Chapter Eight

ᘓ

"Yeah, boss, you wanted to see me?" Bill Mann came in to Frank's office shortly after noon.

"Sit down, Bill."

Bill sat nervously in the chair in front of the CEO's desk. "Yeah? What's this all about?"

"I thought you'd like a progress report." Frank pulled out the video camera. "Here's what your wife did today." He turned the display so Bill could see and hit *Play*. He watched Bill's expression as he saw his wife masturbate then Frank's body entered the picture—and Janet. They fucked wildly and he watched her climax. His shock gave way to delight.

"That's great!" he said when it was over. "I can't believe it! You were right." He paused. "What happened to, um, her hair down there?"

Frank laughed. "I made her shave it off. Well, I should say I shaved it off."

"Wow. And she let you?" He shook his head. "I didn't believe it when you told me Janet was a submissive!"

"Well, I have you to thank too. If you hadn't convinced her that she needed to get a job, I doubt I would've ever been able to get her to overcome her reservations. But it looks like she's well on her way now."

"God, I never would have imagined it. My Janet, a submissive! No wonder our marriage has been dull. I just didn't know how to handle her!"

Frank recalled how this entire adventure had been started. It had begun not long after his divorce. Bill had commiserated with him about it and Frank had responded that Mary "just wasn't the submissive type he'd been looking for".

Bill had expressed surprise at that—and great curiosity. "I didn't think there was any such thing anymore," he had said. "I mean, with the women's movement and all."

Frank's words had shocked him. "Oh there are millions of women out there who repress their submissive side. You should know—you're married to one of them!"

Bill hadn't believed it of course. "No way. She's no doormat!" He saw Janet as a woman with her own mind, a bit demure, sure, but certainly no submissive.

"No, no. I'm not talking about a doormat. Far from it. A submissive is someone quite special—a woman who responds sexually when a man is strong and forceful to her. Not abusive, you understand, just forceful. The alpha male. It touches them on a very basic level."

"Maybe so, but how could you tell that about Janet? You haven't been married to her for ten years!"

"Oh I could tell from those times we sailed together and other occasions. She's just repressed it. She just needs someone to bring it out of her. Then look out!"

The expression on Bill's face had been priceless. Frank could tell he was excited by the idea that his wife might be submissive but confused by it as well.

"I guess I don't know what a submissive really is. Are you telling me that Janet might defer to me and wait on me and all those other things?"

"Yes and no. That's part of it. It's really not about ordering a woman around or making her fix you drinks. It's more about attitude. And power. I believe Janet is a sexual dynamo who would do almost anything to experience love from a dominant man."

"It sounds very interesting but I just don't see it," Bill had said.

"Well, I guess you never will. It's too bad though."

"Why?"

"Because she's not really happy being the demure and proper wife. She needs this, you see."

"Oh and you could make her more submissive, I suppose?"

"Not make her 'more submissive', no. I would merely show you who she really is. But if you're the jealous type, it won't work, so forget it."

Bill had been silent a long time. Frank had let the silence grow. Finally Bill had said, "And just what would you do—that is, if I *wasn't* the jealous type?"

And that had been the start of Frank's little "experiment". Turned out Bill was excited by the prospect of seeing his wife with Frank—or other men. As long as he was part of it of course.

Frank offered to prove it to Bill. If he was right, Bill would have the kind of woman he secretly wanted but dared not suggest—a good wife who could be very naughty and sexy. Frank wouldn't have been interested in the challenge if he hadn't had free rein to see just how far Janet could be taken. A "hands-on" trainer so to speak.

"I'll give you regular reports but it will have to appear that you're ignorant of the affair, okay?"

So they had come to an arrangement. Frank would seduce Bill's wife in order to show him what kind of woman was truly underneath that repressed exterior. Frank would finally get to have sex with a woman he'd always lusted after. And Bill would learn how to be more dominant around her.

"I have to warn you, Bill, being a dominant isn't something you can necessarily teach. It may just not be in you," Frank had said.

"I know. And that's okay. The idea that my wife is fucking other men or being dominated by other men is very exciting. It was something I could never have suggested to her before—I figured she'd freak out and call me perverted. So that's why I don't really think you can do it."

They had shaken on the deal. Bill agreed to give him some room but he wanted hear about every detail.

Now watching Bill view the tape, Frank could tell it aroused him to imagine his wife acting like a submissive slut. He smiled. He bet Bill couldn't wait to go home and fuck her himself.

"You're going to have to give me more tips on this dominant thing," Bill said, breathing a little harder now.

"Just let out a little of your inner caveman. Don't be a jerk, just be strong. I think she will respond to it. If she doesn't or if you find you're trying to be something you're not, then don't push it, okay? Leave that to the experts."

"Okay."

Bill left and returned to work a changed man. To think that his wife would do such things! What else might she do? For the first time in years, Bill felt as if his marriage wasn't doomed to die of boredom. While most men would be jealous of Frank, Bill was actually grateful to him. He never realized that he had his fantasy woman right under his nose and didn't realize it. He only hoped he could live up to her fantasies as well. If not, would she leave him for Frank?

That was the big question, wasn't it?

When five o'clock came, Bill raced home. He walked in to find Janet in the kitchen, chopping vegetables for dinner. He came up behind her and grabbed her around the waist. She pushed back and tipped her neck for him to kiss.

"Hi, Bill. How was your day?"

"Just fine. Still have a job!"

"That's good." She snuggled against him, wiggling her ass on his hard cock.

"Did you find a job yet?"

She stiffened. "Uh, yeah, I did. I'm working at this boutique down on Chester Street," she said. "You know, women's dresses and shoes."

"Great. I'm really sorry you have to do this. I just thought it would be prudent in the short run to have some extra cash in our savings." He paused. "How much are they paying you?"

"Oh just two-fifty a week for part-time. But I'm hoping I can get more later."

"Good girl. Take 'em for all you can get!"

He let her go and turned her around, kissed her tenderly on the lips. She was still holding the knife.

"Careful! Don't want to chop you too! What brings all this on? Usually you come in and plop down in front of the TV."

"What? I can't come in and give my wife a kiss without a reason? Besides, I've been thinking I watch too much TV anyway."

Her eyes widened. "Really?" She put her free hand to his forehead. "You getting sick?"

"Ha-ha." He slipped his hands under her blouse and cupped her breasts. "Maybe we have a little time before dinner for some fun?" As soon as the words were out of his mouth, he realized that was not "dominant" behavior. He was asking her, not telling her!

"I'm flattered but I really have to finish getting dinner in the oven or it won't be ready in time. Take a rain check?"

He nodded and let her go. She turned back to her cutting board. Bill cursed himself. That wasn't a very good start. Could he take lessons in domination? He didn't want to be a wishy-washy guy. What would they call that anyway, the beta male? Or maybe the omega male.

He turned and went to the bedroom to change out of his work clothes. As he undressed, he imagined watching Janet and Frank together. He'd love to be a fly on the wall, seeing how he dominated her. And how she responded to it. It would be like attending a seminar on how to be a man. He sure could use it! He made a mental note to ask Frank to set something up for him. He could hide in a closet. But that bothered him too. It would make him a peeping tom, wouldn't it? Spying on his wife without her knowledge? That might be okay once or twice but he wanted to be present in the room, to sit on the bed while Frank fucked her. To watch her expression. To hear her cry with pleasure. And to fuck her afterward and feel her sloppy pussy accepting his cock.

He had no idea why he felt this way. Wouldn't a "real man" be jealous? If the situation were reversed, could he imagine Frank sitting by and watching his wife be fucked by another man? Somehow he doubted it. *Maybe I just don't have what it takes to be the kind of man Janet needs.*

For the first time Bill was a little worried about starting this "experiment" in the first place. What if she fell in love with Frank? If Janet left him for Frank, he'd be devastated. All the more so because he had started the ball rolling.

He made a mental note to talk to Frank. It was one thing to prove to Bill that his wife was submissive but quite another to steal her away from him. Of course he was making it easier because he liked the idea of watching his wife with another man. What was wrong with him?

He threw on some casual clothes and returned to the kitchen. He was torn. Part of him wanted to just zone out in front of the TV as before. But part wanted to try to break through the shell she seemed to have up around her. Was she feeling guilty? He decided that was probably it. And the nicer he was to her, the guiltier she'd feel.

Dammit. Now he didn't know what to do.

He went into the kitchen. "Anything I can do to help?"

She looked surprised. "No. I've got it. Why don't you go sit down and relax?"

He pulled out a stool at the counter and sat down. "Okay."

She smiled. "It's nice that you want to keep me company but it's okay, really, if you want to catch a game on TV."

Bill found himself becoming a bit peeved. "It's okay. I thought we could talk."

She turned, startled. "About what?"

"About our days. Tell me what it's like, working in a dress shop."

Janet colored a little. Just enough that he would notice because of what he knew. He could picture her on that couch, her legs spread, opening her arms for Frank…

"Nothing to tell really. Everyone is nice. Women come in and they tell you what they're looking for and we try to find something that will fill the bill."

"I imagine that must be hard, trying to find the right outfit all the time."

"Oh no, you'd be surprised. Often we seem to have just the thing they want. But not always."

"Was it hard, standing on your feet all day? Maybe you'd like a foot rub later." He wondered if that was another example of how he wasn't an alpha male, then decided he was just being nice. Dominants don't have to be selfish assholes, do they?

"Wow, that would be great." She paused. "What's gotten into you? You're being so conciliatory."

"Nothing. I'm just grateful you're helping us out. If I lose my job, it will be nice to have that extra money."

She nodded but didn't say anything. He wondered what she was thinking.

"I can at least chop some veggies for you."

"Uh, sure. You can chop this onion."

He started in while she moved to the stove to stir something. He watched her movements, knowing she was nervous. She should be! *She's worried I might find out.* Bill felt sorry for her. He knew she'd only agreed to fuck Frank to save his job. Not that it was really in jeopardy. But still. Now she faced a dilemma. She enjoyed her newfound subservience but worried about what happen if word got out. Well it would, but if everything worked out, there shouldn't be any jealousy or recriminations. Bill had been in on the deal from the beginning—the only wild card would be Janet. How would she react when she found out the whole thing had been cooked up by her husband and his boss?

She'd probably be furious. Unless she'd become truly submissive. Even then, he wasn't sure. He'd have to talk to Frank about that and see what he thought.

There I go again, deferring to the alpha male!

Of course it was a moot point anyway. The whole deal was short-term. Frank had said he'd only need a month, maybe less. She should be fully trained by then. But when would they tell her? He wanted to start watching his wife with other men, ordering her to fuck them, suck them. It made him hard to think about it.

After dinner, Bill made sure he talked with Janet and left the TV off. She seemed surprised but pleased. But when he started kissing her on the couch, she became distracted.

"What's wrong?"

"Um, I don't know. I'm not sure I'm in the mood."

Bill nodded, wondering if she were embarrassed now that she was shaved. He decided this would be the first real test of his attempt at being dominant. "Well, that's too bad because I am. And as my wife, you have to provide me with comfort." He grinned at her.

"Uh, well…"

"Come on. I won't take no for an answer." He pulled her to her feet and propelled her into the bedroom. He began unbuttoning her blouse and she seemed nervous. Her hands fluttered about as her top came off. He removed her bra and sucked on her nipples. They grew hard and she sighed. But when his hands went to her skirt, she pulled back.

"Bill, there's something I should tell you."

He wondered if she was going to confess her "affair". He raised his eyebrows.

"I, uh, was shaving my legs this morning and, uh, I got carried away. I don't know if you're going to like it."

Her skirt slipped down her legs and she stepped out of it. When his hands went to her panties, he noticed he was shaking with excitement. Revealing her bare pussy was like being a kid at Christmas and getting exactly what he wanted. His eyes widened, his mouth came open.

"Wow," he breathed. "It's beautiful."

"You really like it?" She seemed pleased but very nervous.

"Oh yeah!" He leaned down and kissed it. It tasted clean and sweet. She probably showered as soon as she had arrived home from her "lesson". "You should've done this a long time ago! What made you decide to do it?"

"Well, that's nice. I've been reading about it, you know, in women's magazines. Apparently, it's all the rage nowadays. You think I should keep it like this?"

"Yes, I do."

"You don't think it makes me look like a little girl?"

"Not really. You have womanly hips and breasts. It just makes it cleaner and neater—easier to eat."

He pushed her back on the bed and dove in between her legs. He loved the smoothness of her mound against his face. He teased her until she reached a minor climax before he stood to remove his own clothes. Janet lay there watching him. When he was naked, she opened her arms to him and Bill had the image of her opening her arms for Frank. It made his cock even harder, thinking about his wife with another man.

Chapter Nine

ꟃ

Janet parked the car out in front of Frank's apartment and looked around. This time she hadn't worn the undergarments under her robe and she was feeling particularly vulnerable.

Frank had called her Wednesday morning and told her to come over at ten. "This time just wear the robe and sandals. I'll be watching."

She glanced at her watch. It was two minutes 'til. Time to move. She got out and walked quickly to the door. Fortunately his door was set back, protected from view by a small stoop. She rang the doorbell and waited.

He opened it and smiled. "Hello, Janet."

"Hello, Sir."

He blocked her way as she tried to come in. She looked up, startled.

"Take off your robe and shoes."

"What?!" She looked around. No one could see her unless they happened to be walking between the buildings but she still felt very exposed.

"The robe. From now on when you come over, you are to hang your robe over the hook under the mailbox before you ring the bell. Shoes too. When I peek through the peephole and see that you're naked, I'll let you in." He closed the door in her face.

She stood there flummoxed. Then she looked around and decided no one could see her and shucked off her robe, kicked off her sandals. With shaking hands, she hung it up and turned back to the door. She waited but nothing happened. Finally she rang the doorbell again.

Another minute went by and she was starting to shiver—not from the cold but from embarrassment. She wiggled her hips and moved her feet, trying to will the door to open.

At long last it came open and she went past him in a rush.

"God! I was so embarrassed!"

"Don't be. I loved seeing you stand there naked."

"You're going to ruin me!" She was simply parroting her concerns. Her body told a different story. Her nipples were hard. Her pussy tingled.

"Oh come on. I'm sure Bill would be very excited to see you like that."

"Don't bring him into this! I'm doing this for him but, well, it's starting to get out of hand."

"Don't worry. Leave everything to me."

He waited, watching her. She waited too, staring at him. This pleased him since she was waiting for instructions. She was making progress. He moved close, reaching a hand out to touch her mound. Frank felt the stubble there immediately.

"You didn't shave?"

"I, uh, I didn't have time. Uh, Sir."

"I think you did that on purpose. So that I'd shave your sweet pussy and spank it like last time. I think you enjoyed that a bit too much, hmm?"

"Well, I thought you might like to do it, you know, yourself."

"Yes, but that's not what I asked of you when I told you to shave. I said, 'keep it like this'. Remember?"

She looked down. "Yes, Sir."

"So you'll have to be punished for that."

"Yes, Sir." She sounded contrite and a little eager at the same time. Frank had expected this.

"Very well. Go get the equipment from the bathroom."

She hurried off. She returned in a few minutes to find Frank already sitting at one end of the couch. She sat on the other and put her legs across his lap. When he looked at her in a meaningful way, she dropped one leg onto the ground as before, opening herself to him. Janet could tell she was already wet just thinking about what was to come.

But Frank did something strange. He eased her other leg off his lap and stood, pulled out his cell phone and dialed a number. Janet watched confused.

"Okay. You're on." He hung up.

"What was that about?"

"You'll see." He came around to stand by her head.

Before Janet could react, the front door came open and a stranger walked in. She gasped and closed her legs together. Her arms went across her breasts. She tried to get up but Frank held her down.

"Listen to me," he said softly. "You disobeyed me. I asked that you keep yourself shaved and you didn't. So as part of your punishment, George O'Malley here will shave you. He's my next-door neighbor."

"No! You can't!" She tried to turn away from him to hide her body.

Frank held her firmly as the man approached. He appeared to be close to fifty, she guessed, but otherwise was attractive in a rough-hewn kind of way. He had a barrel chest and thick arms and his unruly hair was speckled with gray. His eyes were friendly but hungry as he eyed her naked body. He sat on the couch and patted her leg. "Not to worry, my sweet. Frank explained the rules to me."

"Please, no, Frank! Don't let him do this!"

"Why? Because it embarrasses you? Or because you might like it?"

"Yes, I'm embarrassed! And I have a husband!"

"Leave everything to me. He won't find out unless we tell him. George certainly won't."

The man smiled, showing even white teeth. He kept stroking her legs and her hip until she settled down. He was already getting an eyeful and there didn't seem to be a lot she could do about it. At Frank's urging, she allowed her legs to come apart and felt his eyes on her moist privates. George rubbed her with the damp towel and squirted the shaving cream into his thick hands.

Janet turned her head away when he began to spread it over her stubbly mound, mortified that Frank would allow this. And yet… It did cause a tingle inside her. A naughty thrill. She was a very bad girl. But because she had no choice, she might as well enjoy it a little.

She watched as George took the razor and began to shave. He was very gentle. Frank let go of her arms and she didn't move, fearful of getting cut, but also because it felt good. He used short little strokes, being sure to get all the hairs on top. Frank was helpful in pointing out hairs he missed along the sides and George bent down to get every one, forcing Janet to put one leg up over the back of the couch and one on the floor. She could not be more spread open for this rugged stranger.

He finished without a nick and wiped her clean. Then he leaned over and gently kissed her naked mound. It was a sweet gesture, not an overtly sexual one. Nevertheless, it caused another thrill to shoot through her.

"Now why don't you thank George for shaving your pussy."

Janet felt her face go red. "Thank you, George, for, uh, shaving my pussy."

Both men laughed. "What?" Janet asked, confused.

They switched places and George, now standing by Janet's head, unzipped his pants.

"He was thinking of another way you could thank him," Frank said, sitting between her legs, his hands on both her thighs.

"Oh no! I didn't sign on for this! I'm not fucking this guy!"

"Now you've hurt his feelings! You are really piling up the punishments!"

"Don't worry, miss," George said. "Just a little nibble is all I ask." His cock came out and it was impressive. He leaned up against the couch near her head and put it close to her mouth.

"If you don't, the punishments will only get worse," Frank said. He leaned in close. "Besides, you promised to obey me."

With some reluctance, Janet opened her mouth and took the man's semihard cock inside. She had to help it with one hand since it was so large she feared she might choke. As she started to suck, it began to grow until it was huge. She couldn't get it deep enough into her mouth to be effective. It made her gag. She kept at it for several minutes but he didn't come. Finally he pulled back and patted her on the head.

"That will do for now, Janet."

Janet felt a little embarrassed for not trying harder. She knew Frank would be displeased.

"Would you like to stay and help with her punishments?"

"Well sure."

Her eyes flew open. Her regrets about the man flew out the window.

"Wait!"

"Shhh. You have to learn to obey. These little punishments are merely to steer you, not actually harm you."

Of course he was right—the fear of the punishments was worse than the practice. Janet decided she was really more afraid of George's leering at her while she was having her privates slapped. She would surely climax in front of him—did Frank want that? Would he fuck her in front of him too?

Her fears increased when Frank directed George to open a drawer on an end table. He pulled out an eighteen-inch riding crop and waved it in the air.

"Frank! You can't be serious!" She tried to get up but he held her down.

"Don't make it worse! I'm going to let George slap your pussy a few times. Don't be such a baby."

She eyed the powerful stranger fearfully. Yet her obedience overcame her reluctance and she didn't resist as Frank made her keep her legs apart.

"There's another one, a smaller one, in there too," Frank told George. The older man reached into the drawer and pulled out a crop that was about twelve inches long and handed it over.

"Okay, here's how this works. You are going to spread your legs wide just as before. George will give you twenty slaps on your pussy with the crop. Each time you move your legs together, I will slap both breasts with this." He waved the small crop in the air above her.

"Nooo," she moaned. She was naked, exposed and vulnerable. She was helpless—she might cry, she might scream, she might have a shattering orgasm that would mortify her. Everything was on display.

George took Frank's place between her legs and he moved up to sit on the coffee table, facing her torso. George measured the distance to make sure the leather flap of the crop would land right on her mound. He tapped her there a few times and Janet could feel her clit respond.

He raised it up. She watched fascinated.

Whack!

She screamed and her legs jerked together, trapping the crop in between. Immediately, she felt the *slap, slap* of the smaller crop on her breasts, setting her nipples on fire.

"Keep your legs apart."

How could she stand nineteen more of these?

Whack!

"Pleeease!" This time she managed not to move her legs.

Despite her protests, there was another sensation bubbling up from her loins. Her clit didn't seem to be harmed by the blows—in fact, it seemed to be growing in size, as if it were reaching up to meet the next strike.

Whack!

"Aaaaagh!"

Her legs jerked and Frank's hand moved immediately. *Slap, slap*! Her breasts burned nearly as badly as her pussy.

"I think your screaming is counterproductive. Instead of that, let's have you count the strokes, shall we? You're on number four. If you lose count, we'll start over, all right?"

Whack!

"Four!"

Whack!

"Five!"

"Say, 'Give me another, Sir'."

"Give me another, Sir!"

Whack!

"Six! Give me another, Sir!"

Janet was beside herself. Her clit throbbed and she didn't know if she was on the verge of an orgasm or she was about to be maimed for life. Deep down, she knew Frank wouldn't allow that. She was being punished for not trusting him and letting go. It was hard to do but she hoped she could learn to accept her new role with grace.

Whack!

"Seven! Give me another, Sir!"

George suddenly stopped and leaned down to blow on her tortured clit. She nearly came right then. She felt on the painful verge and knew it wouldn't take much. His fingers came down, patted her and Janet groaned aloud.

"You like that?" Frank asked.

"Yesssss."

The fingers returned and dipped into her sopping-wet slit. She groaned again and tried to hump them so she could climax. She no longer cared that this stranger was fondling her. She closed her eyes. The fingers retreated.

Whack!

Her legs jerked and her eyes flew open.

"Aaaagh! Eight! Give me another, Sir!"

"Almost had to start over there," Frank warned. He raised the smaller crop above her breasts, giving her a chance to steel herself then *Slap! Slap!* Her breasts stung.

The blows continued. She cried out the numbers—nine, ten, eleven, twelve, thirteen. Then another pause. George's fingers returned.

"Yes, please do that," she babbled.

"You like my fingers in your pussy?" he asked.

"Yes, yes, please let me come!"

"Can I come over any time and make you come?"

Her eyes flew open. She saw both men watching her carefully.

"Will you spread your legs for me and let me rub your pretty little clit until you come on my fingers?"

"Yes, please," she said in a small voice. "Anything, just let me come!"

"We're not done yet," Frank said.

Whack!

Her legs snapped together again. Frank slapped her breasts. There was a live current between her nipples and her cunt, sparking and flashing like ten thousand volts. Janet knew she was going to come but wasn't sure she could survive it.

When George reached nineteen, he stopped again. Janet was thrashing her head back and forth. No one had ever done this to her before. To be balanced on the razor-thin edge over a shattering climax that loomed just out of reach was almost more than she could bear. Her pussy throbbed and her breasts ached. She wasn't making sense any longer. All of her attention was concentrated on her pussy.

George's fingers touched her. She nodded, "Yes, yes, yes," not aware she was speaking. She was so wet his fingers were instantly coated. She felt his thick digits move up toward her clit. She tried to help him. "Oh yes, please touch my clit, touch my clit."

"I still owe you one more slap, Janet," he said. "I'm going to rub your clit hard. When you come, I don't want you to close your legs, all right?"

"Yes, yes, yes, please…"

His fingers finally touched her fiery core and rubbed hard. Janet exploded. She tried not to slam her legs together so she arched her back instead, which brought her clit up.

WHACK!

The hardest blow yet landed right on her throbbing clit. She shrieked like a woman being electrocuted and thrashed wildly on the couch. The orgasm was more massive than any she had experienced before. Then she passed out from the pleasure-pain conundrum.

She woke to find Frank gently wiping her face with a damp towel. "Hey there. How are you doing?"

She looked around. George was gone. She raised her questioning eyes to Frank.

"No, I sent him home. He had enough thrills for one day. But don't worry, he'll be back again."

Janet blushed, remembering her promise to him. Would she really have to spread her legs for him whenever he came over? Would Frank allow that? Knowing Frank, he probably would. Why was he so willing to share her with others?

"Come, get up. I want to fuck you now."

She groaned but did as he asked. He laid her over the padded arm of the couch and entered her from behind. She was grateful for the position since her clit still throbbed and she didn't want any more rubbing there. Janet lay there passively while he plowed into her. It wasn't about her pleasure, only his, and she understood it.

As he fucked her, Frank glanced over at the bookcase where a teddy bear sat. It was actually a nanny cam he had purchased yesterday. It had captured the entire scene today. He knew Bill would be pleased. He gave a little wave.

Just knowing that he was turning Bill's wife into a submissive slut brought him to the brink of climax. He began slapping her ass. She brought her head up and gasped.

He came hard inside her and held her ass with both hands. After a few minutes he pulled free. He climbed on the couch in front of her and made her suck him clean.

Frank let her relax for several minutes until she came down from her high. Then he helped her up and walked her toward the door. "Friday, ten a.m." he told her. She nodded weakly and stepped out naked into the alcove. She grabbed her robe and put it on. Her feet found her sandals. He closed the door and walked back to the spare room. From there, he could see her stagger to her car and drive away.

ChapterTen

"My god, Frank, this is great stuff!" Bill was saying as he watched the footage from the nanny cam. They were in Frank's office, the door closed.

"You like? You can see how quickly she's coming along. I'm prepared to take her further—you okay with that?"

"Oh boy, I don't know. Just keep going and I'll tell you if you should stop."

"Are you seeing some results from this already?"

"Yeah, some. I mean, she seems more responsive in bed. But my problem is I'm just not dominant yet. I always seem to say the wrong things."

"I've been thinking about that. We can keep on with me as the dominant one and soon she'll do anything I ask. You could be there, just like George. Of course you'd be a much more active participant."

Bill nodded. "Yeah." He liked the idea. Watching George get his jollies with his wife was a real turn-on. He could picture himself there, seeing his wife writhe and beg for release.

"What's next?"

"Well, that's up to you. But I would like to mark her next."

"In what way?"

"Just a gold ring through her labia or nipple. What do you think?"

"Ohh. Labia. I think that would look very sexy."

"I doubt she'd show it to you! She'd probably take it out first."

"Well, I wouldn't want that! I'd want her to have to explain it."

Frank smiled. "Leave that to me."

* * * * *

Friday morning ten a.m. Janet stood naked in front of Frank's door, her robe on the hook, her sandals lined up neatly underneath, and wondered why she was allowing him to do this to her. She knew she enjoyed it but it was more than that. It was like a drug to her. She had to have the pain-pleasure orgasms that only Frank could give her. She had never thought of herself as a pain slut or a submissive but he was sure pushing her buttons in some way! Now the little climaxes she experienced in bed with Bill seemed weak and pale in comparison. She enjoyed the closeness with her husband but her body needed what Frank gave her.

She stood there for what seemed like two minutes before he opened the door. "Hi," he said. "Come on in."

She went past him into the apartment and stopped still. There in the living room was a strange black man. He was broad-chested and bald and his arms were covered in dark tattoos. Beside him was an odd-looking chair of some type made of metal poles and canvas. The man was bent over a kit that was sitting on the seat and paid Janet little attention.

Janet turned and with wide eyes, silently begged Frank to explain.

"Oh don't worry. That's just James, the piercer."

The man looked up from his kit and waved. "Hi." He had a silver ring through his eyebrow and a stud through his lower lip. He turned back as if he saw naked women all the time. In his line of work, he probably did.

"What is this? I can't do this. Don't make me do this."

"Relax. It's all arranged. It won't hurt much."

"No! I can't explain this to my husband!"

"Sure you can. Tell him you did it for him. He'll go ape over it." He pushed her from behind, leading her to the chair.

James moved the kit and stepped aside, gesturing for Janet to climb on. "No," she said weakly, but climbed on when both men helped her. James began fastening Velcro straps around her thighs and shins. Frank did the same to her upper and lower arms. She was soon immobilized.

James came up and cinched up a final strap around her waist. Whistling a little tune, he bent down and began turning a wheel. Janet's legs began to come apart.

"Where are you putting this? Where are you putting this?" Her voice seemed on the edge of panic.

"Relax," James said. "It's just a little ring on your labia. It'll be cute." He slipped on a pair of latex gloves.

"My…my…?"

"Just one for now," Frank said. "Later on we can add more, don't you think?"

James nodded. "I can show you some pictures if you'd like to see."

"My…my…?"

"I think you'd better get started. I promised George a little treat later and I'd like this to be all done first."

"George?" she squeaked.

James bent down between her legs and nodded. "Good. Nicely shaved I see. That always makes it easier."

Frank patted her shoulder. "Yes, she's learning."

James pulled a small stool out from underneath the chair and sat on it. His head was even with her wide-open pussy and Janet was mortified. James adjusted the chair to bring it down a little until he was satisfied. He dabbed the area with an alcohol swab and looked over his shoulder at Frank.

"Left or right?"

"Hmm. Left I should think."

"Okay." He grabbed a bottle and stuck a cotton swab in it. He gently coated the area around her left labia.

"What are you doing now?" Janet gasped.

"I'm numbing it. You shouldn't feel much more than a pinch."

He picked up a gun-like contraption and laid the fold of skin in it. "Front, back or center?"

"Oh front. We should be able to see it, don't you think?"

"I couldn't agree more."

"Please!"

James squeezed the handles and Janet jumped. "Ouch!" Working quickly, he wiped the excess blood and used antiseptic to clean the small hole. Then he threaded the small gold ring into it and snapped the tongue home.

"You said you wanted it permanent?"

"No!" Janet gasped.

"Yes, please. I wouldn't want her to lose it." Frank's voice was light, teasing.

James picked up a soldering iron with a tiny tip and a small gold wire and bent to his task. There was a hiss and a bit of smoke then he pulled back. "There, all done." He got up, stripped off his gloves and began gathering his tools.

Janet sat frozen on the chair, her eyes wide. She had no idea how to explain this to Bill. He would think she'd gone mad. Why else would a sane, thirty-something woman suddenly get a piercing?

James gave Frank a small bottle. "Just have her dab it with this antiseptic regularly for a week then it should be okay. If she has any discomfort, she should call me and I'll come by and have a look." He gave Frank a card.

"Great. Thanks." Frank took a wad of cash from his pocket and peeled off a few bills, handing them over.

James nodded and pocketed the money. He unfastened Janet and both men helped her out. They made her stand in front of them posing while they commented on the gold ring. When she looked down, it did look very nice. But she still worried how she would explain it.

James folded up the chair and tucked it under one arm. With his toolkit in the other, he nodded his goodbyes and left. Frank approached her and began to fondle her body, kissing her neck and cheek, telling her how proud he was of her. She felt a little light-headed.

Within minutes there came a knock on the door. "That must be him now," he said. "Would you answer it please?"

"I can't! I'm naked!"

"Oh pshaw. He's seen you naked."

"But what if it isn't him?"

"That's what peepholes are for."

Janet felt foolish. She went to the door and peeked through. It was George. She opened it, using the door as a shield for her nudity.

"Well, hi, Janet! I've been looking forward to seeing you again."

She blushed and said, "Look, about the other day…"

"Janet! Are you being rude to our guest?"

"No! It's just that…"

"Come in, George! Janet just can't seem to stay out of trouble! And just when she was doing so well."

George came in and stood there, unabashedly ogling her naked body. "Wow! I love the jewelry! Did you just get that?"

"Yes," she said in a small voice.

"Go ahead, touch it," Frank said.

"No! It's just not right."

"But you promised," George said, looking forlorn.

"That's all right," Frank put in. "You can spank her instead."

Janet's head came up and she stared at Frank. "What?"

"You heard me. If you don't want to let him touch you like you did the other day, then you must be punished."

He took her to the couch and made her drop over the arm. George took the riding crop out of the drawer of the side table and stood behind her. It was all moving too fast. Janet didn't have time to think.

Whack!

"Ow!" He was hitting her hard today!

Whack!

"Please! Frank! Sir?"

Whack!

"All right! All right! He can touch me!"

"He's going to want another blowjob too," Frank said.

Whack!

"Okay! Okay! Just please stop!"

They pulled her upright. She felt woozy and needed Frank to steady her. George came close and Janet stood still, her cheeks aflame. She felt his fingers fondling her and was more embarrassed when she realized how wet she was.

He touched the ring but spent more time on her wet slit, running his fingers up to her clit to coax it from its sheath of skin. She closed her eyes.

"Spread your legs for me, slut," George said, and she found herself obeying.

His fingers probed deeper, eliciting a moan from her. She felt Frank behind her, helping to prop her up as George's fingers dug into her. Her wetness was spread up and down and his fingers teased her clit again and again.

She leaned back against Frank and allowed the man to have his way with her. After all, she told herself, she had promised. And it felt so good. He brought her closer and closer. Her mouth dropped open.

Just before she let herself go, he pulled away and unzipped his pants. She was so close! But she knew what she needed to do if she wanted to climax. Without another word from Frank, Janet dropped to her knees and took his huge cock into her mouth. She struggled to get it in and used her hands to pump the shaft. She heard Frank encourage her and she managed to take more into her throat this time. She wanted to please Frank so she gave it her best effort. She didn't think about how this might look or what it might mean. Her job was simply to please this man.

She heard his voice rise up as she pumped and knew he was close. Janet redoubled her efforts and suddenly George grabbed her head, holding her still. She felt his seed shoot into her mouth and she swallowed automatically. For a few minutes, he held her in place.

"That was wonderful. Now come on, I'll finish you off." He pulled away.

She wanted to lie on the couch but the men didn't let her. She stood again and leaned back against Frank's broad chest while George's fingers found her sensitive spot. He rubbed and she allowed herself to drift, living within the sensations. She could still taste him on her tongue and it made her feel naughty. Her orgasm approached and it surprised her. Was she so easy now? Her mouth dropped open and she shuddered with the climax.

George's fingers left her and she felt them at her mouth. She opened automatically and cleaned his fingers, tasting herself.

"That was great, Janet. I'll see you next week then?" She found herself nodding, imagining him coming over regularly for her to tease him to a climax and for him to stroke her to one in exchange. Would it be so bad?

George left.

"My turn," Frank said, and went to the couch and sat down. Janet came to him, feeling strange, as if it weren't her body that was obeying. She unbuckled his pants and eased his cock out. It was so big and hard! She took it into her mouth and loved it. She could tell he was getting close when he stopped her.

"I want to fuck you," he said, and turned to lie on the couch, his cock a spear pointed at the ceiling. She grinned and climbed over him, pulling her labia apart and aiming his hard cock into her core. The ring felt heavy against her fingers and she wondered again how she might explain it to Bill.

Once she pressed down, all thoughts of her husband vanished and Janet threw her head back, allowing the pleasure to begin. She rode him wildly, thinking about James' fingers on her, George's cock and Frank's monster inside her. They rode together and when she felt him erupt, she came hard, collapsing onto his chest.

When it was time for her to go, Frank gave her the small bottle of antiseptic. Then he pressed two hundred and fifty dollars into her hands. "It's payday today," he said, grinning at her.

She looked at the money. Did this make her a whore? She shook her head and left, grabbing the robe and pulling it tight around her before she headed out to her car.

Chapter Eleven

ꙮ

"What did you do to yourself?" Bill was staring at her gold ring, his eyes wide. They were in bed, Friday night. It was all an act. Frank had been sure to alert Bill to Janet's new jewelry and had showed him the tape. She tried to hide it with her panties but Bill had "insisted" they make love.

"You like? I did it for you, dear," she lied, smiling sweetly.

"Yeah, I do. But, well, it's not exactly something I'd expect from you, is it?"

"I know. But our sex life has gotten into a bit of a rut, you know, and I thought this might spice it up some."

"Wow. That's great. But where did you get it done?"

"Uh," Janet realized she hadn't seen James' card so she had no idea where he worked. "Just a little place near the dress shop. I did it on a whim during my lunch hour."

"Was the, um, piercer a man or a woman?"

Janet's eyes darted away. "Uh, a man."

"So you walked into some shop and let a stranger stare at your naked pussy? Especially now that you've started shaving it and everything."

"Yeah, I did. He was very professional." The image of James' thick fingers fondling her private parts came to mind.

"Huh. I just never would have imagined that from you." He shook his head. "But it's real sexy. I like it. Come here, you." He grabbed her ass with both his hands as he positioned himself against her wet slit. Seemed she was always wet now, he noticed.

Janet grimaced and he saw it. "What's wrong? I haven't even put it in yet."

"Uh, it's nothing. I'm just a little sore is all."

"Oh! Of course. I'm sorry. I should've known that! Does that mean we can't make love?"

"No, but it's better if you do it from behind for now." She turned over on the bed and slipped a fat pillow under her hips. That brought her still slightly reddened ass into view.

Bill knew he could make an issue of it and she would be hard-pressed to explain why. But Frank had cautioned him that it was too early to confront her.

"We need to bring her innate submissiveness to the forefront for a while longer before we allow you to 'find out' about her secret life," he had said. "Otherwise she could retreat from both of us."

Bill had agreed so he said nothing and pretended not to notice. Slipping into her, he reached around to rub her clit, careful not to touch her ring, trying to make her orgasms as powerful as the ones he had seen on the tape. But again, when he climaxed inside her, her pleasure seemed weak and pale in comparison to those he had seen on the tapes. Bill was determined to make her shudder with release like Frank did.

* * * * *

"I've got to tell her, you know," Bill was informing Frank Monday morning. "I feel like a cad. This is my wife after all."

"I know. But you do understand that she has to separate the two of us in the beginning or this never would work."

"Yeah, I know. She sees me as this boring old guy she married. I'm sure she has no idea I am into the idea of her becoming submissive."

"I think you are more excited by seeing her with other men—in a safe environment of course."

"Yeah, I guess so. It's all mixed up in my mind. I like seeing my wife in this sexy new way. I just have to get her to understand that what we did wasn't some horrible trick we've played on her."

"It could be awkward. She might be angry at us both."

"Yeah."

"Working on our side, though, is how she is reacting to her new submissiveness. She's a natural. I know it probably scares her but she really seems to be enjoying it."

"I can tell from the videos."

"And you aren't jealous? That's a big sticking point."

"No, because I made it happen. I mean, I allowed you to make it happen. I could've said no. But I was curious. You told me she was submissive and I didn't believe it. Now I see what you mean but I'm not sure how we join the two parts together. I don't want to scare her away."

"No, I agree. I'm very fond of your wife. I'd hate to let her go."

Bill paused, tapping his fingers together in front of him. He looked at the ceiling for a moment. "Well, I wanted to talk about that."

"Yeah?"

"I think we both know that I'm not a dominant. I try, but I'm just not there. I'm more of a voyeur or a 'nice guy'—you know, that fatal flaw in some men."

"It's not a bad thing."

"No, of course not. I only mean when it comes to someone like Janet, well, she's always going to be drawn to someone like you. I'm safe. You're dangerous. It's clear she likes going to see you but coming home to me where no one is challenging her. You understand?"

"Yes, I can see that." Frank paused. "So you're suggesting we could become a tag team so to speak?"

"Yes, that's what I was thinking. At least until I learn how to become more dominant."

"You could learn as we go. Right now, she sees you as a little too safe, if you don't mind my saying."

"I know. That's why I thought this might work. But if she freaks out when we tell her, well, then I fear everything will end."

"That would sadden you, wouldn't it? You're excited about this."

"Aren't you?" Bill asked.

"Yeah, I am."

"So how are we going to do it?"

"I don't know yet. Let's just take it slow, okay?"

* * * * *

The following Tuesday morning, Janet was outside Frank's apartment at ten o'clock, just as he had ordered. It was odd, coming from her ordinary life over to the excitement that Frank offered. It was as if she were a secret agent.

She hung her robe on the hook, slipped off her shoes and stood naked twitching, looking around for anyone who might walk by. She hated these moments and yet they put her in the right frame of mind for Frank's world. His world excited her.

She heard a whistling behind her and she turned in time to see a man walking a dog along the pathway between the buildings. She froze, not able to move enough to grab her robe. He stopped and stared, and his dog, a German shepherd, barked.

At that moment, Frank opened the door. Janet scurried inside, breathing hard.

"That was wonderful," he said, giving her a big hug. "I really enjoyed seeing you show off your body."

"God! He might call the cops!"

"I doubt that very much. That's just another neighbor, Martin Campbell. But I'm sure he'll start walking by my door regularly from now on."

Janet was embarrassed yet her pussy throbbed. Did she secretly like men staring at her naked body? What was happening to her? Hadn't this started out as simple blackmail?

"Come. Today I have new plans for you."

Janet's stomach lurched but she followed him into the living room. There on the couch was an outfit. Sort of. A blue miniskirt and a plain white blouse. A pair of black sandals lay on the floor.

"Wh-What's this?"

"Your outfit. We're going out."

"Out? Out where?"

"But first, before you put those on, you need to be reminded of your place."

"What?"

He grabbed her and pushed her over the arm of the couch. Taking the crop from the end table, he spanked her several times on her bottom as she squealed and jerked.

"What? What did I do wrong?"

"You've been questioning me again. Plus, you never once called me 'Sir'."

"I'm sorry! I'm sorry, Sir!"

He let her up. She rubbed her ass and looked at the red stripes he had left. Without another word, she began putting on the clothes. She stopped and looked around. "Sir, there's no underwear."

"That's right."

Nodding, she put on the skirt and pulled it up. It came to mid-thigh and she knew if she bent over, the red marks on her upper thighs would be seen. When she pulled the blouse over her breasts, she found it was a little tight. The buttons strained to close and her nipples poked hard against the material.

"Sir, this doesn't fit."

"I like the way it fits."

Janet sat down and put on the sandals. "May I ask where we're going?"

"No, you may not. Come." Frank led her to the door. She followed him out, her shoulders hunched. They got into his BMW. He took the freeway and drove her across town. She recognized the mall as soon as he took the exit. He was going to parade her in the mall dressed like this?

"Sir…"

"Shhh. Trust me. I'll protect you."

She sat nervously, looking around as he found a place to park. "Let's go."

"People are going to stare."

"Good. I like them looking at you."

She followed him, trying to use his body as a shield to her own. He took her inside and she glanced around, her head down, trying not to catch the looks of the other shoppers. But she could see some women frown while men often paused to smile at her. She hurried on.

Frank took her to a shoe store and made her sit down at the back of the establishment. Janet felt a little better being almost out of sight of the shoppers walking by.

"May I help you?" A good-looking urbane man, dressed in a pale blue sports coat and tan slacks, addressed his question to Frank. "I'm Charlie."

"Yes, Charlie. My girlfriend here needs some shoes."

The man looked down at Janet, his blue eyes glinting. "What would she like?"

"Black or dark blue pumps, I think. Tall heels."

He nodded. "Of course." He grabbed a stool and bent down to measure her foot. Janet gasped when she realized he would easily be able to see her naked pussy. She tried to keep her foot on the ground.

"Let Charlie measure you. How else are we going to know what size to get?"

Janet looked up and shot daggers at Frank. But she let the man take her by the ankle and raise her foot up. He held it there and took his time, fumbling with the foot scale, his eyes never leaving her crotch. Finally he determined her size and placed her foot back down. He stood and turned to Frank.

"Nice." Then he turned and went into the back.

Frank winked at Janet. She colored and turned away.

Charlie returned, carrying two boxes. He put them down and sat on the stool. Again he took a foot and slipped the shoe on. The heels appeared to be at least three inches in height. He took his time, getting another look before he had the shoes on.

He stood and nodded to her. Janet stood and tried to walk. The heels were higher than anything she was used to and it was hard to stay balanced.

"Walk back and forth for me," Frank said. "I want to see how they look."

She did, feeling all eyes on her. She knew her ass was wiggling as she moved away from them—she couldn't help it. It had been years since she had last worn heels like this.

"Good. I like those. Let me see the other ones."

Janet returned and sat down. Charlie opened the other box, showing Frank the blue pumps with a heel that appeared to be even higher. She noticed Charlie deferred to Frank, not to her. More evidence of his dominant personality.

Charlie slipped the blue shoes on, getting another look at her nakedness under her skirt. These shoes were even harder to walk in. She worried she might turn an ankle. Bravely she strode back and forth, trying to maintain her balance until Frank was satisfied. She felt a rush of emotions run through her. Quickly she covered the heat she felt by sitting down and putting her sandals back on.

"I like them both. But I was only planning to purchase one pair," Frank told Charlie. "Maybe we could work out a deal?" He waved his hand at Charlie and the two of them walked to a far corner of the store.

Janet paled. She watched as the two men talked, wondering what Frank was offering. She worried she might be asked to give this strange man a blowjob and she couldn't possibly do that!

But why not? she asked herself. *Didn't you suck George?* Why was he doing this to her? Didn't he want her to himself?

They returned. Janet's heart beat loudly in her chest.

"Come," Frank said.

She rose on shaky legs and followed Frank into the back of the store, Charlie right behind her. In between rows of shelving, Frank stopped and turned to face her. "Charlie said we could have half off the second pair if you'd let him masturbate you to an orgasm or he'd give the second pair free if you'll blow him. What would you prefer?"

Janet's mouth dropped open, yet part of her was pleased that Frank was giving her a choice. "Masturbate me," she said at once. She turned to face Charlie. She felt Frank come up close and grab her shoulders.

She leaned back against him and spread her legs. Charlie stepped in close, his breath coming more quickly, the sweat beading on his scalp. His fingers reached underneath her dress and she realized she was quite wet. He gasped when he touched her ring.

"Gosh, you're really wet."

"For you, Charlie, just for you," she breathed, for she knew that would please Frank.

He began to rub and soon found the rhythm, moving his middle finger up along her slit to her clit and back again. Her mouth fell open and her breath quickened. Her legs grew weak and she was grateful Frank was holding her or she might've collapsed.

Charlie's free hand came up and unbuttoned her blouse. She almost spoke up but felt Frank's grip on her arms tighten and knew that he had approved. Her breasts spilled into view and the salesman's hand stroked her nipples. The other one quickened between her legs.

"Oh, oh, oh!" she gasped as she felt the orgasm approach. She felt strange, as if she were looking down on herself from above, watching this slut get masturbated by the sales clerk, her breasts exposed. Why did she allow this?

Suddenly she was up and over the peak and she gave a little cry, sagging into Frank's arms. Charlie held his fingers tight to her spasming cunt. Reluctantly he let her go and stood back.

"Thanks, that was well worth it," he said, licking his fingers of her juices. "Sure you don't want one pair free?"

Janet saw the bulge in his pants and shook her head. She quickly refastened her blouse and adjusted her skirt, pulling it down as low as she could. Her pussy squished with her wetness.

"No, I think that's enough. You heard the lady. Wrap them up."

"Um, may I have a tissue?" Janet asked.

Frank shook his head. "No, I like you like this."

They came out into the lights of the store. Janet could see the eyes of the other customers and salesman on her. She flushed with embarrassment.

Frank paid for the shoes and they left. She hoped they were done but Frank had other ideas.

"Come, let's go in here," he said, pointing to a Victoria's Secret. She groaned inwardly.

The well-dressed female clerk with blonde hair up in a bun tried to hide her surprise when she saw the too-tight blouse with no bra. Her eyes dipped down to take in the skirt and she pursed her lips in disapproval.

"As you can see, my girlfriend is in need of a good bra," Frank said cheerfully.

Janet felt the blood rush to her head.

"Of course." She turned to Janet. "What kind were you looking for?"

She wanted to say, *Big, like grandma's!* but knew Frank would be the one to decide. She looked over at him.

"I think something that lifts and presents, like a demi cup," he said, smiling at the clerk.

The blonde nodded in understanding. She had probably seen lots of men bring in their wives and girlfriends for such games. She gestured for the two to follow her and she came to a display of very sexy bras and panties.

"We have these demi bras and some quarter bras," she said, smiling. The bras were hardly there. Instead of covering her, they would put her nipples on display.

Frank looked through several and picked out a few he liked.

"And how about matching panties? Would you like to see those too?"

"No, I prefer her without panties," he responded.

Janet wished the floor would open up and swallow her. The blonde saleslady flashed her a knowing smile, as if to say, *Aren't you lucky?* Janet didn't feel lucky, yet she couldn't deny how turned on she was. She wanted Frank's cock in her in the worst way. She couldn't help but smile at her own joke—*I mean in the best way*, she corrected herself.

"Do you know your true size?"

"Well, uh, I'm a 36C."

"Most women choose the wrong bra size. I can measure you to be sure."

"That would be great," Frank put in.

The clerk led them to a row of dressing cubicles and gestured to the one at the far end, up against the wall. None of the others seemed to be in use. Frank followed Janet inside. It was big enough for them but the clerk had to stand outside.

She held on to the door. "Now just take off your blouse and I'll measure you."

Janet paled. "But people might see!"

The clerk laughed. "I thought that was the whole idea!"

Janet shot a glance at Frank and shrugged off her blouse. She stood there in the cubicle with only the saleswoman blocking the view of her breasts. She came close and used a tape measure on her, tugging and pulling to make sure she had it right. Janet was sure she could smell the scent of her recent encounter with the shoe salesman.

"Hmm. Looks more like a 38C," she said, stepping back. "I'll get some in the right sizes." She left.

Janet closed the door and faced Frank. "Why are you embarrassing me so? I could get arrested!"

He laughed. "I doubt it. It pleases me to display you. And I know deep down you like it too."

"No! I'm mortified! This isn't like me."

He reached between her legs and scooped up some of her wetness then showed it to her. "I think you're enjoying yourself enough, don't you?"

Before she could reply, the saleslady came back and Janet straightened, covering her breasts with her hands.

"Here we go. Try this on." She handed over a wispy strapless bra all in cream with an underwire. Janet put it on and found it supported her breasts from underneath, her nipples pointing out like bullets amid the lacy edge.

"Oh my," she said. "That's a bit much, don't you think, Frank?"

He frowned at her. "Oh no, I like it."

The saleslady beamed. "Good. I think you'll like this one too."

It was a black-strapped version that left even less to the imagination. Her breasts cantilevered out from her chest, her nipples erect. Janet could tell from Frank's expression that it was just what he was looking for.

"Great, I'll take them both."

"Would you like her to wear one?"

"The cream, I think," Frank said. He watched as the saleslady fastened the first bra around her. Janet quickly put on her blouse. With the extra support, her nipples appeared ready to burst through.

"I think her blouse is a bit tight. But I suppose you like it that way?" the clerk inquired.

Frank nodded and gave her a wink.

After paying for their purchases, they left. Janet hunched her shoulders and followed Frank quickly out of the store. She hoped they were done. He stopped suddenly.

"How's your ass?"

"What? Uh, it's fine." She remembered the whipping he had given her but it no longer hurt.

"Well, you're in for more. You haven't said 'Sir' to me once since we got here."

Her mouth went into an O. She'd been so distracted by the embarrassments she had suffered, she had forgotten. Now her ass burned as if she could feel the crop again. "I'm sorry, Sir."

"Too late." He herded her into a dress shop where rock music blared. He went straight to the rack where several miniskirts were on display. As he was flipping through them, a tough-looking young female clerk came over.

"Help ya?" She had dyed black hair with a purple highlight and a silver ring in her nose.

"Yes, I think so. My girlfriend needs a new miniskirt."

The clerk gave Janet the once-over, raising an eyebrow in surprise. "Are you sure that's the right style for her?"

Janet felt deeply offended but said nothing.

"You think she's too old for a miniskirt?"

The clerk stared at the blue one she had on. "Well, maybe not. She does have good legs." The tip of her tongue touched her upper lip.

"She does, doesn't she? Let's try on these two," Frank said, pulling out a black one and a red one. "I think this is her size."

The clerk took them and led the two back to the dressing rooms. As they walked, Frank whispered to Janet, "If you can make her rub your pussy, I'll reduce your punishment."

Janet's eyes went wide. "How?" she whispered back.

Frank shrugged. He paused outside the rooms and let the clerk lead Janet inside. He winked at her as she went by.

In one of the stalls, the clerk handed Janet the two skirts and said, "I'll leave you here to try them on—"

"No! Wait."

The clerk paused, confused.

"Uh, what's your name?"

"Claire."

"I couldn't help but notice your nose ring," she went on hurriedly. "I just had a ring installed myself and I wondered if you'd like to see it."

Claire raised an eyebrow and gave Janet's body a quick once-over as if she were trying to spot it. "Where?"

"Here," she said, unsnapping her skirt and letting it fall. When the clerk saw she wasn't wearing panties, her eyes bulged. Then she spotted the gold ring nestled amid the folds of skin and her mouth dropped open.

"Wow," she said, staring at it. "That's real pretty."

"It's okay. You can get a closer look."

Claire bent down and looked this way and that. "Did it hurt?"

"Not too much."

The clerk made a face. "You're kinda wet, you know that?"

"I know. Frank—my boyfriend—made me come out today without panties and it always gets me excited."

Claire looked up at Janet. "You're lucky."

"Don't you have a boyfriend?"

"Uh, no." She licked her lips.

"Do you like it?"

The girl jerked. "Huh?"

"The ring."

"Oh yeah. It's pretty." Janet could see her fingers twitch.

"Go ahead, you can touch it."

"Really?"

"Sure." She spread her legs for the girl.

Claire reached out and tugged at the ring. She admired how it looked, so shiny and heavy. "I may have to get one someday," she breathed.

Janet enjoyed how her gentle fingers tickled her throbbing pussy. "Could…could you do me a favor?" she whispered.

Claire's eyes never left the gold ring. "What?" she whispered back.

"I'm so horny. My boyfriend's got me on edge. Would you—?"

"What? What do you want me to do?" She played with the ring and allowed her fingers to slip past it, touching her hot skin.

"Yes, that's it. Just rub it a little. Please?"

"Well, sure," she said, as if that were the most common request she heard from her customers. Claire's fingers began to slide up and around, drawing more moisture from her. Janet leaned back against the wall and spread her legs. Claire moved closer until they were face-to-face. Only her hand moved as they stared into each other's eyes.

Claire found her rhythm and stroked Janet's pussy from back to front, making sure to tease her clit only briefly. Janet nodded, her mouth open, encouraging the younger woman to continue.

"You like it like this, slut? You like my fingers in your pussy, rubbing your wetness, making you weak?"

"Yes, yes," Janet said, rising to another orgasm.

"You like to show off your tits and your cunt for me?"

"Yesss."

"Unbutton your blouse. Show me."

Janet's hands flew up and the buttons parted.

"I like the way your nipples are exposed," Claire said, her finger moving rapidly, watching Janet's face. "I'm going to suck on them."

Janet could only nod, her voice gone. Claire bent down and sucked a fat nipple into her mouth and Janet went over the edge. She gasped and bit her lip to keep from screaming. Her climax took the strength out of her knees and she buckled, sliding down to sit on the narrow bench, her legs splayed apart.

"Oh god!" she said. "Oh my god!"

Claire smirked. "You liked it?"

"Oh my yes." She glanced over her shoulder to see Frank there, peering through a crack in the door. He opened it a bit wider and gave her the okay sign. Then he left. Claire remained unaware. Janet quickly buttoned her blouse.

It took Janet a few minutes to compose herself then she tried on one of the skirts. Frank was called back and he nodded his approval. No mention was made by Claire or Janet what had taken place a few minutes before. And yet when it came time to try on the other skirt, neither Frank nor Claire left and Janet was forced to strip in front of them. She was more embarrassed by her increased wetness than being naked, she noticed. She wished she had a tissue.

When Frank was satisfied with the skirts, Claire talked him into a new blouse. "You can't possibley want your girlfriend to walk around in that too-tight number," she told him. "Let her have a little dignity."

He laughed and agreed with her. Claire found a nice salmon-colored blouse that went well with the blue skirt so she wore that outfit out of the store. At least it covered her better. When they were outside, Frank turned to her.

"You did very well. You escaped most of the punishments."

"Most, Sir?" She was hoping it would be all.

"Yes, I would still like to crop your sweet ass a few times, just because I enjoy it so."

Janet smiled. "Very well, Sir."

They headed back to the car carrying their purchases.

Chapter Twelve

ЅЭ

"You're kidding me."

"No, I'm serious," Frank said. It was Wednesday afternoon and he was giving Bill a recap of Janet's latest adventures.

"I wish I had a video of that!" Bill shook his head, thinking about his wife being masturbated twice—*twice!*—by strangers at the mall.

"That might've been awkward!" They both laughed.

"Well, I want to join in now. I want her to do that for me."

"Um, I still think it's too soon. But I have some ideas on that, if you're willing to wait awhile longer."

"Yeah? What?"

"I'm getting her to accept the intimate touch of strangers. But she's still embarrassed and a little ashamed by it. I want her to get to the point that she'll do anything I say as long as she knows I'm there to protect her."

"Yeah, I see that. But what more do you need to do? Isn't she ready already?"

"No. She hasn't quite let go yet. I'm sure she still feels some remorse over her actions, even though she did them at my behest. She's come a long way but she's not where I think she should be before she can overcome the shock of seeing you there." He pointed a finger at Bill. "Besides, you need to work on becoming more dominant. Otherwise, she won't be able to handle the two worlds colliding."

"I know, I know. I'm working on it. How much more time do you need?"

Frank thought about that. He wanted to take as long as possible. He so enjoyed having Janet all to himself. And yet he knew he couldn't delay Bill much longer. "Give me until the end of next week. Friday. That will give me another four or five sessions with her. I hope that will be enough."

"That long?" He grimaced his disappointment. Then he shrugged. "Okay. I defer to your expertise. But I want to see more videos, all right?"

"All right. I'll do what I can. It's difficult to videotape her when we're out in public."

"You think that's wise, really? Having her out like that? What if she gets arrested?"

"I'm being careful. I don't want to ruin this deal any more than you do."

* * * * *

"Hi, honey, I'm home." Bill came in and kissed his wife.

"How was your day?" Janet tried to fight the wave of guilt that washed over her every time she saw her husband now. Thankfully she had showered and changed her clothes after her recent outing with Frank.

"Good. Same ole, same ole. Haven't heard any more news about layoffs so that's good."

Janet was tired of hearing about layoffs. It brought home to her just how this whole mess had started. She never would have agreed to fuck Frank and therefore she never would have known about the type of orgasms she'd been missing out on. She could've lived her ordinary little life in peace.

Now it was difficult to go back to the boring old sex that Bill offered. He was sweet and all, but her body was left unsatisfied by the minor tremors she received from sex with him. Why couldn't he be more like Frank?

She pulled away and went into the kitchen. Bill followed her. "So what did you do today?"

"Uh, nothing. Worked at the shop."

"Get any more jewelry installed?" He winked at her and she blushed.

"No! That was a one-time treat." *I hope so anyway*, she thought. How would she explain nipple rings?

"Aww, too bad. You know I love it."

"Well, I'm glad you do. But don't get too excited."

"I want to take you to that shop and have some other jewelry installed," he said forcefully.

She looked up, startled. "What?"

"Yes. I'd like to see maybe a gold ring right above your clit. I hear that if you can get a heavy little ring to rest right on your clit hood, it can cause a lot of erotic sensations all day as it bounces around."

Janet stared at him. "You'd want me to do that?"

"Yes. I like the idea of you aroused all day, waiting for me to come home and relieve the itch." He came closer and found her nipples were trying to burst through her bra and blouse. He pinched one through the material. "Or maybe a nice set of nipple rings."

She colored and leaned back against the counter. "That…that's not really like you, is it?"

"Sure it is. I know I've been this boring and quiet guy but I have my secret fantasies too. When you got that ring, it made me think about what I've been missing."

His hand went down to her slacks and he rubbed her gently. "I'll bet I'm making you wet just thinking about it."

"I, uh, I don't know. Maybe." She tried to sidle away but he held her.

"You know what I would like tonight?"

"I can guess!"

"Well, that too. But I'd like you to make my dinner naked with just an apron on." He left her frozen there, her mouth ajar, and went to the drawer, pulling out one. "This would be perfect." It said *Kiss the Cook*. He held it out.

She didn't move. "You can't be serious."

"Oh I'm serious, all right. If you can let a stranger see your bare pussy while he installs a ring, you can cook dinner for your husband naked."

She took the apron and looked from it to Bill and back again. "This is so unexpected." She started to head into the bedroom.

"Oh no! You strip right here. Hand me your clothes. I'll make sure they are taken care of."

Janet shook her head as if she couldn't believe what she was hearing. Suddenly Bill was acting like Frank? She found herself falling into her submissive mode—she couldn't help it. But it surprised her that it was Bill giving the orders.

She unbuttoned her blouse and handed it over. Her bra followed. She started to put on the apron to cover herself but Bill tsked and pointed to her pants. She unzipped them and slipped them off. He took and draped them over his left arm. Dressed only in her panties, she pressed her hands to them and begged, "Can't I keep these?"

"No. Naked." He waggled his fingers at her and she shucked them off.

"I do like this new look," he said, touching her smooth mound over her shiny ring.

"You do?"

"Oh yeah."

He took her clothes into the bedroom while she quickly put the apron over her nakedness. When he came back, she was at the counter, chopping vegetables, her cute peach-shaped ass exposed. He came close and rubbed her bottom. She wiggled it and tried to get away. He grabbed her and pulled her tight to him so she could feel his hard cock against her.

"Now, now, you're going to ruin dinner!"

"Oh yeah, the hell with dinner." He pushed her up against the counter and unzipped his pants.

"Bill! This isn't like you!"

"It is now," he said. He used his knee to pry her legs apart. His cock found her wet slit. Aiming carefully, he pressed himself into her.

"God, Bill!"

He fucked her hard and fast up against the counter. When he came, she gasped with the shock of it. This was more like Frank than Bill! When he pulled back, she looked flustered.

"I have to cook," she said, and went to work, chopping vegetables with a vengeance. Bill laughed and retreated to a stool to watch her cute butt wiggling.

* * * * *

Frank called Janet on Thursday and told her to meet him at six o'clock at his apartment. Six?

"Why so late? What am I going to tell Bill?"

"I don't know. That's up to you. Wear one of the outfits I bought you. No panties. Don't be late."

Janet hung up the phone and worried. This was the first time he had wanted to meet at night. What was that about? Would he take her out to embarrass her further? Or was he planning to have someone come over—someone who could only be there at night?

She shivered and wondered what excuse might work with Bill. She worried about it all day. He'd been acting so funny lately! That business last night with the apron. That was more like something Frank might do! What had gotten into him? She couldn't understand it.

In the end, Janet decided simply to leave Bill a note. He usually arrived home at five-thirty so if she left a little early, she could avoid any nervous lies she might have to tell.

She showered and shaved carefully, making sure she was smooth. She knew if she didn't, some stranger would be down there pawing at her, and she'd have to suck him off as his reward. She put on the cream-colored bra, the salmon blouse, the black mini-skirt and her new black heels. Underneath, her pussy was naked to the world.

She penned *Gone to the movies with Joyce, be back later* and left the note on the kitchen table. Joyce was an old friend whom she hadn't seen in a while so Bill would probably buy it.

She left the house at five-twenty and drove to Frank's apartment but didn't park in front. Instead, she parked at the far end of the lot and simply waited. When it was five 'til, she drove up and parked closer.

She was very nervous when she rang the doorbell. What in the world would he do to her today? He opened it at once and smiled at her. "Hello, Janet." He was dressed in slacks, a blue shirt and a sports coat.

"Hello, Sir." He stepped aside and let her in. She looked around the living room but there was no one there. She waited, her eyes questioning him.

"I thought I'd take you out to dinner."

Her heart melted. So that's all it was! "Well, thanks, that's nice of you."

"There's just one little twist."

Her stomach twisted and her eyes grew wide. What now? Her pussy felt hot.

"I bought something for you." He went to the end table and opened the drawer. She feared he might bring out the riding crop but he pulled out a package. He brought it over to her.

"See? It's a remote-controlled vibrator."

She'd heard of such things but had never tried one. It was more kinky stuff from her kinky lover. Janet smiled. Frank looked so eager, like a kid at Christmas. He opened the box and brought out the toy. It was a cylinder about two inches in diameter and four inches long with a short wire that hung down from one end. He put in two small batteries and handed it to her.

"Here, this goes inside your pussy. And don't take it out until I tell you to."

She took it, feeling foolish. Did he really want her to put it there? Yes, he did, so she sat on the couch and spread her legs. The cylinder was made of smooth plastic except for at the end near the wire where it had a wide rubberized band. She had no idea why it was made this way. Janet caught Frank's eyes on her as she slid the device into her. She was wet so it fit easily, all except that part at the end. That took a bit of work. When she stood, she felt full. And she suddenly realized why it had that rubber band at one end. It was so her vaginal muscles could hold it in place. Otherwise, it might slip out onto the ground.

"Okay, it's in. Now what?"

Frank showed her the remote, which had four settings. He threw the switch to the first one and Janet felt a buzzing between her legs. A wave of pleasure rolled through her.

"Wow," she said.

He moved it to the next setting and the sensation increased in intensity. Her mouth came open and her breathing grew shallow. Janet grabbed the arm of the couch to steady herself.

"That's enough," she gasped.

"Well, let's just see what the others do, shall we?" He hit the third position and the sensations came and went as the device went on and off at regular intervals. It never gave her a chance to rest and she found it was worse than the second position. She actually felt as if she might climax right here and now.

"Oh god, Frank, I'm going to come!"

"Wait! Let's try this last one." He thumbed the button and the sensations suddenly cut out. For a moment she thought it was broken but then the buzzing started, a rolling motion that made her weak in the knees. It stopped then started again, more powerful than before. She sat down heavily on the couch and splayed her legs apart, her hands on her knees. It cut off, leaving her breathless. This last position of the switch was the cruelest for it came and went with no notice. One moment she was fine, the next she was gasping. And it wasn't regular so she could prepare. It was just random surges of pleasure that knocked her off her feet.

"Ohhh looks like we'd better save that for special occasions," Frank said, shutting it off. Janet gasped in relief.

"Y-You're not g-going to do that while we're at dinner, are you?"

"Well, sure. But I'll be careful. Wouldn't want you to climax in the middle of your baked potato!" He laughed.

He gathered up his keys and they went out.

In the car, Frank flipped it to the first position and Janet had to grab the armrest to maintain her sanity. And that was just the weakest setting! "Sir, I don't know if I can do this."

"You might come?" His eyes slid from the road to her.

She nodded.

"Well then, I'll have to be careful. But I do enjoy teasing you so."

"God, you're going to kill me." Secretly however, she had never felt so alive.

"By the way, what did you tell Bill?"

"Uh, that I was going out with a girlfriend to a movie. I just hope he doesn't check on me."

He nodded, a slight smile on his lips. "Okay, we're almost here so I'll give you a little break." He flicked off the remote and Janet sighed with relief.

The restaurant was upscale and Janet was pleased. With their constant worry about money lately, she and Bill would've been hard-pressed to afford something like this. The table wasn't quite ready so they went into the bar for a drink. Just as the waitress approached, Frank flicked on the device to the first setting.

Janet's mouth dropped open and she gripped the arms of the chair.

"May I get you something?" the perky blonde waitress asked. She didn't seem to notice Janet's discomfort.

"Yes, I'll have a martini on the rocks with a twist of lime. How about you, Janet?"

"Um." She bit her lip. "I'll have a…glass of white…wine."

The waitress nodded and left.

"Sir!" she whispered. "Please!"

"You don't like that setting? How about this one?" He flicked it to the second one. Janet's eyes bulged and her eyes immediately glazed over. She began breathing shallowly. The bar was too noisy to hear the vibrator working inside her so her actions seemed oddly out of place.

The waitress returned with a tray and Frank shut off the remote just as she approached the table. Janet blew out a breath. "Here you go," the server said cheerfully, setting the drinks down.

Janet took a big sip of her wine and stared daggers at Frank as he paid for the drinks. When the woman left, Janet leaned forward. "You're going to cause a scene!"

"I know—isn't it grand?" But he left the remote off for a while.

Frank excused himself to go to the restroom, giving her a chance to think.

Janet felt the heat of the moment and realized she had never had a man willing to play such wild sexual games before. Was she being a fool or had she been missing something in her life all these years? She wasn't sure. But she had to admit, she felt safe with Frank despite the risk. He took her to the edge but he made sure she never crossed over into real danger.

Frank returned just as their name was called and she stood, wondering if he would spark the vibrator as they walked to their table. Fortunately, he was being good and she made it safely. But as soon as she sat down, she felt the vibrator start up.

"Oh god!" she whispered, feeling the buzzing throb in her pussy. "I can't eat this way."

"Really?" He grinned. "This I gotta see."

"No, you can't!" She feared she might really climax in the middle of this crowded restaurant. She looked around, seeing all the other diners going about their business, not aware of the little drama being played out in front of them.

Fortunately at that moment, the buzzing ceased.

"All right, I'll let you pick." He grabbed the menu with both hands.

"Good," she said, picking up her menu. She read the choices and made her selections, stopping now and again to peek over the top and make sure Frank wasn't cheating.

As the swarthy waiter approached, Janet suddenly felt the vibrator start up again, this time at a higher setting. Wave after wave of pleasure rocked her. She glared at Frank, who had one hand in his coat pocket. "What are you doing?" she gasped. "You promised."

"I promised to let you read the menu. Now I'd like to see you order."

"Please," she begged. "I can't…" She squeezed her legs together hard just as the waiter arrived to ask what they'd like to order.

"Ladies first," Frank grinned. Janet groaned.

"Uh, I'll have..." she couldn't concentrate. All she could think about was the orgasm building in her body, causing her to flush with chagrin. "Oh god!" Her dam broke and she climaxed, her legs tightly held together, her teeth clenched as she tried to hide it. The waiter seemed alarmed. *He must think I'm having a seizure,* she realized.

As soon as the peak crested, she gasped out, "I'm okay!" She took a deep breath. "Just a cramp." Fortunately, the buzzing stopped. She shivered and took a sip of water. She glared at Frank who shrugged his innocence.

"Are you sure you're all right?" the waiter asked.

"Yes. Fine. Uh." She concentrated on the menu as she ordered.

The waiter looked at Frank as if to confirm what he saw. Frank shrugged again. He ordered and the waiter went away, shaking his head.

"That was horrible! I could've died from embarrassment!"

"No, I doubt that. It was fun, wasn't it?"

"No! It was too much. I feel like I'm on display."

Frank reached his hands across the table and took both of hers. "That's exactly what I want. You are a lovely, sexy woman and I want you on display."

"Why? Why do you like that so much?"

"It pleases me. You know how some men like to see their wives wear sexy outfits? Or flirt with other guys? It turns them on. Seeing you learn to live a little turns me on."

Janet couldn't believe how overly sexual Frank had become. Had he always been like this? She couldn't picture him with Mary—she had been so strait-laced. Perhaps he was letting himself go as well. They were exploring the dark side of their psyches together. She couldn't imagine Bill having a dark side like this. If he could see her now, he'd probably divorce her.

For a brief moment, she wondered if that would be so bad. Would Frank want her if she were single again? Could she stand it, being treated like a sex goddess all the time? She felt a little shiver run through her and decided, yes, maybe she could.

But of course she'd never leave Bill! She wasn't that kind of woman!

The game with the vibrator seemed to be over and Janet was grateful. They ate their dinner in peace and she tried to push the memory of herself climaxing in front of the waiter behind her. He must think she's a total slut! But her pussy wanted more. She felt like slapping it. And that brought on the image of her on the couch with George slapping her bare cunt with the riding crop. She closed her eyes.

"Something wrong?"

"No, nothing." She looked startled.

"You seem distracted."

"No, I'm okay. I, uh, just have to go to the restroom." She stood and excused herself.

The restroom was small, just two stalls, and appeared to be empty. As she sat on the toilet, she debated taking the vibrator out. Then she remembered Frank's order that she leave it in until he said so. Why was she so readily obeying him? Why did it give her such a thrill? She dressed and washed her hands, shaking her head and wondering where this would all end.

"Probably with the end of my marriage," she muttered.

She came out into the narrow hallway and was shocked to see Frank standing there—with the waiter.

"Hi," he said casually. "This is Omar, your waiter."

"What—?"

"I offered him a choice. A tip or to see you have another orgasm."

"You…you told him?" She couldn't believe it.

"Guess what he chose?" He grinned at her.

This was too much. "No, Frank, I can't."

"Of course you can. Remember, I will protect you. Now is there anyone in the restroom?"

"Uh, no…but really, I can't."

"Relax, he's not going to do anything George or the others haven't already done. You don't have to think about it. Just obey." He turned to Omar. "You know what the limits are, right?"

The waiter nodded, his dark eyes steady on Janet. "I thought I saw you come there at the table. Mr. Ramon said I could touch you, make you come for me."

Janet found herself in another place. It was as if her mind had left her body. She was looking down at herself, nodding dumbly. They pushed her back into the ladies' room. Frank stood by the door in case someone wanted to come in. Omar pressed her up against the sink. His hand went underneath her skirt and began to fondle her. She was so wet! She couldn't believe she was actually doing this. Part of her wanted to scream but she was so excited she said nothing. Her eyes met Frank's and they stared at each other as Omar's fingers rubbed her clit, bringing her to the brink. Her mouth came open and her breath caught in her throat.

"Oh no," she breathed, feeling another climax approach. How could this be?

"Rub his cock," Frank whispered, and Janet's hand went automatically to the waiter's pants. His cock was hard and threatened to burst out. "Unzip him," he ordered.

Janet nodded, her mind lost to the sensations in her pussy. She was being controlled like a puppet. Her fingers eased the zipper down and his cock sprang free.

"Rub him like he's rubbing you," Frank said, and she did. It felt so good to hold it. But it really felt good to have Frank watch her do it.

Her orgasm came like thunder upon her. She gasped and threw her head back as the wave broke and she cried out. Her hands fumbled on his turgid cock. She sagged against the sink and nearly lost her balance. Omar caught her.

Her embarrassment suddenly became acute. "Oh no!" She hid her face in her hands. She could smell Omar's musk and quickly pulled them away.

"Now look," Frank chided. "You've gotten him all hard but you're all done."

"What?" She looked down to see Omar's cock still straining red and purple beneath his olive skin.

"Go on, finish him."

"But, Frank…"

"Do it or there will be more punishments. Perhaps Omar would like to participate…"

Janet's hands went back to the waiter's cock, shocked that Frank might allow him to whip her. She pictured herself spread out on the couch, Omar staring at her naked body. No, no, no! It was better to end it here. Her hands began to move up and down, trying to milk his seed from him.

God, his cock was so nice! She found the angle was wrong so without thinking, Janet eased down to her knees and began to jack him off in earnest. His cock bobbed in front of her and she had a wicked thought. She could almost taste the cock head.

"Go ahead," Frank said.

"No…" she breathed. She wasn't about to suck on this stranger's cock. That was too much! But it surprised her that she wanted to.

Fortunately, the mood was broken when Omar gasped and streams of white began pumping out of his cock. She jerked back but it landed on her chin and neck. She let go and stood then turned and caught a glimpse of herself in the mirror. A slutty wife with ropes of semen on her face looked back. She felt suddenly ashamed. Janet grabbed several paper towels and began to clean up.

"Thank you, ma'am," the waiter said behind her. "You are wonderful." He zipped up and left.

Frank leaned over her shoulder. "Don't feel bad. That's exactly what I wanted you to do. In fact, I would've loved it more if you had sucked his cock."

She stared at him in the mirror, her face flushed, beads of sweat on her forehead. "Please, Sir, go away. I want to get cleaned up."

He nodded and disappeared through the door. She was left alone with her thoughts.

Chapter Thirteen

ꟓ

My god, what is happening to me? Janet sat in her bathroom, staring at her reflection. It was Friday morning and Bill had already left for work. He had been asleep when she'd gotten home and left early before they had a chance to talk. Janet was grateful, for what would they talk about? *I nearly allowed a stranger's cock into my mouth! And the worst part was, I wanted to do it!* Of course, she had already allowed George's cock into her mouth but somehow that was different. That had been Frank's neighbor, not some strange waiter!

Even now, the idea of sucking on that beautiful cock excited her. But she knew nothing about the man. He could be diseased or dangerous. She was being a fool! Then why did it cause her such excitement?

She wondered if this was how men felt most of the time. They could fuck anything. Was Frank releasing her inner slut? *Is that what I've become?* She wanted to talk to him about it. She was so confused.

The phone rang. Her stomach lurched and she both hoped and dreaded that it was Frank.

"Hello?"

"Hi, baby. How are you?" She closed her eyes.

"Frank, uh, Sir, last night…" She couldn't go on.

"I know. You're concerned. But relax. Don't worry so much. I was right there watching you, protecting you."

"But you didn't know anything about him! He could've been…well, dangerous."

"Well, of course I spoke with him before I brought him back there. I would never cause you harm."

"It was…risky."

"But you have to admit, you liked it, didn't you."

Janet said nothing, her mind whirling.

"I'd like you to come by today. But not until eleven. That should give you some time to recover."

Her pussy throbbed, but her voice said, "So soon? Please, Sir, don't make me do any more dangerous things."

He sighed over the phone. "If you knew that the person was perfectly safe and wouldn't cause you any problems, would you feel more comfortable?"

"You mean…" Did he want her to take another man's cock into her mouth…or pussy?

"Yes. I like being in control, watching you with other men."

"That's easy for you to say. You're not the married one."

"Come on, hasn't your marriage perked up lately? I can't believe this sexy new attitude of yours isn't rubbing off on Bill."

The mention of her husband's name made her feel guilty. "How would you know?"

"I don't. I'm just guessing."

"Well, it's none of your business." She had to admit that Bill did seem more interested in her. Fucking her up against the counter was brand-new behavior. Was she giving off vibrations?

"Be here at eleven," he said abruptly, and hung up.

She felt a twinge, arguing with him like that. She knew he would punish her. Her ass tingled and her pussy felt hot. His "punishments" opened her up to new pleasures. Once he spanked her, she would do just about anything. Would he bring George over? Or someone else?

For a moment, she imagined Omar's hard cock was in her hands again and she found her mouth had come ajar. She snapped it closed.

Eleven o'clock Janet was standing nude in his alcove, her robe hanging next to her, sandals below. She waited, trying not to think about anything. A jingle of a chain startled her and she turned to see the same man with the dog behind her on the sidewalk.

"Hi," Martin said. "Nice to see you again."

She blushed and turned away, offering only the view of her backside. He was not so easily deterred. He came up the walk and stood not five feet behind her. The dog pulled at his leash and nosed the crack of her ass. She jumped forward, nearly slamming into the door.

"Hey! Get your dog off me!"

"Sorry. I was just wondering why you're standing here nekkid."

She looked over her shoulder. "Go away!" She pounded on the door. "Frank!"

The door opened and the man made a hasty retreat. Frank smiled. "I like to see you getting to know the neighbors. I hope you weren't rude to Martin."

She rushed past him into the apartment. "God! Why do you do this to me?"

"Because it pleases me. But more importantly, it excites you." He stepped forward and ran the tip of his finger along her slit. She was dripping wet. "See?"

She blushed and turned away. Her body was betraying her. She looked around the room and saw, thankfully, that it was empty. Good. She wasn't sure she could take any more surprises.

"Come, sit down." He led her to the couch. "I thought I would explain some things to you."

"Yes?" She eyed him warily.

"I know you've been wondering why you've been feeling so…strange about the things we've done together." He gave her a small smile. "I mean, beyond the obvious cheating aspect."

Janet found herself nodding.

"It's simple really. I've been showing you the real person underneath your calm exterior."

"Oh yeah?"

"Yes. You're a submissive, Janet. It excites you no end."

Was she really? "You think so?"

"I'm sure of it. Look at you." His hand waved over her naked body. "You are so sexy right now. Coming over here and stripping down, doing what I ask of you—even sucking George's cock—it makes you feel alive, doesn't it?"

"I'm not sure 'alive' is the right word. More like 'embarrassed'." But she knew he had a point.

"No, I've seen your face, your eyes. This drives you wild. You can't hide it."

She shrugged. "I'm not sure I like all the sharing."

"Then why do you do it?"

She had no immediate answer. To say "because you asked me to" seemed too simplistic. She could recall, back when she was fifteen, she had briefly dated an athlete who was very popular. Brett had been seventeen and in the hierarchy of high school, a senior was a grizzled veteran compared to a naïve sophomore. Brett was strong and confident. Every time she had been in his presence, he had made her knees weak. He too had been dominant, she realized later. If he hadn't been so unskilled at it—ordering her around and generally being a jerk—she would've stayed with him. Though she found his personality ultimately repelling, she had been deeply excited by the sex-charged atmosphere he had created. She had wanted to be his little pet, although she hadn't been able to define it at that early age.

She had never found that thrill again in a relationship—or in a marriage. First David then Bill—both safe choices. Now

Frank was reawakening that naughty little girl again. And unlike Brett, Frank was a master of domination.

"I can't really say."

"Come on. You know. You've always known. This is who you are inside. This is why Bill seems so boring and I seem so, well…intriguing."

"Maybe so. But where do we go from here? Jail? Divorce court?"

"I'll keep you out of jail. I can't guarantee the other." He gave her a soft smile.

That stunned her. Was he really trying to steal her away from Bill? Was she so easily led? Even if she was, could she stand a life with Frank and all that it would entail?

"Frank, I'm not sure I'm ready for this 24/7. I mean, don't get me wrong, this has been…exciting." To say the least! "But I'm not ready to leave Bill for you."

"Of course not. At least not now. Maybe not ever. That's okay. I'm only giving you what you need. Where it goes from here depends on you—and Bill."

"Bill! You mean, if he found out?" She shook her head. "He'd probably kill me. Or you."

"I doubt it." Frank seemed to choose his words carefully. "Maybe Bill would be grateful for a man like me."

"What?"

"Think on it. He's clearly not a dominant personality yet you love him in your way. He's safe, right?"

Janet tipped her head, not willing to give it a full nod. But he was right of course.

"Whereas I'm…well, just how you put it earlier—risky. Dangerous. And sexy. Just what you need but won't admit to yourself."

"I admit it. I mean, part of it. I'm here naked, aren't I?" She hugged herself, feeling suddenly exposed.

He came close and put his arms around her. She closed her eyes and enjoyed the warmth of his embrace. She could just stay here forever, safe in his arms.

"Here's what I think," Frank went on. "I think Bill wouldn't be angry. In fact, I think he'd be excited."

"What? To know I've been fucking you? No way."

"Yes. Just a hunch, you know. But I think if you talked to him about his secret fantasy, it would be to see you with another man."

She pulled back. "That's so…weird. I can't see it." And yet Bill's comments of the other day filtered back into her mind. How he was excited with the thought of the man fondling her as he pierced her labia.

"That's because he'd be afraid of losing you. He probably thinks he could never find a woman like you ever again. But you see, he really shouldn't be with you. He should have a nice, church-going woman who bakes cookies for Greenpeace. You, on the other hand, need someone to awaken the sexy beast inside."

"Yeah, well, maybe I should just keep you both!" She laughed at her own joke and quickly realized Frank wasn't laughing with her. "That was a joke, Frank."

"I know. But sometimes our jokes have a ring of truth to them." He took her hand. "Come. I'm going to make beautiful love to you—after I spank your cute little ass." He dragged her to the bedroom. Janet went along willingly, her body trembling with excitement.

* * * * *

Janet thought a lot about what Frank had told her as she drove home, another two hundred and fifty in her purse. She didn't like taking the money—it made her a whore. Why did she ever agree to this arrangement? Did she even have to ask? Her pussy had been well fucked and her bottom still tingled from the spanking. He had been gentle with her today and in some ways she felt disappointed. Considering how surprisingly bold Bill had been the other night and how careful Frank had been today, it was as if their personalities were starting to meet in the middle. She wasn't sure she liked that.

It was far easier to keep the two men in her life completely separate. Let Bill be the nice guy and Frank the alpha male. She would happily bounce between them for months, years even. Hah! As if she could keep this charade up for years! No, she was headed for disaster, living on borrowed time.

She was sure Frank had just been gentle because of her confusion over her newfound submissiveness. Letting the waiter touch her like that had been so shocking. And exciting. She had to admit it to herself, even if she wouldn't to Frank. She trusted Frank and he took her places she'd never been. But did she really want to go there? Did she want to let other men fuck her? To be a slut, doing things she never would do if Frank hadn't made her? Would he make them pay her too?

Was that her secret fantasy? As if in response, her legs clutched together, squeezing her deliciously sore pussy.

Her mind returned to what Frank had said about Bill. That maybe he'd like to see her with other men. Did he know something she didn't? Could he tell that from working with Bill all these years? Maybe men gave off vibes that would indicate such things—vibes women couldn't see. Like a male intuition. They have "gay-dar", or so they say, why not some sort of radar about women's secret fantasies?

She grinned at herself. What a ninny! Bill could never be like that.

Could he?

Janet pulled into her garage, grateful that the return trip had been uneventful. To think a few months ago, if someone had told her she would soon be driving across town practically naked to meet a dominant lover who spanked her and showed her body off to strangers, she would've laughed it off.

She showered and dressed then puttered around the house, pretending to clean, but her mind was in turmoil. She had no idea how she might resolve the two halves of her personality or how Bill might react once he found out. If he found out. Janet felt it would be better if he never did.

At five-thirty, Bill arrived home and greeted her with a surprisingly passionate kiss at the door. She was pleased but a bit taken aback.

"How was your evening yesterday?" he asked.

"Fine. Cindy says hi."

"I thought you went out with Joyce."

Dammit! "Oh right. Sorry. Did I say Cindy?"

He smiled. "What movie did you see?"

She thought fast. "Uh, that new one with Brad Pitt. It wasn't very good."

Janet was glad she had showered before Bill came home. Otherwise Bill would've smelled his scent on her and would know she was cheating on him. Cheating on him…the words stung her. She had gone far beyond trying to save Bill's job. Now she knew she needed this for herself. Her pussy seemed to hum with pleasure. A well-fucked woman is a happy woman. And a submissive woman being spanked and fucked by a dominant man is a happier woman. Why couldn't Bill do those things? Was she just supposed to accept things the way they were? Could she go on as Frank's submissive little mistress and hope Bill didn't find out?

"You seem to be staring? Did something happen?"

She startled. "Uh, no. Nothing. Just girl talk." She went to move past him but he reached out and grabbed her arm.

"You, uh, look really pretty tonight," he said, his eyes watching her face for her reaction.

She smiled, tentatively. "Oh? Thanks."

From his expression, Janet realized he was at a loss for things to say. He let go of her arm and she continued into the bedroom. She felt sorry for him. She could tell he was interested in her and yet she would have to turn him down. He might notice her sore pussy or reddened ass and discover her secret. She remembered the other night when Bill had demanded she wear only an apron to cook his meal—that had been so unlike him! It had made her wet and their lovemaking had been exciting. Why couldn't he be like that all the time?

* * * * *

For Bill, standing in the living room, staring at the empty hallway, he felt lost. Knowing Janet had recently had sex with Frank made him hard yet he couldn't seem to keep up the dominant style. It wasn't in him. He remembered he had acted that way after coming fresh from Frank's office where he had been filled in on Janet's latest adventures. It had excited him. He had to face it—he was a pale imitation of Frank. Fact was, he needed Frank. But his boss might wind up stealing Janet away if he wasn't careful. What would hold her to him except loyalty? It's not as if they were getting along well lately. Their sex life was boring and they didn't have much to talk about. Was their marriage doomed?

Bill realized the only way he could avoid being replaced was to be Frank's assistant in all the things Janet needed as a submissive. He wanted to learn but he knew he also needed Frank's strength to dominate her. He'd have to share. That was better than the alternative, but would it be fine with Frank? Or Janet?

She was going to find out anyway, why not tonight? Or would he ruin things? She might be shocked and react badly, ruining it for both of them. No, he decided, he would wait until he could talk to Frank. That made him shake his head—here he was, deferring to the alpha male yet again. It was as if he had been born this way—a nice guy but no womanizer.

And certainly no dominant. He had always considered himself respectful of women. Was that just another way of saying he was a wimp?

He sighed and flipped on the television.

Chapter Fourteen

ଌ

Bill corralled Frank in his office shortly after nine, Monday morning. Frank was startled to see him. He was still seated behind his desk.

"What brings you up here—aren't you supposed to be monitoring the milling project?"

"Yes, I'm going down there in a second. I just had to talk to you first—it's about Janet."

Frank raised an eyebrow. "Yes?" Had Bill spilled the beans?

"Well, I..." he looked away. "I'm not sure how to say this."

Frank wondered if Bill wanted to call a halt to their little experiment. He wouldn't blame him if he did—Janet was falling further under his spell and Bill might soon become an afterthought. She needed Frank's strength. What did she need from Bill?

"Just say it—we don't have time to beat around the bush."

Bill nodded. His face seemed flushed. "I don't want to lose her."

The lie came out before he even thought about it. "I'm not trying to steal her away."

"Maybe not. But I see how she is now. She's, uh, different. I think she compares me to you and I come up short."

Yeah, I'd agree with that, Frank thought. "It's just the difference in our personalities," he said soothingly. "You're comfortable and I'm risky."

"And she likes the risk. I know it. I'm not blind." He came close to the desk and looked Frank in the eye. "Look, Frank. I know you probably have the power to steal Janet away from me." He raised his hand when Frank had been about to speak, cutting him off. "No. I know you'll tell me it won't happen, that you respect me too much, blah, blah, blah." He paused then put both hands down on Frank's desk and leaned forward.

"This is the embarrassing part so just let me get through it." He took a deep breath. "I need you. I know that sounds crazy. I know I should be jealous or angry with you and how this thing has gotten out of hand. But I know the truth. I'm not dominant. You are. Yet she's my wife. So I have a proposition for you."

Bill had Frank's full attention now. He sat up straighter and met Bill's gaze.

"If you'll work with me, I think we, uh, can go on as a team. That is, if you're willing to share." He laughed at the irony of that. "What I mean is, well, you know I don't mind sharing her in this way because I get to see a whole other side to her. I know it excites her. So I would like to be part of this and I won't object to you taking the lead, providing you don't harm her and you don't cut me out."

"I would never harm Janet," Frank said at once.

"I know. I just thought I should say it."

"So let me get this straight. You're willing to go along with my wishes? To essentially 'own' Janet?"

"Yes, as long as you don't try to sneak around behind my back. And of course as long as Janet is willing. And she would have to be in on it. No more secrets."

Frank nodded slowly. It just might work. In fact, it might be the best solution. Having come out of a bad marriage, he was not eager to jump back into one. He simply wanted to keep Janet around and see how much of a submissive she really was. It was early in this game they were playing. In most such situations, there would come a time when something would be expected of him—Janet would want to leave her husband and run off with him. Under Bill's plan, he could continue exploring her fantasies as long as Bill came along for the ride.

That was the tricky part, he knew. To let Janet in on the secret too soon could be ruinous. She might react badly, especially if she found out that Bill had been in on it from the beginning. Or having Bill around might conflict her so she couldn't let go of her inner submissive.

"The key is Janet," he found himself saying. "As far as I'm concerned, I think it could work. That is, if you really don't mind seeing her actually fuck other men, including myself."

"No, and maybe there's something wrong with me, but I find it, uh, stimulating. But you knew that. I mean, come on. She's become a completely different woman."

"I just wanted to make sure. Hearing about it or watching it on video is quite different from being there while it's happening."

"I know. I wouldn't have come to you if I didn't think this was a solution I could live with."

"You're not just saying this because you fear you'll lose Janet otherwise?"

"To tell you the truth, I've already lost her. I'm hoping in this way I can get her back."

Frank nodded. "All right. But how we tell Janet is going to be tricky." He steepled his fingers together. "Let me think on it. Go back to work."

Bill nodded. "I hope you come up with something good." He left.

Frank sat at his desk and imagined how this might play out. He didn't want to shock Janet but he didn't want her to think about it too much either. Her knee-jerk reaction would be shock and withdrawal. Especially if she realized this was all cooked up from the beginning between her husband and him. It would be better if she didn't know that.

As he sat there, ignoring the paperwork in front of him, an idea began to form. He pushed at the edges, reshaped it and found it just might work. The question was, did he have sufficient control over Janet?

At lunchtime he called Bill back into his office. His project manager seemed eager.

"Yes? You figure out how to break it to Janet?"

"Maybe. But it's going to take another week to set up."

"Really?" He seemed disappointed. "What's the plan?"

Frank outlined it. Bill's eyes grew wide. "You really think that will work?"

"I think so. It's the best I could come up with."

"You really think you can get Janet to accept fucking other men that quickly?"

"She's on the way. She's already allowing men—and women—to touch her and bring her to orgasm. And she's sucked my neighbor's cock. It's just a matter of time."

"God, I would love to see it."

"Well, I'll try to film some of it. I can't guarantee it. But you'll be seeing it yourself soon enough."

"Okay. I'll leave it to you. Just tell me when you think she's ready."

* * * * *

Tuesday morning, Janet stood naked outside Frank's apartment, shivering slightly. The days were getting colder and she didn't enjoy being exposed like this. Her skin had goose bumps.

She heard a "woof" behind her and turned to see Martin and his dog behind her. *How did he know when she'd be here? Did Frank tell him?*

"Hi."

"Hi," she said, trying to keep her back to him.

The dog strained at his leash and the man allowed it to pull him forward until the dog's nose disappeared between Janet's legs.

"Stop that!" she shrieked, and jumped. She grabbed her robe and wrapped it around her body.

The door opened and Frank stood there, tsking quietly. "Are you being rude to my neighbor?"

"But his dog was nosing me!" she explained.

"You know what I told you about the robe."

"I know! I know! But—"

"No 'buts'." His voice was firm and she found herself nodding. The robe slipped off and she hung it up. She didn't move as the dog returned to sniff at the crack of her ass.

"Did she hurt your feelings?" Frank asked Martin.

"Well, yes, I believe she did."

"Martin, why don't you come inside and let Janet apologize to you?"

Frank led the way inside and Martin pulled the dog's leash. Janet stumbled through the door.

Inside, Frank steered her toward the living room and made her get on her knees. Martin busied himself by tying the dog's leash to the leg of the kitchen table. She looked up with alarm when Martin came into the living room and began fumbling with his zipper.

"Sir?" She watched wide-eyed as Martin's cock sprung free.

"I want you to suck on Martin's cock, just like you do George's," Frank said.

Janet heard alarm bells going off somewhere deep inside her. But she ignored them. Frank's commanding voice made her reach up and gently steer Martin's cock to her lips. He thrust into her eagerly and she had to pull back to better control it. Her tongue worked hard to please it. This cock was smaller than George's and she could take it easily. She found herself enjoying bringing him pleasure and worked her mouth up and down on his turgid shaft.

"Oh god," Martin breathed.

She felt his cock stiffen and knew he was close. "Fuck!" the man gasped, and his cock erupted in her mouth. She tried to swallow it but much of his sperm spilled out down her chin and onto her breasts. The dog howled.

He pulled away. "God, that was good. Thanks, Frank." He zipped up.

Martin untied the leash and pulled the dog toward the door. "Come on, Rex. Let's go home."

The dog seemed disappointed. He whined as he followed his master out, looking back at the naked woman kneeling on the carpet. "Maybe some other time, huh, Rex?" Martin laughed and they were gone.

Janet returned to her senses. She looked up at Frank, lust evident on her face.

"Oh I'd bet you'd love to make love right now, wouldn't you?"

"Yes, Sir." She looked coy and gave him her best come-hither look.

"Well, first I have to punish you then we'll talk."

"P-Punish? For what?" Even as she said it, she remembered. She had put on her robe, strictly against Frank's orders. She shivered, knowing that his swats only made her hotter.

"I'm sure you know why."

He pulled her to her feet and positioned her over the upholstered arm of the couch. She could imagine how inviting her ass must look, thrust up at him like this. She wiggled it slightly. Frank removed the riding crop from the drawer and showed it to her. Her eyes widened and she prepared herself for the pain. The pleasure, she knew, would follow close behind.

Whack!

She shivered. "One, Sir."

Whack!

"Two, Sir!"

Whack!

"Three—"

The doorbell rang. Janet froze for a second then tried to get up. Frank held her down forcefully. "Don't get up," he warned, "or I'll double your punishment."

He went to the door and opened it. "Ahhh, James! Come in!"

Janet thought she might die. Why was he here? She craned her neck to see the large tattoo artist come in, struggling with his portable chair. His bald head glistened despite the cool air. He caught sight of Janet, her ass up, and turned to grin at Frank.

"I see you're in the middle of something. Want me to come back later?"

"Oh no! I'm just punishing her for disobeying my order. She won't mind if you watch, will you, Janet?"

She didn't know what to say. Of course she would mind! But she remembered that James had already seen her naked—intimately so. The image of his thick fingers fondling her labia came to mind and she simply shook her head at the two men. She knew Frank wanted something else done to her body. What this time? And how would she explain it to Bill?

"Good! Why don't you set up your chair while I finish, hmm?"

Janet turned away, unable to watch. She could feel James' eyes on her as Frank moved back into position.

"Now, where were we?"

"Uh, three, Sir."

"Okay."

Whack!

"Four, Sir!" Now that James was watching, she felt more exposed and the blows seemed to intensify the pain. At the same time, she could tell her pussy was sopping wet and distended. God, would Frank fuck her in front of James? Had he no shame?

Whack!

"Five, Sir!"

Her voice rang out with each blow. By ten, her ass was wiggling around, trying to cool off. By fifteen, tears were flowing from her eyes and she was begging him to stop.

"If I stop, what will you do for me?"

"Anything! Please, anything!"

"Will you let James here put in another piece of jewelry?"

"Yes! Yes, I will!" She'd figure out a way to explain it to Bill.

"Will you reward him when he's done?"

"Yes…" Her head came up. "Re-Reward him?" She could see herself once again on her knees sucking on the big man's cock. "Yes, I guess."

"You don't sound very convincing." He raised the crop.

"Yes! I'll suck him off! Please!"

"I don't know. What do you think, James?"

"I'd rather fuck her."

Frank turned back to her. "He'd rather fuck you."

"Nooo," she gasped. "I can't! I'm married."

"Hey, you fuck me and you don't seem to mind."

"That's…different."

"Very well."

Whack!

"Ow! Please!"

"It's all right," Frank said. "I completely understand."

Whack!

"All right, all right! I'll let him fuck me. But he has to wear a condom!"

"What do you think, James?"

"That'll be fine." He gave her a wolfish grin.

Frank dropped the riding crop on the couch and began to rub her ass, speaking soothing words. Her skin seemed on fire but his touch helped. He paused to grab a tube of cream from the end table and rubbed it into her reddened skin. It cooled her at once.

"Aahhh, that's good. Thanks, Sir." Janet felt her pussy contract and hoped Frank would fuck her now. She didn't care if James watched.

"Okay, let's get you into the chair."

She groaned and got to her feet. She felt a little unsteady and needed Frank's hand to guide her. Janet got in and allowed the men to fasten her into position. She knew what was coming next. James cranked the handle and her legs moved apart, showing her hot, wet pussy to his gaze. She feared she'd climax as soon as he touched her.

"What are you going to do to me?" she squeaked.

"What did you decide on, Frank?"

Frank came over and bent down. "I've always heard that a heavy gold ring fastened through the skin above her clit would bounce against her all day—if she wasn't wearing panties—and drive a woman crazy. Do you know if that's true?"

James nodded. "Yes. It can keep a woman on edge."

Janet tried to sit up, not believing her ears. That's just what Bill had said! At least she knew she'd have a good excuse when he saw it—she'd say she did it for him. "Will it hurt?"

"Not any more than the last one did," James said, slipping on his latex gloves and bending to his toolkit. "Don't worry—I'll be gentle."

Because she was shaved, the skin above her clit was already clean. James wiped the area with an alcohol swab and Janet sucked in her breath from the cold, anticipating what was coming. Still, she couldn't take her eyes off James' hands as he prepped her.

"To be effective, the ring has to be on the heavy side—at least fourteen gauge," he said. "Those will have a ball about three-sixteenths in diameter." He found a small plastic envelope and held it up for Frank to see. "Like this."

Janet watched as Frank took the envelope and peered at the ring inside. She couldn't quite see and craned her neck, curiosity evident on her face.

"How do we know if it's right for her?"

"We put it in temporarily and let her try it out. If it doesn't work, I'll remove it and replace it with a larger one."

"Show me a large one."

James found another small envelope and held it up for Frank to see. To Janet, it looked huge. "This is the largest. It's an eight-gauge with a one-quarter inch ball. But I would suggest you start with the smaller one."

Janet held her breath. That would be too big for her delicate clit! To have that heavy ball bounce against it all day—how could she function?

"Very well. I'll defer to your judgment." Janet let out a lungful of air.

He handed it back and James took the smaller ring and dropped it into a shallow dish of alcohol. Janet could see it now—it was a small gold ring, similar to the one through her labial lip but thicker. The little ball at the end looked plenty big to her. At the other side, the ring thinned out in the middle into a prong that she knew would be fastened through her clit hood. She felt a shudder go through her.

James spread salve over the area and Janet felt the skin grow numb within a few seconds. She was grateful for that. The piercer took the ring from the alcohol bath and measured it against her, finding just the right spot so the heavy end would rest right on her desperate clit whenever it poked from its protective hood. He marked a spot with his pen. He held the top in place with one gloved finger, lifted one side of the ring up and dropped it a few times directly on her clit and Janet nearly came right then.

She gasped aloud and Frank smiled. "You seem a little horny," he said.

"God," was all she could say. She eyed the bulge in James' pants and wondered how it would feel when he drove into her.

James put the ring aside and picked up the same tool he had used before. Janet gritted her teeth and looked away. She could feel his fingers pinching but it didn't hurt. When he pressed the tool against the narrow flap of skin, she felt a sharp pinch and jerked a little, more out of shock than pain. James worked quickly, swabbing the area to clean up the blood before threading the thin prong through the double hole.

"Do you want this one permanent too?"

"Yes, but let's make sure it's the right size first."

James nodded. He reached forward and flipped the ring a few times. Janet's mouth opened and she moaned.

"I think that hits the right spot," he said, grinning. "Let's have her try it out." He unfastened the straps and helped her shakily to her feet.

When she stood, she felt woozy and hung on to Frank. She looked down at her jewelry. Now she had a very prominent ring in front and a winking ring nestled among the folds of her labia. Her body was no longer her own it seemed. She belonged to Frank. Whatever he wanted to do to her, he would. She had no say. Now she was about to be fucked by this bald bear of a man.

Her head cleared and she pulled away from Frank, curious to see how the ring affected her. She could feel the weight of it already. Cautiously, she took a step then another. Her mouth dropped open and her knees felt weak.

"My god!"

"Feels good?"

"Oh my god!" The ring thrummed against her most private, sensitive spot, just hard enough to make her body quiver with lust. It was like a low-level buzzing. Walking across the living room would be a challenge, going to the grocery store would be an impossibility.

"I don't know if I can walk with this thing in me," she said breathlessly.

"Sure you can, you just have to get used to it," Frank said.

"Oh my god." She came back and Frank took her arm to steady her.

"So I guess that's the right size then."

"Yes, Sir. I couldn't stand it any bigger."

Frank turned to James. "All right. Let's make it permanent."

They eased Janet back onto the chair. James leaned forward with the soldering iron and soon had it fastened securely. He took another small bottle of antiseptic and handed it to Frank. "You know the drill. Dab this on twice a day for four to five days and she'll be fine. Let me know if you see any swelling."

Frank helped Janet off the chair. "I want to watch you fuck him now."

She glanced over at James, who flashed her a big smile. Janet could see that the bulge in his pants had grown. It was as if she could already feel it inside her and she went to him, dropping to her knees. The ring thudded against her clit, driving her forward. She fumbled for his belt.

"She's pretty eager, isn't she?" Frank said.

"Yeah," he said, watching her as she opened his pants and eased out his large black cock. She loved the contrast against her white skin. Her mouth opened and she took in as much of it as she could. "Oh yeah, baby, that's good."

As she tongued him, her hand dropped down to her ring and flipped it up and down, up and down. Each time it struck her clit, she felt an indescribable thrill. Her pussy was weeping with need.

The cock was hard in her mouth and she wanted to feel it thrusting into her. She got up and took James' hand, nearly dragging him over to the couch. She flopped down over the padded arm and thrust her butt up at him.

"Please," she said. "Fuck me now."

James was only too happy to oblige. He steered his rock-hard cock to her slit and rubbed it up and down, coating the tip with her juices. Then he lined it up and plunged deep inside of her with one stroke.

Janet cried out and climaxed at once, her body shaking with release. But James had barely begun. He stroked in and out, in and out, his big cock rubbing her in new places, and Janet came again. And again.

Frank stepped forward and pulled a condom out of his pocket. "I thought you wanted one of these," he said, holding it up for her to see.

"Go away," she gasped, feeling another climax rock her.

"Would you like him to come inside you?" Frank persisted.

"God, yes! Fuck me! Fuck me!"

The sensation of James' thick cock rubbing and sliding in and out was heaven to her. She didn't care about Frank watching, she didn't care about the new ring, she didn't care about Bill. All she wanted was to feel his seed erupt within her.

She didn't have long to wait. James began moving faster and faster, pounding his huge cock inside her wet pussy. She began to squeal as a tidal wave of emotions built inside her. Then he bellowed and thrust himself hard against her. She could feel his cock squirting and throbbing and she climaxed again.

"God! Goddamn! Oh god!" she cried out, hugging the couch, her face beaded with sweat. "Damn!"

James stayed inside her until his cock shrunk then pulled out.

"Clean me," he ordered.

She immediately got up, turned around and dropped to her knees, taking his wet cock into her mouth. There was no hesitation. She used one hand to cover her pussy, which fairly gushed with the fluids trapped inside.

"Sorry," she muttered, "I seem to be leaking."

"It's all right. Go into the bathroom to get cleaned up while I see James out," Frank said.

In the bathroom as she sat on the toilet, feeling James' seed drip into the water, Janet felt the first pangs of remorse. She had fucked another man! A stranger! And without a condom! How could she? But another part of her answered, *Because it was so fucking good*. She giggled.

Her hand returned to her new ring and idly flipped it, sending tiny waves of pleasure through her. This could become a new habit, she mused.

After she cleaned up, she returned to the living room, feeling the ring bounce with each step. Now that she had been satiated, the sensation was a little easier to bear. Still, it made her acutely aware of her clit at all times.

James had already packed up his equipment and left. Frank sat on the couch, sipping a glass of wine. There was another glass on the end table that he gestured to. She picked it up and took a swallow. It was a very good wine. She sat on the couch and waited with no embarrassment about her nakedness.

"You were magnificent," he said. "I'm so pleased."

"But that was so risky! It's not like me." She worried about diseases.

"You can relax. I had James take a blood test. He's clean."

That shocked her. Not because of the results but because Frank had thought this through ahead of time. He anticipated that James would fuck her unprotected!

"Why do you like to watch me fuck another man? Most men would be jealous."

"Not me. I like it because I made it happen. And I controlled it. I love my little submissive girl."

She smiled. Somehow he always made her feel better. When he's in charge, she got as much or more out of it. She needn't worry. Then a thought intruded.

"What about Bill?"

"What about him?"

"Well, I just fucked a stranger. And I've been fucking you for weeks. What if he found out?"

"What if he's like me?"

"What do you mean, Sir?"

Frank took another sip of wine before answering. "He might like to see you with other men—have you thought of that?"

"No." She couldn't imagine it. Bill would be hurt and probably jealous. Wouldn't he? Of course, she couldn't imagine Frank watching her fuck another man either.

"I'd like you to find out."

"I can't do that!"

"Why not? You could have a discussion about secret fantasies and see what happens."

"And what would I tell him my secret fantasy is? That I love to fuck his boss…and any others he tells me to?"

He shrugged. "That's up to you."

"God."

He put down his drink and came over to her. He took the glass from her hand and set it on the coffee table then helped her to her feet. He placed a gentle hand alongside her face. She trembled at his touch.

"Look, Janet, I think you know that I'm crazy about you. I knew you were submissive from the beginning and now that I've awakened that part of you, I doubt you want to go back to your old life. Am I right?"

She could only nod. Then she said in a small voice, "But I'm scared."

"I know you are. You're worried about Bill and what might happen to you. But let me ask you—do you trust me?"

She gazed into his eyes. "Yes, Sir."

"Good. Then continue with that. Let yourself go."

She nodded. "So you want me to ask Bill about his secret fantasies? What if his secret fantasy isn't watching me with others? What then?"

"I don't know. We'll have to take it one day at a time. We could simply continue doing what we're doing and being careful about it."

She snorted. "You call this being careful?"

"I call this giving you—and me—what we both need." His hand went to her breast and stroked it, using his thumb to caress her nipple. "There's nothing wrong with that as long…well, as you once said, 'as long as it doesn't get out of hand'."

Janet chuckled but he noticed she pressed her breasts forward at his touch. "I think this got out of hand a long time ago."

"And you love it."

"Yes, I do. I never knew I was like this. You bring out the worst in me."

"No, honey, I bring out the best in you." He kissed her.

Chapter Fifteen

ഇ

Janet was vacuuming, trying to figure out the best way she might ask Bill about his secret fantasies. It would have to be either right before or right after sex. Before would be better, she decided. She'd get him all excited then ask him to confess. She would have to share too. Hmm, how to best tell him about the recent resurgence in her fetish toward submissiveness?

What's up with that anyway, she wondered. Why are some women so turned on by it? Must go back to caveman days. Otherwise, it doesn't make sense in today's modern world where men and women are supposedly equal. It certainly involves trust—she would never have been able to free her submissive side if Frank had been abusive or derisive. No, he had the right tone about it. She felt safe and protected, which allowed her to do some amazing, sexy things. Like driving across town nearly naked. Or stripping down at Frank's front door. Or, and her body gave a little shiver, fucking that beast of a man James.

She had showered for a long time after she arrived home. Afterward, she dabbed antiseptic salve around the reddish skin where the ring pierced it. When she dressed, she made sure she wore underwear and tight jeans so she could have some relief from the constant throbbing in her clit. Her skin still hurt a little from the piercing, but how would she feel once that went away? She would be horny all the time.

She couldn't describe her feelings. It was a jumble. But one fact stood out clear in her mind. She had enjoyed it. All of it. The exposure, the piercing, James' cock—everything. It was nasty, it was sexy, it was dangerous—and she had loved it. Frank was right—giving in to one's baser instincts was very freeing. As long as she had a safety net. Janet had no desire to die or catch some horrible disease. But Frank was always there, watching out for her. He even planned ahead, in the event she fucked James without a condom. She could really trust him.

Could she trust Bill like that?

She found herself vacuuming the same spot over and over so she shut the machine down and put it away. To keep from pacing, she went to the kitchen and prepared a pot roast, putting it in the slow cooker. She checked the time—not quite one. Had all that happened this morning? It seemed as if she had been at Frank's for a long time, yet it was probably less than two hours.

It felt strange not having Frank around right now to tell her what to do. Was she so far gone she needed him to tell her how to run her own household? *God, what an idiot I am*, she thought. *He's gotten under my skin.*

Janet went to the sink and pulled out some cleaning products, a sponge and an old toothbrush she used for the grout. Then she went into the bathroom to clean. She could spend hours in there and it allowed her to put everything out of her mind except what was in front of her.

* * * * *

Bill came home at five-thirty tired but with a tingle of excitement. Frank had told him what Janet would be asking him. Let her bring up the subject, he had warned. All he was supposed to do was confess his secret fantasy—no more. Don't spill the beans yet, his boss had warned him and he knew Frank was right. He still wasn't sure how it would all work out in the end but he couldn't wait. He wanted to see how Janet performed with Frank. And other men. Frank had shown him the video of her with James. The idea that his wife would be so out of control with desire that she'd fuck that big black man had made him so hard he had to sneak into the restroom after he had left Frank's office and masturbate. He hadn't done that before—but then he'd always been "muffled" in his life. He always took the safe route. For the first time he was beginning to feel alive.

Bill was no fool—he knew Frank thought him boring. Hell, Janet thought him boring too. And they were right, he *was* boring. Well, that was about to change. Even if he couldn't become the man that Frank was, at least he could come along for the ride. Frank wouldn't be able to steal her away if he was an active participant, right?

"Honey, I'm home!" He put his coat on the hook by the door and found Janet in the kitchen.

"Hi, Bill. How was your day?" She offered her lips for a brief kiss.

"Good. Real good." He kissed her then pulled her to him and patted her rump. She melted into his arms. "I don't like you in jeans."

"What?"

"Jeans. They're too restrictive. I prefer skirts. I like to reach up and touch your skin."

She stared at him. "I never knew that. You've never said it before."

"Well, I'm saying it now. Why don't you go change?"

Janet looked at him a long time. He could tell she was worried about revealing her clit ring.

"But I'm right in the middle of dinner."

"Now don't argue with me or I'll have to spank you," he said with humor in his voice, but his eyes indicated he was serious.

Janet nodded and disappeared. He waited, checking on the pot roast and turning the heat down on the vegetables she was steaming. He whistled a happy little tune.

She returned wearing a plaid, wraparound skirt. She was barefoot. Bill felt his cock start to harden just looking at her. When she returned to the stove, he cupped her cute little ass and squeezed.

She jumped. "Hey now! I'm trying to cook here!"

"Yeah, we wouldn't want to ruin dinner." He rubbed his hands over her thigh, feeling the edge of her panties. He let his fingers slip underneath the material.

"Bill! Now stop it! I can't cook with you doing that. Besides," she added, "you'll ruin the surprise."

"Surprise? What surprise?"

"Never mind. You'll have to wait. Now shoo! Go watch some TV. I'll call you when dinner's ready."

He let the moment pass since he knew everything would come together soon enough. He'd get to see her clit ring up close and personal. Frank had cautioned him that she'd still be sore, but a guy could look, couldn't he?

He decided against TV and stayed in the kitchen, chatting with Janet as she finished preparing dinner. Bill had trouble keeping his hands off her and he enjoyed seeing her squirm with embarrassment at his touch. He knew she was worried about his reaction to the clit ring and trying to figure out how she might ask him about his secret fantasies.

Of course she needn't have worried. He planned to be honest in both cases—he would be thrilled.

They ate dinner in near silence, they had run out of small talk about their days and the elephant in the room was Janet's secret. Bill tried to be nonchalant but his nerves jangled. He felt like a kid on Christmas Eve who couldn't wait for morning.

After dinner he helped her clean up, making sure he put his hands on her at every opportunity. She dodged his efforts at first but soon gave in.

"What's gotten into you today?"

"I'm just attracted to my lovely wife," he said. "Nothing wrong with that, is there?"

"No, of course not." She licked her lips. "It's just not like you—I mean, normally."

"Well, today it is." He cupped his hand against her lovely round ass. He rubbed it and she danced away to wash a pot that had been left in the sink.

Bill would not be denied. He knew she was just delaying the inevitable. Finally she gave up and allowed him to pull her into the bedroom.

"So what's this surprise you've been teasing me with?"

"Uh, well, you, uh, seemed to be so excited about my little ring that I, er, got before," she began nervously.

Bill just nodded and raised one eyebrow.

"Yeah, well, I decided to get another one," she blurted out, suddenly turning bright red.

He pretended to look shocked. "You mean, down there?" He pointed.

She nodded. "I thought about nipple rings but decided against them."

Bill wondered about that. Had she really? No, of course not. That was just part of her invented story. He knew it had all been Frank's idea. But now that she brought it up, he'd have to suggest it to Frank for the next time. Maybe by then he could watch James fuck her.

"So show me!"

Janet looked embarrassed as she pulled up her skirt. She held it against her stomach and used the other hand to pull down her panties. "Now I hope you like it because I did it for you."

Ha! What a lie that was! But he said nothing, his eyes riveted on the V of her legs.

The ring came into view, hanging near the bottom of her naked mons. It was thicker than he had imagined, far thicker than the delicate gold ring through her labia. And the ball appeared heavy as it rested atop her swollen clit. *God, how that must arouse her all the time! What a wonderful idea!*

"Do you like it?"

Bill realized he had been staring, his mouth ajar. "Uh, yeah! It's great. Can I touch it?" He cursed himself when he realized he wasn't being Dom-like again.

"Sure. But be careful. It's still sore."

"Okay." He reached out and gently flipped it up and watched it thud down on the skin right above her clit, which seemed to swell before his eyes. He looked up in time to see Janet briefly close her eyes. "Did that hurt?"

"N-N-Noo," she said softly.

He gave it another flip and she jerked as if a small current had jolted through her. *Wow,* he thought. *This is going to keep her on edge all the time! Especially if she doesn't wear panties!*

"I like what it does to you," he said.

She nodded, her mind seemingly elsewhere.

He flipped it again. And again. Janet licked her lips.

"I don't want you to wear panties anymore."

"What?" She came back to focus on him.

"You heard me. I want this little ring to keep you on edge for me all the time."

She opened her mouth then closed it again. She seemed to be selecting her words carefully. "But why? I mean, when I'm at home alone, why do you care?"

"Because I want you to be thinking about me and waiting for me to come home." He caught the brief flash in her eyes and knew she was thinking about Frank, not him. But that was okay. He was going to get just as much out of it as Frank would. Or at least he hoped so.

"I think we need to, uh, celebrate," he said, unbuckling his pants.

"Wait. No. I'm still pretty sore. And I have to put this stuff on it all the time for a couple of days until it heals."

Bill wasn't sure why she was being so coy. Didn't she just fuck James right after she had it done? Of course, he realized at once, she would've still been numb then from the cream James had spread on her pussy.

"Well, you've got to do something. I can't look at your beautiful new jewelry without getting really hard."

Janet nodded and dropped to her knees in front of him, her skirt falling down again. She took his stiff cock into her hand. Bill smiled. A few weeks ago, his wife would never voluntarily suck him off like this—not without a lot of begging! Her training with Frank was kicking in. Bill wanted more.

"Open your blouse," he said as forcefully as he could.

She paused, staring up at him. Her hands went to the buttons and she opened them, revealing her lacy bra.

"Take it off. In fact, get naked."

"Bill, I can't—"

"I'm not asking you. Don't worry, I won't fuck you. Not tonight anyway."

She stood and began removing her clothes. He watched, feeling his cock grow even harder. When she was naked, she eased back down to her knees and took his cock into her soft hands. Her mouth opened and she began kissing the tip of it. Bill was in heaven. His boring old marriage was suddenly not so boring anymore.

He imagined her sucking off other men, learning how to do it right and being rewarded by shots of semen in her face. God, it made him impatient. He wanted to see her doing that right away. Why did he have to wait?

Janet took more of his cock inside her mouth and used her tongue to tease him. She couldn't quite deep throat him yet, he noticed, but her hand felt very good around the shaft.

"Oh god," he said as he felt his seed boiling up.

Just as he released, he grabbed her head and held her in position, squirting his hot seed into her mouth. She choked and gasped and he finally relented, letting her go so she could catch her breath.

"God, Bill! I could've choked! You should warn me first!"

"Sorry," he said. "I was just so turned on."

She seemed to recover and grabbed her robe from the end of the bed. "It's okay. I'm glad to help you out and all—it was just startling, you know."

Bill knew the evening wasn't over. He wondered how Janet might approach him with the subject of fantasies. He didn't have long to wait.

"Uh, Bill," she said, sitting again on the edge of the bed, her robe wrapped around her.

Bill buckled up his pants. "Yes?"

"I never knew that that was one of your, uh, interests before."

"What? Blowjobs?"

"No," she said at once. "I mean, you know, the piercings."

"Well, I guess there's a lot you don't know about me then."

"You never said anything before. We've been married ten years and you've never said anything!"

"Should I have? You might've thought I was weird or something."

"No, no! I wouldn't have! In fact, I find it, um, highly arousing."

"Really? It's a pretty common fantasy among men, I'll bet."

"Piercings? Nah, I can't believe that."

"Oh no. It's true. I'll bet if you asked ten men on the street, eight or nine of them would tell you it turned them on."

"I wonder why."

"Dunno. Maybe something about marking our territory or something."

"Ewww. That doesn't sound very romantic."

"You know what I mean," he said hurriedly, sorry he had explained it so poorly. "Kinda like putting a tattoo on your wife that says *Property of so-and-so,* you know?"

"That's not much better. I'm not your property."

No, he thought, *you're Frank's property.* "Which is why I've never confessed my secret fantasies to you before."

She caught the opening he gave her. "Fantasies? What other fantasies do you have?"

"Oh no! I'd just get into trouble!"

"No! No you won't, I promise."

"Well, you'd have to tell me yours too."

"Me? I, uh, I really don't have any."

"Then I don't have any either."

And there it was. He wasn't going to make it easy on her. She would have to confess that she was submissive first. Tit for tat.

"All right. I'll tell you one of mine if you tell me one of yours."

"One of? You have more than one?"

"Well, of course, silly. Every woman does. For example, I'd like to fuck Brad Pitt but that's probably not a surprise to you."

"Oh I didn't know you were counting fantasies that were impossible to achieve."

"That's what fantasies are, silly."

"All right. I'll tell you one of my fantasies but only if you tell me one that we could actually make come true. Deal?"

She eyed him, biting her lower lip. "That wouldn't mean we'd *have* to make it come true, right?"

Bill had every intention of that but he wasn't going to give her any excuse not to be honest with him. "No, of course not. I'm just trying to stick with plausible fantasies here."

"Okay." She took in a deep breath. He could see her hands shaking. "I have this, uh, fantasy of control." She stopped.

Bill pretended not to understand. "Control? You like to be in control?" He frowned.

"No!" she said too quickly. "You know, when I read romance novels, I always like the ones about a strong man, coming in and sweeping the fair maiden off her feet. Taking her away to make love to her."

"Oh I get it! Wow, I didn't know that about you. You like the strong men, hmmm?"

She lowered her eyes. "Yes."

"Well, that's great! I would love to help that dream come true!"

She lifted her eyes and gave him a quick smile. He knew what she was thinking—*You don't have it in you. Not like Frank.*

And she was right.

"Now it's your turn. What's your fantasy? Your main one, I should say."

"My main one? Hmm, let's see." He made a show of pretending to think about which one to mention. "Well, you're probably going to be shocked," he said at last. "But I'd, uh, like to see you with other men."

He looked away as if embarrassed. When he glanced back, Janet was sitting on the edge of the bed, her mouth agape.

"Really?" she said. "You'd really like that?"

"Only if I could be there of course," he added quickly. "I wouldn't want you to get hurt or anything. I'd want to have control over it."

"Wow," she said. "I would have never thought of that about you. I would've assumed you'd be jealous."

"I would be if you were having an affair," he said pointedly, watching her face. She had the presence of mind not to react. In fact, she looked frozen. "You know, behind my back. But if I could select the men you, uh, entertained, and be present during it, I would find that a turn-on."

Silence descended over them as they both thought about each other's confession. Bill could tell Janet was in shock while he was trying to figure out how to take her to the next step. He realized he might've treaded on dangerous ground by telling her he would be angry if she had an affair. Had he just painted himself into a corner? How was he going to tell her he knew all about Frank without having her feel betrayed and used?

Janet apparently had been thinking the same thing. "But why would you care if I had an affair, if you secretly wanted to see me with other men?"

"Because I'd be afraid he'd steal you away from me," he said before he thought, and realized it was exactly the truth.

"Oh, so it's not so much the affair, it's losing me."

"Right. I love you, Janet. I would love to play little sex games and such but I wouldn't want to lose you over them."

She smiled and opened her arms. He sat next to her and they hugged for a long time. "Don't worry," she whispered. "No one's going to steal me away."

Chapter Sixteen

ᘛ

Janet got on the phone to Frank the next morning.

"Frank?"

"Yes, my beautiful little submissive?" He was in his office. Bill had been in earlier, giving him a full report, but he was alone now.

Her words came out in a rush. "He told me! You were right! He said he'd like to see me with other men! Can you believe it?"

"Really? Wow. That's great." He wasn't about to let on that he knew it all along.

"Great?" She paused. "I don't know, I'm a little worried."

"Worried? Why? It would seem to fit into our plans neatly, don't you think?"

"Well, sure," she said. "That's what worries me. It seems too good to be true."

"Now don't borrow trouble."

"I'm not trying to. I just worry he'll be jealous and hurt, no matter what he says."

"If you feel that way, we can just keep on the way we're going."

"No, I can't do that either. He's bound to find out sooner or later." She paused. "I'm damned if I do and damned if I don't. The thing is, I'm not sure how we should proceed from here."

"Why don't you agree to fulfill his fantasy? Can you think of someone—I mean, other than me?"

"But why? I don't want anyone else."

Frank smiled into the phone. "Well then, why don't you bring it up and if he asks who would be a good candidate, casually say that you find me handsome and you've always been attracted to me. See if he goes for it."

"I can't do that! I'd be too embarrassed! Besides, you're his boss!"

"Hmm. That could be a little awkward. I could talk to him. You know, sound him out."

"What could you say? 'I've always wanted to fuck your wife, Bill, why don't I stop by tonight?'" She laughed derisively.

"I would hope I could be more subtle than that. Why don't you just leave it to me?" He knew that's what she secretly wanted—to let him be in control.

"Well, okay. But I'm worried."

"Don't be. Trust me."

He hung up and sat back. A big grin slowly spread over his face.

* * * * *

Bill stopped by after lunch. "You called? Did you hear from her?"

"I sure did. And she's ready for the final phase, I think. We have to be careful of course."

"You think she'll go for it?"

"Why not? She really wants both of us, you know. You are her husband and have been a safe and honorable man for ten years—maybe a little too safe. I provide what's been missing in her life since she was a teenager."

"So you're agreed then? You won't try to steal her away from me?"

"I don't really think I could, the way she loves you," he said, choosing his words carefully.

He didn't relish the idea of sharing her. But half a loaf was better than none. Maybe something would change later. He eyed Bill. *Maybe he'll fall in love with another woman. Or we'll open a plant in Beijing and I'll put him in charge.*

He smiled and said, "Now when she comes to you and suggests that you fulfill your fantasy, act shocked but not too shocked. Tell her you'd like to think about it but you're really surprised she'd be willing to do it, etcetera, etcetera."

"I know what to do."

"Do you? How will you react when she says she's always had an eye on me?"

Bill grimaced. "I dunno. My first reaction would be jealousy, I suppose."

"Well don't be jealous. That's what she waiting for. She'll pull back at once. Just act a bit surprised. Say, you might be willing but you wouldn't want to lose your job over it or something. Get her to talk about her fantasy as well. Don't just make this about you."

Bill nodded. "I get it."

"All right. We're on the home stretch now. Be careful."

* * * * *

Janet was having a glass of wine, her second, as she sat in the upholstered chair and waited for Bill to come home. Ever since his little confession last night, she'd been nervously trying to figure out how to get Frank involved without her husband freaking out. It was one thing if they invited a total stranger in here—someone they'd never see again, but Frank! That would be weird, no matter how it was approached.

She heard the garage door open and she gulped down the rest of her wine before pouring a third glass. She sat immobile as Bill came in from the garage.

"Hi, hon," he said casually, bending down to kiss her. "Having a cocktail without me?"

"Uh, yeah. I just felt like one. Hope you don't mind."

"No, not at all." He went into the kitchen and grabbed a beer out of the fridge. "How was your day?"

"Good. Real good."

He sat down across from her. "Really? You act like there's something on your mind."

She took another sip. "Well, yeah. About last night..."

"You mean our little fantasies? Oh well, I figure it'll never happen. I hope you weren't offended by mine."

"No, no! I wasn't." She caught his eye. "It's just that..."

He waited.

"You've had that fantasy for a long time, haven't you?"

"Yes, but I don't dwell on it," he said.

"But you never said anything to me."

"It's not something one would necessarily share with one's wife."

"Are you shocked by my submissive fantasy?"

"No! Not at all. I find it sexy. I just always thought of you as this modern woman. I figured if I ever suggested something like that, you'd be frying up my balls in the skillet."

She laughed. "No... Well, maybe yes. I would probably have reacted like a tough feminist. That was the way I, uh, saw myself as an adult after all. But deep down there's a woman—actually a little girl—who wanted to be...um, I don't know. Punished." The last word was barely a whisper.

Bill had an image of Janet bent over the couch as Frank spanked her. He could feel himself get hard. "Same here. I'm not supposed to like seeing my wife with another man. But I can't help that it excites me."

A silence fell. Janet took a deep breath. "Well, I'm willing to let you have that fantasy...if I can have mine."

Bill pretended to be shocked and pleased. "Really? You'd do that?" He sank back into the couch and rubbed his forehead.

"You're not disappointed in me?"

"Not at all! Wow! This would be like a dream come true!"

"But not with just any man, you understand."

"Oh of course. You'd like one of those, whatchacallits."

"Dominants."

"Yes. Dominants. Someone who knows what you want and how to do it right."

"Exactly. I'd be worried if you just went out and picked out a man at a bar. You know, he'd probably be crude and hurtful."

"Yeah, but how do we find someone like that? Someone who is dominant but also willing to share?"

She nodded. "That's a tough one."

He finished his beer and stood up. "Well, we'll have to think on it for a while, I guess. Maybe you could ask some of your girlfriends..."

"Frank," she said softly, almost a whisper.

He turned. "What?"

She was suddenly embarrassed. "Um, what about, er, Frank?"

Bill looked surprised—it wasn't hard to fake. "Frank? My boss?"

"Yeah."

"Why him?"

"Well, I know he's always been attracted to me."

"You could tell? I mean, did he flirt with you behind my back?" He narrowed his eyebrows questioningly, trying to seem like a suspicious husband.

"No!" she said a bit too quickly. "But a woman can tell. He's always been a perfect gentleman with me." The lie came out so smoothly he almost believed it.

Bill got another beer. "You think he's a dominant?"

"Well, sure. Isn't he?"

"Now that you mention it, yeah, you're probably right. At least at work. But I don't know how he is with the ladies. He didn't seem that way with Mary when they were together."

"No, he didn't. But then that might've been Mary's issue, not his."

"You mean that she wouldn't go along with any such games."

"Right."

"You think that's why they got divorced?"

Janet took another sip of wine. "It's possible."

"Hmm. Interesting." He took a big drink from the bottle. "I don't know, Jan. He could fire me or something."

"Oh no! He wouldn't do that!"

"How can you be so sure?"

"Well, if he did, he'd never see me again."

Bill smiled broadly. *This might work after all,* he mused. "So you're saying it would be kinda like a Mexican standoff."

"That's a crude way of putting it but yes."

"Hmm. I don't know."

"It's just an idea. I just want to please you."

"I appreciate it, I really do." He sat on the edge of her chair and leaned in to kiss her. She kissed him back with passion.

"Maybe I could just be your dominant guy," he suggested.

"Um, maybe." She didn't sound encouraging. "But that wouldn't solve your fantasy."

"Well, it might eventually. I could do that dominant thing and later bring in guys for you to, you know…"

Janet put a hand on his forearm. "Bill, I love you and you're the sweetest man I've ever known. But I just don't think you're the Dom type."

He sighed. "Maybe you're right." It was a conclusion he'd come to weeks ago. "So how do we do it?"

"You mean, talk to Frank?"

"Yeah. I don't want him to think I'm weird or anything."

"No, of course not." She thought about it. "How about if we invite him to dinner? Say Friday night?"

"So soon?"'

"This would just be a sounding-out session. I wouldn't expect we'd make any overt suggestions or anything. We could delay, if you'd feel more comfortable."

"No, it's all right."

"Are you sure?"

He stood and took a swig of his beer. "Sure I'm sure. Why not?"

Chapter Seventeen

ꟸ

"Frank, I gotta hand it to you—you're a fucking genius."

Frank beamed. He was seated behind his desk, an unlit cigar in one hand. "See, I told you. I know what your wife wants. She's just as excited about this as you are."

"Yeah, but we're going to have to take it easy," Bill said. "She thinks this will just be a 'sounding out' session Friday. We wouldn't want to spill the beans."

"We won't. We've come too far to ruin it now." He rubbed his hands together, his cigar trapped in the crook of one finger.

"So how do we play it?"

"Leave that to me. Just follow my lead, okay?"

Bill nodded and headed for the door. He paused with his hand on the knob. "And since when did you smoke cigars?"

Frank laughed. "I don't. I just feel in a magnanimous mood today and I had this leftover from a client visit. It makes me feel like a big shot."

Bill grinned and shook his head as he left. Frank leaned back in his chair and put his feet up on his desk. He shoved the unlit cigar into his mouth and interlaced his hands behind his head.

"It's all coming together," he said to the empty room.

* * * * *

By Friday afternoon Janet was a nervous wreck. What had she gotten herself into? "Oh what a tangled web we weave..." she quoted aloud to herself. She felt as if she were on the verge of a precipice, about to leap over. Why had she fallen under

Frank's spell anyway? Why couldn't she leave well enough alone?

She checked her watch. It was after five already! Bill would be here soon to help and Frank was scheduled to arrive at six. She hurried to check the roast before heading into the bedroom to change.

She had already showered earlier and had been cooking in her robe and a pair of granny panties—anything to keep her clit from being stimulated by the ring! Now she had her outfit all laid out—a conservative dress that buttoned up right to the neck, a sturdy bra and another pair of granny underwear. At the last minute she replaced the grannies with something a little more sexy, not even knowing why she was doing it. Was she trying to impress Frank? Or Bill?

In either case, she would make sure her clit ring was held immobile. She wasn't going to walk around on edge all night!

The phone rang, interrupting her. She picked up the receiver in the bedroom, thinking it was probably Bill.

"Hello?"

"How's my little submissive today?"

"Frank! Oh god." She felt suddenly weak and sat down on the bed, pulling the robe closer about her. Her worlds were colliding and she had set things into motion!

"What's wrong? Are you nervous?"

"Duh! Frank, I can't do anything that would hurt Bill, you know that. Please, be on your best behavior tonight!"

"Hurt Bill? I thought this was his fantasy too."

"You know what I mean—you're his boss. It could get awkward."

"I know. I promise to behave—if you'll do something for me."

"What?"

"Don't wear panties tonight."

"I can't!"

"Of course you can. If you don't, I may have to spank you in front of Bill!"

"No, you can't! You wouldn't!"

"I'll bet Bill would like that."

"What? The spanking or no panties?"

Frank laughed. "Both. But I'm sure he'd like it if his wife were naked under her dress."

Janet remembered what Bill had said, how he liked her in a skirt so he could run his hands up under it. Of course he'd like it if she went without panties—but wouldn't he think she was doing it for Frank, not him? That could cause jealousy. Not only that…

"But I can't! That damned ring will drive me crazy!"

"That's the whole idea, Janet. Look, I know I've been lax with you lately, allowing you to work through this, but I really must insist. You know deep down you want to obey me."

His voice sounded so commanding, so confident. Janet found herself falling under his spell again. It would be so easy to allow him to guide her. Then her concerns about Bill intruded.

"God, Frank, I'm all atwitter here. You've got me going one way and Bill another."

"That's not really true."

That stopped her. "W-What do you mean?"

"Bill wants the same thing you do—and I do. He just wants an excuse for it to happen. You told me he wanted to see you with another man—maybe more than one. I think if you give him the right opening, he'll take it."

Janet licked her lips. "And you think me not wearing panties is that, er, opening?" The double entendre made her smile and she had to admit, it did cause her a tingle of excitement, just thinking about it.

"Yes, exactly. And I'll be checking so don't disobey me. You know that I'll have to punish you sooner or later."

Another throb went through her pussy and she closed her legs together. Her hand stole down to feel the shape of the ring through the thin material and she wondered how she could possibly do what he asked.

"Are you sure about this?"

"Yes, I'm sure. I promise you, if Bill shows any jealousy, I'll back off."

"All right," she said softly.

"Oh and one more thing."

Inwardly she groaned but her pussy grew wetter. "Yes?"

"I'm sure you've picked out some boring dress that will cover you from head to toe practically. Pick out something else. Something sexier—and shorter."

"Frank!"

"You know, you haven't been calling me 'Sir' lately—you'll have to be punished for that too."

"Oh god," she moaned. Frank knew just what buttons to push.

"Remember. You wouldn't want to disappoint me further. I can't wait to spank that perfect ass."

Her hand reached into her panties and flipped the ring up and down, up and down. New waves of pleasure rolled out from her clit, like tiny waves in a puddle. "Yes…Sir," she said.

"Good girl. See you soon." He hung up.

Janet rose and looked down at the dress she had picked out. It was a very safe choice, she realized. Too safe. Maybe Frank was right—she was going about this the wrong way. Open the door a little, see what happens.

She dropped her robe and stripped off her panties. Naked, she took the dress to the closet, feeling the thrum of the ring against her clit. She placed the dress back and looked through the others. A shiny green dress caught her eye. It was elegant and sexy at the same time. She hadn't worn it in almost a year—since the last time Bill had taken her out to dinner for their anniversary. The top wasn't too low cut but it allowed a little bit of cleavage to show. And it came to just above her knees so it wouldn't be too short. She nodded. A good, safe choice that would please both Frank and Bill.

She hung the dress on the door and went to put on her bra. A lacy one without an underwire would be perfect. It would allow her to move and be comfortable but still cover her well. She looked at herself in the mirror. Her shaved pussy looked exposed, the gold ring prominently displayed. She shivered.

Janet sat and put on her makeup. Not too much. She wanted an understated look. When she was satisfied, she rose and checked her watch. Five-twenty. She hurried to slip into the dress. She liked the way the satin felt against her skin. Tugging it into place, she strode around the room experimentally, trying to see how it felt with no panties on. She stopped at the mirror and looked. Without a panty line, she looked damned good and just naughty enough to be dangerous.

Smiling at herself, she turned this way and that. Then she heard the garage door open and hurried to put on her shoes, her mind filled with new doubts.

She met Bill coming in from the garage and kissed him hello.

"Well, don't you look wonderful!" he said, hugging her. His hands went to her ass and he cupped her to him.

Janet thought he might notice her lack of panties and complain but he said nothing. "Thanks, dear. Now let me finish dinner. You'd better go get cleaned up."

He headed for the bedroom while Janet went to check on dinner. She slipped on an apron to protect her outfit and started the vegetables. Her mind seemed to bounce around from sexy slut to demure wife and back again. She noticed her hands were shaking.

Bill came out just before six in a comfortable shirt and slacks and offered to fix her a drink.

"Oh god, yes," she said at once without thinking.

"Are you nervous, dear?" he teased.

"Yeah. I don't know how this is going to work out. It could be a disaster."

"Oh relax. You said so yourself, we're just going to play it by ear. If it seems too weird, I'll be the first to call it off, okay?"

She nodded, relieved to hear him say it. "Okay."

He fixed her a glass of wine and she gulped down a big swallow. He just shook his head and grinned.

The doorbell rang and they both froze for a second. Then Bill came to her and put his arms around her. "Just take it easy. It's only Frank. Think of him as an old friend, not my boss."

She nodded, thinking about "only Frank", and had a visual of him spanking her with the riding crop, making her so hot with desire she couldn't stand it. Ha! If Bill only knew!

He went to the door and Janet took another slug of wine. How was she going to survive this night?

Frank came in, all hale and hearty and full of cheer. Janet stood in the doorway to the kitchen and waved at him. He waved back and smiled. She suddenly realized she still had on her apron and felt foolish.

"Thanks for inviting me over, Bill! I don't get out much since the divorce."

"Happy to have you. Can I fix you a drink?"

"Sure!"

They went to the bar and Janet took the opportunity to head back into the kitchen, feeling the ring bounce with every step. *Oh god! What have I gotten myself into?*

She took the vegetables off the heat and drained them. She double-checked the roast. *There! Everything will be ready by six-thirty,* she told herself. She could hear the murmur of the men's voices in the living room and wondered if they were talking about work—or about her.

Her thoughts were interrupted when Frank came into the kitchen alone. She startled and stared at him, her eyes wide.

"Now I know where the expression 'deer in the headlights' comes from," he said, smiling.

"Hi, Frank. I was just getting dinner ready. Should be done soon."

"No rush. We can sit and talk and have a drink first, can't we?" He came closer and she found her breathing quickened.

"Sure. What's Bill doing out there all by himself?"

"He's picking out some music. He said he had some good CDs he wanted me to hear." He was close enough now to touch her. She tried to back up but the stove was in the way.

"Ah, g-good," she said. She tried to step to the side but Frank's hand caught her hip. She froze. She could feel his hand rub against her dress.

"Good," he whispered. "I see you're not wearing panties. I'm pleased."

"Uh, yeah." She slipped sideways and escaped his hand. He didn't try to stop her. She looked past him to the living room but didn't see Bill anywhere.

Her nerves were jangling and she tried to think of some small talk to distract him—and her—from the emotionally charged atmosphere. "W-Where did Bill go?" she said, trying to sound light.

"He said something about looking for a particular CD he had in the bedroom. I don't know. I'm sure he'll be back soon." He moved toward her again and put his hand on her upper arm. She shied away.

"Look, I know you're nervous. I said I would protect you and I will. But I do want to touch you now and again and I don't care if Bill sees. Remember, we're exploring tonight. Let's see where this goes. Don't be so tense."

She nodded and didn't move again when his hand returned to her arm. He rubbed her gently and Janet remembered all over again why she had fallen under this man's spell. If she hadn't been married...well, that was another story.

His other hand came up and rubbed her other arm. She relaxed a little, enjoying the sensation of his strong hands on her. She closed her eyes. But when she felt his lips on hers, she drew back in shock.

"Frank!" she whispered. "Don't!"

She checked out the living room but Bill was still missing. What was taking him so long?

"Don't fight it, Janet. I know what I'm doing."

"He might see!"

"He might like it."

She closed her eyes and shook her head. Turning back to the stove, she pretended the vegetables needed stirring but they were already perfect. She put them into a serving dish and then into the microwave to be reheated just before dinner.

Frank was still in the kitchen, watching her.

Then, thankfully, she heard Bill's voice. "I found it!" He came back to the living room. Frank turned and went out, and when she glanced back, they were standing near the CD player, talking in low tones.

"How did it go?" Bill asked.

"She's as nervous as a cat," Frank said as they pretended to look over the CDs. "Even though we've both said what we wanted, she's really worried about having us together like this."

"How should we play it?"

"I'm going to touch her occasionally in front of you, just a pat here and there. Then sometime during the evening, you get her aside and tell her how much it turned you on to see that. Act really excited about it."

"That won't be hard to do! I can't wait to see you do that Dom thing with her!"

"We have to play this note perfect or we're going to blow it. So ease her fears."

"I noticed already that she's not wearing panties. Was that your idea?"

Frank smiled. "Yep. I called her a little while ago. She was reluctant at first but she went for it. I had a feeling she would."

"I almost said something about it when I came in! But I caught myself in time."

"Good thing or you would've increased her anxiety. Now we've got to concentrate on getting her to relax."

"Well, the wine should help."

"Yes. That reminds me—"

Bill held up a hand. "All taken care of. She asked me to buy at least two bottles and I only bought one. I'm going to regret my 'oversight' and run out to buy more in a few minutes, just like we discussed."

"Good. And we'll hear the garage door when you return, right?"

"Right. Except I'm going to park on the street first and take a peek."

Frank nodded. "Fair's fair. Just don't expect too much so soon. We'll probably just be playing a little slap and tickle."

Bill laughed. "Gotcha."

Chapter Eighteen

ꟸ

Janet heard strains of gentle jazz filling the living room. She smiled and wondered who was seducing whom. *Maybe Bill has a thing for Frank! Ha!*

Bill came into the kitchen and opened the door to the fridge. "Hon, where's that bottle of Chablis we had in here the other day?"

"What? We drank that, remember?"

"Oh. Right." He looked disappointed.

"Why? Didn't you buy more like I asked?"

"I bought a bottle of red to go with dinner. Was I supposed to buy more?"

"Oh Bill! I told you to buy at least two bottles! I'm sure we're going to run out."

"Sorry, I forgot. Don't worry. I can run out before dinner and get some. It will only take about fifteen minutes."

Janet paused, her eyes wide as she thought about that. "Never mind. I'm sure we can drink ice water with dinner."

"No, no! I won't hear of it." He grabbed his keys off the counter. Before she could say anything else, he went to the doorway and called to Frank.

"Hey, Frank, I forgot to get some wine. I'm going to run out for a few minutes. Don't start dinner without me!"

"Want some help?"

"No, no, you stay here and keep Janet company. I'll be right back."

Bill left quickly. Janet heard the garage door open then close. Her heart began beating faster. She leaned back against the sink, waiting for what was to happen next.

Frank came into the kitchen at once and approached her. She didn't move. He stopped just a foot away and they stared at each other for a long moment. Then he reached down to slide his hands underneath her dress along both legs. She made no sound, no protest, as he raised his hands slowly, touching the smooth, hot flesh of her thighs as he went.

Her mouth came open and she breathed softly, almost a whimper. His hands reached the globes of her ass and she shivered involuntarily. Frank stepped closer, drawing his hands around behind her, grabbing the fullness there and bringing her up against him to feel his hard cock. Her ring was trapped in between and it seemed to throb against her clit, causing little jolts to her nervous system.

"Oh god," she whispered.

He pressed himself against her and she could feel the heat there. He said nothing, he simply used his hands and his hips to rock his hardness up and down her hot cleft, his eyes on hers the entire time. Now that Bill was gone, it was easy for Janet to fall under his power. Her body responded. She wanted nothing more than to feel this man's cock slide into her.

She began to breathe more heavily. Her eyes closed and she found herself drifting, her entire being concentrated on her pussy. She didn't stop him when he pulled her dress up past her hips, clearing the cloth from between them. Now only his slacks separated his cock from her wetness. He held her close with his left arm.

The sound of his zipper only excited her further for she felt safe and obedient in his arms. She trusted him completely. If he wanted to fuck her before Bill got home, that was just fine, Sir, just fine. Nevertheless, her mind remained alert for the sound of the garage door.

He pulled away for a moment and when his cock returned, it was bare and hard against her damp pussy. She sucked in a breath and pressed against him, enjoying the sensation of her juices spreading over his shaft.

Both of his hands returned to her ass cheeks, squeezing them hard and keeping her tight against him.

"I want to spank this lovely round ass," he whispered in her ear.

She shuddered with delight.

"I want Bill to watch as I whip you until you are bright red and begging for mercy."

Hearing her husband's name sent out tiny alarm bells but Frank's cock's constant rubbing soon caused them to fade into the background.

"I know he'd like to watch us," he said. "He'd like to learn what you really want."

She frowned, not sure if that were true but it sounded encouraging. She pressed her clit against his shaft and rocked with him. The ring caught between only exacerbated the sensation.

"You're a slut and a submissive and you need this," he said.

She could only nod ever so slightly. God, she wanted him inside her!

"Once your husband sees how you really are, I'll probably invite James over to put in nipple rings and have George and Martin watch along with Bill. Then they could all take turns fucking you."

"God," she said, throwing her head back. "Goddamn it." She was close but she couldn't quite get there. She needed him inside. Janet pushed up on her tiptoes and reached down to coax the tip of his cock into her sopping cunt but he wouldn't let her.

"Please, Sir," she said.

"Please what, slut?"

"Please fuck me!"

"But your husband! He'll be coming home soon. Do you want him to find you like this, humping his boss?" His voice teased her.

"Eeeeeee," she said, her body struggling now to move his cock. Her fingers slipped over the wet tip as she rubbed it against her clit. She brought her fingers up to her mouth and could taste his pre-cum. It drove her wild.

"What was that?"

"Yeeeees," she said. "Yes, I want to fuck you now. I don't care if Bill sees!"

He was relentless now, rubbing against her, driving her to the brink. "No, it's more than that, my little sub. You *want* him to watch as you fuck me."

"YES!" she shouted. "God, Sir, fuck me! Quick!"

With some effort, he pulled away, leaving her poised on the edge. Her eyes flew open to see his wicked smile.

"No. It's not time until I say so," he said. With some effort, he tucked his rock-hard cock back into his pants and zipped up. Janet was splayed back against the counter, her dress still halfway up, her legs apart. She could see some of her wetness on Frank's slacks and knew she was a sopping mess.

"How could you?" she gasped. "I was so close!"

He came forward, grabbed her arm and half turned her then gave her a sharp swat on the ass. It shook her out of her reverie and calmed her. Her dress fell down and covered her. She reached underneath, trying to rub herself to a quick climax but Frank held her arm and shook his head.

"There will be none of that tonight. If you come, it will be at someone else's hands. Or cock."

"You are so mean."

"You are so mean, *Sir,*" he said. "That'll cost you too."

"Am I supposed to call you 'Sir' when Bill is here too?" she said mockingly, aware that it would come back to haunt her as well when he tallied up her "punishments".

"No, not at first anyway. We'll work that out, don't worry."

The sound of the garage door startled her. She straightened up and smoothed down her dress. She thought she could feel herself squish with every step as she hurried to finish dinner. Frank stepped back and returned to the living room, tugging at his pants as he went.

Good, she thought. *Hope he gets blue balls!*

* * * * *

Bill came in, two wine bottles in hand. His cock was so hard he held one of the bottles in front so as not to give away his delicate condition. He had returned a few minutes earlier and had parked in the driveway. He had snuck up to the window to the living room to watch the scene. He could observe them through the opening into the kitchen. To see his wife pressing up against Frank like that, wow! She clearly was hot for him. She seemed to be humping him as if she had been desperate to get off. He wondered what Frank had said or did to her that drove her wild like that. She had never acted like that when they were making love.

He put the wine on the counter and excused himself. Janet said nothing to him—in fact, she seemed more flustered than he did. He nodded at Frank and went into the bathroom, unzipped his pants. His hard cock was aching. He took a washcloth and ran it under cold water then pressed it against his cock, trying to cool it down. It had the desired effect and soon he was able to tuck it back into his pants.

He washed up and went out. He sat down next to Frank on the couch.

"Wow," he whispered. "I saw part of it. Wow."

Frank grinned. "Janet is so horny she's ready to do just about anything, whether you're here or not. We'll get started after dinner, okay?"

"You bet." He looked down at Frank's pants. "Looks like she got a little on ya."

"Yeah. Just ignore it. When she sees it, she'll be embarrassed. She'll wonder if you've noticed. We'll let it play upon her mind."

Bill smiled.

"Dinner's ready!"

They got up and went to the table. Janet tried to be the perfect hostess but she was clearly flustered. Bill noted that she spotted the damp smears on Frank's crotch and looked away at once. She forgot to rewarm the vegetables then she neglected to put out a serving spoon. And she couldn't remember where the electric knife had been stored when she went to carve the roast.

Bill opened the wine and made sure everyone had plenty, especially Janet. She seemed all too happy to drink up—probably to calm her nerves.

The conversation started out smoothly. They talked about the lovely meal and both men congratulated Janet. But when the conversation turned to work, Bill noted Frank had decided to up the ante.

Frank turned to Janet and asked, "So tell me, Janet, Bill says you've been working at a dress shop for a while. How's that working out for you?"

Janet froze, her fork halfway to her mouth. She stared at Frank then glanced over at Bill. "Uh…"

"Tell him, honey. You seem to have been enjoying it," Bill offered helpfully.

A tiny shudder ran through her. Bill could imagine her thoughts—"working" at being fucked or pierced. His cock grew hard again and he had to shift in his seat.

"Uh." She struggled to find her voice. "It's, uh, fine. Just a temporary job, you know. I help rich ladies find the right, er, outfits."

"I'll bet that can be fun, working with all those new fashions," Frank said, giving her a big grin.

"Sure." She turned to Bill. "More roast, honey?"

"No, no thanks. I'm stuffed. It was a great meal, dear."

"What's the store's top-selling designer?" Frank wasn't ready to let it go yet.

Janet stared at him as if to say, *What are you doing?*

"Uh. I don't know. Vera Wang, maybe?"

Frank nodded. He and Bill exchanged glances. When Bill looked back at Janet, she was studying her meal. He looked back at Frank and gave him a quirked eyebrow and his boss shrugged.

When they were done, Janet and Bill cleared the dishes. Frank volunteered to pitch in but she shooed him away and told him guests didn't have to help. He went into the living room.

"So what'd you guys talk about while I was gone?" Bill said in a low voice while they loaded the dishwasher.

"Talk?"

"Yeah. Didn't you talk?"

"Um, no, we didn't talk. I, uh, let him hug me."

"What?" He pretended to be shocked.

"I know you want to be present. But I thought I should let him know I was interested so I didn't protest."

"What exactly did he do?"

"He, uh, held me close. You know, just a good hug."

It had been more than that! But Bill didn't say anything. He wanted to let her see he wasn't going to be jealous about it. He could tell she was watching him closely for a reaction.

"That's great, honey!"

"Really? You think so?"

"Well, sure. It's what we want, isn't it?"

"Yes. I just want to make sure it's what we both want and not just one or the other, you know?"

He took her hand in his. "I know. And I really appreciate it. I mean, just hearing about how he was with you gets me excited, even if he is my boss."

She smiled. "Well then, I should tell you it was a very good hug. I could feel his, well, you know."

"No!"

"Oh yeah. I know he wants me. But he's probably thinking I want to have an affair. I don't know how to get him to consider the idea that you'll be there."

"Yeah. And we don't know if he's a real Dom, do we?"

She looked at him, puzzled. "Oh he is, trust me."

"What do you mean?"

"The way he came in here and took me in his arms left no doubt. He wasn't tentative or worried I might scream. He saw what he wanted and came in and took it. That was very Dom-like."

"I'll bet it turned you on."

"Oh yeah." She saw the expression on his face and added, "But I wouldn't trade you for him so don't look so hurt. It's like visiting an amusement park. Fun for a day but I wouldn't want to live there!"

He laughed and gave her a kiss.

"Now I'm just about finished in here so go out and keep our company waiting," she said. "Shoo."

Janet took a deep breath when Bill left the kitchen. Things were moving rather fast and she wasn't sure if she liked it. She thought Bill might exhibit some jealousy but he seemed eager for things to continue. Apparently, having Frank as his boss didn't bother him as much as she thought it would. Her pussy throbbed and she wondered just how far they would go tonight. Somehow she couldn't quite see her husband watching as Frank put her through her paces. Wouldn't she be too nervous and self-conscious to go through with it? She shivered.

Janet took a deep breath and tried to calm her nerves before returning to the living room. Bill had taken the upholstered chair, leaving a seat on the couch next to Frank. She sat down, trying not to think too much about the situation. Now that she was close to Frank again, her pussy seemed to respond to him, swelling with heat and need.

"Well, that was a lovely meal, Janet. Thanks so much for inviting me. Since I became a bachelor again, I don't get too many home-cooked meals," Frank said. He reached over and patted her leg.

She nodded. "You're welcome anytime, Frank. We should've invited you over sooner." She glanced down and noticed that Frank had not moved his hand. She looked up at Bill and he gave her a sly grin.

Okay, if this is what he wants, she thought, and turned slightly toward Frank, allowing her skirt to ride up a half inch. It was all the encouragement he needed. His hand slid up another inch, taking the material with it.

"That pot roast recipe was really good too. It was so tender it about fell off my fork."

"Oh that's my mother's recipe. I can't take credit. Slow cooking is the key."

Bill got up. "I'll be right back." He headed down the hall toward the bathroom.

Janet turned toward Frank. "You're being pretty brazen! Are you sure Bill will go for this?"

"I'm always brazen around you, babe." He reached over and unbuttoned her dress between her breasts, exposing the tops of her lacy bra.

"Frank!" She looked down the hall.

"You know this is what Bill wants. You should stop worrying so much. If he objects, he can speak up." His hand moved up under her skirt, about halfway up her thigh.

She jumped and pulled away. Frank let her go. She sat back against the cushions and caught her breath. "God! I just feel so funny! I just can't believe Bill will go for this. I know what he says and what you say, but still, it's hard to accept."

"I know. But you heard him. It's his fantasy—and yours. You just have to let go a little. He's not going to fly into a jealous rage—trust me on this." He reached out and pulled her closer to him.

She allowed it and settled in next to him. "I don't know why I'm so nervous. Bill's been clear about this and he's been giving me encouragement. I guess since I've been cheating on him for so many weeks now, I feel like I've already betrayed him."

"Ah, see, that's guilt talking." His hand returned to the skin along her collarbone and he stroked her there as he talked. "You'd probably feel better if you had found out earlier what fantasy Bill had, right? Then you could've talked it all out before you got caught up with me."

His touch felt good. She closed her eyes. His other hand returned to the inside of her leg to rest against her hot skin, but she didn't react. "Yeah, that would have been better," she said.

"But you must remember—it's my fault, not yours. I blackmailed you, remember?"

Janet did remember but it seemed so long ago. They had come far since then and blackmail no longer had anything to do with it. "I could've stopped it," she said, her voice languid and weak.

"No you couldn't have." His hand drifted down across her chest to tickle the tops of her left breast. "I was in control of you. You couldn't help it."

She nodded, drifting. His other hand pushed up her dress a little farther.

"You had to do what I said or Bill would lose his job. You're the heroine here."

"No, I'm not."

"Hey, I'm in charge here, remember?" He leaned in and kissed her cheek. "You're just building up the punishments for later."

She gave him a half smile. "I wonder what's taking Bill so long?"

"He's probably giving us some time. I'm sure he's aware of your awkwardness."

"Yeah. Maybe."

His hand moved up until it touched her throbbing pussy. She jumped and pushed him away with some effort. "I'm sorry, Frank, uh, Sir, but I have to go talk to Bill. I just want to make sure I'm…I mean, he's okay with this."

Frank shrugged. "Sure. I understand. I'm not trying to ruin your marriage here. Only enhance it."

Janet smiled at him and stood. She smoothed down her dress, acutely aware of how sensitized she felt. It was as if her whole body were tingling, especially her breasts and sex.

She moved down the hall and found Bill in their bedroom, standing at the closet. "Bill?"

He turned. "Oh hi. Are you ignoring our guest?"

"I was just worried about you. You took off so quickly…"

He came to her and took her into his arms. "No, it's okay. I wanted to leave you two alone for a bit. I know you're all confused but I'm telling you it's all right."

"You really mean it? Frank is, uh, taking full advantage of your absence."

"I know. And if you don't want him to, by all means, call a halt to it. But if you're enjoying it, well, then…"

"You amaze me, Bill. You really do."

"Hey, you asked about my little fetish. Now let me ask about yours—is Frank, uh, dominant enough for you?"

"Oh yeah, I think he is," she said. "I mean, so far." *If you only knew,* she thought.

"Good. So go out there and have fun."

"But what about you? I don't want you hiding out in here."

"I'll come out when I'm ready. And when I do, I expect you to be enjoying your, uh, submissiveness. This is a win-win, dear. Okay?"

"You're not just saying that, are you?"

"No. I'm not going to freak out. I know that probably doesn't make sense to you but there it is. I like seeing you being dominated."

"Okay." She kissed him. "I feel better now."

"Good. Now scoot." He turned her around and gave her a playful slap on the ass.

She came out into the living room energized. So it was all right! Bill was being wonderful about it! He didn't act jealous at all. Maybe this really does turn him on. Who would've known?

"Stop," Frank said.

Janet froze, puzzled.

"Lift up your dress. I want to see you."

She smiled coyly and wondered if Bill could hear him. She stood in front of the couch and slowly lifted her dress to her waist.

"That's enough."

She held her position, feeling his eyes on her sex, making her hot and wet. God, how she needed to be fucked! The teasing earlier had left her body thrumming and having his eyes on her made it more intense.

"Legs apart more."

She obeyed, her body shaking.

Suddenly, she felt hands on her bare ass and turned to see Bill standing there behind her—he had snuck up silently. She jerked and then settled down, feeling safe in Bill's hands. No one was angry, no one was jealous. Her two worlds came together in that moment and it was all right. Janet breathed a little easier. She kept her eyes on Frank as Bill fondled her pale, soft globes.

My god! I'm here with my two favorite men and I'm half naked and wet!

She could almost climax just from the emotional waves crashing over her. No one spoke for a few minutes, giving her time to get used to this wildly improbable situation. She could see the erection in Frank's pants and she could guess there was a similar tent forming in her husband's. All because of her!

"Oh my," she whispered.

Chapter Nineteen

ꟸ

Frank wanted to exert his control over Janet right away—and Bill too, for that matter.

"You've been very bad, Janet," he said soothingly.

Her voice reflected her alarm. "What? How so, uh, Sir?"

"You didn't believe Bill when he said he wanted to see you with other men. You questioned his wishes for you."

"It was a lot to accept."

Frank watched as Bill stroked her ass. She trembled and leaned back against him.

"Come here."

She came to him at once, leaving Bill's hands cupping air. He went to a chair and sat down, his eyes alight.

"Kick off your shoes and lean over my lap."

He could see in her eyes that she knew what was coming next. But she obeyed after one quick glance back over her shoulder at her husband. She settled over his lap, her ass up invitingly. He eased her skirt up, exposing the rounded shape. His hands gently rubbed her pale skin. Underneath, he felt her shiver.

"I'm going to spank you now, Janet. Bill is going to watch you get punished. He's going to see what a submissive slut you are."

She made a near-soundless groan deep in her throat. He raised his hand and brought it down hard.

"Ulp!"

"Why don't you count for Bill, slut?"

"One, Sir!"

Whack!

"Two, Sir!"

"Tell Bill what you are."

"I'm…a slut, Sir!"

Whack!

"Three, Sir!"

"And why is that?"

"I don't know!"

Whack!

"You can do better than that."

"Four, Sir! Uh, I guess I like the power of a strong man."

Unstated of course, was the fact that Bill wasn't. Frank wanted Bill to hear it from his wife. He wanted Bill to understand that he needed Frank as much as Janet did.

Whack!

"Five, Sir!"

Frank could feel her body vibrate now. Her ass was reddening nicely. He knew if he touched her slit, she would be wet.

"Spread your legs apart, slut. Show your husband how wet you are."

She groaned but obeyed. Frank could smell the light scent of her arousal.

Whack!

"Six, Sir!"

Bill got up and moved closer. Frank could see the sheen of wetness between her legs and ran his finger up along her slit. She jerked involuntarily. He held up his finger to show Bill the honey he had collected.

"Look at you, showing yourself off like this!"

"Oh god!"

Whack!

"Seven, Sir!"

"You like this, don't you, my pet?"

"Uh…"

Whack!

"Eight! Yes, Sir! I like it!"

"What does it do to you?" His hand rubbed her abused skin, soothing her.

"It…makes me hot."

"It brings out the slut in you, doesn't it?"

"Yes, Sir."

Bill was silent, his eyes wide and alert. Frank could see the bulge in his pants and knew how much he was enjoying this scene. It was time to exert his authority, to show both of them who was in charge.

"Tell your husband how you saved his job."

"What?"

Whack! Whack!

"Nine, ten, Sir! Okay, okay! Bill, Frank blackmailed me! He made me fuck him! He said he would fire you if I didn't!"

Bill came forward and touched her shoulder. "Really? He did that to you?"

"Yes!"

"That wasn't all, was it?" Frank pressed.

"Oh god!"

Whack!

"Eleven, Sir!" She gasped. "Bill, he made me get this jewelry! And he made me, oh god!"

Frank raised his hand and she rushed ahead.

"He made me suck off one of his neighbors! And another neighbor saw me naked! And the piercer…oh god!"

"What did the piercer do?" Bill asked.

"He, uh, fucked me, Bill. I'm so sorry!"

"You let another man fuck you!" Bill's voice seemed to waver on the knife-edge of jealousy and joy. The jealousy part was an act to convince Janet that he didn't already know all the details. Yet Frank knew there was some truth to that emotion. "Why didn't you come to me and tell me what was going on?"

Frank stepped in. "I still hold all the cards," he said, nodding at Bill. "I could fire him tomorrow if I felt like it."

"See? I had to, Bill."

Bill nodded, going along. "I understand."

"So you'll give your wife to me whenever I want her?" His hands kept rubbing her, eliciting another deep sigh from the submissive woman.

"Uh, yes, I guess I have no choice," Bill said. There was a question in his eyes and Frank knew what it was. Bill wanted to be present at every session. Frank had other ideas and he wanted to see how far he could press them.

"And she's mine to do what I want? Including making her fuck and suck other men?"

Bill didn't answer right away. His brow furrowed. Frank gave him an impatient tip of his head and Bill shrugged.

"Uh, sure. If I can be—"

"Did you hear that, slut?" Frank interrupted. "I can fuck you anytime. I can give you to other men like James or George or Martin."

"Well, now, I—" Bill began.

"Would you like to see your slutty wife fuck another man?"

Bill's eyes glazed a bit before he regained control. "Yeah," he said, licking his lips.

Janet groaned.

"Touch her, see how turned on she is."

Bill came forward and ran his fingers up along her core. She jumped.

"Yeah, she's sopping wet. She wants it."

"Slut, get up and take off your clothes."

She rose on shaky legs and turned to face her husband. Frank watched as a wordless conversation passed between them. He could guess what they were saying. She was asking him if he really was okay with this and Bill responded positively, although Frank could tell he had some doubts now. Now that Frank was exerting his control, Bill wasn't entirely sure he liked it. Yet this is what he said he wanted. Frank knew Bill was wrestling with second thoughts.

He waited, exerting his will on them like an invisible wave of energy. It was a critical moment. If Bill objected, everything could come apart. Janet would revert to the shy, loyal wife. Frank believed that Bill was subservient too and given the right push, he would fall into line. As long as he made it seem like his own idea.

Frank gave Bill a long look as if to say, *This is what you wanted, right?*

Bill gazed back at him and slowly nodded.

Frank reached out and gave Janet a slap on the rump. "Come on, slut! I don't have all night!"

A final look passed between husband and wife then Janet began to remove her clothes. She stripped slowly, her dress peeling away and down her legs. She kicked it away. Her hands went to her bra and unhooked it, allowing it to fall as well. She stood naked in front of them, her eyes downcast.

"I'm going to fuck you now, Janet, and your husband's going to watch. If he's very good, I might let him fuck you too." He winked at Bill to let him know he was kidding, but in reality he wasn't. He hoped that soon he would have control over both of them.

He guided Janet to the upholstered arm of the couch and draped her over it. There would be no further preliminaries. He would fuck her hard and fast and show Bill who was boss. He expected her to feel awkward—Bill too for that matter.

Frank knew it was one thing to watch your wife being submissive on a video and quite another to watch it in person. He might even want to step in to "rescue" her, although she didn't need rescuing. She needed to let herself go.

Her ass was so invitingly red with his palm prints, Frank found himself rock-hard at the prospect of fucking her. He unzipped his pants and pulled out his cock.

"Keep your eyes on your husband," he ordered, and plunged into her.

Janet gasped but kept her eyes open. A look was exchanged between husband and wife. Something changed there and Frank hoped they were both understanding who was in charge now.

He fucked her quickly, not caring if she climaxed or not. Considering the situation, it probably would be hard for her to come. She couldn't help but feel she was betraying her husband somehow. Perhaps she was waiting for him to grow angry or stop them. But he just stood there, his mouth half open and watched as his wife was plowed by his boss.

Frank came hard and thrust up against her, feeling his cock throb inside her. He pulled out at once and ordered her to clean him off. She squeezed her legs together to keep his semen inside as she kneeled down to take him into her mouth. Frank watched Bill's reaction but it did not change.

"My turn," Bill said when Janet was finished.

Frank nodded at Janet. "Yes, my little submissive, you have my permission to fuck your husband."

Both of them glanced at him but neither one challenged him. Good, he thought. Let them get used to his power. A stronger man would have objected but Bill seemed willing to go along.

He watched as Bill fucked Janet, smiling when he observed that her eyes were on him the entire time. Her husband came quickly and pulled out.

"Clean me, slut," Bill ordered, and Janet looked to Frank for his nod before she obeyed.

Frank smiled. Things were going well.

Chapter Twenty

ജ

It had been a busy three months. Frank had a lot to deal with at the plant after Springfield Mills was bought out by a competitor. There had been several duplicate jobs that had to be eliminated, including Bill's. Fortunately his control over both Bill and Janet had remained strong. Janet of course needed what he gave her. And Bill seemed happy to allow Frank to be the alpha male as long as he was allowed to hang around like a puppy to observe.

Frank had thought that when the word came down to lay off Bill everything would come apart—all his careful work could've gone for naught. But Frank was a resourceful man and he always seemed to have a few cards up his sleeve. He found a way to make even this work to his advantage.

He remembered the day, just a month ago, when he had called Bill into his office for the news. Frank had been using Janet regularly by then and had even exerted control over when Bill could make love to her. As long as Frank brought in a powerful man or two regularly to fuck her while he watched, Bill was happy to go along.

"Bill, sit down," he had said, seeing the man's puzzled expression. No doubt the plant had been full of rumors ever since the merger had occurred, yet Bill probably thought his job was safe due to their intimate arrangement.

"Bill, I won't beat around the bush. Since the merger, Consolidated Steel has decided to use their own project manager at this plant. I did everything I could to stop them but I only have so much power now."

Bill's mouth came open. "You're…laying me off?" His face darkened. "You can't!"

Frank held up a hand. "I know, I know. This wasn't supposed to happen like this. I swear—I never wanted this." Truth be told, he didn't. He was happy with the way things had worked out between the three of them. But now, how could he pass up this opportunity?

"What the hell am I supposed to do? You were supposed to protect us!"

Bill was getting worked up so Frank pulled his trump card out quickly to head him off. "Now wait. Hear me out. I have been able to pull a few strings."

Bill's angry expression stopped in mid-rage and he held himself in check. His eyes were alert, expectant. He waited for Frank to save him.

"You know how the U.S. steel industry is on the wane? Well, there's good and bad news coming from that. Sure, it's bad for jobs here but it also opens up new jobs…" he paused. "Overseas."

Bill's eyes narrowed. "What?"

"Consolidated has a plant in Shanghai. They need a project manager who can supervise operations—in other words, be a co-plant manager, working hand in hand with the Chinese manager. I convinced them that you'd be perfect for the job. You'd handle the English-speaking side of things, which means you'd be in direct contact with the bosses at Consolidated. The Chinese manager would deal with the employees."

"You want me to move to Shanghai?" Bill was thunderstruck.

"It's only temporary," Frank told him. "The reason the job is open is that the current manager is being transferred to Consolidated HQ with a fat promotion. He was in Shanghai less than two years. Think about that."

To his credit, Bill did pause for a moment to digest this new information. "So you're saying that if I do well there, I could come back in a reasonable amount of time?"

"That's what I'm saying. You'd have invaluable experience. You'd be one of the go-to guys for Consolidated."

Bill nodded. "I suppose there's a raise in this somewhere?"

"Of course! Twenty-five percent. Plus, most of that will be earned tax free."

Bill sat back. He blew out a breath. "Wow. That's...that's very generous of you. Thanks. I'm sure Janet and I can learn to love China for a couple of years."

"Yes, well, about that. There's a catch—Janet stays here."

"What?! No way."

"Yes. That's the deal. If you refuse, then the job goes to a man Consolidated is putting up."

Bill stood, his anger rising. "You can't do that! All I have to do is tell Consolidated you're blackmailing me in order to steal my wife and you'll be out on your ear."

"Very possibly true," Frank agreed. "But you'd be out of work as well. Think about it. I'm a CEO. I can always find another company that needs good management. What kind of job would you find?"

Bill held his tongue as he thought about it.

"Besides," Frank added, "I'm not stealing your wife. I already have her. I'm just borrowing her until you return. You've seen how she is with me. She needs me. If you go along with this, I promise I *won't* try to steal her. When you return for visits, I'll step aside and leave you two alone, if that's what you and she want. And when you return for good, we'll all sit down and discuss where we want to go from there."

Frank had no intention of giving Janet up. He knew once Bill left the country he would be out of sight and out of mind. When he returned, Janet would be so conditioned to being Frank's submissive that Bill would no longer have any hold on her. She would refuse to go back to her old life with him. Let him cry and moan then, he thought. It would be too late. Bill wouldn't want to do anything to jeopardize his job and future.

He'd find a way to rationalize it—he'd tell himself how he and Janet hadn't been getting along for months, years even. Or he may even find himself a cute little Chinese girl to take Janet's place. A lot could happen.

"I'll have to think about this," Bill said. "I'm not happy. You promised me you'd keep things the way they were."

"I know. But I had no control over the merger, you know that. I was happy the way things were going too—we could've gone on for years, I think. But once I found out they were replacing you, I had to act fast. This is a good deal. You don't know the favors I called in to make it happen."

Bill tipped his head. "Yeah, well, thanks, I guess. I'm not sure I want to trade my wife for my job though."

"You don't really have to. She'll be here when you come home to visit. Plus, you'll have free rein to fuck any of those subservient Chinese gals while you're over there."

Bill's eyes glazed momentarily as he imagined it. A thin smile came to his lips. "Well, let me think about it." Without another word, he left.

It hadn't taken long for him to decide. Frank made sure to prep Janet for her part of the argument. She convinced Bill it was a golden opportunity and he'd be a fool to let it slip through his fingers.

"I'll be here when you get back," she had said. Frank had told her it wasn't really a lie—a lot could happen in two years. Or three. And Janet would be "here" when he eventually returned. But by then, he probably wouldn't want her. She would be completely under Frank's spell.

So Bill had taken the job. He had left a week ago. And Frank was preparing to move as well. He had found a cute little house on a wooded half acre outside town and knew instantly it would be the perfect place to continue Janet's training. For now, Janet was staying at his apartment. She and Bill had sold their home and split the proceeds. In many ways it was like a divorce, although they were still legally married.

The thought that Janet was home, waiting for him naked and moist, her hands chained to her waist belt so she couldn't masturbate, sent a thrill through him. She had come a long way in just a few months. After another year, she would be his perfect little submissive. He would take very good care of her and protect her from harm. And she would learn so much about the Dominant/submissive lifestyle.

He smiled and sat back in his big leather chair.

Also by J.W. McKenna

About the Author

ẟ

J.W. McKenna is a former journalist who took up penning erotic romance stories after years of trying to ignore an overly dramatic—and often overheated—imagination. McKenna is married and lives in the Midwest, where polite people would be shocked if they knew what kind of writing was being done in their town.

J.W. McKenna welcomes comments from readers. You can find her website and email address on her author bio page at www.ellorascave.com.

Tell Us What You Think

Why an electronic book?

We live in the Information Age—an exciting time in the history of human civilization, in which technology rules supreme and continues to progress in leaps and bounds every minute of every day. For a multitude of reasons, more and more avid literary fans are opting to purchase e-books instead of paper books. The question from those not yet initiated into the world of electronic reading is simply: *Why?*

1. ***Price.*** An electronic title at Ellora's Cave Publishing and Cerridwen Press runs anywhere from 40% to 75% less than the cover price of the exact same title in paperback format. Why? Basic mathematics and cost. It is less expensive to publish an e-book (no paper and printing, no warehousing and shipping) than it is to publish a paperback, so the savings are passed along to the consumer.
2. ***Space.*** Running out of room in your house for your books? That is one worry you will never have with electronic books. For a low one-time cost, you can purchase a handheld device specifically designed for e-reading. Many e-readers have large, convenient screens for viewing. Better yet, hundreds of titles can be stored within your new library—on a single microchip. There are a variety of e-readers from different manufacturers. You can also read e-books on your PC or laptop computer. (Please note that Ellora's Cave does not endorse any specific brands.

You can check our websites at www.ellorascave.com or www.cerridwenpress.com for information we make available to new consumers.)

3. ***Mobility***. Because your new e-library consists of only a microchip within a small, easily transportable e-reader, your entire cache of books can be taken with you wherever you go.
4. ***Personal Viewing Preferences.*** Are the words you are currently reading too small? Too large? Too... ANNOYING? Paperback books cannot be modified according to personal preferences, but e-books can.
5. ***Instant Gratification.*** Is it the middle of the night and all the bookstores near you are closed? Are you tired of waiting days, sometimes weeks, for bookstores to ship the novels you bought? Ellora's Cave Publishing sells instantaneous downloads twenty-four hours a day, seven days a week, every day of the year. Our webstore is never closed. Our e-book delivery system is 100% automated, meaning your order is filled as soon as you pay for it.

Those are a few of the top reasons why electronic books are replacing paperbacks for many avid readers.

As always, Ellora's Cave and Cerridwen Press welcome your questions and comments. We invite you to email us at Comments@ellorascave.com or write to us directly at Ellora's Cave Publishing Inc., 1056 Home Avenue, Akron, OH 44310-3502.

Cerridwen, the Celtic Goddess of wisdom, was the muse who brought inspiration to storytellers and those in the creative arts. Cerridwen Press encompasses the best and most innovative stories in all genres of today's fiction. Visit our site and discover the newest titles by talented authors who still get inspired - much like the ancient storytellers did, once upon a time.

ELLORA'S CAVE
ROMANTICA PUBLISHING